W9-CFB-355

Also available from Linda Lael Miller

THE CARSONS OF MUSTANG CREEK
A Snow Country Christmas
Forever a Hero
Always a Cowboy
Once a Rancher

THE BRIDES OF BLISS COUNTY
Christmas in Mustang Creek
The Marriage Season
The Marriage Charm
The Marriage Pact

THE PARABLE SERIES
Big Sky Secrets
Big Sky Wedding
Big Sky Summer
Big Sky River
Big Sky Mountain
Big Sky Country

McKETTRICKS OF TEXAS

An Outlaw's Christmas
A Lawman's Christmas
McKettricks of Texas: Austin
McKettricks of Texas: Garrett
McKettricks of Texas: Tate

THE CREED COWBOYS

The Creed Legacy
Creed's Honor
A Creed in Stone Creek

STONE CREEK

The Bridegroom
The Rustler
A Wanted Man
The Man from Stone Creek

THE McKETTRICKS

A McKettrick Christmas
McKettrick's Heart
McKettrick's Pride
McKettrick's Luck
McKettrick's Choice

MOJO SHEEPSHANKS
Arizona Heat
(originally published as
Deadly Deceptions)
Arizona Wild
(originally published as
Deadly Gamble)

THE MONTANA CREEDS
A Creed Country Christmas
Montana Creeds: Tyler
Montana Creeds: Dylan
Montana Creeds: Logan

LINDA LAEL MILLER

Country STRONG

HQN

Doubleday Large Print Home Library Edition

ISBN-13: 978-1-64385-510-3

Country Strong

This edition published by arrangement with Harlequin Books S.A.

HQN | 22 Adelaide St. West, 40th Floor Toronto, Ontario M5H 4E3, Canada

Printed in the United State of America

To animal lovers everywhere.

Dear Reader,

Welcome to the town of Painted Pony Creek in the Big Sky State of Montana. **Country Strong** is the first of three stories based in this town; it will be followed by **Country Proud** and **Country Born**.

The heroes of these books, longtime friends, are Cord Hollister, Eli Garrett and J.P. McCall. Central to this first one is Cord, who owns a horse ranch and a horse-training business. You'll also meet Shallie Fletcher, a woman from his past, who becomes part of his life again.

And you'll meet Eli, the local sheriff, and J.P., a military veteran, and you'll learn more about them in **Country Proud** and **Country Born**, and see how they find love, too.

In this book, this series, you'll experience everything that's important to me and, as I know from past contact with

my readers, to you, too: a strong sense of community, a love of country and small-town life and, above all, the importance of human connections—especially family and friendship.
The possibility of redemption. The importance, too, of a sense of humor, which can help us through hard times and make good times even better. The same goes for the role of music and how it enhances our lives.

And I can't imagine what my own life would be without dogs, cats, horses, birds...I'm an "animal person" all the way, and I'm fortunate that almost everyone I know is, too. (I'd love to hear **your** animal stories, dear reader. Write me at the website or address below. Send pictures if you'd like.)

Ultimately, it all comes down to love, doesn't it?

I'm grateful to have these beliefs in common with my editors, Paula

Eykelhof and Michele Bidelspach, and my agent, Irene Goodman. I'd also like to extend my appreciation to a number of people at Harlequin Books, a division of HarperCollins: Dianne Moggy, Margaret Marbury, Loriana Sacilotto and Susan Swinwood.

My family—daughter, Wendy, and niece, Jenny, and their respective (and respectful!) partners are vital to my personal and professional lives. So, of course, is the rest of my family. And my longtime friend and fellow animal lover, Debbie Macomber.

Much gratitude to my many loyal readers!

You can reach me at my website, www.lindalaelmiller.com, and at my snail-mail address, PO Box 19461, Spokane, Washington 99219.

PROLOGUE

Eighteen years before...

Sparks rose from the crackling bonfire in lazy, twisting spirals, the tiny stars of some miniature universe, soaring high above the loud party on the stony banks of Painted Pony Creek, blazing brilliant red-orange trails against the night sky for a few glorious moments, then, inevitably, fading to ash. Drifting slowly earthward, so briefly bright, then gone.

Shallie Fletcher, seventeen and prone to finding cosmic meaning in just about everything, sighed. Sparks continued to flare, then vanish, only to be replaced by more.

Not that she'd ever shone, let alone soared.

That was for other girls, girls like her best friend, Reba Shannon.

An ache formed in Shallie's throat as she watched her best friend wrap her dazzling self around Eli Garrett, there at the faint, flickering edge of the firelight, but the ache didn't stem from jealousy.

Oh, no. What Shallie felt, that hot summer night, was remorse.

And guilt. Mostly because of what Reba was busy doing. But Eli was certainly doing **his** part...

He was making a damn fool of himself, which was his own fault, since he'd had too much beer, like a lot of the other guys and not a few of the girls. High school was over. Graduation was a full week in the past, but the parties, it seemed, might go on all summer. Or until the whole class ended up in jail for underage drinking, whichever came first.

Shallie, raised in foster care by her aunt and uncle, both of whom swilled cheap vodka from midmorning until they passed out sometime after the eleven o'clock news, quietly avoided alcohol. Tonight, knowing what she knew—what **everybody** knew, except for Eli and his two closest friends, John Patrick McCall, known as J.P., and Cord Hollister—she'd considered diving head-first into a bottle and curling up at the bottom, like the storied worm in a jug of rotgut tequila.

If she'd been drunk, after all, she could have forgotten for a little while that she'd stood by and watched, saying nothing, not for just a day or a week, but for **months**, while Reba, beautiful, narcissistic Reba, played her game. While she convinced each of them that she was in love with **him**, and him alone.

Shallie hadn't been the only one who could have, **should** have, spoken up. But that didn't really matter now, did it?

She'd known Eli, J.P. and Cord since kindergarten. A tomboy, Shallie had been part of their circle from day one, when they'd decided, for whatever reason, to befriend the scruffy foster kid from the run-down motel south of town.

In the early years, she'd gone every-where with those three—fishing and swimming in this very creek, horseback riding, and even to Saturday afternoon matinees at the Silver Buckle Theater, before it closed for good.

She'd eaten supper with their families, in their clean, orderly houses. In her early teens, J.P.'s older sisters, Clare and Josie, had given her clothes, brushed and braided her hair and, when the time came, taught her a million things she would've had to learn by trial and error otherwise.

How to make the most of her features with a minimum of makeup, for instance, and which colors looked best on her. They'd insisted that being smart was a **good** thing, more important than being pretty or popular, though both of those things were fine, in and of themselves. A girl just had to remember that being pretty didn't mean jack-shit if you were ornery or a liar or a cheat. Popularity, the very popular McCall sisters agreed, was fun all right, but it didn't have much substance in the long run.

It was great to be class president or prom queen or a cheerleader, but some people got stuck, Clare and Ellie maintained, and accomplished little or nothing after graduation.

Who wanted to peak in **high school**?

Watching them, Shallie wondered about her own future with her friends. With Reba. And with Eli, J.P. and Cord. Especially Cord...

Was it better to say something right now?

Or do nothing?

CHAPTER ONE

Evening of Thursday, June 6

The night Reba Shannon's ghost materialized in the cramped storeroom behind Sully's Bar and Grill, where Cord Hollister and his best friends, J.P. McCall and Eli Garrett, sat playing their usual every-other-Thursday game of five-card stud, the famous big sky was fixing to bust wide open and dump a shitload of rain.

Cord, never the anxious type, had been curiously uneasy all day. Woken up that morning with the small hairs on his nape and forearms rising and an odd twitch in the pit of his stomach.

The storm had been brewing even

then, but it wasn't the impending gully washer that was getting under his hide. He was used to violent storms, having lived in God's country from the age of three; hell, he **relished** them, always had. Could stand at a window for hours, watching lightning slash jagged rips from sky to ground, dance along the rods on the barn roof, roll itself into a fiery ball and tumble from one end of the horizon to the other—and back again.

The wilder the show, the better Cord liked it.

Which was a damn good thing, since on the Montana plains extreme weather was common enough,—blazing hot summers, apocalyptic blizzards in winter, flash floods and the deep, sticky mud residents called gumbo in the spring, when the rains came and the snow began to melt high in the Rockies.

Some springs were mild; creeks and rivers, freshly thawed, stayed politely within their banks.

Flowers dotted the meadows, and the grass grew green and rich and plentiful on the range.

But if the winter had been hard, the snowmelt descended from the high country in dark, churning torrents, taking out roads, drowning fields and ranges.

Life was tough everywhere, Cord knew, but it took a special kind of stick-with-it to farm or run a ranch in Montana, even with decent equipment and enough capital to make it from one season to the next. Smaller outfits went under on a regular basis, all too often taking the hard work, hope and sacrifice of several generations down with them, but a surprising number held on, somehow.

Folks out here had plenty of backbone, and they kept their complaints to themselves.

The old-timers were particularly durable; the Four Horsemen of the Apocalypse could ride in, wreaking their predicted havoc, and these veterans of peace and war, hardship and plenty, would swear up and down it was nothing compared to that drought or wildfire or recession way back when.

As far as these descendants of pio-neers were concerned, the West in general—and Montana in particular—was no place for the timid or the easily discouraged.

And, being neither, Cord pretty much agreed.

So, no, it hadn't been the weather that made him jittery.

As the clouds gathered, darkening from pale gray to an ominous shade of ebony over the course of the day, a prelightning charge pulsed in the air, almost audible.

And then, between one heartbeat and the next, she was there.

The specter blew in through the rear door of Sully's place, the creak of its rusty hinges muted by a blast of thunder and, as if to ratchet up the drama a notch or two, a bolt of lightning struck just the other side of the vacant lot behind the bar, briefly illuminating the figure from behind.

Although her arrival was relatively

mundane—no shimmering ectoplasm, rattling chains or harrowing moans—the effect was still creepy, in a Wes Craven kind of way.

Cord, who was holding his first decent hand of the evening, one jack short of a royal flush, instantly dropped his cards.

J.P. turned in his chair, following Cord's gaze, and abruptly froze.

Eli, focused on his cards, took a while to shift mental gears and notice that Cord and J.P. were staring at something behind him.

Frowning, he swiveled, registered the slender haunt standing just inside the cardroom, rain lashing through the opening and pooling on the uneven floor around her feet.

"Holy shit," he whispered.

"Reba?" J.P. murmured, very quietly, like a man talking in his sleep.

J.P.'s retired service dog, Trooper, didn't move or make a sound.

The shadow-woman closed the door with visible effort and moved toward them, dumping a shabby backpack on

the nearby floor. She stopped just inside
the wavering circle of light that fell over
the round table where they sat, motion-
less, stricken to silence. They didn't even
think to stand in the presence of a lady,
normally a reflex as automatic as
breathing.

Not that any of them drew a breath.

Finally, Trooper bestirred himself,
stood at attention, emitting a low, uncertain sound, more whine than growl.

"At ease," J.P. told the animal, although he didn't look away from the
thin, bedraggled girl hovering at the edge
of the light.

Cord, finally over the initial shock,
and plenty embarrassed by his reaction,
shoved a hand through his hair and pulled
himself together.

Mostly.

The girl wasn't, **couldn't be**, Reba,
but the resemblance was downright
uncanny. She had Reba's coloring—
caramel-brown hair and those remark-
able amber eyes, her high, elegant cheekbones, too—but she was impossibly

young and a few inches shorter than her look-alike.

That she was related to Reba, and closely, was a sure bet, but she was no ghost back from the grave.

Of course she wasn't.

She'd given Cord one hell of a turn, though, and shaken J.P. and Eli up, too.

Had Reba had a sister? As Cord recalled, she hadn't said much about her family; in fact, she'd given the impression that she didn't have any kin at all.

Like this girl, Reba had just **appeared** one day, seemingly out of nowhere. Claiming to be eighteen, she'd landed a job cleaning rooms at the Painted Pony Motel, and started building herself a social life—which had consisted of hanging out with high school seniors and turning up at dances, football games and keggers when she wasn't working.

She'd almost certainly been closer to twenty; Cord had no doubt she'd lied about her age. As far as he knew, nobody had found Reba's preference for running with a younger crowd odd.

She'd had a way of deflecting questions, delicate or otherwise, laughing them off.

Now, here stood this young girl, literally the mirror image of the Reba they'd all known eighteen years ago.

They say everybody has a double.

Cord hadn't believed that—until now.

The resemblance could be coincidental, he reasoned, but that seemed a lot more unlikely than a biological connection. She had to be Reba's sister, niece, cousin...

Or daughter.

Was this girl, somewhere in her teens, Reba's **child**?

That possibility jarred Cord, colliding with a few **other** possibilities rolling around in his head at the moment.

Thinking he ought to say something, he opened his mouth, but his brain, busy with calculations, refused to cooperate. He couldn't form a single rational word.

Finally remembering his manners, Cord got to his feet and, awkwardly, J.P. and Eli stood up, too.

Eli was the first to recover the power of

speech.

"Who are you?" he asked the visitor. That was Eli, direct to the point of bluntness. In his line of work, as the local sheriff, that was a plus, though it often hampered him when it came to ordinary communication.

"Tonight," she said with a little shiver, which she tried to hide, "my name is Zelda."

Cord was still thrown by the mere fact of this woman-child, but he recovered enough to ask, "What is it the rest of the time? Your name, I mean."

She made a face and jutted out her chin, at once obstinate and defensive, her bare, skinny arms wrapped tightly around her middle, as though she thought she might splinter into pieces if she didn't keep a firm grip.

"Whatever I decide it will be," she replied crisply, but her bravado was clearly slipping now.

Cord took his denim jacket from the back of his chair and draped it around her shoulders without comment, while

J.P. silently offered her a place to sit, drawing back a chair, indicating it with a gesture of one hand.

She sank gratefully onto the wooden seat and surveyed the scarred tabletop, strewn with poker chips and cards dropped and forgotten when she made her grand entrance.

"How old are you?" Eli demanded.

"Twenty-two," the girl said, after the briefest hesitation.

"Bullshit," J.P. muttered, watching her, studying her, as they all were.

By then, the dog had lost interest, no doubt concluding that the new arrival represented no threat to his master and could therefore be safely ignored. He was curled up alongside J.P.'s chair again, as he'd been all evening.

"Okay," she admitted, with an exaggerated sigh of long-suffering tolerance, "I'm seventeen. Which is why I had to come in through the back door, since this joint is evidently a saloon or whatever."

"All right—Zelda," Eli persisted, "back

to the point of this conversation. Who are you, and what are you doing here?"

She studied her overlong fingernails, which were painted a troubling shade of greenish purple, dusted with glitter and noticeably chipped. Then she raised her Reba-eyes, wide and brown-gold, swept a haughty glance from Eli to J.P. to Cord, and finally swung it back to Eli.

"That was **two** questions," she pointed out mildly. "But I suppose, since you're the county sheriff, you have to grill every stranger you see."

So, she'd done her research. When in doubt, google.

"That wasn't an answer," Eli said.

"Zelda" raised her shoulders briefly, then lowered them again. Gave another little sigh, as though put upon. Lord, but teenagers could be a pain in the ass.

"You'll have plenty of time to quiz me later," she said, sitting up straight and tossing her head so that long tendrils of wet, tangled hair tumbled back over her left shoulder. "For now, I'm calling the shots."

The gesture was familiar, another echo of Reba, and so was the big talk.

"Unless," she went on, assuming a thoughtful expression, "you plan to run me in on a vagrancy charge or something."

"I could do that," Eli warned, but he was wearing down, Cord could see that. Hell, they all were.

It was surreal, as if they'd slipped out of the world they knew into some parallel dimension, where the rules were very different. Here, in this new place, it seemed that Reba wasn't dead and gone, long before her time. Her presence was palpable.

And she wanted something.

Cord hadn't gone to Reba's funeral; none of them had. Wouldn't have known she'd died if Brynne Bailey hadn't come back to Painted Pony Creek to take over her parents' failing restaurant and mentioned it one morning, when the three of them stopped by for breakfast.

Breast cancer, Brynne had said. About two years ago. It had been a shockingly quick decline. All very sad. She hadn't attended the services, either, since she'd been out of the country at the time on a research trip for her job with an art gallery back east, but she'd seen a notice on social media and sent flowers.

She hadn't said anything about Reba having kids.

Shaken again, Cord refocused his attention on Zelda.

She was wearing a skimpy tank top and stylishly ragged skinny jeans. He registered that much. And there was a tattoo on the rain-beaded skin at the base of her throat. A musical note. A double one with two stems.

J.P. got out his cell phone, peered at the screen. He needed glasses but was too vain to wear them in public, so he squinted a lot.

"Calling the cops?" the kid asked in a tone breezy with impudence. She darted a glance in Eli's direction. "That seems unnecessary since the head honcho is right here."

"Listen," J.P. interjected, ignoring her

remark, "can we get down to the pro-
verbial brass tacks here?" He slipped
his phone back in his shirt pocket and
glared down at the girl, marking off each
point on a finger as he made it. "You're
seventeen years old. You just turned up
in the back room of a seedy beer hall in
small-town Montana, during the middle
of the goddamned storm of the century.
None of us ever saw you before and
given the size of this place, that means
you aren't a local. It follows that you're
a runaway, and maybe in some kind of
trouble, too. Somebody, somewhere, is
worried sick about you."

Some of the zip went out of the girl.
"Nobody's worried about me," she said,
with a note of sadness none of them
missed. Again, she examined their
faces, each in turn. "Cord Hollister, J.P.
McCall and Eli Garrett. That's you guys,
right?"

"Right," Cord admitted, grimly amused. Google **did** have a lot of answers
—and, in his opinion, anyway, a lot to
answer for. "How about returning the

favor and telling us who you are and why you're here."

"I'm hungry," she said, as if she hadn't heard a word he said. "And I could really use a cup of hot coffee, strong, with three sugars and real cream. None of that powdered crap."

J.P. sighed. "I'll get you a hamburger and some java," he told her. "On one condition, of course—that you stop jerking us around and tell us what's going on here."

She smiled Reba's smile, and Cord, for one, felt as though he'd been gut-punched. "A hamburger would be awesome," she told J.P. sweetly. "Make it a deluxe, with a double order of fries, extra cheese and bacon, crisp."

"Not until you give us some answers," J.P. retorted.

"Okay, but I intended to spill my guts all along." She flung another glance at Eli, full of defiance. "I didn't thumb my way halfway across the country to watch a bunch of yokels play poker in some backwater dive. I have a very good reason for being here." A worried pause. "Does that mean I don't get the burger?"

J.P. merely shook his head, walked to the inside door, which led to the main tavern, shoved it open a crack and called, "Hey, Molly. Mind taking an order?"

At last Cord and Eli sat down.

It was a relief to Cord, since his knees had turned wobbly.

Molly, a plump, sweet-faced woman they'd all known since childhood, appeared, pad in hand, trying to peer past J.P.'s shoulder and get a look at the girl.

Having lived in Painted Pony Creek since her teens, Molly knew just about everything that went on there, and she planned to keep it that way.

Now whispers were exchanged, Molly's demanding in tone, J.P.'s easy-going and smooth as could be.

Molly sighed audibly. "Willie isn't going to like it, that girl being on the premises, I mean. She can't be more than sixteen years old, and the state could pull his liquor license—"

"The kid isn't drinking, and technically, she's not in the bar," J.P. pointed out. "We'll take full responsibility for her. Just bring the burger and fries, okay? Coffee, too. Lots of sugar and cream. The wet kind."

"Not the low-fat stuff," the girl specified decisively, before adding a belated "please."

"Burgers all around," Molly said, putting pencil to pad with a flourish. The space between her overplucked brows remained furrowed, though, and her eyes narrowed as she took in Cord, then Eli, then J.P. "The three of you have been swilling beer since you got here, and I'll bet those peanuts I brought with the first round are all you boneheads have had to eat since lunch."

"Fine," J.P. agreed, looking back at his friends for confirmation, receiving none, and proceeding anyway. "Burgers all around. Put them on Eli's tab—or Cord's. I paid for the pizza last week."

Molly took advantage of J.P.'s distraction to slip past him and trundle purposefully across the room, all pudgy dudgeon in her mom jeans and Johnny Cash T-shirt, to stand next to the girl's chair.

"You in trouble, little gal?" she asked in her forthright way. Molly wore too much makeup, and her dyed blond hair was piled on top of her head and sprayed to immobility, but she was as kindhearted as they came.

"I'm all right," the girl said politely.

Molly looked skeptical. "You're not from around here. I know every kid in this town, and I would've seen you."

"No, ma'am, I'm not." She seemed so small and fragile in that moment, wet and skinny and pale, her eyes raccoon-like, encircled by smudged mascara, and so world-weary that Cord ached to look at her.

She was a baby—seventeen, if she was telling the truth, which was by no means a given—far from home. The thought of her or any young girl hitching rides along lonely highways made him cringe.

God knows what she'd been through on the road, what had prompted her to bolt in the first place.

"You tell me your name, honey," Molly coaxed. "I'll get in touch with your folks. Whatever happened, it can be made right."

"Molly," Cord interrupted, his voice a little shaky with an emotion he couldn't quite identify. Not that he tried. "The kid's fine for now. What she needs most is a plate of hot food and some strong coffee. We'll figure out the rest in good time."

Molly ignored him, except for a shushing motion of one hand. "Speak up, little girl. Your family must be beside themselves, wondering where you are. Far as they know, you could be dead in a ditch somewhere. So give me a name—or better yet, a phone number—and I'll get word to them."

Nothing. The visitor seemed to shrink inside herself, as though trying to disappear, and she wouldn't meet anybody's eyes.

Since Cord had gotten nowhere with Molly, J.P. gave it a shot. "We're fixing to starve to death here," he cajoled, with just the right amount of slick cowboy charm. "How about mustering up that grub?"

Another rumble-and-roar rocked the skies overhead, momentarily halting the exchange.

When the cracking of thunder subsided, long seconds later, Molly shook a finger at J.P. and proclaimed, "Wouldn't surprise me if that was a message from the good Lord Himself, J.P. McCall, telling you to watch your mouth and show some respect for your elders."

J.P. laid a hand to his chest, fingers splayed. "Why, Miss Molly," he teased, "I have the utmost respect for my elders, and for you in particular."

Molly's mouth tightened, and she shook her head in mock disgust, although a twinkle danced in her pale blue eyes. She gave the girl one more searching look and reluctantly left the room.

No one spoke right away, despite the

lull in the storm that would have made conversation feasible.

Eli gathered the cards back into a deck and thumped the edges against the tabletop, end over end. Repeatedly.

He tended to fidget when he was thinking.

J.P. got out his phone again, swiped to his favorite app and frowned at what came up on the screen. Punched a few keys, probably checking his sizable stock portfolio to find out if he was richer than he'd been five minutes ago.

Cord settled back in his chair and folded his arms, watching the girl as Trooper roused himself, got up off the floor and rested his muzzle on her blue-jeaned thigh.

Tears glimmered in her eyes as she laid a gentle hand on the dog's head and whispered, "Hey, buddy. How ya doin'?"

"You have a dog of your own?" Cord asked casually. "Back home, I mean?"

She bit her lower lip, shook her head. "Not anymore," she said wistfully.

"You look a lot like somebody we used to know," J.P. ventured, having put his phone away.

Eli stopped making that infernal noise with the cards, and Cord was grateful.

"Do I?" The girl's aplomb was back, just like that. Gone was the defeated, rain-drenched waif, wandering the countryside on a stormy night, taking shelter in the cardroom behind Sully's, replaced by a fiercely determined she-warrior. "Well, then, I guess that'll make it easier to convince you."

There was a long moment of pure tension, stretched to the snapping point, and then Cord asked, "Convince us of what?"

She took her time answering. "I'll get to that," she said, sitting up very straight now, still stroking Trooper. "After we eat."

Eli leaned forward, his face solemn. "No more games," he said. "You're the spitting image of Reba Shannon. What's your connection to her?"

The kid hesitated, then opened her

mouth to answer—or dish out more guff —but Molly came through the swinging door with an eloquent crash, carrying a tray. The mugs rattled when she plunked it down hard in the middle of the table, and coffee splashed around in the carafe.

"The burgers will be ready in a few minutes," she announced with a sniff.

And then she was gone again, snit and all.

"What was **that** about?" the girl asked.

J.P. was pouring coffee with a slight smile on his face. "Molly hates a mystery," he said lightly. "She'll be in a fine fuss until she knows what's going on, right down to the last detail. Chapter and verse."

The girl helped herself to one of the mugs and added plenty of sugar and thick cream before lifting it to her mouth.

"What **is** going on?" Eli tried again. He might have intimidated a lot of teen-agers with his official status, his dark scruff of a beard and his practiced glare, but this one merely sipped coffee and smiled with her eyes.

She must have downed half that first cup before lowering it and saying softly, "Reba Shannon was my mom."

Was.

The reminder packed a punch. Reba, a vital force, was gone.

"Oh, don't worry that I'm scamming you. I actually have a birth certificate." She flinched. "I can show it to you later, okay, Mr. Sheriff?"

It still seemed impossible...Except that, no, it wasn't. Reba's death was hard enough to believe and, in some ways, to accept. But she had a **kid**? Seventeen or eighteen? He wasn't going to think about the potential implications of that. Implications not just for him but for all three of them. That kind of reflection would have to wait...

"We won't worry about it now," Eli said. "But back to Reba..."

The girl must have read something in their faces. "You knew, then? That she died?" she asked.

"Yes," Cord answered at some length,

his voice so hoarse it hurt. "We knew."

Accusations sparked in the amber eyes. "I don't remember seeing any of you at the funeral."

Cord's own eyes scalded, and he couldn't look at either J.P. or Eli. Didn't dare.

"It was too late by the time we found out," Eli said.

"Would you have shown up, any of you, if you'd known earlier?" It was a challenge; she knew the answer.

Unfortunately, she was right.

The ensuing silence blocked out even the bull-bellow roar of the storm.

"Probably not," Cord said.

The girl bristled again, bit her lower lip.

The truth was, Reba had done her share of damage during her months in Painted Pony Creek. He wasn't about to lay that on this frightened, broken, lonely child, but facts were facts.

The rain slackened suddenly, reduced to a rhythmic patter on the rooftop.

The girl sat very still, huddled inside Cord's jacket, meeting no one's gaze, saying nothing but exuding hurt and fury and confusion, all at once.

J.P. and Eli were looking down at the tabletop.

Trooper, his head now resting on the girl's lap, gave a despondent little whimper.

Molly, with her questionable timing, broke the stalemate by bumping the door open with one swing of her hips and bustling in, food-laden tray gripped in both hands.

She set the tray down, right on top of the scattering of poker chips, nearly overturning the coffee carafe in the process, and left again, still in a huff.

The girl came alive at the sight of the burgers and fries nestled in battered plastic baskets, the paper linings spotted with plenty of grease. She extended one hand toward the grub, drew it back again.

"Go ahead," Eli said quietly. "Eat."

She practically did a swan dive into the food.

Cord didn't reach for a basket, and

neither did Eli or J.P.

They were all hungry, Molly had guessed right on that score, but Cord, for one, felt as though he was walking a tightrope. A single move, however slight, would send him smashing onto the ground.

Or so it felt.

Watching the child gobble down a hot meal, evidently the first she'd had in a while, Cord let his thoughts wander, and they went straight to Reba. Vibrant, beautiful, dangerous Reba.

A Category 5 hurricane of wind and ice and fire, all wrapped up in one trim and entirely unpredictable package— that was the Reba he'd known and, yes, loved, with all the testosterone-fueled passion of a seventeen-year-old hotshot kid.

It was an old story, a typical rite-of-passage thing. Reba had played him, big-time, along with Eli and J.P., of course. Left them wondering what else she'd lied about.

Oh, she'd been an enigma, all right.

And that had been part of her attraction, he supposed.

The whole thing might not have jammed up his gears the way it had if he'd been the only dimwit pawn on her chessboard, but Eli and J.P. had been part of her game, as well.

As young and perennially horny fools will do, they'd fallen for Reba's elaborate stories, all three of them, each believing himself to be her one-and-only true and forever love.

Cord had long since come to the conclusion that he'd believed the lies because he'd **wanted** to believe them. He'd suspended his innate common sense, ignored the excuses, the fault lines and inconsistencies in her stories, and his friends had done the same.

It was a dangerous thing, wanting so badly for something to be true that you dismissed all contrary evidence, he reflected now.

Suddenly, a memory of the last time he'd seen Reba overwhelmed the present and pulled him back into the past...

One August night after graduation, he and J.P. had returned early from an out-of-town rodeo and put in an unexpected appearance at a friend's party, both of them all slicked up and secretly eager to surprise Reba.

Well, they'd surprised her, sure enough.

Surprised themselves, too.

Found her in the shadows just beyond the reach of the crackling bonfire, wrapped around Eli Garrett like a roll of freshly glued wallpaper, the two of them kissing as if they were trying to swallow each other. Oblivious to the revelry, the laughter, the joking, the swilling of keg beer, they might as well have been alone on the planet.

The sight had struck Cord with the impact of a mule's kick, busting through the thin layer of denial like a revelation from on high.

The crowd, noisy and fluid a second before, had gone into instant freeze-frame.

With that silence came a second realization, almost as humiliating as the first.

Everyone in Painted Pony Creek had known what Reba was doing that summer. Everyone except J.P., Eli and Cord himself.

He'd glanced J.P.'s way, seen his own reaction reflected in his friend's face.

Finally noticing that something was up, Eli and Reba had eased apart, Eli's expression wary, Reba's confused, then startled, then panicked.

Eli had pried himself from her loosened embrace, and she'd clung to him for a moment before she let him go.

Although Cord would have liked that fateful evening to end in calm, rational discussion, three close friends reasoning things out, coming to terms with the obvious, it hadn't gone down that way.

Instead, after a few heated words, they'd lit into each other, then and there.

If half the varsity football team hadn't separated them, they probably would've done some lasting damage.

They'd emerged with bloodied knuckles, world-class shiners and fat lips.

Superficial stuff, not that unusual, considering the ways of teenage boys,
especially ones raised rough-and-tumble,
country-style.

Sadly, the real injuries ran much deeper.

The bond of trust, something they'd
depended on, even held sacred, albeit
unconsciously, had been broken. All
three of them felt betrayed, sold out by
the two people they'd believed would
always have their backs, no matter what.

Reba, meanwhile, had quietly disappeared, caught a ride back to the
Painted Pony Motel, packed her stuff
and skipped town.

No explanations, no excuses and
certainly no apologies.

She was just gone.

For good.

Her absence should have calmed the
troubled waters a little, but it hadn't.

The three amigos, inseparable since
first grade, were on the outs, and it had
felt permanent.

Glancing at his friends now, Cord could
hardly believe it.

That fall, they'd gone their separate ways without so much as a goodbye.

Cord had entered his freshman year at the University of Montana, Eli opted for a criminal justice course over in Seattle, and J.P., who had completed a special ROTC program in his junior and senior years of high school, joined the army.

J.P.'s first leave happened to fall at Christmastime and, prior to starting more high-level, if-I-tell-you-I'll-have-to-kill-you training, came home to be with his family.

Cord and Eli were back in town, too, for winter break.

They probably would've gone right on freezing each other out if they hadn't been tricked into showing up at the same dinner table on Christmas Day.

Cord's late granddad, that sly old coot, had orchestrated the setup, with plenty of help from J.P.'s and Eli's families. They'd celebrated on neutral ground, at Bailey's, the run-down restaurant on Main Street. It was the whole boisterous bunch—parents, grandparents, siblings, aunts and uncles, cousins and friends. These days, under Brynne's management, ever since her parents had retired to Arizona, the place had been fixed up. Cozy. Comfortable. Art on the walls. And it even had a liquor license now.

Back then, Bill Hollister had booked the place for a private party and had later invited guests to his home, where he (discreetly) provided some wine, beer and bourbon for the occasion.

Cord, Eli and J.P. had all balked, of course, once they arrived at Bailey's and realized what was happening, and Bill had gone so far as to announce that nobody was going anywhere until they stopped acting like dad-blamed idiots and talked things through, man-to-man.

Their respect for the old man kept them from storming out.

They'd eaten turkey and all the customary trimmings in seething silence, but, after the pecan pie was served, the mood seemed to mellow.

Holiday tunes played on the jukebox, prompting aunts and uncles to get up and dance to numbers like "Rockin' around the Christmas Tree" and "Jingle Bell Rock." Colored lights blinked and glowed around the frosted windows and spilled onto the snow beyond, and a tacky aluminum tree filled a corner of the room, fake presents glittering beneath it.

Cord had half expected to look out the window and see Jimmy Stewart running down Main Street, shouting lines from the final scenes of **It's a Wonderful Life.**

Merry Christmas, Mr. Potter!

Merry Christmas, you wonderful old building and loan!

It was almost magical, and irritating as hell.

The whole troupe had gone back to the Hollister ranch house, and Cord, Eli and J.P. had found themselves in the small storeroom off the kitchen, seated on crates, avoiding each other's eyes.

"I'll lock you in if I have to," Cord's grandmother had said sweetly from the doorway, dangling a ring of keys in one hand and giving them a jingle.

J.P. had shaken his head with a resigned

chuckle.

Mimi Hollister had smiled warmly and closed the door.

Finally, the ice had been broken—or at least cracked a little.

At first, the exchange was grudging, a word here, a grunt there.

Cord couldn't recall precisely what was said, but there'd been some sniping, at least in the beginning, followed by the usual questions, such as, "How's school?" and "What's it like, being a soldier?"

Once they'd exhausted the mundane stuff, there was nothing to do but get down to the real issue. Settle things, one way or another, and move on, as friends or not.

Reba's name hadn't come up right away. She was the live hand grenade, ready to explode, at their feet.

Then Eli's face had split into a wide grin, and he'd said, as near as Cord remembered, "It took me a while to work it out in my head, but I figure the person I'm really pissed off at is myself."

Nobody needed clarification; he was referring to the night the shit had hit the fan, when they'd all shown up at that end-of-school party and run smack into the hard truth.

Eli had gone on. "Look, we screwed up. Royally—all of us. We fell for the same girl. It happens. Punches were thrown. But maybe knocking each other around was as close as we could get to pounding on **ourselves**. Did you ever think of that? That we did the best we could, with the precious little we knew?"

"Seems to me," J.P. had mused, "that we should've blamed **Reba**." He'd paused. "Especially since we talked about everything in those days. There weren't any secrets between us. So why didn't we talk about her?"

"I've wondered that myself," Cord had admitted. "Reba played us for fools, no question, but the fact is, we let her do it. On some level, we knew exactly what the deal was."

"What are we?" J.P. had demanded. "Stupid?"

"Well," Eli had drawled, "yeah."

"Not to mention horny," J.P. had said.

They'd all laughed then, and that was when the mending began, like a broken bone knitting itself back together, into a stronger whole.

The process of rebuilding had been gradual but steady. After that Christmas party (and the subsequent drinks at the Hollisters'), they'd kept in touch, met up when time and circumstances allowed. Eventually, the breach had closed forever, and that was a damn good thing, considering all that had yet to unfold.

A day would come—hell, more than one—when they'd need each other more than ever.

Cord didn't want to think about those things now, hard as it was to avoid them with Reba's double sitting right there, sharing their table. He didn't want to spend any more time recalling the past. Even the toughest cowboy had his limits, and this current matter was enough to handle for the moment.

He made a conscious shift back to the

present.

Thankfully, he hadn't missed much.

The girl had eaten her fill, which was plenty for such a small person.

She sat up very straight, wiped her mouth and hands with a paper napkin, crumpled it and asked brightly, "Where were we?"

Where indeed? Cord thought.

"You were telling us that Reba was your mother," Eli said evenly.

"Yes," the woman-child agreed. "And about how she died and none of you came to the funeral because you didn't know she was dead and all that."

The gibe registered, as it was meant to.

"So then it was just you and your dad," J.P. prompted. "Any brothers or sisters?"

"I'm an only child," came the reply. "No step-siblings or half siblings. And I didn't have a dad. Just a stepfather, who remarried six months after we buried Mom and wanted me out of the picture ASAP."

"Grandparents?" Eli suggested hopefully. "Aunts and uncles? Cousins?"

She shook her head and, for a moment, amber fire flashed in her eyes. "Nope. None of the above."

"Who took care of you?" J.P. asked. "After Reba...died?"

"Mostly," the girl said, "I took care of myself." She paused, looked down at Trooper, and an expression of such sorrow crossed her face that Cord's heart cracked right down the middle. When she raised her head, tears glimmered in her lashes. "They gave away my dog."

Cord swallowed hard, near tears himself. "Who did?"

He wanted names, addresses. Wanted to track down the heartless assholes and rearrange their faces, feature by feature.

Which was why he didn't ask for specifics.

The reply was almost flippant. "Who else? The stepfather and his bimbo bride. I freaked out, and guess what? They gave **me** away, too. Next thing I knew I was in a foster home. And that was only the first."

J.P. muttered a curse, shoved the splayed fingers of one hand through his dark blond hair and glanced Cord's way, as did Eli, gauging his reaction. Until he was three years old, when Bill and Mimi Hollister had appeared out of nowhere and rescued him, he'd been in and out of the foster system himself. His father, Bill and Mimi's son, had died before he was born. He hadn't seen his mother, Julie, since he was removed from her custody at the age of two and had no actual memories of her.

At the moment, there was no room in his mind—or his heart—for thoughts of those long-ago days. Most of what he knew about his early past he'd learned from Bill and Mimi. What he felt now was fury, and deep empathy for the girl huddled inside his jacket.

Before he or his friends could find words, Reba's daughter went on.

"Don't go feeling sorry for me," she warned. "Bad things happen to everybody."

Eli sucked in a breath, huffed it out. He

was back in cop mode, but he spoke gently. "So you ran away from the latest foster home?" he asked.

"No," she said, with obvious pride. "I applied for emancipation and I got it."

Though he suspected the kid knew how to lie—like her mother—Cord believed her. She wouldn't be the first minor to go before a judge, make her case for independence and walk out as an adult, at least in the eyes of the law.

Evidently, J.P. was still hung up on her vanished pet. "Who does that?" he murmured. "Who gives away somebody else's dog?"

"Dooley's okay," the girl said. "It wasn't easy, but I found him. He went to a shelter, and he was adopted right away. He has a nice family now."

Cord pushed back his chair, stood and turned his back on the small group. If he lost his composure, he didn't want anyone to see.

He heard J.P. and Eli get up, move toward him. J.P.'s hand came to rest on his shoulder.

"You all right, cowboy?" Eli asked gruffly.

Cord nodded. Turned to face his friends and spoke quietly. "I guess I forgot, after all these years of good living, what a shit-hole this world can be, especially for kids."

"I'm not a kid," the girl called out from her place at the poker table.

Her words broke the tension, and Cord cleared his throat, shook his head again.

"So much for private conversation," Eli said, with a wry grin.

"Do you guys want to know why I'm here or not?" She sounded impatient now, and little wonder. She was cold, tired and wet.

Cord, Eli and J.P. returned to their chairs. Stared pointedly in her direction and waited for what they all figured was coming.

"One of you," the child announced, "is my father." A pause. "Make that **sperm donor**. A **father** would've been there when I needed him, or at least checked up on me once in a while."

CHAPTER TWO

Shallie Fletcher pulled into the weedy gravel parking lot of the Painted Pony Motel on Thursday evening and sat for about five minutes, motor running, windshield wipers splashing back and forth in frenzied futility as heavy rain sheeted the glass. Peering through the watery blur, she braced herself against another kind of deluge—memories of growing up here, cleaning rooms after school and on weekends, wanting nothing so much as to get away.

But the past, like the storm, would not be ignored.

One June night, a week after her eighteenth birthday, humiliated and ashamed beyond bearing, Shallie had packed the few belongings worth taking with her, waited until she was sure her aunt and uncle were sleeping off that night's shared fifth of cheap vodka, and sneaked out. In those first moments of freedom, she'd had no particular destination in mind. Any sizable city would have done, as long as it was far away and full of strangers.

Like many teenage runaways, Shallie hadn't given much thought to the dangers waiting for her out there in the big, wide world; in retrospect, the risks she'd taken, hitching rides with strangers, sleeping in rest-stop bathrooms, stealing food when her money ran out, made her shudder.

She'd really been quite sheltered back then, despite her half-assed upbringing, and ridiculously naive, as well.

Rain hammered at the roof of her car as she resisted yet another overwhelming temptation to shift gears, do a three-point turn and lay rubber getting the hell out of there. Again. But Shallie was through running away, wasn't sure it was even possible. After all, here she was, parked in the same old lot, in front of the same forlorn pile of weathered boards, broken gutters and dirty windows.

There was a certain inevitability about it.

Besides, she'd spent the last years carefully reinventing herself. She wasn't that unwanted child anymore; she was the person she had **decided** to be, strong, educated, responsible and self-confident. And that person had business in Painted Pony Creek, Montana. Business of one kind and another...She drew in a shaky breath and loosened her white-knuckle grip on the steering wheel. She sat still and took in her surroundings.

Even through the torrent, she could see that time had been especially unkind to the small motel at the side of a forgotten road. In its heyday, long before her time, the place had been a going concern, conveniently situated at the edge of a busy highway.

Then, in the early 1960s, a wide, well-paved interstate, long under construction, finally opened to traffic. The Painted Pony Motel was suddenly irrelevant, too far off the newly beaten path to attract more than a few of the random travelers who, along with hikers, hunters, fishermen and vacationing families of limited means, had sustained it.

Seeing the place now, through the eyes of an adult, Shallie marveled that it hadn't been bulldozed years ago, the land cleared for grazing or a trailer park or a crop of Christmas trees.

Instead, the Painted Pony kept its sad, slump-shouldered vigil, hunkered down like some beaten creature awaiting the next blow.

The paint was peeling away from the clapboard walls, and the roof sagged. The neon Welcome to the Painted Pony Motel sign, though still clinging to its weathered metal post out by the road, was dark, every letter burned out and coated with grime.

There was an enormous spider-shaped

crack in the office window, as if someone had bounced a rock off the glass,
or plugged it with a bullet. The word
Vacancy glowed, dimly hopeful, in the
lower right-hand corner, as in days of
old, though only the **V** and the two **c**'s
had any juice.

The whole effect was glum, and more
than a little spooky. It wasn't hard to
imagine Norman Bates somewhere inside, sitting in his rocking chair, wearing
his dead mother's clothes and cradling
an ax in his arms.

The image brought a badly needed
smile to Shallie's face, if a flimsy one. The
motel was, and probably always had
been, a depressing place, but it hadn't
been a house of horrors. Not for her,
anyway.

Della and Norm Schafer, Shallie's legal
guardians from the day she was abandoned as a two-year-old, in Room 2,
hadn't physically abused her. Granted,
they did apply for, and receive, foster
parent status and money, largely because there was a legitimate family

connection, since her mother had been Della's half sister...Still, life hadn't been easy.

Dysfunctional even then, discouragement ground into them by chronic hard times, the Schafers had fed her, provided her with clothes, mostly hand-me-downs and thrift store finds, and new shoes, twice a year. They'd kept her in school and, once a week, they'd sent her (and, of course, their own kids) to church.

Neither Della nor Norm would have dreamed of setting foot in God's house themselves, and they hadn't been shy about saying so. Church was for hypocrites and cowards, they'd maintained, though every Sunday morning, they'd sent their little brood off to hear the Gospel and drop a coin in the collection plate.

Throughout Shallie's childhood, they'd treated her with the same disinterest and sometimes scorn as they had their twins, Bethanne and Russ, who were five years older than Shallie and none too pleased to have a toddler shoehorned into the cramped bedroom they shared in the "family quarters" behind the motel's front office.

At first, the twins had largely ignored the newcomer.

Later, when bored, they'd teased and sometimes bullied her. They'd spent whole days pretending she was invisible, so convincingly that Shallie, still too young to start kindergarten, began to believe them. Maybe, she remembered thinking, she wasn't real at all. Maybe she'd just made herself up.

To a four-year-old, the possibility made sense.

All her life, all that time spent living with the Schafers, she'd known that no one was going to protect her. She couldn't depend on Norm or Della—they weren't mean, but they paid little or no attention to the kids, unless they were forced to. Their interests usually didn't veer past the bottles of low-end booze they gulped down and the equally low-end reality TV shows they devoured. Nor could she depend on Russ, who'd made clear that he had no use for her. Especially after an incident that involved her smacking him—hard enough to cause a bloody nose—when he'd tried to make her eat a stinkbug...

Bethanne seemed to resent Shallie as much as her brother did.

Shallie had **herself**, that was all.

But maybe at the time—and even now—that was enough.

Tonight, years later, sitting in her car with rain strafing the roof like bullets, Shallie sighed. She'd had to defend herself, and she didn't regret it, but she felt profoundly sorry for the child Russ had been, overweight, unattractive and not considered bright, with a father who made fun of him. Held him in contempt.

Della hadn't been much kinder.

Little wonder Russ was still hiding out in the Painted Pony Motel after all these years, even as the roof threatened to fall down around his ears.

Bethanne, if her social media posts could be believed, had fared better than her brother had. At first, anyway...

She'd split for the big city of Helena the day after high school graduation, rented a room in a private home, landed a job in a big-box store and put herself through cosmetology school. Eventually, she'd married and moved with her husband to a small town in West Texas. She was now Bethanne Robertson. She'd opened her own beauty shop and never returned to Painted Pony Creek— except briefly for her mother's funeral— as far as Shallie knew.

For a while, Shallie and Bethanne had kept in touch via the internet, but gradually, they'd stopped emailing. Shallie, officially a "friend," had still checked Bethanne's Facebook page now and then, but she never updated her own information on the site, and there'd been nothing from Bethanne in more than two years. Where was she now? Shallie had no idea whether she was still married, still had her business, still lived in Texas.

From the little Shallie **had** been able to

learn, mostly by reviewing the social media pages of high school classmates, Bethanne had started off doing well, which Shallie already knew. But recently —according to various rumors—she'd bounced between various county jails in Texas and court-mandated stints in rehab.

And indeed, there were rumors aplenty —Bethanne had joined a cult, met up with a serial killer, moved to Boise, found religion, remarried, witnessed a crime and gone into witness protection. Interesting theories, to Shallie's mind, but **only** theories, mostly gossip and speculation at that, none of them supported by any evidence she could see.

In her opinion, Bethanne might well be dead. Despite some earlier success, she'd disappeared from everyone's life, from social media, from sight. She'd been, or had certainly become, hell-bent on self-destruction, according to what several people claimed to have heard or observed. Most likely, she'd succeeded, with or without the help of another person. Was there any way of knowing?

Shallie had been secretive about her own location, in case Norm and Della came to expect some form of financial—or other—support. Some kind of pay-back...Della had been killed, ironically by a drunk driver, three years after Shallie left.

Norm had followed his wife a few months later, dying of "complications" after minor surgery. Although the online obit hadn't said so, Shallie figured he'd been felled by a combination of grief and that bottom-shelf vodka.

In both cases, she'd sent brief notes of condolence, first to Norm and Russ, and then to Russ alone, accompanied by small checks. She hadn't enclosed a phone number, however, or given a return address.

She had, in fact, gone so far as to mail both envelopes to a friend in Oklahoma City, who'd sent them on so they wouldn't bear a Seattle postmark.

Silly, she thought now. It wasn't as if any of the Schafers would have bothered to track her down and force her to come back into their lives.

In the end, only Shallie herself, odd girl out, forever under-foot, treated as an inconvenience when she'd been noticed at all, had escaped the glum legacy of Norm and Della Schafer and their combined neuroses. How had that happened?

Okay, yes, she hadn't emerged entirely unscathed; she had issues, and some of them stemmed directly from things that had happened right here, but at least she hadn't been trapped, like Russ, or irreparably damaged, like poor Bethanne —as it now appeared.

For whatever reason, Shallie had not only survived, she'd thrived, for the most part. She'd made some stupid mistakes, especially in the beginning, but she'd eventually gotten her act together after fleeing the town of Painted Pony Creek and this dump of a motel.

She'd come a long way...and she'd managed to create a life pretty much on her own terms. She'd landed in Seattle, after knocking around for six months or so, found a job—cleaning in a hotel (she'd certainly had the experience!) —and a room in a decent boarding-house. Later, she'd put herself through art school and now worked as an illustrator; she'd saved her money, made friends, been married to a good man, even though that marriage had ended in divorce, and developed a passion for horses. Her best friend, Emma Grant, ran a therapeutic riding program for kids with physical and/or emotional challenges, just outside Seattle, and Shallie had spent every spare hour volunteering there and loved it. She and Emma had discussed how she might quit her graphic arts job and then they'd become business partners; she was currently on an unpaid three-month leave so she could explore that option— and pursue the other reason she was here...

The horses and the children had taken her out of herself, healed her in the broken places, taught her courage and persistence and the power of gentle persuasion.

She'd still be in Seattle right now, she reflected, if she hadn't come to a decision about her life and particularly her past. If she didn't have something urgent to do. Well, to be honest, she had three priorities.

And the first of them, in some ways the most urgent, had brought her back to a place she'd vowed never to set foot in again—no matter what.

Never say never, she thought ruefully.

Time to quit procrastinating and get started.

Resolved, Shallie took a long, deep breath, held it, thrust it out in a forceful gust. Then she shut off her car and pushed open the door.

She was immediately drenched by a cascade of rain, almost as if she'd been singled out for a private deluge.

That quickly, the long day on the road caught up with her. Ever since landing at the airport in Billings, renting a car, setting out, she'd felt a tension that was no longer familiar to her.

She was exhausted, weary down to her bones.

You can do this, Shallie reminded herself. **Get moving, before you drown.**

Taking her own advice, she shut the car door behind her and hurried toward the seedy motel's tiny office.

Tonight, she had only one person from her past to face, and the sooner she did that, the sooner she could move on.

Reaching the door, she shoved hard and fairly hurled herself over the threshold. She'd half expected to encounter Russ first thing, but the office was empty.

Shallie paused, catching her breath, dripping rainwater onto the gray carpet, which had probably been some other color once upon a time. Even through the soles of her wet shoes, she could feel the stiffness of the pile and gave an involuntary shudder. God only knows when the rug had been vacuumed last, let alone shampooed.

She looked around, still lingering by the heavy glass door, which had fallen shut behind her.

The walls were even dingier than she recalled. There were cobwebs in the corners, and clutter covered the reception desk—magazines, junk mail, old newspapers and several coffee mugs. There was no computer, and the telephone was the same one Shallie remembered from her childhood, black and heavy, with a rotary dial. From where she stood, she could see that the numbers had been completely worn away.

The handbell still occupied its place on one corner of the desk, so Shallie reached out and gave it a brisk tap. A clamorous **ting** followed.

And she waited.

As her breathing slowed and her focus expanded, Shallie became aware of the drone of a TV set beyond the office wall, where the family had lived.

It was easy to imagine Russ settled in his dad's old recliner, staring morosely at the screen and drowning his resentments in booze.

"Hello?" Shallie called, finally, when

several minutes had passed and no one had appeared.

She was chilled, soaked to the skin, and she was ready to be done with this damn day, **more** than ready for a hot shower, a cold slice of pizza left over from a drive-through lunch, and eight solid hours of sleep. If not more.

"Hold your horses!" a male voice, surely Russ's, called. "I'm coming!"

Apparently, the son-and-heir had inherited his parents' flair for business, in addition to Motel Hell—and not much else, Shallie would have bet.

Finally, Russ lumbered in, a great hulk pushing the limits of ragbag sweatpants and a ratty T-shirt printed with some now unreadable but probably inflammatory slogan. Never the middle-of-the-road type, Russ had always chosen the course most likely to piss off as many people as possible.

Like his father before him, he had been aggrieved from birth, had scores to settle with the known universe and all its occupants.

Recognizing her, Russ came to a dead stop. With one sweep of his eyes, he took her in, head to toe.

"You," he said, affronted it would seem, not only by Shallie's presence, but by her very existence.

Maybe, Shallie thought, numb with fatigue, she should've waited until morning, come here in daylight. She could have booked a clean, pleasant room at the new-looking hotel in town, one with maids, room service and a Wi-Fi connection.

Except that she'd made a plan and intended to stick with it.

Like it or not, she was going to stay right here at the Painted Pony Motel, preferably in Room 2, where she'd been abandoned. There, she hoped, some dim fragment of memory might surface. A glimpse of her mother's face, a murmured goodbye, a promise to return.

Anything.

Not that the odds were with her on that score—years of online searches had yielded no information whatsoever about Christine Fletcher—but if there was the slightest chance that being back in the same surroundings might trigger some glimmer of recollection, she had to try. This was the biggest unanswered question of her life.

It was time. Time to go back to the source. To search in a more concerted, more serious way.

Besides, Shallie couldn't drive another mile, not after the day she'd put in. So, she clung to that one flimsy hope and resigned herself to a lumpy mattress, a moldy shower stall and a slice of rubbery pizza for supper.

"Hello, Russ," she said quietly.

"What do you want?" he demanded, his tone curt.

Shallie raised her shoulders slightly, lowered them again. "A room?"

"Here?" Russ frowned. He seemed not only confused but suspicious now.

No, Shallie replied in her mind, **at the high-end lodge I passed when I came through town. The one that doesn't look like something out of a horror**

movie.

"Here," she confirmed, hoping her voice sounded steady.

Russ studied her again, no friendlier than before. And he still hadn't moved. "Why?"

Shallie sighed. She was really too worn-out for a sparring match, verbal or otherwise.

"Come on, Russ. I have my reasons. And I know you have rooms available— the vacancy sign is on." Some of it was, anyway. "There aren't any other cars in the lot, either."

Russ spread his hands, his expression one of sly mockery. "Take your pick," he said. "If you insist on being our guest."

Wondering who the "our" might refer to, then promptly deciding she didn't care, Shallie glanced at the rack on the wall behind the desk, where the room keys hung on tarnished hooks. No fancy magnetized cards at the Painted Pony; these were actual metal keys, with numbered plastic fobs attached. Most of the lettering was worn away, like the digits on the telephone dial.

"I'll take Room 2," she said, about to open her purse, which, she realized now, was pressed between her right elbow and her rib cage as though she'd expected to be mugged at any moment.

Russ arched his brows and set his bulk in motion. "Interesting choice," he remarked dryly. "Room 2, I mean. Since that's the one Crazy Christine dumped you in." He didn't wait for a response. "I don't suppose you remember, you were so little, but I was the one who found you that day. Did I ever tell you that?"

"Yes, actually, you did." **Only about a thousand times.**

He extended the key, fob dangling. "You were screaming at the top of your lungs," Russ reminisced as if she hadn't spoken. "You were naked, except for a wet diaper, and calling for your mama. By then, she was long gone, of course."

Shallie resisted a sudden impulse to defend this woman, her mother, who was and most likely would remain a total stranger to her. Della's story, when she could be persuaded to discuss the matter at all, had been pretty basic. Shallie was the daughter of Della's half sister, Christine, which was why Della hadn't been asked to sign a registration card when she checked in that long-ago day. She'd been "family."

And oh, yeah, Della Schafer had been all about kinship.

All Shallie really had was a name and a birth certificate. According to that, her father was "Unknown" and her birthplace was Chicago.

The real reason the Schafers had taken her in was, of course, far more prosaic—their monthly check from the state, very little of which had been spent on Shallie, or even Russ and Bethanne, but that was neither here nor there.

The one thing Shallie had really wanted from the Schafers—the truth—had not been forthcoming.

Which was why she'd started an investigation of her own.

It hadn't been easy or productive, any more than her search for Bethanne.

There were a lot of Christine Fletchers in the world, as it turned out, and none of the dozens Shallie had contacted over the years had admitted to leaving a two-year-old daughter behind at the Painted Pony Motel a quarter of a century ago. More like thirty-plus years now.

She'd studied grainy photos online, hoping to spot a resemblance to herself, since she'd never seen a picture of Christine, hard as that was to believe. She'd surfed social media sites, pored over newspaper archives, looked at birth and death records in more states and counties than she cared to remember. She'd checked out cemeteries, mental hospitals, halfway houses and prisons.

All without a single lead.

So, here she was, back at good old square one. Her (mostly amicable) divorce from Rob had sparked an even greater need to know about Christine Fletcher — who she was, who her people were, what she'd been about. Della and Norm were both gone, of course, and Bethanne might be anywhere, including a pauper's grave in some unknown place, but Russ was still around, and if he knew anything, Shallie was going to get it out of him, one way or another.

She also meant to question as many of the locals as she could corner; some of the older people might remember Christine and be willing to talk.

Had Christine been mentally unbalanced, as Russ and Della and Norm had all claimed? Maybe. Parking a toddler in a crappy motel room and taking off for the unknown wasn't exactly normal behavior.

But wasn't mental illness a better excuse than not loving a child enough to keep her?

"Who was she?" Shallie asked, surprising herself. She hadn't planned to jump in like this; the plan called for patience. Caution. "My mother, I mean."

Russ shook his head. "You **know** who she was," he said with an exasperated sigh. Perhaps he was missing a rerun of some stupid reality show or merely wanted to drink in peace, but he wanted Shallie out of there, that much was obvious. "Crazy Christine. Mom's half sister."

"Okay," she said, resigned, taking out her billfold. Russ knew more than he was saying, she was sure of that, but she didn't have the energy to probe. Not tonight. She'd try again tomorrow, see if she could coax some forgotten detail from his booze-soaked brain. Not that Russ was a **bad** guy, and who knew what he might remember. Maybe if she asked the right questions...

"Put your wallet away," Russ told her with a dismissive wave. "This is on me." He turned to the wall and retrieved the key for Room 2.

"I don't mind paying," she said evenly.

Russ folded his arms, shook his head again. "You're family," he said, with a note of mockery or, worse, pity.

Shallie put her wallet back in her purse. Moved, key in hand, to the outside door.

At least the rain was letting up; she

hoped that was a good omen.

"Shallie?" Russ's voice was quiet, almost kind.

She didn't turn around or speak. But she did stop.

"What business could you possibly have, way out here in Buttcrack, Montana?" he asked.

She ignored his profane description of the town, although it probably described **his** view of it. "Here's the deal, Russ," she replied, still facing the door. "You tell me what you know about my mother —not Della's version, but what you, yourself, remember—and I just might answer that question." She wondered if he realized she'd actually **given** him her answer, or part of it, anyway. Her need to learn whatever she could about Christine Fletcher.

Russ was silent.

Shallie pushed open the door and stepped out into the drizzle. This time, it felt good, the rain, warm and gentle and, somehow, soothing.

CHAPTER THREE

Now what? Cord Hollister asked himself, as he drove the winding road to the ranch, the girl sitting silent in the passenger seat of his truck, arms wrapped tightly around her backpack. Thankfully, the rain had tapered off in the last hour, now reduced to a drizzle.

After some whispered discussion back at Sully's, he and J.P. and Eli had decided it made the most sense if he took the girl home—to stay with Mitch and Tina Robbins, the ranch foreman and his wife.

Thank God, when he called Tina, she'd readily agreed to take her in. Tina and Mitch were good people, and since their own brood was grown-up and gone, there was plenty of room in their spot-less double-wide trailer for one skinny, bullheaded girlchild.

Maybe Tina could get something out of the kid, like her real name for one thing. Cord wasn't buying the "Zelda" bit, and he was getting tired of thinking of her as "the girl" and its few variations.

"I looked you up online," said the mystery child. "You know, Google. I looked you all up. That's how I knew who was who. You're pretty famous. Are you rich, too?"

Cord laughed. "I'm not famous out-side the horse-training world," he said. "And I guess I do all right, moneywise." **Certainly well enough to pay child sup-port, if I'd known I might be a father. Damn it, Reba, any one of us, all of us, would've stepped up if you'd told us you had a child—and that we might each be the father...**

"I like it, that you work with horses," she said.

"You like horses?" It was a start.

"Better than people, most of the time."

Cord smiled at that, but he felt another ripple of sadness, too, remembering that story about her dog. If it was true—and it **felt** true—it was a real heartbreaker.

A lot of people liked animals better than their fellow human beings, he supposed, and he could empathize. He'd often thought the world might be a better place if the critters had it to themselves.

They were quiet for a while, man and girl; the silence was weary but companionable enough.

"You could teach me how to train horses, like you do," ventured his might-be daughter. "And how to ride..." In some ways, maybe a lot of ways, Cord hoped this spunky little hellcat really **was** his, and not just some clever con artist looking for a mark.

If it hadn't been for her heart-stopping resemblance to Reba, he probably wouldn't have believed a thing she said. That resemblance couldn't help awaking a few very specific memories of Reba.

The post high school party, of course, the one that ended in disaster for his most important friendships. An evening of laughter at the old pre-Brynne Bailey's. A walk in the woods, with plenty of moments spent leaning against trees, kissing...

Cord shook his head, dispelling those memories.

"I could teach you," he replied after a moment. "But I'd have to know your name, for a start. Not a made-up one, either. The real deal."

She considered that. "It's stupid," she said, at some length. "My name, I mean."

"Your mother must not have thought so," Cord observed carefully.

A long pause ensued.

"It's Charlotte," she admitted with marked reluctance.

Cord repeated the name in the silence of his mind. Liked it.

"What's wrong with 'Charlotte'? I think it's kind of pretty. Classy, even."

"It isn't **me**," said Charlotte. "Do I **look** classy to you?"

"Whoa, back," Cord said. "The tattoo maybe not, and your clothes have seen better days, but I reckon you'd clean up all right."

"Gee, thanks." She glowered at him. "What do you have against tattoos?"

"Nothing," Cord responded truthfully. **Except when they're on the neck of a teenage girl who might have my blood running through her veins.**

The turn onto the ranch road was coming up in a few hundred yards, so he signaled a left and slowed the rig.

"Is that it? Your place?" She pointed toward the large house on top of the rise, lit up against the gloom, thanks to Tina. She'd be waiting there, all down-home sweetness and good will, with fresh coffee brewing and some hearty dish ready to be popped into the micro-wave.

"That's it," Cord confirmed.

"It looks big."

"It is. But it isn't fancy, so don't think you're headed for the Ponderosa."

"What's the Ponderosa?"

"Never mind," Cord answered, with a tired grin. His grandfather had loved the old TV Westerns, especially **Bonanza** and **Gunsmoke**, and Cord had been raised on the reruns. He still spoke the lingo.

They bumped along the dirt road for a couple of minutes, and Cord stopped the truck beside Mitch and Tina's SUV.

The barn loomed in the darkness, more shadow than substance, but the house glowed like a Christmas tree.

"You're about to meet one of the kindest women on the face of the earth," Cord said after shutting off the engine. He knew he sounded serious, and that was fine because he was. "We're giving you the benefit of the doubt, kiddo, but I'm telling you right now that if you try to jerk Tina around, lie to her, or hurt her in any way, you'll have me to deal with."

The kid's eyes were wide. "Okay," she told him. "I hear you."

Cord shoved open his door. "Good," he said.

Bandit and Smoky, part-Lab mutts,

rushed to greet him, barking with that foolish joy particular to the canine crowd.

Cord glanced at Charlotte, about to tell her not to be afraid, that the dogs were harmless, but she was already approaching them, laughing at their enthusiasm.

"Hey, guys!" she crowed, ruffling their ears.

Tina stepped out onto the wraparound porch, her petite, slender form rimmed in light from the kitchen behind her.

"Hush up, you critters!" she called. "You'll scare our company away!"

"Remember what I said about messing with Tina," Cord said in a low voice.

"I'm not **completely** without manners, you know," Charlotte retorted in a loud whisper.

Tina was headed toward them, and they met in the middle of the yard, the dogs still half-frenzied with delight. For those two, every arrival was cause for celebration.

"Hi," Charlotte said warmly, extending a hand to Tina. "I'm Carly."

Carly, Cord thought. The diminutive

did suit her better than Charlotte.

Tina pulled Carly into a brief, tight hug, then held her at arm's length, running a motherly eye over her. "Lord, child, we need to get you inside so you can warm up." She cast a disapproving glance in Cord's direction, but she was already steering the girl toward the house. "You could catch your death in those damp clothes."

Carly seemed to lean into Tina just a little as she allowed herself to be hustled across the wet grass, and Cord, walking behind them, felt his spirits rise a notch. Until that moment, he'd wondered if the kid was ever going to let down her guard.

Well, she had with the dogs, which was an encouraging sign, certainly to someone like him. But he hoped he'd see more of who she was—and not just because she reminded him of Reba. That had its pluses and its minuses. But because she might be his **daughter**. Or Eli's. Or J.P.'s. Regardless of whether she was his kid or "honorary niece," she'd be part of his life. She'd change his life. And he'd change hers, he vowed. They all would.

Please God she wasn't lying! But, considering her Reba-ness and her age, he'd begun to decide she probably wasn't.

He watched as she and Tina hurried inside. All the way to the side porch and in through the kitchen door, Bandit and Smoky frolicked on either side of the females, a two-dog party. Big as they were, they were still pups, and it showed.

"Wow," Carly murmured, looking around the large, old-fashioned kitchen. "Time warp. It's the 1950s all over again."

The kitchen, in fact, was much as his grandmother had left it, right down to the wood-burning cookstove, scuffed linoleum floor and avocado-green appliances. The rest of the house—thanks to his ex-wife, Jenna—not so much...

Jenna had only been interested in their bedroom and the rooms on public display, the ones she could show off to guests (not that there were many, outside of Cord's friends). Besides, she'd counted on Tina to provide the majority of meals.

Tina had been after him to update the kitchen, too—brought up the subject once a week on average—and he always promised he would. Eventually. He glanced around; Mimi's needlework still hung on the walls, and her embroidered dish towels lay neatly folded in the cabinet drawer they'd occupied since she'd come to this house as a young bride. These things were deeply important to him. It was all about family. And memory...

Carly went straight to the iron beast against the far wall, warming herself in the woodsmoke-scented heat it gave off. Looking back over one shoulder, she frowned curiously. "Why are there two stoves?" she asked.

"A reasonable question," Tina said with a twinkle. She wore her silver-gray hair in a short, curly bob, and her brown eyes smiled behind her stylish glasses.

Tina was one of those people who lit up all over when she smiled.

"**That** stove," she went on, pointing to the green range, "barely works. The oven won't heat up half the time, and two of the burners are out of commission. And don't get me started on the fridge."

"Seems to me," Cord said dryly, "that something **already** got you started."

Tina made a **pffft** sound, followed by a dismissive gesture. She was focused on Carly, one hundred percent. "At least the other stove works, and there's a microwave," she said. "Are you hungry?"

Carly shook her head, and the tiniest smile curved her mouth. "No," she said, watching Cord. "So are you, like, a hoarder or something? Or just really, **really** behind the times?" She pointed to the tattoo on her neck, a reminder of their conversation in the truck. "Like, hello, this is a whole new century. Ink isn't just for sailors and guys in jail and guys who ride motorcycles anymore, and what **is** this stuff on the floor?"

Cord laughed, sent the dogs to their beds near the woodstove with a quiet word and a motion of one hand. They obeyed, collapsing onto the matching sheepskin pads with sighs of resignation, their brown eyes rolling toward Carly, liquid with devotion.

He was chilled, since the kid was still wearing his jacket, and he felt drawn toward the stove, but Carly was already there, and he didn't want to crowd her. She reminded him of a fawn, spindly legged and easily spooked.

"It's called linoleum," he said, looking down at the scrapes and scratches, noticing the places where the pattern had worn away. "As for the 'ink,' as you call it, no comment."

"Oh, yeah. Linoleum. I've heard of it." Carly was grinning and more relaxed than before.

Cord credited Tina, who was busy pouring coffee, with keeping the tension level down.

"Sit," Tina told Cord briskly. "You make me nervous, standing there like a telephone pole."

He chuckled, went to his customary chair at the long trestle table. Once, it had been his grandfather's place, and sitting there still felt odd, even after almost twelve years.

"Will this keep you awake?" Tina asked Carly, with sudden concern. Late-night coffee was an institution on the ranch, but the girl was a newcomer.

"Nothing keeps me awake," Carly replied, leaving the stove at last and taking a seat on one of the long benches lining either side of the table. Then, as an afterthought, she added, "Well, coffee doesn't, anyway."

Cord wondered what **did** keep her awake, but he wasn't about to ask.

He still felt the need to give the kid space and, besides, he wasn't sure he wanted to hear the answer. God only knows what she regarded as the twenty-first century norm.

"Well, you drink up, then," Tina said cheerfully, addressing the girl, setting three steaming mugs of hot java on the table. "Soon as you've warmed up a little, we'll head over to my place. You can take a hot bath—or a shower, if you'd prefer—and I'll rustle up pajamas for you. You're about the same size as my Susan. She keeps some clothes at our place, since she visits pretty often."

Carly cupped her hands around the mug in front of her, breathed in the rising steam with obvious appreciation. "Thanks," she said, and she sounded sincere.

Cord watched her and wondered if the kid was behaving herself because of the don't-mess-with-Tina edict he'd issued earlier, or if she simply enjoyed being mothered.

No question, Tina had a gift for that.

"You're entirely welcome," Tina said, patting Carly's shoulder gently as she passed, heading for the much-maligned refrigerator to grab a dairy carton.

To Cord's amusement, she sniffed the contents—in Tina's opinion, he played fast and loose with expiration dates—before coming back to the table and sitting down in Mimi's chair at the other end. She settled herself for a few minutes, watching fondly as Carly loaded her brew with plenty of sugar and sloshed in a generous dollop of cream.

It was an ordinary moment, but suddenly something warm and bittersweet welled up in his chest and overflowed. He didn't try to identify the emotion, he just let it ride.

Despite the coffee, Carly soon began to yawn.

Tina smiled. "Let's go home," she said, rising from her chair.

Carly visibly registered the word **home**, nodding, eyes closed. "Okay," she agreed.

Cord stood, too, out of long habit, and waited while Carly said goodbye to the dogs, then snatched up her grubby backpack, ready to go. She was at the door before she stopped and turned to Cord, starting to shrug out of his jacket. "I almost forgot to give this back."

"Keep it for now," he said.

She considered that briefly, then nodded. "Okay. Thanks."

"The car's unlocked," Tina told Carly, after a brief and awkward silence. "I'll be with you in a minute."

Carly paused, then went out.

"Who is this child?" Tina asked, as soon as she and Cord were alone.

Cord shoved splayed fingers through his hair. Sighed. "I'm not sure," he replied honestly.

Tina's eyes widened. "What?"

"I'll tell you what I know, which is damn little, by the way, but not tonight, if that's okay with you." He was bone-tired, though he knew sleep would be elusive, if it came at all.

"Of course it isn't okay with me," Tina answered sweetly, "but since you look as if you've been dragged backward through a knothole, as my grandmother used to say, I'll cut you some slack."

Cord laughed. "That's mighty big of you, Tina," he teased.

"Just this once," Tina was quick to respond. "Tomorrow, we talk."

"Fair enough," he agreed, feeling even wearier than before. The next day would be full, since he had a private client scheduled to show up bright and early for a one-on-one version of his basic horse-training course.

Damn if he hadn't forgotten all about that.

"It slipped your mind, didn't it?" Tina chided, though kindly. She could have made a good living as a phone psychic, the way she went around reading people's thoughts. "That you've got a student coming first thing tomorrow morning?"

"Yeah," he confessed. "It did."

"Well, then, you'd better get some rest. You have a reputation to maintain. The man who knows all there is to know about horses, and then some." Tina approached, stood on tiptoe and kissed his cheek. "Too bad you don't understand **people**, as well."

"Hey," Cord objected, a little miffed. "I 'understand people' just fine."

Tina glanced toward the door. "Do you? Including teenage girls?"

"Come on, Tina. Nobody understands teenage girls."

She smiled. "I do," she said. "I raised

three of them." She cocked a thumb in the direction Carly had gone. "That child is lost and so hungry for a place to belong it makes me want to cry just looking at her."

"Maybe she is," Cord allowed. "And maybe she's a first-class grifter." Despite his increasing confidence that the girl was telling the truth, or at least a substantial part of it, he wasn't entirely willing to let that remaining doubt go. He wasn't sure why. Out of self-defense? Not wanting to risk being hoodwinked or taken advantage of? If he bought her story too readily and then found out he'd been had, he wouldn't just feel like a fool, he'd be wounded, and deeply.

Tina rapped lightly on his chest with one fisted hand. "She's no such thing, Cord Hollister. I have no idea why Carly's here, but I can guarantee it isn't part of some devious plan to fleece anybody."

"If I were you, I'd reserve judgment on that score. She turned up out of no-where, and she's got one hell of a story, as little of it as she's been willing to tell."

"Well," Tina said, on her way out, purse in hand, "you're **not** me. And furthermore, you're too suspicious for your own good. You automatically mistrust anybody you haven't known your whole life."

Cord could have argued that he trusted plenty of people—he dealt with strangers all the time in his line of work —but he didn't have the energy. All he could muster was, "You, on the other hand, would trust the Devil himself if he played on your sympathies."

Tina merely shook her head.

A moment later, she was out the door. Seconds after that, he heard her car start up.

Cord crossed to the sink and watched her headlights slice through the drizzle as she drove away.

He sighed.

Maybe Tina was right, and he **was** too suspicious. But he prided himself on a sense of reality and the smarts to see through scammers.

Still, he knew one thing about Carly—

she had to be Reba's daughter, with that hair and those eyes. But in spite of the likelihood that one of them **was** her dad, it was still possible that Reba had hooked up with someone else (or several someones) after she'd left town...

Better to keep his guard up until he knew what was what.

A simple DNA test would tell the tale. Provided the kid could be persuaded to take one.

Come to think of it, Eli and J.P. might balk at the suggestion, too. They might not be all that eager to find out they were somebody's dear old dad—or that they weren't. And maybe **that** was the real point. In any case, he knew he was willing to do it, and eventually they all needed to. But that was tomorrow's worry.

As if on cue, his phone rang. He pulled it from his shirt pocket, squinted at the screen and saw J.P.'s mug grinning back at him.

Cord almost let the call go to voice mail, but in the end, he couldn't. This was his friend and J.P. might need help of some kind; independent as he was, J.P. still had the occasional bad night, when the flashbacks kicked in and he was back in Afghanistan, or he just plain panicked for no apparent reason. But fortunately that was rare these days.

PTSD was tricky, though. And it had a way of sneaking up on J.P. out of nowhere.

So Cord took the call.

"What?" he barked, because that was always his response when J.P. phoned him; any hint of concern or, God forbid, **sympathy** would sting the man to the quick.

Cord collapsed into his chair and reached for his coffee, which had gone cold.

"You **know** what," J.P. replied, sounding peevish. "Is the girl there?"

Relieved, Cord released the sigh he'd been holding back. "No," he answered, rising and crossing to the sink to empty his coffee mug. "She went home with Tina, as planned. They just left."

J.P. hesitated, then asked, "So, do you believe the kid?"

"I believe she's Reba's daughter—you can't fake that kind of resemblance—but beyond that, I'm not sure." Self-defense tactic kicking in again...

"If she's not telling the truth, she's a damn good liar."

"It's not as if they're uncommon. I've known plenty of them, and so have you. Reba, for instance."

A brief silence fell.

"Cord, she's seventeen. Do the math."

"She **says** she's seventeen. She could be older than she claims—or younger—and that would make all the difference." Cord closed his eyes for a moment, recalling his earlier and growing certainty about her. He braced himself. "Don't forget Reba lied about her age. **And** she put one over on all of us. Who's to say there wasn't another fool involved, somebody we don't know about."

"But the girl says she has a birth certificate and that she's willing to show it to Eli. He should be able to find out if it's real or a fraud. And if it's real, that'll answer the question about her age."

"True."

"Also," J.P. went on, "I don't think there was anybody else. Not then, anyhow."

"Don't be a sucker," Cord said, but without rancor. "Reba had the chutzpah to juggle the three of us—and we were **best friends**—for the better part of a summer. One more idiot wouldn't have thrown her at all."

Another silence, longer than the last.

J.P. broke it. With a verbal sledge-hammer.

"How many times did you sleep with Reba?" he asked.

It was a question they'd never asked each other, which wasn't surprising, considering that they'd rarely talked about Reba after that one Christmas at Bailey's. And it was a damn personal question, to boot.

"Once," Cord heard himself say.

He carried his mug to the coffee maker, decided against another shot of caffeine and retraced his steps, putting the cup in the sink.

"Yeah," J.P. murmured reflectively. "Me, too."

"What about Eli?"

"Hell, I don't know. I think it might be a different story with him. You remember how they were all over each other, he and Reba, at that party."

"So, if the kid's on the level, Eli's the most likely candidate."

"Or not," J.P. said, and the quick way he responded lent the words a defensive note. "They were necking, after all, when we saw them, not having sex. She and I did our share of necking, and I reckon you could say the same."

Yet again, Cord asked himself what the hell Reba had been trying to pull that summer. Yes, she'd been wild, unpredictable and often reckless, but she'd never struck him as cruel.

He shook his head. What did **he** know?

He'd fallen for Reba—excusable, since he'd been a dumb-ass kid amped up on testosterone at the time—but then he'd proceeded to date all the wrong women he could find, all through college. In fact, he'd actually **married** one of them, Jenna Clifton, despite dozens of red flags. He'd met her at a college reunion the same year his grandmother died.

Just as his dad, Bill and Mimi's only son, had gone ahead and married a young woman he barely knew.

Toby Hollister had met his future wife, Julie Welch, in an LA club one hot August night, while he was stationed in San Diego. Within a month, Julie was pregnant, so they'd eloped to Las Vegas, tied the knot and proceeded to live unhappily ever after.

Not that Toby lived that long.

He'd been killed in a freak accident on base, when Julie was six months along.

"Yo, Hollister," J.P. interjected crisply. "You still with me?"

"Yeah," Cord said wearily. "I'm with you."

"I'm worried about you, old buddy. Lately, you've been downright drifty. And that isn't like you."

"I think a lot," Cord answered, mildly annoyed. "You ought to try it sometime. Thinking, I mean."

J.P. laughed. "Not just drifty, but prickly, too."

"Asshole," Cord muttered.

"I rest my case."

"Did you call about Carly, or did you just feel like pissing off one more person before you turned in for the night?"

"Carly? That's her name?" J.P.'s tone was almost wistful.

"According to her, yes. Short for Charlotte. Keep in mind, she was calling herself 'Zelda' a few hours ago." He figured he understood why she'd done that—her own form of self-defense.

"What is it with you?" J.P. snapped. So much for wistful. "She's a **kid**, and five will get you ten, she's in some kind of trouble. Why not give her the benefit of the doubt?"

"I'm doing that," Cord replied reasonably. "She's here on my ranch, isn't she?" He paused. "Or you want the kid at your place, J.P.? Come and get her."

"Whoa. Dial back on the attitude a little, will you? This is **me**, your old pal J.P. McCall. And I'm on **your** side."

Chagrined, though he'd be damned if he'd let on, Cord took a deep breath, held it for a few seconds, exhaled slowly.

Before he could pick up the conversational ball, J.P. went on again. "Look," he said, "I know you've got trust issues, but right now, you need to let all of that go. We have to get a handle on this situation, Cord."

"'Trust issues'?" Cord bit out. What did that mean and what did it have to do with anything?

J.P. sighed expressively. "That's what I said," he replied. "Your ex betrayed you. So did Reba, even though that was years ago. Plus, the kid—Carly—mentioned being in foster care. I'm guessing that brought up some stuff you don't want to deal with. And believe me, I know all about bad memories."

"Okay," Cord managed, still furious and well aware that his mood was irrational. "Can we move past that, please, and discuss the problem at hand?"

The problem.

He didn't have a lot of memories of those early years, but recalled being referred to as "the problem" by a foster parent or two before Bill and Mimi found him and brought him home. Now here he was, sticking the same label on Carly.

"Let me rephrase that," he added, before J.P. could start up with the amateur psychological analysis again. "We ought to be talking about the girl."

"Right," J.P. said. "**Carly.** Reba's daughter and, most likely, yours, Eli's or mine. What are we going to do, Cord?"

Cord rubbed the stubble on his jaw. He'd shaved that morning. Maybe he ought to give up and just let his beard grow in.

"We can settle the matter easily enough, it seems to me," he said calmly. "All we need to do is have our DNA tested, see if one of us is a match."

J.P.'s response was slow in coming. "I'm not sure I want to know yet, one way or the other," he finally confessed. "Eventually, but I don't feel ready..."

"Maybe none of us is ready, with the possible exception of Carly herself," Cord answered, feeling hollowed out and more than a little bit lonesome. Considering what all had happened in **one day**, that wasn't surprising. And he knew J.P. had to feel much the same...

He'd thought he'd be happily married by now, with a passel of kids, but things hadn't turned out that way and, deep down, he was disappointed.

He was thirty-five years old, and what did he have to show for it, besides his work? One short, tempestuous marriage to Ms. Wrong, a mistake from "I do" right on through to the final showdown, when his bride backed a rented truck up to the front door and had her three brothers load up most of the furniture, the still-unused wedding china and silver, the whole shooting match. She'd stripped the walls of the expensive art they'd chosen together, helped herself to half the pots and pans, even taken the aspirin from the medicine cabinet.

She'd tried to make off with his **dog**, for God's sake! Out of spite, no doubt, since Jenna didn't much care for animals —or maybe she'd planned on holding poor Clyde for ransom.

Turned out she didn't much care for ranch life in general.

Or him.

And there went his mind, wandering again. Maybe J.P. was right, and he ought to find himself a shrink, have his head examined.

Nope, not gonna happen.

"You off in the hinterlands again, buddy?" J.P. prompted.

"I'm here," Cord insisted. **For now.**

"What if Carly won't agree to a DNA test?"

"That would be a little suspicious," Cord replied carefully, remembering J.P.'s observations earlier.

Hell, maybe he **did** have trust issues.

If so, he was entitled to them. He'd been screwed over often enough, hadn't he?

Fortunately, or maybe out of simple

mercy, J.P. let his comment pass without remarking on it.

"Eli ought to be in on this conversation," he said.

"Yeah," Cord agreed.

"How about getting together for breakfast tomorrow, at Brynne's? The three of us. We can hammer out a plan."

"Can't," Cord said in all honesty. "I have to work."

Until Tina had reminded him an hour ago, the obligation had slipped his mind completely. A new client, Ms. S. Fletcher, was due to arrive by 6 a.m. at the latest, and the way his luck had been running, she'd actually show up.

It was unlike him not to thoroughly vet applicants for his program, since it was rigorous and as apt to break prospective horse whisperers as make them, but he'd been rushed at the time, dealing with another commitment, so he'd merely skimmed the details. Then he'd banked the hefty deposit, which included room and board in the guest suite, and emailed the woman a set of dates and a few release forms, which she'd promptly returned.

She was from Seattle, this Ms. Fletcher, and while he had nothing against the place, it was big, and these days that bothered him. He wasn't interested in big-city life and hadn't been for years. Besides, he was in no mood to teach some lame-ass city slicker the basics of salvaging a damaged horse, particularly the kind of equine misfits and delinquents and no-hopers he took on. Or to teach people to train and work with therapy horses, since there was more and more interest in that, and some of his horses —despite or more likely because of their abusive backgrounds—were good contenders for that kind of life.

Damned if his brain hadn't gone off on another tangent, he thought, landing back in the here and now with a jolt. The mind trip must have taken no more than a second or two, though, because J.P. didn't miss a beat.

"Work?" he challenged. "Really? Cord, this is important."

"I know that, J.P., but so is my work." Cord was proud of his restraint. If he'd been a lesser man, he might have pointed out that, unlike J.P., who had parlayed a government settlement into a fortune by trading stocks, he had to earn a living.

"See you tomorrow night?" J.P. asked. "You, me and Eli at your place for dinner."

He couldn't resist. "Assuming Eli can take the time off," Cord pointed out. "Some of us have jobs, you know."

"Eat your heart out," J.P. shot back. "And besides, what you do isn't a job. It's a **calling**—and you'd do it even without the fat fees your clients pay you to work your magic."

Cord didn't take the bait—which sounded more like a compliment. He was too tired to wrangle with J.P., who'd been known to argue one side of a question, then turn right around and argue its opposite just as convincingly.

"Tomorrow night," Cord capitulated. "Bring food."

J.P. didn't answer, didn't bother with a goodbye. He just ended the call.

CHAPTER FOUR

Cord took the dogs outside to lift a hind leg one more time.

When Bandit and Smoky were back inside, settled on their beds by the stove, he made his way to the large master bedroom, remodeled at Jenna's insistence; she'd dug in her stiletto heels right away and said she wasn't about to settle for a bunch of old folks' furniture or those musty curtains in **her** bedroom. Or that positively **dreadful** wallpaper.

A besotted bridegroom at the time, Cord had hired the appropriate contractors and given her free rein.

That was bad idea number two. Nobody's fault but his own, since he'd agreed to it. Bad idea number one: marrying her in the first place.

Thanks to Jenna, and his own wimpy agreement to changes he'd never wanted, the once-homey space was barely recognizable as the room his grandparents had slept in for nearly sixty years. Gone were the heirloom quilts and the samplers Mimi had embroidered, along with the matched pair of rocking chairs as well as the potbellied stove that had kept them toasty warm on cold Montana nights.

Now everything in the bedroom was high-tech, from the lighting to the gas fireplace, velvet-soft carpeting and designer drapes. When it came to decorating—not to mention spending money, **his** money—Jenna had been in a league all her own.

Not content with the spacious accommodations at the end of the hall, she'd had a wall knocked out and turned Mimi's beloved sewing nook into a bathroom suited to a movie star. She'd had that formerly humble chamber fitted with a massive marble bathtub, his and her johns, and a counter almost as long as the bar at Sully's, with a backlit mirror running the length of it. The sinks were marble, like the tub and the floor, and sported gleaming copper fixtures, the gracefully arched faucets perfectly positioned to smack a man hard on the forehead every time he bent to splash water on his face or spit while brushing his teeth.

Even now, with Jenna long gone, living in Brooklyn and remarried to a rich lawyer almost twice her age, Cord felt like a squatter in both rooms, as if he were bunking down in somebody's palace on the sly, or had sneaked into some obscenely expensive hotel without paying. A part of him expected to be found out and sent packing at any moment.

Tonight, though, he appreciated the space-age shower stall, big enough to hold a crowd, for its multiple sprayers, strategically arranged to strike whole muscle groups at the same time, thus working the knots out of a cowboy's weary, banged-up carcass with well-aimed blasts of steaming hot water.

He stripped, stepped into the shower, turned the copper-and-crystal handles, and took his time lathering up and rinsing off. The water pummeled him from all directions, and he stood there for a good fifteen minutes, letting it pound him into some semblance of relaxation.

Afterward, he stepped out onto the cushy bath mat and dried himself with an equally cushy towel, not even minding, for once, that the damn thing was pink.

Every towel he owned these days was some shade of pastel—lavender, mint green, baby blue, pale yellow.

It was embarrassing.

Jenna had basically cleaned the place out when she left, so why the hell hadn't she taken the girly towels and fussy bed linens?

Probably because she knew he hated them.

He swore, glaring at his steamed-over reflection in the three-acre mirror.

Any thought of his ex-wife was a trap he could generally side-step by running a few lines of one of his grandfather's all-time favorite tunes, "Thank God and Greyhound," through his head, but tonight, he'd fallen right into the pit.

He was definitely off his game.

Resigned to human fallibility, including his own, Cord brushed his teeth, wiped some steam off the mirror and took in his reflection.

He looked slightly derelict, definitely needed a shave.

It could wait until morning since he'd have to do it again anyhow. And it wasn't as if he'd be subjecting some woman to a beard-burn.

Leaving the bathroom, Cord was confronted by the bed, as he was every night.

As decadent as any piece on display at Versailles, the head-and footboards were ornately carved with fat baby angels and blooming roses, every inch covered in gilt, and the damn thing was big enough to hold half of Marie Antoinette's court, powdered wigs and all.

Jenna had left the monstrosity behind simply because she'd tired of it, and was ready to buy something new. Plus, like the towels, she'd surely guessed he hated that bed.

Revenge by household goods. Trust her to find a new twist.

Once again, Cord considered bunking in his old room, now more of a junk depository, at the opposite end of the hall. The drawback where that idea was concerned? The bed was too short and too narrow and, besides, he didn't want to give Jenna the satisfaction of running him out of the master bedroom, even if she'd never know she'd scored a point.

He knew the solution, of course— get rid of the stupid bed in his current room, the matching dresser and bureau, the massive end tables, the Easter- egg-colored towels, the whole kit and caboodle.

But it wasn't all bad.

Cord kind of liked the fireplace, even if it was a touch too fancy; he could clean up the old rocking chairs and bring them back in. It would be nice, if he ever met and married the right woman, to sit there on a chilly evening, side by side, talking or not, reading maybe, or just being together.

The bathroom might be a monument to conspicuous consumption, but it was woman-friendly, for sure. If he swapped out the treacherous faucets for something more practical and had the marble floor covered with, say, stone tile, he could deal.

Trouble was, he never seemed to find the time for remodeling projects. Most days, he worked from sunrise to sunset, and beyond.

Today, with the scene at Sully's and then Carly's appearance, he hadn't worked with any of the horses since early that afternoon. Thank God for Mitch Robbins! He'd make up for it tomorrow, especially since he'd have his new client to contend with. And thinking of Mitch made him wonder how the older man would react to the presence of a teenager in his home. It should be fine, he told himself. Mitch was a kind, generous and tolerant man, and as Tina had pointed out, they'd raised three children of their own.

He and Mitch spent a lot of time together, maintaining the property, caring for the horses, doing whatever needed to be done.

And whenever Cord had a few extra hours, he generally spent them with J.P. and Eli, playing poker, riding horseback for the pure fun of it, or just sitting around on one of their porches, drinking beer and shooting the shit.

Like him, his buddies were having a dry spell when it came to romance, and they'd probably have been better off searching for a good woman out there, one they could settle down with.

Instead, they were gun-shy, all three of them, for reasons of their own.

If they didn't want to wind up as crusty old bachelors, still playing poker in Sully's back room every other week, having breakfast at Bailey's far too often and spending most of their free time with each other, something had to change.

J.P. and Eli knew that as well as Cord did; they weren't stupid. They also weren't eager to risk getting burned again.

That, Cord supposed, was a form of cowardice, but as much as he despised his own reluctance, he couldn't seem to shake it.

For a while now, maybe since Jenna, Cord had sunk into a kind of inertia where dating was concerned. True, he'd never deeply loved his ex-wife—hindsight confirmed that he'd loved a **version** of her, one he'd outlined in his own head. Her behavior, her exploitation, had quickly confirmed the mistake he'd made. Yes, he'd initially been convinced he loved her, certainly been attracted to her. But more than ever, he realized that, for her, he'd been a means to an end.

The sad truth was that he'd loved only one woman in his life—Reba Shannon. And he'd loved her with the vehemence of youth. Were those feelings, which he'd been remembering today, which he'd been **experiencing**, simply a holdover from the past? One that had suddenly emerged because of her daughter? He hadn't thought much about Reba in recent years, but she'd been on his mind today. These were the questions that crowded his mind.

Time to forget about Reba. She was gone. And forget about Jenna, which he more or less had. Time to leave **those** bad memories behind.

And time to pull his head out of his ass and get it back on his shoulders. **Stop looking for what might have been and take some interest in what is, here and now.**

Painted Pony Creek was a small town, yes, but it had its share of attractive, available women. Over the years—and Cord wasn't proud of this—he'd slept with a few of them and shut down at the first sign that something lasting might be taking root.

There'd been Katie Dupree, for instance, a pretty redheaded RN, divorced, with two great kids.

Cord hadn't loved Katie, though something might have developed, given time. But he'd fallen head over heels for those kids, two little boys with hair like their mother's and hope in their hearts—hope that they might, just might, get themselves a dad to replace the one who'd left them behind to move to another state, marry another woman and start himself a whole new family.

Cord had stopped seeing Katie as soon as he realized the kids had him tagged as a stepfather. He ended the relationship not because there was anything wrong between them, but because he was afraid of hurting her in the long run and, worse, hurting those innocent kids.

Katie was understandably angry and confused at the time but, blessedly, life had turned out more than okay for her. Less than a year later, she'd married newcomer Zach Fairfield, a family physician.

Zach, a widower with no children, had

tired of asphalt, traffic and smog, and wanted to live a simpler life. When old Doc Fillmore finally retired, Zach bought his practice and started seeing patients right away, keeping Doc's small staff— Millie, the bookkeeper, and Sandra, the receptionist—on the payroll.

This made him popular in the community because Millie was seventy-five if she was a day as well as opinionated and a little forgetful, and unlikely to be hired anywhere else, and Sandra, although sweet, wasn't qualified to do anything besides answer phones and book appointments.

Zach had also hired Katie, who'd been employed at the hospital outside town since earning her degree but was ready for a change.

She'd told Cord once, over coffee, long after their breakup, that she'd fallen in love with Zach not because of his good looks, quick wit and sexy Australian accent, but because he was able to look past Millie's advancing age and Sandra's constant chatter and see them for the good-hearted, caring people they were.

So that was that, where anything that might have happened between Cord and Katie was concerned.

Katie was happy, Zach was happy, the kids were happy.

Cord? He was happy, too, for the most part.

He loved his work, the ranch, the state of Montana and the town of Painted Pony Creek. He was healthy and financially secure, if not out-and-out rich, like J.P.

Only one thing was lacking: a family of his own, starting—call him old-fashioned—with a wife.

So far, obviously, he was batting zero on that score. After repeating several variations of the Katie scenario, Cord had given up on finding Ms. Right any=time soon. Sex was easy enough; he knew several women who were as emotionally unavailable as he was, with no desire to lasso a husband, which should have been a win-win.

Except it wasn't.

Bed hopping had been all right when he was younger—better than all right, actually—but these days, it always seemed to leave him lonelier than before. Not that he indulged in it all that much.

He wanted **lovemaking**, not just sex. Somebody to confide in and listen to. Somebody to laugh with and, if the occasion called for it, cry with, too.

She didn't have to be beautiful.

She didn't have to be skinny.

She just had to be **real**. In it for the long haul.

Basically, Cord wanted to love a woman the way he loved his job, his "calling," as J.P. had said earlier—without reservation.

He'd learned a lot from his brief marriage. First of all, that he and Jenna had been a bad combination from the get-go.

He'd been faithful to her, but since the marriage only lasted eighteen months, he hardly deserved a medal for that. If they'd stayed together much longer, he might've gone looking for love in all the wrong places, as the song had it.

The plain fact was that no matter how much Cord groused to J.P. and Eli—and himself—about Jenna's failings, he'd definitely been part of the problem. As soon as he'd realized the extent of his mistake, which was about a month after the wedding, he'd begun to withdraw.

He hadn't half tried to make things work.

Next time he got married—if there **was** a next time—he'd make damn sure he found the right woman first.

Then, damn it, he would **stay the course**, the way he did in his work.

Once Cord took on a horse, he didn't give up on the animal, period. He put in as many hours as necessary, met every challenge, no matter how difficult. He was all in, every time, and somehow the horse always came to understand that, some more quickly than others.

In the company of horses, Cord was his best self, the man he wanted to be, knew he **should** be, not just in the saddle or the corral or the round pen, but everywhere else, too.

It might sound crazy; obviously, women weren't horses, and only so many parallels could be drawn, but Cord wanted that same level of do-or-die commitment—on his part **and** hers—when and if he married again.

He wanted to be that person as a lover and, eventually, as a husband and father. As a man.

All of which was fine in theory, but in this age of instant downloads and delete keys, it seemed to Cord that everything moved too quickly. People didn't take the time to get to know each other, up close and personal; they evidently preferred digital relationships to the flesh-and-blood kind, racking up "friends" on their social media pages and mostly ignoring the people they saw every day of their lives.

It didn't take a shrink to figure that one out. Real, face-to-face **human beings** could be troublesome. They needed time and attention. More than a chirpy text or a 140-character "tweet" or a post on some cyber wall.

Oh, yeah. Things got messy with the three-dimensional types.

Plenty of people seemed to prefer communicating from a comfortable distance. That way, you didn't have to engage. But Cord believed you could still be generous. You could drive somebody to the hospital in the middle of the night— whether it was a male friend, an elderly person, a woman you were seeing. You could help people move, let them sleep on your couch when they needed a place to stay or give them a ride home when they'd had too much to drink.

Cord didn't frequent social media sites; he had a PR firm to promote him and his training programs online. But he did a lot of business on both his phone and his laptop, often without talking to another living soul.

So maybe he didn't have any right to criticize other people's ways of interacting with their fellow mortals.

Jenna, for one, would've had a lot to say about his style of communication—

and none of it would be good. Granted, she wasn't the most objective person he knew, but she had a knack for calling bullshit.

A few minutes later, all these random thoughts stopped circling his brain like so many squawking crows, and he was left with the present dilemma. Carly.

Carly, who might—or might not—be his daughter.

If he'd fathered the girl, he had a responsibility toward her. One he'd willingly accept. But it was about **more** than responsibility. He had to think about her lost years—all those years lost to the three of them. And the fact that after Reba's death, she'd been through so much, including a hateful stepfather who'd given her dog—and her!—away. Then a year of neglect, of fielding the foster care system, finally managing on her own. At seventeen!

It was all so wrong.

Even if she belonged to J.P. or Eli, she definitely qualified as an honorary niece, and that was no small thing, either.

And if she didn't belong to any one of them...well, she was still a mixed-up kid, apparently alone in the world and headed for trouble, if she wasn't already in it up to her musical tattoo.

No getting around it, Carly needed help.

Cord rolled onto his side and reached out to take his phone from the charger on the nightstand.

It was 1:12 a.m.

He grinned.

Not too early to call J.P., he decided.

He pressed the appropriate key.

"Cord?" J.P. mumbled. "What the hell—? Do you know what time—?"

"I changed my mind," Cord said cheerfully. "About meeting up for breakfast tomorrow, I mean. I'll be at Bailey's as soon as the chores are done."

J.P. yawned loudly. "What about your client?"

"She'll keep," Cord replied. "You want to call Eli or shall I?"

"No need. He has breakfast at Brynne's pretty well every morning, with or without us. You know that."

"Right. Well, I'll let you get back to sleep."

"That's mighty generous of you."

"You gonna unfriend me, old buddy?"

J.P.'s chuckle was husky. "You should be so lucky."

With that, he hung up.

Cord, still wide-awake, propped himself up in bed, went through the contact list on his phone and found S. Fletcher's email address. Waking J.P. in the middle of the night was one thing; waking a client was another.

Quickly, he thumbed out a message. **Something has come up**, he wrote, **and I'll be unavailable until around 9 tomorrow morning. We'll start your training then. Sorry for any inconvenience. Cord Hollister.**

He hit Send, and the phone made a cute little zipping sound.

He hated "cute," but sometimes it couldn't be avoided. More like, he always forgot to turn off all that cheerful shit.

Thinking maybe he could sleep now that he'd made a decision and acted on it, Cord switched off the bedside lamp and was about to set the phone aside again when it chimed, alerting him to a new message.

It was probably incoming junk mail, Cord figured, but he checked anyway.

I hope you don't make a habit of changing plans at the last minute, Mr. Hollister. Consistency and order are important to me. Nevertheless — (never-the-freaking-less?) — **I will do as you ask and arrive promptly at 9 a.m. S. Fletcher.**

Cord set the phone on the nightstand with an annoyed **thunk**.

Great.

S. Fletcher was serious about learning what he had to teach, which was a good thing because the course was tough. Tough enough to weed out the wanna-bes and ensure that the ones who made it through were fit to work with horses.

She seemed a little on the snippy side, though, and that **wasn't** so good, because it meant they were likely to butt heads along the way. But if S. Fletcher turned out to be a bossy pain in the butt, class would be dismissed early, either because she told him what he could do with his course and stormed off, never to be seen again, or because he returned her money and showed her the road.

Cord stretched, yawned and settled in to get a few hours of sleep.

He woke at 4:15 exactly, as always, threw back the covers and got out of bed.

After grabbing a cup of cold coffee, left over from the previous day and nuking it in the microwave, he showered, shaved, put on some clothes and returned to the kitchen, his boots dangling from his right hand.

The dogs were already at the kitchen door, yipping anxiously and wriggling their hind ends, so he let them out, then followed as far as the porch steps, where he sat down and tugged on his boots.

The horses—his own four and the two special boarders—would be wanting their feed.

Last night's storm had blown itself out and the sun was about to rise, though it was still just a faint line of orange-red light rimming the eastern hills. The still-cool air smelled of hay and horsehide, wet grass and manure.

He'd lit the stove, and the pleasant scent of woodsmoke rode the breeze, too. Cord smiled to himself. Plenty of folks still chased off the early-morning chill—even in summer—by lighting a fire in a cast-iron stove, and he found that comforting.

He set aside his reheated coffee—he'd make a fresh batch when he was through with his chores—and headed for the barn.

The dogs gamboled alongside, delighted with themselves, with life in general.

Cord grinned, watching them.

Take a lesson, cowboy, he told himself. **You're alive and on your feet, and**

that's reason enough to be happy.

He spent forty-five minutes with the horses, talking to them as he worked—filling the feeders, making sure the automatic waterers were operating, doing a little grooming as needed. He told them about Carly and how they'd meet her, and about the new client who'd be arriving soon. Some of the other local ranchers would no doubt consider him a bit touched in the head, carrying on lengthy conversations with horses, dogs and even the occasional bird.

Finally, he turned four of them out for the day. The remaining two included a Thoroughbred gelding named Chief with a serious attitude problem; Chief was now his. So was a shaggy little black-and-white mare, a pro bono case brought to him by a volunteer with an animal rescue group just two weeks before.

He'd named the mare Annie, and every time he thought of her, another crack opened in his heart. She'd been abandoned, turned loose to fend for herself, and she'd had a rough time of it out there all alone; she was scarred and slat-ribbed and her hooves had grown out, then split.

Annie was still terrified of everything— the other horses, the dogs and Cord himself. Now she huddled in a corner of the stall, hide quivering, and stayed well back from the feeder.

He'd trimmed her hooves when she'd first arrived, washed her down and applied salve to her wounds, and she'd borne his attentions meekly, shrinking from every touch of his hand.

He would get through to her, no doubt about it, but the process was going to take a while. He'd officially adopted her, which was how he'd gotten three of the four horses he owned. Rebel, his sorrel gelding, was the only one of the bunch who'd had a good start in life—he'd been born and bred right there on the ranch, near the end of Bill Hollister's working days.

For a while after Cord's grandfather

died, Rebel was the only horse on the place. With Cord away at college, finishing his last year, Bill had found new homes for all the others and he'd stopped taking on extras to train or just redeem.

That summer almost thirteen years ago, when Cord was about to begin a veterinary studies program, Bill had suffered a heart attack and died in his sleep, leaving Mimi almost catatonic with shock.

Cord hadn't been in much better shape than his grandmother, and even Rebel, a yearling at the time, had seemed to feel the loss. Bill had spent a lot of time with that colt, and it had been heartbreaking to see the animal standing at the pasture fence, watching for his friend to come out of the house.

Cord had decided to stay home instead of attending veterinary college, to keep the ranch going and look after Mimi, who was never the same after losing her husband. Mimi had died almost six years later, and despite an autopsy, cause of death was never established with certainty. Cord had always believed that grief was the reason.

The horses were a large part of what had helped him get through his own grief. The hours had been long, the work hard, but Cord had never minded those things; Bill had taught him well.

He'd worked with Rebel, using the techniques the old man had taught him, and coming up with a few of his own. Without that horse, and plenty of support and encouragement from Eli— J.P. was still in the military then—Cord thought he might have lost his way.

Word had gotten around. Cord Hollister, people said, had a way with a problem cayuse, just like his granddad, and then they started bringing him their misfits to train, some of them valuable, some simply beloved. Their troubles ranged from simple things, like an animal that refused to take the bit or accept a saddle or cross a creek, to serious cases of trauma, such as abuse, injury and neglect.

As his reputation grew, so did his business. Within two years, Cord was not only working with equine outlaws on the ranch, he was traveling all over the country to work with prized race horses, jumpers and the like.

Thanks to popular demand, he'd begun holding clinics and teaching his methods, and he was good at it. Recently, he'd also contributed to some therapy training when requested and found it immensely satisfying, especially after observing J.P.'s positive experience with Trooper. The right horse, like the right dog, could be a lifesaver in more ways than one.

He was no extrovert, far from it, but he soon discovered that he liked teaching owners and aspiring trainers almost as much as he liked spending time with their horses. He admired men like Monty Roberts and Buck Brannaman and had studied with both of them, even after he had students of his own.

Now here he was, an acknowledged expert, with all the work he could handle.

Sometimes, it still surprised him.

More surprising yet, he'd never once regretted not going back to school and becoming a veterinarian.

He had a special affinity for all animals, but especially for horses, and at times, he felt it bordered on the mystical.

He spoke gently to the little mare, who was still keeping her head down and her hind end pressed against the far wall. Mentally, he joined his heart to hers.

"You're gonna be all right from now on, Annie-girl," he said. "You have my word on that."

CHAPTER FIVE

Tina walked into the kitchen and marched straight to the coffee maker.

She was wearing her bathrobe over a pair of cotton pajamas, there were fluffy slippers on her feet, and her head bulged with pink foam curlers.

She helped herself to coffee, gently hushed Bandit and Smoky, and joined Cord at the table, motioning for him to sit back down as she settled herself in the chair to his right.

"Is something wrong?" Cord asked. He'd never seen Tina dressed—or **not** dressed—like that, let alone with curlers in her hair and her face bare of make-up. "Mitch is okay?"

"Mitch is fine, and so is Carly, not that you asked about her," Tina replied, sounding a shade terse.

"I was about to!" he insisted.

"I'm here because I might not have a chance to talk to you once the day gets started, what with your chores and the new client coming and all."

Cord wasn't all that reassured since Tina could have called him. Under different circumstances, the pajama tableau might have seemed amusing, but he'd begun to feel a little anxious. "Is this about Carly? Did something happen?"

"No," Tina answered, sharpening the word to a fine point. "Nothing **happened**. The poor girl took a hot bath last night, crawled into bed and fell asleep right away. In fact, she's probably still sleeping."

"Did she tell you anything?"

"No," Tina repeated. Maybe the coffee was mellowing her out a little. "But she did tell me, before her bath, that it would be all right if I washed some of her clothes. I asked her first, of course."

"Tina. What's the problem? **Is** there a problem?"

"This coffee is terrible," Tina said, before going back to the pot for a refill.

"Damn it, Tina," Cord growled once she sat down again. "What are you getting at?"

Tina sniffed, as if she'd taken offense, then relented. Slightly. "Everything that child owns is in that awful backpack of hers. I had to open it if I was going to do her laundry, didn't I?"

Cord said nothing.

"Anyway, Carly needs new clothes. Especially underwear."

"Is that what you came here to say? That Carly needs some decent clothes? Hell, I could have told you that last night. You saw what she was wearing!"

Tina puffed up with annoyance. "Will you just shut up and listen, Cord Hollister? Or are you going to keep interrupting me?"

Cord drew a deep breath, let it out slowly. Relaxed his shoulders. "I'm listening," he said, pleasant as could be.

He'd just remembered that J.P. had invited himself and Eli to supper tonight. They were supposed to make a plan regarding Carly.

He'd told J.P. to bring food, but that didn't mean he would. Cord figured he'd have to prevail on Tina for help with the barbecue supplies. Before he could mention it, though, she returned to their original discussion.

"I found something in Carly's backpack, Cord," Tina said. "Besides ratty underwear, two pairs of jeans that probably came from a thrift store and a couple of T-shirts."

"What?" Cord demanded. His imagination was in over-drive—he pictured Tina coming across drugs, or the paraphernalia to use them.

"Money," Tina almost whispered. "A **lot** of money. In a roll with a rubber band around it. And I'm talking larger bills. Twenties, fifties and up." Coffee forgotten, she shaped her hands to indicate something about the size of a baseball. "And one of those ultrathin laptops, the kind people wait in line all night to buy. How could she afford something like that, Cord? She didn't even have **food** in that backpack, or a toothbrush."

"Maybe the bankroll used to be thicker," Cord said, thinking about that expensive laptop. He wasn't trying to be funny, which was a good thing since nobody was laughing, including him.

"There's probably a reasonable explanation," Tina said weakly.

"Right," Cord said, pulling his phone from his shirt pocket.

"What are you doing?"

"Calling Eli."

Tina blinked, clearly confused, and Cord realized he hadn't told her anything about Carly, beyond the fact that she'd needed a respectable place to spend the night.

He returned the phone to his pocket. "According to Carly," he began, "her mother was someone J.P., Eli and I knew, way back when—and I say **was** because she died a couple of years ago." He paused at the sorrowful expression on Tina's face. "Do you remember a girl named Reba Shannon?" he continued. "She worked at the Painted Pony Motel for about six months, including the summer after we graduated from high school."

"Vaguely," Tina said. Then added, "Not really." A moment later, **"The Painted Pony Motel?"**

"Yes," Cord replied, with exaggerated patience.

Tina looked mildly puzzled, then horrified.

Even back in the day, the joint had been something of a rat-hole, and not many people stayed there, except for low-life types passing through on their way to somewhere else. Or "guests" who wanted a cheap—really cheap—place for a night or two. Or those who didn't know better. The more discerning ones probably chose to sleep under a tree instead or got themselves tossed in jail for a couple of days. At least there, they could count on clean bedding and a decent meal.

So how had Norm and Della Schafer, a pair of drunks, scraped up the money to pay Reba to clean rooms? Why had they **needed** anyone to clean rooms, when they certainly didn't have a lot of regular or long-term guests to mess them up?

"I remember now. She was the girl you and Eli and J.P. got into that big fight over—Reba, I mean—and the three of you stayed mad at each other all the way to Christmas." Tina was tapping her lower lip with the tip of an index finger, thinking hard. "And I remember those poor children. Russ and Bethanne and —wait, it's coming back to me. The younger one..."

The name, long forgotten, came to Cord's mind instantly. "Shallie," he said, with a strange pang of—what? Sadness? Regret?

"Yes," Tina said. "That's it. She was Della's niece, I think."

Cord nodded. "Sounds right," he said, wondering about the girl he'd barely known during her teenage years—and his. She'd been part of his group of friends when they were kids; later, in high school, she'd become an outsider, always on the fringe, but not because the others rejected her. No, Shallie Fletcher hadn't been shunned or bullied. She'd turned into a sulky, obstinate little rebel in those days, spoiling for a fight. With anybody, about anything.

He'd never really understood why. Was it Reba's influence? He suspected now that Shallie had felt both jealous of Reba and, at the same time, connected with her in that best-friends way.

She'd appeared on the scene when he and Shallie were in twelfth grade. He'd fallen almost instantly for Reba, and lost all awareness of any other girl. Including Shallie.

Until the night she'd suddenly confronted him with avowals of undying love.

He'd been stunned by the outburst, stricken to silence. And turned his face away from her attempted kiss.

Still raw from Reba's betrayal and the loss of his two best friends, the friends he'd counted on, he wasn't ready for this, for Shallie, for **anyone**.

Shallie wasn't unattractive; she might have been really pretty, in fact, with her compact, shapely body, good skin, thick chestnut hair and large, luminous brown eyes, but by that stage she was doing everything she could to play down her best features. Worn too much make-up and ugly, oversize clothes, boots more suited to a lumberjack than a seventeen-year-old girl. Not to mention the fuck-you attitude and the force field it created.

She'd looked very different that night, he remembered, although he hadn't noticed at the time. He'd only registered her blue cotton sundress, goo-free face and clean, carefully styled hair later on, much later, when he'd gained some perspective.

Sitting at his table with Tina, he re-called now that he'd tried to be kind but he'd hurt Shallie. Hurt her badly. He knew that. That was the thing about telling the truth—it might be right, but it could also do harm.

She'd left town soon after, and Cord hadn't seen her or thought about her since.

A possibility ran swiftly through his mind. An unlikely one, but...He'd just come across the name Fletcher. His new client. **S. Fletcher.** It couldn't be. Could it?

"Hey," Tina said, snapping her fingers an inch from his nose. "Where were you just now?"

"Remembering a few things," he answered. He'd been doing a lot of that lately, and it was starting to worry him.

Tina's face softened as she regarded Cord. "Like what?"

"Never mind," Cord replied. "Did you ask Carly about the money and the laptop?"

"Of course I didn't. I had no business snooping through her stuff. I said I'd do her laundry, not invade her privacy."

"Her privacy," Cord repeated. "But if we're going to figure out what's going on with her, if we're going to help her, we need more information than she's been willing to give us so far." He paused, considering. "Suppose Carly **wanted** you to see what was in that backpack? Why else would she have let you near it?"

"I didn't think of that," Tina admitted. She looked so serious, and so funny in that crazy getup, Cord had to suppress a laugh.

"If I ask any questions, she'll know I snooped. She'd never trust me after this. She might even run away."

"**Or** she might be relieved that you took the cue, hoping you'd care enough to confront her."

"I don't know," Tina fretted. "My girls would've been furious if I'd rummaged through their belongings the way I did Carly's."

"Your girls had a mother and a father and a solid, loving home. They were happy, confident kids. They probably never gave you any **reason** to check out their stuff."

"My daughters weren't angels," Tina pointed out, most likely in the interests of modesty, but Cord could tell she thought they came close, and he would have agreed.

"Take some credit, will you?" Cord teased, with a grin. "You and Mitch were good parents. You paid attention. Set rules. Loved your kids without spoiling them." He took a sip from his mug. "They were lucky to have you, and vice versa."

Tina sighed. "It wasn't easy, you know," she said softly. "Girls—especially when puberty arrives—are **never** easy."

"True," Cord allowed, thinking, not for the first time, how much he liked and respected this woman and her decent, hardworking husband. "But if my grandparents were here, they might just point out that raising boys is no picnic, either."

"I miss them," Tina replied, standing, smoothing her bathrobe with both hands, suddenly self-conscious. "Mimi taught me how to cook and clean and raise children. I didn't know beans about being a wife and mother when I married Mitch. And Bill was like a father to me— the father I never had."

Cord got to his feet. Laid a hand on Tina's shoulder. "They were good people, my grandparents," he said hoarsely. "I was lucky, too. The way your girls were. And still are."

Tina smiled, rested her hand over his. "So were Mimi and Bill, Cord. And they knew it. It about broke them both when Toby was killed. They kept going because of **you**. You needed them, and they needed you. You were their second chance, their reason to go on."

Cord felt his eyes burning, and his throat thickened.

Tina touched his cheek, still smiling.

Cord nodded, but he didn't trust himself to say anything.

Tina laughed. "Just look at me," she said, "standing here in my **bathrobe**, for heaven's sake, and in curlers! Mimi would've delivered a lecture on ladylike behavior and personal dignity." Her expression turned tender. "I'm out of here," she told him. In the next moment, she headed for the door, car keys plucked from her pocket and jingling cheerily.

Reaching the threshold, she turned to face Cord. "Whoever she turns out to be," she said quietly, "Carly is a good kid. In trouble, maybe, but good. Trust me on that."

Cord nodded, hoping Tina's instincts were right. "You don't have to ask her about the money and the laptop," he said. "Carly isn't your responsibility."

"I'll play it by ear," she replied, after a moment of thought and a brisk nod of her curler-covered head. "Like I did with my own kids."

With that, she was out the door and gone.

CHAPTER SIX

Cord loved early summer. By now, at six thirty in the morning, the sun was already progressing to the middle of the sky. After yesterday's rain, flowers in the ditches along the road were blooming with wanton delight. Every once in a while, he'd find himself grinning at cows and their calves, grazing diligently in their pastures.

He took the almost empty road with care, always concerned about an animal —a deer or coyote, perhaps a sheep or young horse—darting in front of his truck. Half an hour later, he turned into the dirt parking lot at Bailey's, sprang out and entered the restaurant. He noticed that J.P.'s Jeep was parked in its usual location. He also noticed a sign announcing an event on Sunday evening—Classic Country Night.

Cord joined him, first greeting Trooper, who was lying half under the table. J.P. grunted, "Hello," and Cord helped himself to coffee; he had to admit, once again, that Tina had a point. This was **much** better coffee than he often drank at home. His own fault because when he bought it himself, he always got the cheap brands—he never seemed to learn. Brynne appeared then, carrying a laden tray over to another customer in one of the booths.

"Hey, Brynne Bailey!" he called out, then started to sing, "Brynne Bailey, won't you please come home?" J.P. took up the chorus, just as Cord saw Eli standing in the doorway.

Reactions from the few people there— except for Brynne—were good-natured. She merely groaned. "I am home, you dum-dums. Oh, not you, Troop, my darling. You're the smart one here. I'll bring you a treat in a little while." The Lab wagged his tail excitedly. **Eat** and **treat** were two of his favorite words. Two of **every** dog's favorite words.

"Trooper, don't suck up to her," J.P. said. But he wasn't serious. Trooper was less a service dog now than a companion; he no longer wore the vest. At the age of almost nine, he'd reached retirement, but J.P. wasn't giving him up. The dog still played a role in helping him maintain his stability. J.P. no longer suffered from the constant anxiety and frequent panic attacks he'd endured after Afghanistan, but as Cord knew, they could still strike and without warning.

Another good thing—Trooper was welcome everywhere in Painted Pony Creek.

As Eli approached, Cord asked, "Did you hear what she called us? Dumdums!"

"Hmm. I'm sure she's got her reasons. Maybe I should arrest you both for creating a public disturbance."

Brynne reappeared to take their

orders. "Sounds good to me. Now, what do you guys want?"

They all ordered that morning's special, the breakfast burger. As she left, Eli announced, "All right, gentlemen, this meeting is called to order."

J.P. glanced at Cord. "Is 'gentlemen' better or worse than 'dum-dums'?"

Eli ignored them. "Let's get serious. What do we do about...Zelda?"

"It's Carly, not Zelda. She told me last night."

"Fine. Carly, then."

"Carly for short, Charlotte for long."

"What's her last name? Same as her stepfather's, whatever that is? Or maybe Reba stuck with Shannon for her own kid."

"Don't know. Didn't think to ask. I'll find out, though."

"Man, that stepfather and wife number two were real assholes," J.P. muttered.

"I assume you'll get her name from the birth certificate. Or maybe not, depending on when Reba married this jerk." Cord took out a pen and began writing on a napkin. "Okay. Last name. What else?"

They waited until Brynne had dropped off their meals and left again.

"Education," Eli replied, digging into his egg-topped burger with fries.

Cord added that to his list. "Yeah, I'll bet she didn't finish high school."

"Bet Reba didn't, either," J.P. put in.

"The big question," Eli went on, "is... what exactly does she want from us?"

Cord shrugged. "She wants a father. **Her** father." He paused to take a slurp of coffee.

"Listen, is she after money, you think?" asked Eli, ever the suspicious lawman. "Maybe she's here to rip all three of us off."

"She'd be entitled to some kind of money. At least from her birth father," J.P. insisted. "Whomever that turns out to be."

Which reminded Cord, not that he'd really forgotten..."Uh, I have to tell you something," he said, looking directly at Eli. "Tina was getting Carly's laundry from her backpack—and found a whack of bills. Twenties, fifties and up. Plus a high-end laptop."

Eli almost choked on his coffee. "Whoo, boy," he sputtered. "What the hell is **that** about?"

"Well, considering the filthy crap clothes she was wearing," J.P. began, "and the fact that she was hitchhiking..."

"Yeah," Cord said. "Doesn't connect."

"Unless she managed to steal from one or more of her rides?" Eli shook his head. "I could look into it, but I'd need to know where she's from, where she was living. And where she's been since she took off from wherever it was."

"Okay." Cord picked up his pen. "Writing that down."

"Now," J.P. began. "As to DNA testing..."

"Can we leave it for the moment?" Eli asked. "Till we know her a bit better, till we're sure she hasn't got an agenda of some sort?"

Remembering that scene eighteen years ago, the two of them, Reba and Eli, all entangled, Cord wondered whether Eli had an agenda himself, a personal reason for his request. Did he suspect he stood a good chance of being the father? If so, like J.P., he might not be ready to face it—either way. "We also need to know that she'll agree to testing." Cord turned back to his note-covered napkin. "DNA. Is she okay with the test? And if not, why not?"

"At the moment, it's hard to tell whether she wants one father or three," Eli said. "Maybe she'd like to keep us all hanging. See what she can get…"

J.P. snorted. "But it practically sounds as if she could buy us all out. How the **hell** could she come up with that kind of cash without stealing—"

"Shut up." Eli nudged him, which had Trooper lifting his head warily. "Oh, hi, Brynne. I think we're ready for our check."

She paid no attention to him and bent down to hand the dog one of the promised treats she kept in the kitchen. "Oh, Troop, you are totally the best of

this bunch."

He gobbled his biscuit and wagged his tail appreciatively.

"You know what?" she said to the dog. "You're not only smarter, you're better-looking and a lot nicer than some of the customers here."

Cord grinned at that. "Check, please. Some of these **customers** actually work for a living."

They always took turns settling up, with Eli paying this time around. Cord noticed that he left a substantial tip.

"See you all tonight," Cord said as he folded the napkin and tucked it in his pocket, then walked toward his truck. "Everybody still okay to come over for dinner? Say, at seven?"

The other two nodded. "Sure," J.P. agreed. "Should we include Zel—Carly?"

"Probably not, but let's see how it goes." And they all headed off, with Trooper taking the lead.

When Cord returned to the ranch and parked—pleased that it was only 8:45

—he saw a car. A sedan. Had to be a rental. And it had to be S. Fletcher's.

Yep. There was a woman crouched beside the car, playing with the dogs. Maybe **S** stood for Susan? Sherry? Sandra? Well, he'd find out soon enough. He couldn't see her clearly, just that she had long chestnut hair.

He got out of the truck, started to walk toward her...and almost stumbled. **Another** familiar-looking woman—the very day after meeting Reba's daughter. Now he knew for sure that **S** stood for Shallie.

Both dogs came racing up to him; he stooped to pet them, then rose to confront the woman. "Ms. Fletcher?" He probably sounded incredulous. Or confused.

"Yes, Mr. Hollister. Cord."

"Are you..."

"Shallie. Yes."

He took a few steps backward and leaned against the nearest fence. The paddock. Yep, here was another shock from the past. Did life **have** to be so complicated? "Wow," he finally said, staring at her. "Shallie. From the Painted Pony Motel."

"That was a long time ago."

"And then you disappeared. But here you are again."

She nodded. She was well dressed in formfitting black pants and a long green-and-blue-plaid shirt. She obviously had confidence, something she'd never possessed as a teenager. And money, which she'd never possessed, either. He was astonished, absolutely astonished, by the change in her situation.

"Let me take you to your suite and then we can have coffee, a chance to catch up." As if he needed more coffee—or maybe with some Jack Daniel's thrown in.

"Thank you." He carried her bags inside and showed her to the client suite, which was up a flight of stairs across from the stairs that led to his bedroom. The suite was another Jenna renovation —she'd had a guest room built in what used to be his grandfather's office and work space. Not that they'd needed a guest room at the time. But he had to admit that with his business flourishing, it came in handy.

As she unpacked, Shallie studied the room. There was a simple but comfortable-looking bed, a rustic bedside table and matching desk with an old-fashioned lamp, a padded chair. A small but adequate bathroom. The suite was part of the deal, part of what she'd paid for, and it was certainly good enough. It also meant she didn't have to worry about getting here from the new place in town or, God forbid, the Painted Pony Motel.

She hung her clothes in the closet, left her current book, a print copy of Michael Korda's **Horse People**, and her iPad on the table and slung her purse on the doorknob. Once she'd checked email she made her way downstairs, feeling both excited and apprehensive.

Because she still remembered how she'd once felt about Cord, how attracted she'd been, despite his very obvious feelings for Reba. The man she'd embarrassed—and embarrassed herself in front of—all those years ago. It'd been an adolescent crush, but after her divorce, she'd found herself thinking about him again. And now, after meeting Cord in person, meeting the man he was today, she couldn't seem to get him out of her mind.

Waiting for Shallie, Cord busied himself responding to email on his cell—his PR firm in Chicago, his lawyer as well as an old college friend now living in LA.

Eventually, Shallie came downstairs. The dogs tumbled around her, hoping for something edible to be thrown their way.

Cord gestured her to a chair and she sat, both dogs following her to the table, their tails in frantic action.

"Sit!" he ordered, but Shallie said, "They're fine."

"You're encouraging disobedience?"

"What, to their lord and master? No, I just want to make their acquaintance.

Their names are?"

"Bandit and Smoky." He pointed at each in turn. "Coffee?"

"Yes, thanks."

"Anything to eat? I can manage toast, scrambled eggs or—"

"Thanks again, but I already ate. Stopped at that coffee place off the highway, had a yogurt." She gave an exaggerated shudder. "What a relief. I was afraid I'd have to force down a doughnut."

Cord didn't get it. For him, a doughnut was, if not superior to a yogurt, certainly preferable.

"Okay, if you're sure..." He poured her a coffee, set cream and sugar on the table. **Of course** she didn't use sugar.

After one sip, she frowned. "I don't mean to be rude...but this is shitty coffee."

Predictable—and exactly what **he'd** thought that morning. "Can you do any better?" he challenged, already knowing what she'd say.

"Oh, yeah. Start by not buying the

cheap stuff." He couldn't argue with that.

"Fine. Well...fill me in on what's been going on with you." He wondered how she could afford a trip like this. A wealthy ex? A successful career? "What happened after you left town?"

"I ended up in Seattle, where—as you know—I still live. At first I worked in a hotel," she said with a grimace. "As a cleaner. Not what you'd call challenging or...unfamiliar work. You might recall that Reba and I both did it, back in the Painted Pony days. But I managed to get a scholarship to art college in Seattle and after that, I started working as a graphic designer. Got married. Didn't last, but we're still friends. Sort of." She paused. "What about you?"

"Similar. Married, didn't last. She's out East now, in Brooklyn. And we're **not** friends." He paused. "However, I've been involved with horses, thanks mainly to my grandpa. Business-wise, I'm doing okay."

"Obviously. I, uh, learned about Hollister Horses on the internet. And social media. You have quite the presence,"

"I've got a good publicity team." Cord leaned down to alternate between stroking Bandit's head and Smoky's. "So, on another subject, how's your cousin Russ? Any idea? I never run into him."

"I saw him briefly. Seems all right. Much the same really." With a shrug she added, "The place is a mess, though."

"Then I guess that's much the same, too."

She didn't disagree.

"And Bethanne?"

"She **was** doing well. I'm not sure what's happening now. She got married, moved to Texas, had her own business — but we haven't been in touch in two or three years. I should've asked Russ..."

"He probably wouldn't have a clue."

"Yeah," Shallie said with a sigh. "I'll try to get hold of her at some point, see what's going on."

Their next topic of conversation had to do with her interest in horses. "I became familiar with them through a friend in Seattle. Emma Grant. She teaches therapeutic riding, and I've occasionally helped her out and, in fact, I'm hoping to join her business. But—" she smiled widely "—I love **all** animals."

"I can tell."

"Not always the human kind, though…"

They caught up on life in Painted Pony Creek and on personal news, then discussed a variety of other topics, ranging from politics to global affairs. An hour later, ten o'clock by then, Tina and Carly entered the kitchen. Once again the dogs bounded to their feet. And Shallie looked at the girl with an expression of deep shock. "Who **are** you?" she asked. "You remind me of someone I used to know—and love."

"I'm starting to hear that a lot around here," Carly replied.

Shallie stood, insisting on a hug. "You look so much like my friend Reba from years ago. Reba Shannon."

"She was my mom."

"What do you mean, **was**?"

"She died. I'm on my own now. How

did you know my mom?"

"I'm...from this town. We met while I was in high school." Cord saw that Shallie still seemed to be in shock at the girl's revelation. "I...hadn't heard. I'm so sorry." He knew that for a matter of months back in her late teens, Reba had been a crucial—and probably confusing—part of her life. And then, like Shallie's own mother, she'd disappeared...

"What about you?" she asked the girl. "Why are you here? Just visiting?"

"I'm trying to...sort things out."

Cord caught Shallie's eye and shook his head slightly; she didn't pursue the question. "Uh, Carly," he said. "This is Shallie Fletcher. And, Shallie—" he pointed at his housekeeper "—meet Tina Robbins."

Tina held out her hand. Shallie clasped it, murmuring a vague greeting.

"Okay," Tina said. "Let's plan on lunch for around noon. Would grilled cheese sandwiches be all right? With some left-over coleslaw."

Everyone agreed and then Cord gave

Shallie a tour of the property, accompanied by his dogs. An hour or so later, they returned to the house for the promised lunch. Carly helped, while Shallie set the table and Cord checked his schedule for the next week. Then, once they'd eaten, Carly loaded the dishwasher; she was fitting right in, he thought. He explained that he was hosting a barbecue on the back deck for his friends Eli and J.P. that evening, a frequent Friday-night event. The girls were more than welcome but might prefer to have dinner on the porch. Up to them.

"Actually," Shallie said, "I'd like to take advantage of this chance to get to know Carly. I'm sure there'll be other opportunities to see Eli and J.P."

Carly nodded vigorously. "Yeah, we should talk, you and me."

Tina immediately offered to prepare something. "Any dietary restrictions?" she asked Shallie.

"Well, I'm mostly vegetarian."

"No problem."

And Cord—although a rancher—didn't

find it a problem, either, even if he did eat meat. Tonight's guys' meal was going to be chicken and burgers...Just as well the girls were going to be dining on the porch...

He announced that he and Shallie would have their introductory session at two and suggested she might want to rest for a while, after her travel the day before.

"Thanks. That's a good idea." Yawning, she hurried up the stairs.

Shallie stretched out on the bed and closed her eyes. Still hard to believe she was here—back in the old hometown. Well, not that much of a **home**, but all she'd had. And despite Della and Norm's inadequacies, she supposed they'd done their best.

There was definitely more to the story of Reba's sudden appearance at the motel almost twenty years ago—and her equally sudden disappearance. Shallie wondered if she actually wanted to find out. She'd have to think about that...

One thing she'd definitely do while she was here, and that was create a relationship with Reba's daughter. She'd felt an immediate connection with the girl and thought they might have a certain comfort to offer each other. And perhaps Carly could tell her more about Reba, her one-time best friend, and what she'd been like in her later years.

Everything seemed to bring back the past—being here in town, seeing Russ at the run-down motel, meeting Carly, who was the very image of Reba. Above all, seeing Cord again in this still familiar and yet very changed house. Talking to him. She hoped she was coming across as natural and sure of herself. Maybe she could replace that embarrassing memory of declaring her love in the face of his complete lack of interest.

She was afraid to hope for a second chance with Cord, much as she wanted it. But she told herself a second chance was unlikely, since there hadn't been a **first** chance. At least they could resume a casual friendship...And, most important, she'd learn what she was in Montana to learn—about Christine Fletcher, about horse training, and, yes, about Cord. Because, maybe, just this once, things had changed. Or **could** change...

It had begun to occur to her that she should hire a private investigator to find Christine or find out what had happened to her. Eli, as a professional in law enforcement, might be able to suggest someone.

Shallie checked her cell phone. A text from her closest friend, Emma, who'd encouraged this trip. Another from her ex, Rob, who—she still believed—had her best interests at heart. She sent quick responses. It was now 1:40, and she should probably change her clothes and her state of mind—away from the past and into the present. She pulled on a pair of new jeans and a T-shirt featuring the logo of Emma's company, Horses Help, an adorable pony and equally adorable little girl. A quick brush of her hair and she was ready for whatever the afternoon would bring.

Cord was waiting for her in the kitchen, yet another cup of coffee in hand. He grinned as he told her, "No comments, okay?"

Shallie grinned back. "Okay. At least not about the crappy coffee."

"All right. Ready to go?" He poured the remainder of the foul-looking brew in the sink. "We'll start with the introductions. Oh," he said, "nice T-shirt."

She followed him out to the barn, and he had her speak to each horse for ten minutes or so, stroking their noses and foreheads. For today, he focused on his two recent rescues. Chief, a chestnut Thoroughbred, was skittish, but Shallie fell instantly for Annie, the shaggy little black-and-white mare. And it was obvious that Cord felt the same way. He explained their histories, or what he knew of them; Annie had been neglected and abandoned, while Chief had been mistreated by an impatient employee at a racing stable. Cord had now adopted both of them.

Shallie was appalled by what these horses had endured, but so grateful that they'd found a better life. Cord emphasized the need to bond with them, to convey a sense of calm and of **love**. A sense that the horses could trust her, that they could afford to feel secure. He guided Annie outside, into the paddock, talking to her all the while, and then Shallie took over as he watched.

She crooned to the little mare in a soothing voice, clasped her halter, led her through the field, stopping now and then to move back and forth in rhythm with her. Cord stood against the fence, smiling.

"I just adore her," Shallie said as they brought Annie back to her stall.

"And she adores you. I think we've made a good start for today. Now, what would you like to do while I meet with my foreman, Mitch?" He pointed at a gray-haired man obviously waiting for him. As they approached, Cord said, "Shallie Fletcher, this is Mitch Robbins, Tina's husband."

They shook hands and Shallie told him how much she'd enjoyed meeting Tina. "I look forward to spending more time with both of you," she said truthfully.

"You will be, and you'll meet our family, too. Maybe at the music night on Sunday. Our son-in-law, one of them, is with The GateCrashers, a popular band around here, and they'll be performing."

"Sounds good!"

She went into the house, thinking maybe she could help Tina begin preparing their supper, but found Carly in the kitchen alone, arranging a platter of raw vegetables. "This is for us. You and me," she explained. "There's ranch dip in the fridge."

"Of course. What other kind would there be?" she said, and was gratified by Carly's laughter. "Where's Tina? And the dogs?"

"Dinner's not till about six. She's gone to get a few groceries. Cheese and stuff for us, chicken or whatever for Cord and the guys. And the dogs are lounging on the back deck."

Shallie nodded. She leaned against the counter, watching Carly's careful positioning of carrots, small celery sticks, radishes and raw green beans. "So," she finally began. "Tell me about yourself."

"You already know the basics," Carly said with a shrug but without meeting her eyes. "My mom, Reba, died a couple of years ago and I've been on my own ever since. And one of those three guys here is my dad. She told me so." She turned to the sink, washing a tomato and paring a cucumber.

This was the first Shallie had heard of it, but recalling that final summer, the whole situation made sense—and it explained why Carly was here. She needed to know about her father, just as Shallie needed to know about her mother.

She took a deep breath for courage, then said, "Carly, at the time, and I'm talking almost twenty years ago, Reba and I were very close. So, I feel as if... we're sort of related, you and me."

"You were at that awful motel with my mom?"

"Yes! How did you know about that?"

"Well, she told me, of course. No details. Just about working there and her affairs with those three guys." Pause. "I don't even know what happened, why she left or anything. I mean, she didn't know she was pregnant with me yet, but..." Carly squinted up at her. "Any chance we really **are** related? That Reba was your cousin or something?"

"No, but I feel like we were. We...lost touch after a while." In fact, after Reba left, they weren't in touch again, ever. Shallie had tried social media, less pervasive back then, but it had revealed nothing of any use.

"Listen," Shallie said. "Can we talk later? Over our private dinner on the porch?"

"Okay. I don't feel like hanging out with the guys tonight, anyway. And then later, Tina will take me back to her place." She gave Shallie a conspiratorial grin as she added, "I love Tina, but Mr. Smart-ass Hollister can be a bit much. Even if he does turn out to be my dad..."

Shallie responded to that comment with a grin of her own. She still planned to catch up with Cord and get to know Tina—but she had to spend time with this girl, who was not only Reba's daughter but possibly Cord's.

With Tina's help, Cord arranged a couple of salads, a shallow bowl of marinated chicken wings, burger patties, plus buns and all the usual condiments. Tina brought out three plates and cutlery. And oh, yes, there was beer in a cooler. Then he started the barbecue.

Minutes later, J.P. arrived with Trooper; Cord's dogs acted like hosts and never showed an instant's aggression toward him. Eli appeared soon after; both guys were toting beer and J.P. handed his over, apologizing for not bringing food as promised. Cord simply rolled his eyes.

"What are we having?" Eli asked.

"Burgers and chicken wings."

"Hey, we're burger guys!" Eli made a face. "Aren't chicken wings kind of effete?"

"They're not feet, they're wings," Cord responded. "And where did you learn such an...**effete** word?"

"Ha ha."

"So Shallie and Carly are eating on the porch?" J.P. asked.

"Excellent deduction." Eli smirked. "Since there are only three plates out here."

Cord handed out beers. He'd previously told them about Shallie's arrival—and both were intrigued. Eli asked if he and Shallie had talked about Reba.

"Yeah, some," Cord replied.

"So, why exactly is she here?" he asked.

"She's interested in pursuing the horse training and learning more about horse therapy. She has a friend back in Seattle she might go into business with."

"Is that the **only** reason she's here? Does Reba have anything to do with it?" J.P. questioned.

"Not as far as I know, but maybe she will now that Shallie's met Carly."

"I'd like to see Shallie," J.P. said. "Some real memories there."

Cord nodded but didn't refer to the night she'd tried to kiss him. He'd never told his friends about that...Out of embarrassment? Or sympathy?

"A sweet girl," Eli agreed. "Although she kind of disappeared from view—and I mean **before** she took off from the motel. And who could blame her for leaving that dump?" He took a sip of his beer. "I'd like to see her, too. But we don't want to barge in on their privacy, hers and Carly's. Shallie and Reba were best friends, so she and Carly need a chance to connect."

"Don't worry," Cord said. "She's here for two weeks. We'll arrange something."

"I'm sure we will," Eli said. "Still, it's quite the coincidence that they both showed up here at the same time."

"True." Cord busied himself with the burger patties. "Destiny? Or maybe just chance."

"Hey!" J.P. chortled. "Your canine corps has expectations."

Bandit and Smoky leaped up and raced around the house to the front. "I guess they're both there now, Carly and Shallie," Cord said. "These guys can smell food—even vegetarian food—a mile away. And they know they're not getting anything here."

On the rather flimsy pretext of checking on the dogs, he went over to the porch. Shallie and Carly were indeed there, the adoring dogs at their feet. He didn't know what they'd been talking about but there was a sudden silence when he appeared. Shallie raised her glass of wine, smiled at him and said, "It's from Washington State."

Cord knew that—he was the one who'd bought it, after all. He gave her a thumbs-up. "Oh, Tina told you she and Mitch ended up going to Bailey's for Friday-night dinner?"

"Yeah," Shallie said. "And remember, Mitch suggested we go there Sunday night?"

"Sure, we can do that. It's Country Classics Night."

"Yes, please!" Carly begged. "I'd **love** to."

Cord wandered back to the deck and his friends, although the dogs stayed on the porch.

As soon as he returned, Eli brought up the inevitable subject of Carly. Cord had to admit he didn't have answers to this morning's questions yet. "I'll ask Shallie to see if she can come up with some information," he said. "They seem to be getting on well."

And that led to speculation about Shallie. "Well, like I said, she's really interested in horses, plus she's thinking about working with a friend of hers. And ...maybe she wanted to, uh, revisit the scene of her ever-so-delightful childhood."

"And her charming cousin or whatever he is," J.P. murmured.

"Changing the subject," Cord said, "what about the music night at Bailey's on Sunday? Country Classics with The GateCrashers. You must've seen the sign this morning. Carly and Shallie would both like to go, and I said we could do that. Either of you want to join us?"

"Hell, yeah!" Eli said. "Haven't seen The GateCrashers in a while."

"Also a good chance to spend some time with Carly and Shallie."

Cord got up again to visit the front porch. And again, Carly and Shallie abruptly stopped talking. He caught a reference to Reba but couldn't tell what that was about. He thought he'd lighten the atmosphere and tried to tell them a joke.

"Hey, did you hear the one about the dog who walks into a bar?"

"He ended up under the table?" Shallie asked.

"Yeah, just like Trooper!" He'd have to share that with J.P. "Good one. Did you make that up?"

"Sure did," she said, and Carly applauded loudly.

Cord brought out the wine bottle and refilled Shallie's glass, which was almost empty. Carly declined another sparkling water.

"Thank you." Shallie raised her glass to him.

"Oh, and we're definitely on for the music night on Sunday. Eli and J.P. are planning to join us."

Carly grinned. "Three for the price of one?"

"So to speak." He wondered if Shallie knew that the three of them were Carly's possible fathers—but assumed from the confidential tone of their conversation that she did. "Well, I'll let you get back to your meal..."

They seemed to be enjoying their veggies and cheese, if the amount they'd already consumed was any indication. He returned to the back deck, this time accompanied by the dogs hoping for burger bits. "Forget it, guys."

As he sat down, he caught the middle of a conversation. "Yeah," Eli was saying. "I'm starting to have some concerns about Eric—" Eric Worth, his nephew, son of his sister, Sara "—but I'm—"

"What's going on?" Cord interrupted. "Is everything okay?" Although he knew immediately what a stupid question that was.

"Well, no. Sara's worried about him, and I'm getting a bad feeling..."

"Why?"

"You know he dropped out of school this spring. And Sara told me he's out and about at all hours. He won't tell her where he's been. And she doesn't like his loser friends." He briefly closed his eyes. "I wouldn't admit this to anyone else. I can't help thinking about a few very recent and very sneaky crimes, although there's absolutely no evidence tying any of them to Eric. You know the crimes I'm talking about? Targeting ranchers and farmers, releasing their animals. Have you heard anything?"

Cord frowned. "Yeah. A little. Perry Roberts told me his enclosure gate had been pried open. And a sheep got out, got hit in the road. Can you believe that? If there's anything I can't stand, it's cruelty. Especially to the innocent, like animals."

Eli nodded grimly. "I hate to even suggest it, and I can't accuse Eric—or anyone—without solid evidence. But like

I said, his mom's worried, and so am I."

"We should all keep an eye on him," Cord said.

J.P. agreed, told them he'd do what he could. Soon after, and by now it was nearly ten and the lights inside and out were on, Tina reappeared in the Robbinses' car to collect Carly. Cord asked Shallie if she wanted to join the guys. She shook her head. "Not tonight, thanks. I'm just too tired. Soon, though."

"I have a question for you. I want to ask if you'll help me out…"

"How?"

"By getting some information about Carly. She's been hesitant to share anything, and I haven't been very good about asking. It's…kind of uncomfortable, you know. She says one of us is her father—you've heard that, right? She told you?"

When Shallie nodded, he went on. "You can see how this situation affects all of us. But we don't know where to go from here."

"DNA testing is the obvious way,"

Shallie said.

"How do I approach that?"

"Let me think about it. Can we talk more tomorrow? Maybe you can give me your questions then?"

"Okay," he murmured. "See you in the morning."

Shallie finished her wine and went inside with the empty glass while Cord gazed after her. A minute later, she came back out to clear up the dishes and the remains of the meal, and to wish the dogs—and him—a good night.

Except it wasn't going to be. Because he'd be thinking about her, wanting her. And wondering what **she** was thinking— and whether she wanted him, too.

CHAPTER SEVEN

Saturday morning, Carly accompanied Tina to the main kitchen for breakfast, where Shallie met them. Tina announced that she was buying some additional groceries—mostly to stock up on vegetarian options.

"Thank you," Shallie said. "I really appreciate it."

"Least we can do," Tina responded. "You're our guest."

"I'll have some toast and coffee, then go out for my session with Cord."

Carly gave her a goodbye hug and followed Tina out to her car.

After buying local vegetables, eggs and cheese, plus several packages of decent coffee, Tina took Carly to a Western-wear store to get her some new jeans, a long-sleeved T-shirt and new running shoes. Carly thanked her but didn't know what else to say. She'd realized the very first morning, after Tina had collected her laundry, that she must have seen the cash. Carly wasn't sure how to address that, how to explain—and wondered if she should've offered to pay.

Tina drove by a run-down motel south of town—the Painted Pony, of course—and asked Carly if she wanted to go inside, check it out. Carly declined. "Later, okay?" No way was she up for this, seeing the place her mother had spent all those months in. "What a dump," she muttered. "Was it always this bad?"

"I wouldn't say it was ever what you'd call high-end, but it was definitely better than it is now."

"Is it still in business?"

Tina shrugged. "If at all, I'm sure he doesn't get many customers."

Carly wondered who "he" was, but didn't ask. Next thing she realized, they were in the parking lot at Bailey's, and Tina said they'd have a quick lunch there, her treat. Which made Carly feel even guiltier.

She changed the subject. "Look! The sign for Classic Country Night. Cord said we'd go."

"Great! We'll all sit together."

"Oh, Brynne's not on shift right now," Tina said as they walked inside. "Probably just as well for the moment."

Another reference Carly didn't understand.

They sat down at a small table near one of the side walls, and Carly glanced around, admiring the art on the walls. The collection included paintings, photographs and prints. Tina explained that Brynne had an art background and that a few of these were by locals. She pointed at a photograph of wild horses. "That one's by a friend of Susan's who's very talented. It's not only beautiful in itself but it represents our county. Wild

Horse County."

"Wow," Carly breathed. "So gorgeous! And I didn't know that, about the county name."

A waitress, name of Miranda, brought them menus and rhymed off a list of specials. The last thing Carly felt right now was hungry but she ordered a small serving of nachos. Tina asked for a salmon salad sandwich with fries.

Before the food arrived, Tina looked her directly in the eye. "Carly, sweetie. I know there are a lot of...issues and questions about your background and why you're here. To be honest, Cord confided in us. I understand you might have reason to keep certain facts to yourself. And I won't interfere. But can you tell me one thing?"

Carly stared back at her, hardly able to speak. It was going to be about the money, wasn't it?

"When I got the laundry in your back-pack—with your permission—I found quite a lot of money. All I want to know is that you have it legally and legitimately."

Bingo. Carly sighed. The whole situation made her feel awkward. Nervous. "You mean did I steal it? No! I promise you. It...it's what was left of my mom's. She got it in cash and gave it to me shortly before she died. She didn't want to risk my stepfather—Duncan—taking it out of her account." Carly was almost embarrassed at what a skillful liar she'd become.

Tina nodded. "Okay, that sounds reasonable."

Yep, skillful, and convincing, too. More than nervous, she felt guilty about lying to the woman who'd been so kind to her. So...motherly.

"Oh, good, here's our lunch," Tina said.

Carly couldn't manage too many of the nachos and asked that the remainder be wrapped up. When they got back to the trailer, she put them in the refrigerator and grabbed her laptop from her room. "I'm going to sit outside for a while and catch up on email." She helped Tina take the groceries to the main kitchen, then walked in the direction of a tree with branches that nearly reached the ground, a tree that would keep her hidden. A cottonwood, Tina had told her. Carly looked around and saw no one. Time for the next YouTube installment, a project she'd begun soon after starting her journey. She'd done it for various reasons, including the hope of memorializing this part of her life, sharing it with others—and the opportunity to make some much-needed money; she'd been more successful at that than she'd expected, thanks mainly to the fans she'd gained and their generous donations.

Accompanied by Bandit and Smoky, she moved carefully toward the paddock and, standing well back, made a video of the two horses there. "Hi, it's Charlotte. Welcome to **My 3 Dads**. You might remember that I'm in Montana now—and I'm close to finding my father, but not there yet. Thank you for your interest in my journey and for all the financial help you've given me." After making sure there was no one in the vicinity, she got some video of the landscape, careful not to show any discernible details. "This is where one of my Possible Dads happens to live. Nice, huh?"

She'd recently begun to sing on her YouTube videos and, standing a few feet from the paddock, launched into John Denver's "Take Me Home, Country Roads." Seemed like a good choice!

When she saw Shallie and Cord, both on horseback and trotting in her direction, she stopped, shut down YouTube and turned off her computer while they were still some distance away. As they approached, she moved toward them and said as blithely as she could, "Hi, I was just catching up on email and Facebook. And now I'm going for a walk."

She had no intention of giving them a chance to find out what she was doing. When she did let them know, **whether** she did, would depend on how things went, who turned out to be her father and, more important, how he reacted.

They left with a friendly wave.

"Whew. That was close." Yeah, she'd really become an accomplished liar—but wasn't sure if she was doing this for her own protection or theirs. Keeping up such a big lie, such a complex one, had become a burden.

For the briefest of moments, she was tempted to call them back, to tell the truth, here and now.

Saturday evening, feeling pleased with the day's results—both his session with Shallie and his work with Mitch—Cord sat on the porch holding a bag of chips and a beer, sipping slowly. The dogs flopped hopefully at his feet.

Tina and Mitch showed up, and Cord offered them a drink; they both accepted. Handing Mitch the chip bag, he went inside to get him a beer. Tina joined him. "Don't worry, I'll pour my own wine," she said. "Had dinner yet?"

Cord shook his head, and she shook hers, making a disapproving sound with her tongue. "That's what I figured. I'll put together a few snacks for us, okay?"

"Thanks! I did feed the dogs, though."

"Well, you've got your priorities straight."

Cord grinned in unfeigned agreement and joined Mitch on the porch again. They discussed today's progress and their plans to hire local workers to harvest hay in a month or so. "How are your girls doing?" Cord asked. "Anything new with Susan?"

At twenty-nine, Susan was the youngest and single; she headed up the town's small library. "She's all excited about starting a weekly blog. She's calling it **Painted Ponies and Favorite Books.**"

"Nothing new with Caroline and family," he went on. Caroline, the oldest, and her husband, Peter Carson, had a ten-year-old girl, Ashley, and an infant son named Mitchell, so she was, for now, a stay-at-home mom while he ran an accounting business. "Peter's just thankful tax season's well over."

Elspeth, the middle daughter, was married to Aaron, helped him with his music career and did English tutoring on Skype. "She's got quite a few students now. And Aaron—Oh, that reminds me. Are you going to the Country Classics thing at Bailey's on Sunday? Like I told you, Aaron and his band are a big part of that. And there's going to be an open mic hour."

"Yeah. Carly and Shallie both want to go. And I always enjoy The Gate-Crashers."

Tina walked onto the porch just then, carrying a platter of cheese, ham and crackers in one hand, her glass in another. Cord jumped up to take the tray. "Couldn't help overhearing. Carly's really looking forward to it. You've probably heard our whole family's planning to go. Well, except for the little ones."

Cord nodded. "Eli and J.P. will probably come, too." The three chatted in a low-key fashion for ten minutes or so, until Shallie emerged from the house. "Sorry," she told them. "I fell asleep. Um, I was wondering if I could take everyone to dinner tonight? As a thank-you for last night? To Bailey's? I keep hearing about it but haven't been there yet."

"Thank you," Tina said, "but we're already going there for the Country Classics show, and two nights so close together is probably one too many, especially since Carly and I had lunch there today. We're—"

"Okay," Shallie broke in. "I'll cover our dinner there on Sunday."

"If you're sure…"

"I'm sure. In fact, I insist. Meanwhile, what are we having for dinner tonight? I guess we can't order pizza?"

"Not easily," Tina said, "but I can fix homemade pizza. Oh—here comes Carly."

"Pizza! Yay!" Carly jumped up the porch steps, laptop in its shoulder bag. "Hi, everyone! Tina, let me help with the prep."

Cord had to smile at her enthusiasm and noted again that she was making an effort to cooperate, to become part of the household.

"Thanks, sweetie," Tina said. "I think

we have all the ingredients—including premade crusts. Sorry if that's cheating."

"I'll chop veggies," Carly offered, following her inside. "That's kind of my specialty now."

Shallie waited until after they'd left to speak to Cord. "Thanks for this afternoon. Going riding was exactly what I needed. I know we don't have horse-related plans for Sunday, but please let me give you a hand with cleaning the stalls."

"You don't need to," Mitch said, as Cord began to say, "It's not part of the deal—"

"I realize that, but I'd like to. And it's not as if I've never done it before." She gave them what Cord thought was a rather awkward smile. "Now, I'll go and do my bit for the pizza-making extravaganza."

Half an hour later, Carly came out to tell them dinner was ready—a variety of homemade pizzas, two vegetarian, two with sausage, all with plenty of cheese.

Additional chairs were brought onto the

porch, and everyone gathered there with their slices of pizza and drinks. Cord called the pizza "Better than any take-out," which made Carly smile.

A lively discussion of favorite country-western songs followed. "What are you hoping The GateCrashers are gonna play tomorrow night?" Mitch asked. He explained that the band was popular throughout Wild Horse County and sometimes performed farther afield. They even had a couple of CDs out.

"Johnny Cash," Tina replied. "Patsy Cline. Willie Nelson. Hey! Any of you planning to volunteer for open mic?"

"I like listening to music, but I can't sing worth a damn," Cord said. "I'd clear the place out in two seconds flat—and I mean **flat**."

"I don't know many of the songs," Shallie put in. "You, Carly?"

Carly shrugged. "I'll be there to listen." She stood up and began collecting dishes from the table.

Cord wondered why the rush, but decided to pitch in. "Thank you, Tina,

Carly, Shallie, for an exceptional meal,"
he said formally as he stood up and
began moving leftovers to the fridge.

Mitch seconded his thanks and
suggested he, his wife and Carly head
back to the trailer. "Long day tomorrow."

Cord agreed, and so did Shallie—
based on her quick good-nights and her
even quicker flight up the stairs.

Damn. He'd hoped to talk with her
tonight, just a pleasant How-are-things
exchange—and he still had to give her
the list of questions for Carly. He'd
check the crumpled napkin tonight and
transcribe his notes.

He thought about what he'd say to
Shallie tomorrow. He'd explain, in more
detail, why he felt uncomfortable with
the idea of asking Carly himself, even
though he might be her father. Or more
likely **because** of it...

**I don't want Carly to think I don't
trust her**, he'd tell Shallie. **I <u>do</u>, but
according to Eli, we need that information. Just to...confirm things. And
I can sense she'd rather talk to you**

than me.

He imagined Shallie's response. She'd agree, she'd have some suggestions of her own—and then their conversation would become personal. About where they were in life and where they hoped to go.

Late Sunday morning, Cord finally relented and let Shallie help with the stall cleaning. She was appropriately dressed in worn jeans, a long-sleeved cotton shirt, old running shoes. And she looked as good as she had in the new clothes she'd had on the other day. She wore a ponytail tied on top of her head, and beautiful as her long chestnut hair was, this style revealed her elegant cheekbones and her smooth forehead. He had to force himself to stop watching her as they had their breakfast of decent coffee and microwaved leftover pizza.

As she'd said last night, it wasn't as though she'd never cleaned stalls or groomed horses before; she explained that she often assisted Emma at the

Horses Help stables. "I don't have a problem with the housekeeping part of working with horses."

With Mitch there, too, the work went quickly; the three of them mucked out the stalls, delivered fresh hay and fresh water, then brought the horses back to the barn.

All the while, they exchanged horse stories, some of them emotional, others amusing. Cord especially liked the one Shallie told them about a horse of Emma's becoming "best friends" with a cat owned by the people who rented her the property. Napoleon the cat would leap onto the stall railing, then he and Charlie the horse would nuzzle each other.

As he prepared to leave, Mitch said he'd never enjoyed a session of stall cleaning more. "I'm going to tell Tina your cat and horse story. She'll love it!"

Afterward, Shallie said she was going up to her room to shower.

"Me, too," Cord said. "I mean," he added with a slightly embarrassed grin,

"I'm going up to **my** room, not yours."
Her laughter made his gaffe seem
worthwhile. They all converged in the
kitchen at around six, Shallie wearing
black jeans, a fringed shirt and sandals.
Carly was in new-looking jeans and a
glittery tank top (which Cord was pretty
sure belonged to Susan). She ended up
driving to Bailey's with Tina and Mitch,
while Cord gave Shallie a ride. Their
conversation continued on the theme of
what she called "interspecies relationships." Surprising how many stories they
both knew. "Emma, more than anyone
so far, helped me learn about animals,
about how they relate to each other and
how we relate to them," she said with a
smile he couldn't miss even in the dim
interior of the car.

Damn it, she was beautiful. And smart
and charming and compassionate...
Why hadn't he been aware of that all
those years ago? Well, because it **was**
a lot of years ago. They were young,
immature. He'd been in love with Reba
and hardly aware of any other girl at the

time. But he had to question the depth of
his love for Reba, now that he realized
how seductive the idea of the one who
got away could feel with time. Their relationship, his and Reba's, hadn't come to
a natural end and he'd probably given it
more of a place in his heart than it really
deserved. Back then, any possibility for
him and Shallie never had a chance. His
fault.

They arrived at Bailey's to discover Tina,
Mitch and family already there. Carly,
too, of course. Brynne had arranged for
two long tables to be pushed together
to accommodate their group. Tina introduced Shallie to Elspeth and Aaron, the
musician, to Caroline and her husband,
Peter, and to Susan. Cord introduced her
to Brynne, who was looking her usual
elegant self, wearing a simple off-white
shift, her midlength blond hair straight
and glossy.

Eli, J.P. and Trooper sat down with
them; the men and Shallie exchanged
hugs, promising each other that they'd
reconnect and share histories later on.

The place was starting to get crowded. Miranda, their server, brought the women wine, while the men all ordered beer.

During their leisurely dinner, which Tina described as "pubbish," Brynne made her usual point of coming by to bring Trooper his treat and enthusiastic praise, and he responded with equal enthusiasm.

Then she stopped abruptly, staring at Carly. "Oh, my God. You look just like—"

"Reba, yes. My mom."

"Oh, my God! I knew Reba died, but I didn't realize she had a daughter. It wasn't mentioned in the obituary."

"That's because her asshole husband wrote it."

"I'm so sorry about your loss. Our loss, too. Anyway, welcome. Hope we have a chance to talk soon. Catch up on..."

"My mom's life?"

"Yes, I'd like that. She and I lost touch so long ago, and I happened to find out online that..." Brynne paused. "You must really miss her."

Carly nodded, and Cord saw her rub

her eyes with both hands. Standing up, she moved into Brynne's waiting hug. Brynne hurried off and Cord found himself repeatedly glancing over at Shallie, who was sitting across from him, between Carly and Susan. He was relieved that she seemed to be enjoying herself as much as everyone else and told himself to stop looking at her. But as much as he tried, he couldn't resist stealing glances at her.

At precisely eight, Aaron and his band started tuning up, then launched into their first song, the Johnny Cash classic "Ring of Fire." Their first set also included (ironically enough) "I'm a Long Gone Daddy" by Hank Williams and Bob Dylan's **Nashville Skyline** song, "Girl from the North Country," big crowd favorites. The band left the stage for a short break, to the accompaniment of delighted applause.

When Cord looked over at Shallie again, he noticed that her expression seemed reflective, even a little wistful. Despite the fact that she obviously had friends, an ex she had a cordial relationship with, a career, enough money—he sensed there was something missing. At least in the current version of her life, as there was in his...He couldn't keep from hoping that her enjoyment tonight had something to do with his presence. Just like his enjoyment was tied to **hers**.

The next set began a few minutes later, and requests were invited. "'I Walk the Line,'" Eli called out, and the band, as usual, gave Johnny Cash his due with their energetic and poignant rendition.

Susan Robbins raised her hand next. "How about some Patsy Cline?" And the band obliged with "Walkin' after Midnight."

Four or five other songs were performed, and finally Brynne spoke up, making the last request for this set. "Sorry. Can't resist, but I'd like to hear 'Friends in Low Places' by Garth Brooks."

When the song was over, Eli asked in a tone of mock innocence, "Hey, Brynne Bailey, was that a comment on your restaurant?"

"What do **you** think?" she scoffed. And the set ended with laughter.

After the break, Aaron invited audience members onstage to sing. One drunken cowboy—or would-be cowboy (if his "uniform" of jeans, vest, hat and boots was anything to judge by) requested "Streets of Laredo" and sang in a rather wobbly voice—just as wobbly as his walk. Aaron ended the guy's performance early with a loud "Thank you, John," and helped him off the stage.

Next was a young couple who sang Loretta Lynn's "Van Lear Rose," followed by an elderly man with a surprisingly robust voice. Gentleman Jim, as he was known, sang "Your Cheatin' Heart."

Cord wondered if he could get Mitch to perform one of Bill Hollister's favorites, Willie Nelson's "Always on My Mind." He remembered his grandfather singing it in his husky voice, remembered his grandmother smiling. He was about to lean over and ask when Carly suddenly got up and walked quickly to the makeshift stage. Cord was shocked and so, obviously, was everyone else at their table.

Carly whispered something to Aaron, who introduced her. "Everyone, this is Carly, and she's new to town. She's gonna sing 'One of These Days' by the great Emmylou Harris."

Carly tapped her foot and started singing. Her voice was...astounding, clear and yet so expressive. So emotional. Aaron led the audience in vigorous applause.

When she returned to the table, everyone stared, first at her, then at each other. Cord noticed that several young people at a nearby booth were exchanging nudges and whispers, pointing at Carly, some even checking their cell phones. **Rude**, he thought, wondering whether she'd noticed. But the evening was over, and their group prepared to leave. Both he and Shallie congratulated Carly on her performance as she got into Tina and Mitch's car. Carly thanked them but remained impassive.

Back at the house, Cord suggested another drink—tea, wine, beer—and some conversation. They sat on the porch with the dogs, she with her spritzer, he with a beer, and talked about their astonishment at Carly's talent. "Did she get that from her mother?" Had Reba been able to sing? They tried to remember and agreed it wasn't something she did often, but she'd had the ability. It only happened occasionally, like the time she'd sung "Piece of My Heart" to Cord, with his arms around her, on another one of those campfire nights. She'd stopped abruptly when she became aware of the attention she was attracting. From Shallie among others...

"'Piece of My Heart,'" Shallie said now, speaking quietly. Yes, she'd been there that night. He recalled, however faintly, the look on her face back then. A look he hadn't quite been able to interpret. Disgust? Anger? Confusion? The only reason he remembered it at all was the difference between **her** reaction and everyone else's. The others who'd been there had either laughed or cheered them on.

He wondered how Shallie felt about that memory—especially since he'd begun to question how **he** felt.

After a few minutes' silence, she asked, "How would you feel if it turns out you're Carly's father?"

"Fine—but there are other possibilities."

"Yeah, two of them. It's ultimately going to be about the DNA."

He sighed. "Do you have any sense of her willingness to go through a test like that?"

"We haven't discussed it yet. I didn't find the right opportunity today, and you haven't given me the questions yet. But I promise I'll talk to her. If you're sure you can't do it?"

"I'm sorry. I'd rather you had that conversation with her. This time, anyway. Like I told you, I'm really not comfortable with it, and I'm not convinced she would be, either."

"I want whatever's best for Carly.

And," she added, "for you."

He nodded his thanks, so moved by her simple statement he could barely speak. Her next remark changed the mood.

"But don't forget you, Eli and J.P. have to do the test, too."

"There isn't, shall we say, universal acceptance of that plan. They don't seem ready to find out, one way or the other."

"I'll bring up the subject with her. But you **have** to talk to the guys."

"Agreed, but no rush."

"If you say so," she murmured.

"I'll print out the list of questions for you. Pretty basic stuff—mostly confirming family background."

"Okay."

"One more thing. I didn't tell you about the money. A couple of thousand dollars, in cash, in her backpack. We have no idea where that came from. Tina confided in me that Carly said it was money from Reba—but I'm not sure I believe that." He shook his head. "And

I'm not sure whether Eli should be investigating this."

"**What?** Two thousand dollars? Where would Carly—" She stared at him. "You're thinking it's theft?"

"Hope not!" Then he said, "If you do learn anything about it from Carly, I need you to share it with me, just so she's not blamed for some crime she didn't commit."

"I'd have to let her know. You understand that, right?"

"Yes. But we'll leave it for now," Cord said. "Ready to go inside?"

"Sure." She stood up and the dogs stood with her. "Everybody in." They happily trotted after her, and Cord locked the front door.

As she stood by her stairs, he walked over. "Thank you," he whispered. "I appreciate what you're doing for Carly. For both of us."

She leaned toward him and gave him a light kiss. He kissed her back, equally restrained, then said, "What the hell? Let me kiss you properly."

"I'd like that!"

"I've been waiting for this..." Waiting and hoping...

Shallie didn't say she'd been waiting, too, but she didn't hold back when he kissed her. She said with that kiss what she didn't say with her words.

This is only the beginning, he told himself. The beginning of a new way of being together.

Carly felt vaguely hungover when she got up—although she certainly hadn't had anything, other than water, to drink. And her experience with hangovers was minimal, anyway. No, her feelings this morning had to do with regret. And fear.

Showing off like that, impulsively getting up to sing, had been a mistake, especially since she'd done that Emmy-lou Harris song on **My 3 Dads**. She supposed the truth was that she hadn't been able to resist. Even worse, those kids sitting in a booth near the back—she'd seen them watching her and she

was positive one of them had said
"Charlotte" as she walked by.

She'd been so careful, but this was
a small town. What if the news got
around? What would Cord and the guys
—and Tina and Shallie—think? Not to
mention that she'd lied to Tina about the
money...Would they understand why
she was doing this? And earning money
at it, via ads and the contributions to
PayPal, since her YouTube channel was
continuing to grow in popularity. She
been cashing out some of the money
deposited in her bank account, stopping
at banks and ATMs along the way.

The other day, sitting under that
spreading tree, she'd spent some time
thinking about why she was doing this.
She'd decided from the start that it was
a way to commemorate her journey.
But now it occurred to her that she was
commemorating her mother, as well.
And she was connecting with others,
communicating with them, even if it was
just through the internet. She'd also
started to see her YouTube channel as

a chance to perform. Which brought her back to last evening.

On the drive home, Tina had said she was "a performer at heart." It seemed that way to Carly, too.

She knew it was very old-fashioned and even risky to insist on turning a chunk of her payments into cash and carrying it around. That was, she figured, partly due to her mom's tendencies when it had come to money; she'd preferred to have it in her wallet rather than in the bank—not that she'd had much in either place. Carly gathered this went back to her early days and her uncertain income working in low-end motels and bars...And she and her husband, Duncan, hadn't really shared their money with each other; they'd covered whatever expenses they'd individually agreed to cover and no more.

Still lying in bed, Carly felt herself grow tense. A tension that came from thinking about the past and worrying about the present. She stretched, but that didn't relax her or wake her sufficiently to get up. Reaching for her cell phone, she saw it was already nine thirty.

Should she get out of here? Leave Painted Pony Creek? Then what about finding her father? And her friendships with Tina and Shallie, which had come to mean a great deal to her in such a short time? Her relationships with Cord and the guys were something she'd miss, too.

No, she had to see this through. But if she stayed—and she **would** stay— she knew she'd better keep a low profile from now on.

She forced herself to sit up, begin another day.

CHAPTER EIGHT

Monday morning. Time to get up. Or maybe not... Shallie wasn't quite ready to join the world downstairs. Or the one outside.

She decided to call Emma in Seattle, catch up on the latest news.

Their most recent conversation, the day after she'd arrived, had been brief. But now they'd have an opportunity for a lengthier talk.

"Hi, Shallie, how **are** you?"

"Not bad. Good, actually. How about you?"

"Same. Got a busy day coming up. One of my regular clients—Jordan? Remember him? The ten-year-old boy with autism."

"Of course. Is he doing okay?"

"I'd say so. He's really bonded with darling little Carrot Cake."

"She's a lovely orange girl, and really, truly a darling."

"How are the horse lessons going? Details, please."

Shallie explained what she and Cord had been working on—introductions to the various horses, and the time spent patiently relating to them, especially the rescues. Riding. Cleaning stalls.

"And the girl you told me about? Your friend Reba's daughter?"

"Carly. I think I've made some headway there. We talk quite often, and she's shared some of her history with me, sometimes asks for advice. She…needs me."

"Yeah. She needs a friend. And a mother."

"Not to mention a father." Shallie had recently informed Emma of the three-fathers situation.

"I don't even want to ask," Emma said,

"but any progress there?"

"Well, Cord's asked me to talk to her about...certain things, including a DNA test."

"If it turns out Cord's her dad, how would **you** feel about that?"

"Okay." And she meant it. The subject of Cord had first come up when she'd investigated his business. She'd told Emma only a little about her memories of Cord and the feelings she'd had for him, or about Reba—but Emma had easily guessed there was more. In a previous call, Shallie had mentioned learning from Carly that Reba had died. She'd described how shaken she was, not only by Reba's death but by the fact that she'd had a daughter.

They left the subject of Cord and Carly and spoke about mutual friends, Country Classics Night and their favorite C&W songs, their delayed plans to take a trip to San Francisco.

Shallie took a deep breath, audible to her and probably Emma, and said, "I'm thinking of hiring a private investigator to research my mother's history and, if possible, find out where she is now."

"Do it! You can afford it."

"Who knows what I might learn? Could be bad news. But I **have** to do it. And you're right, at this point in my life, I can afford it." Her share of profits from the house she and Rob had owned in Seattle had left her with enough money to do that. And change her life if she wanted. She'd been living in a small apartment, in the same building as Emma, since the divorce and, for the first time, had a substantial bank account.

She deeply valued Emma's friendship, valued having someone to rely on, to exchange experiences with, to **laugh** with. Especially since the end of her marriage...She suspected Emma knew she had a crush on Cord. Emma had always been able to read her emotions, even when Shallie herself tried to deny or disguise them.

"Back to your mother...If you don't pursue this, it'll bother you for the rest of your life."

"You're right. Only question is, how do I go about it? Check the internet?"

"Didn't you say that one of those three guys—the three stooges, or whatever—is a cop or a sheriff? Ask him."

"Oh, my God! Of course. Why didn't that occur to me?"

"Hmm. Maybe you're not thinking straight, for one reason or another. Maybe a reason named Cord?"

"Okay, okay. I think I've told you too much," Shallie said with a quick laugh. "But seriously, thanks for being there for me."

"Goes both ways."

"You can count on it. Well, I guess I should go down and get some coffee. And find out what we're doing for the day."

"All right, I should get going, too. But I have to tell you something first. I'm not sure how you'll feel about this and I hope you won't be upset, but I heard that Rob's seeing someone—**not** the one he had the affair with, though. And, Shallie, he might be moving in with her."

Shallie knew Emma believed, or used
to, that Rob was hoping to reconcile, get
back with her; she'd never believed it
herself. She realized that as little as a
week ago, hearing about Rob's new
relationship would have upset her, maybe devastated her. But her life felt different now.

"If this is what he wants, I'm fine with
it," she said.

"Good. Keep me posted on the PI thing.
And, Carly," Emma added. "Talk soon,
and much love."

"Same to you."

Shallie dressed quickly in the usual
old jeans, a cotton plaid shirt, running
shoes. That reminded her—she needed
to talk to Cord or, more likely, Tina about
laundry.

She walked slowly downstairs, considering how to approach him about
asking Eli to recommend a private
detective. He was in the kitchen by
himself.

"Hi," he greeted her, holding up a mug.

"Yes, please."

They exchanged the standard pleasan-
tries as they sipped their coffee (better
than yesterday's)—the weather (warm
and sunny), the dogs (happy lounging on
the porch) and plans for the day (session
starting at ten thirty, Shallie continuing to
work with Chief).

Cord offered her waffles with syrup;
normally, she would've declined. Not
her kind of food at all. But she simply
nodded and said, "Thanks."

While he toasted the frozen waffles,
then poured maple syrup into a small
pitcher, she thought over the request
she planned to make. Ten minutes later,
food finished, coffee drunk, she said,
"Can I ask you a question? I, uh, need
some information."

"Sure, fire away."

Not an image she cared for, but she
launched into an explanation, trying not
to make it too complicated. She talked
about Christine Fletcher's disappearance, her own need to learn exactly who
this woman was—other than "Della's
crazy sister"—and what had happened

to her. Was she still alive? Shallie admitted that her search for Christine was the other "main reason" for coming to Painted Pony Creek. That, in fact, it was her **first** reason and how delighted she was that his training course had fit in perfectly. "So I decided I could make it a double-purpose trip." She didn't include her third, still-private, reason—that she'd wanted to see if there was any chance of a connection, any hope of a future with Cord.

"So, my question is, do you think Eli would be willing to recommend an investigator?"

Cord agreed to talk to him, after pointing out that this kind of research, especially in such a complicated situation, could be costly.

"Oh, I should've said! I'm willing to pay."

He gave her an inquiring glance, but she didn't give him any further information. "I'll get in touch with Eli right now and, depending on his schedule, we'll set up a time to get together."

"Thanks!" She could tell that she sounded a little breathless. Out of gratitude for Cord's generosity, his immediate willingness to help. Out of relief **and** anxiety now that the answers she needed might actually be within reach. She felt he understood her sense of urgency.

He got up and retrieved his cell phone, removing it from its charger, then returned to the kitchen, put it on speaker and tried Eli. He got hold of him right away, then described what Shallie was looking for. To her relief, Eli said he'd be happy to look into it and already had someone in mind..."Why don't we meet at Bailey's tonight? J.P., too, if he's interested. He generally has something useful to add."

She saw Cord grin at that. "Yeah, and maybe the oh-so-smart Trooper will have some ideas, too."

"No doubt."

Shallie called out, "Hi, Eli, and thanks!"

Then she and Cord discussed the day's plans. "I'll have you focus on Chief," he said, providing a little more information than he had earlier. "I want you to prepare him for slow, careful rides, possibly as a therapy horse sometime in the future. I'm interested in moving Hollister Horses in that direction. And at this stage, I'll bet you know more about it than I do because of working with your friend. You've obviously learned a lot from her."

"Thank you. I'll tell Emma you said that."

"Please do. Shall we go and visit Chief?"

As they walked to the stable, Cord said, "Is it all right if I ask why you're looking for your mother now? I mean, she's been missing for thirty-some years."

"Like I told you, it's one of the reasons I'm back in Painted Pony Creek. You're the other..." She hoped he'd assume she was talking exclusively about his business—and wasn't sure exactly why she felt she needed to keep business and personal matters separate, at least for the moment.

"Your mother, Christine Fletcher, disappeared from the motel in the middle of the night when you were two. I kind of remember that. I mean I remember hearing about it from you when we were …twelve or so."

"Yes. And as for why I'm doing this now, there are a few reasons. My divorce, which happened because my husband was unfaithful…" She paused, but thankfully he didn't comment. "Also the fact that, aside from having absolutely no information about my father— he's 'unknown' according to my birth certificate—I know next to nothing about her, either. I've made a real effort to find her on the internet, but no luck. So…this is the biggest gap in my life."

"You might recall hearing that my mother basically abandoned me, too, but I was fortunate enough to end up here with my grandparents. Fortunate enough that they searched for me."

"That's something else we have in common," Shallie told him, wondering if she was going too far. "Besides being brought to this town at a young age, going to the same school, growing up with relatives...Both our mothers disappearing from our lives."

"True. And I know your situation was a lot harder than mine. Frankly, I've never been interested in looking for my mother."

Shallie sighed. "I get it. But you probably learned more about her from your grandparents than I ever did about Christine. Plus, Bill and Mimi were a thousand percent better than Norm and Della. I certainly remember that!"

"I have a lot of faith in Eli and his connections. I'm sure you'll learn something soon."

Shallie smiled. "I keep hoping it won't be bad news. Although at this point, I guess the only bad news would be no news."

By then they'd reached Chief's stall.

Carly pulled on her brand-new jeans, courtesy of Tina and Cord, and another of Susan's T-shirts, this one with a logo promoting The GateCrashers. She went to the trailer's compact kitchen, where Mitch was just finishing his coffee.

Both he and Tina raved about her performance the previous night, praising her with extravagant descriptions. "So beautiful."

"So emotional."

"By far the best of the open mic singers." They couldn't seem to say enough good things.

Lowering her head, feeling embarrassed and yet pleased, she thanked them.

Tina even suggested Carly could probably work with Aaron at some point if she wanted; he'd been impressed, too. They'd talk to him about it, she said, with Mitch nodding enthusiastically. That offer was the last thing Carly had expected. She felt highly complimented —but she couldn't possibly...

Ironic that she'd worn this T-shirt!

When Mitch had left and they'd eaten some scrambled eggs, Tina asked if Carly wanted to go "downtown." They'd hit the drugstore, she said, maybe the magazine stand, the deli.

Carly felt reluctant, for more reasons than she wanted to explain, but she agreed, which had more to do with Tina's kindness than anything else. Carly **needed** to show her gratitude and she could do that by acceding to Tina's wishes. In the process, she could pick up some stuff she needed—nail polish remover and suntan lotion.

They drove to the small drugstore, halfway up Main Street. Was there a town anywhere in the country, Carly wondered, that **didn't** have a Main Street? Once there, she said, "I have a few things I need to buy. See you in ten?"

"By the exit," Tina agreed.

Carly selected the items on her list, plus some volume-enhancing condition-er and a new hairbrush. She was on her way to the cash register when—just as she'd feared—she saw two of the girls she'd seen last night at Bailey's. They saw her, too, and started to approach, calling, "Hey, Charlotte! Carly?"

In a panic, Carly dropped her intended purchases on a random shelf, turned and race-walked out of the store. Great! She didn't need them recognizing her, identifying her, asking questions or spreading gossip. She wasn't ready to be revealed, and if it had to happen, **she** wanted to be in control. So she had to escape. Now.

She waved at Tina, standing in line at the cash, then ran to the car, parked half a block down Main. Luckily Tina had left it unlocked. Another small-town thing, she supposed. She slumped in the passenger seat. She had no idea whether those girls knew Tina, whether they'd ask what was going on and why she'd been so rude—and who **was** she, anyway? Worse, what if they mentioned **My 3 Dads**?

What could she say to Tina about taking off like that? What remotely plausible excuse could she offer. **I had to go to the bathroom? I felt sick? I had to make a call?**

Five minutes later, Tina returned to the

car. She got in, making much work of putting away her purchases, storing her purse, buckling her seat belt, never looking at Carly. Finally, she turned to her. "What was that all about?"

Carly decided, for now, to go with the feeling-sick excuse. At some point soon, she'd tell the truth; she owed that to Tina, not to mention Cord and Shallie. "I felt...like I had to throw up."

Tina's expression instantly became sympathetic. "Oh, you poor thing! Are you feeling any better?"

"A little." Actually she felt worse. Now she really did feel sick to her stomach, nauseated by her lie.

Yes, she wanted to tell the truth— **would** tell the truth. But how? When? Maybe she'd get Shallie's advice.

As they came back inside after another successful session, Shallie said, "Looks like Carly and Tina are still out. Why don't I fix us sandwiches?"

"Thanks." This wasn't typical of his clients. But Shallie was more than a typical client. Not that he'd ever had a history with any of the others. "I'll go check my calls while you do that." In his study, Cord found a voice mail message from a potential new client and phoned back. "Mr. Lewis?" he said when a man answered. "It's Cord Hollister."

"I'm Leonard, but call me Len. As I mentioned, my wife and I are interested in doing one of your horse-training sessions." He chuckled, and Cord liked the sound of his laugh. "I suppose that should be **people**-training sessions."

"Some of both. I'd be happy to work with you. However, I have a current client who's staying in the suite, so…"

"Not a problem," Len assured him quickly. "My wife, Mary Jean, and I are recently retired and—as it happens—we have a nephew living in your town. We'll be able to stay with him. It's Ted Lewis, your fire chief, who's also in a band called The GateCrashers."

"Of course! And is that how you learned about my business?"

"Yep. And I should add that we're

considering getting involved with a therapy group, one that focuses primarily on kids."

Cord heartily approved and they made arrangements for the older Lewises, from Missoula, to arrive next Monday.

Cord thought about this new situation and decided he'd ask Shallie to stay for an extra week, maybe two, at no charge, on the pretext of requesting her help with the Lewis sessions. Not that he didn't believe she'd do an exemplary job; he knew she would. But he didn't want her to leave. It was too soon to tell her that, though.

He'd come to realize that not only did he want her to stay, he wanted her to stay **here**, with him. The more he saw of her, the more he liked. There was so much he hadn't recognized—or under-stood—in the past, and he hoped he could make up for that now.

Shallie had waited to begin eating her sandwich until Cord returned to the kitchen. She was sitting at the table, skimming a copy of **The Atlantic** she'd found on the coffee table. He joined her and took a bite of his ham-and-cheese, with its tomato and pickle garnish. "Mmm."

She bit into hers—plain cheese—and smiled in response. The dogs crept out from under the table and, mouth full, Cord told them to settle. To her obvious amusement, they did, flopping down near the kitchen door.

Shallie told him about an article she'd read, outlining the history of dogs' relationships with humans. "It goes back at least ten thousand years. And dogs chose us—at first for practical reasons, mainly food."

"So they're the smarter ones."

"I'm sure Brynne would confirm that," she said with a grin.

"Don't get me started!"

"Well, when she's right, she's right."

"**She'd** say so—and I think Eli would, too. You know," Cord added, "J.P. and I have the impression that he's...interested in her."

"Good! I never knew Brynne well back then, and I'd like to know her better. But I love the idea of Eli being interested in her. He's always been such a serious guy. And she seems smart, someone with real social skills. I could see them as a good match, and I hope she's just as interested in him."

"We'll see. I hope so, too." Her enthusiasm pleased him. Probably because it sounded like approval. Which was how he and J.P. felt. The relationship, if it **was** one, had only reached its very early stages. Nothing formal, nothing spoken, as far as he knew.

After that, they talked about Russ, speculated about Bethanne and recalled some incidents from what felt like the long-ago past. "Do you remember that time Reba decided to cut Russ's hair?" she asked.

"Yeah, he wasn't seen in public for weeks!"

"She ended up shaving one side of his head. He freaked out, then ran off."

They both laughed. "Poor guy," Cord

said.

"Eventually, he went to the barber on Main, who at least evened it out, although then he looked totally bald rather than half-bald. I don't think he ever forgave her. And you can imagine how Norm turned the whole thing into a big joke."

"Poor guy," Cord said again. "I mean Russ, not Norm!"

"I'm trying to remember what he called him. Razored Russ, that was it. Oh, and Shaved Schafer."

"No wonder Russ isn't exactly sociable."

"Reba felt kind of bad," Shallie said. "But not **that** bad."

"Figures," he muttered. "Do you want a coffee, a glass of wine, a beer?"

She accepted a wine, he served himself a beer and then leaned back in his chair. "I have a proposition for you."

Shallie raised her eyebrows.

"Not that kind!"

"Okay, then. So it's the boring kind?"

He ignored that. "Here it is. I have some

new clients coming in a week, and they'll be staying at their nephew's place in town. Ted Lewis—remember him? You met at Country Classics Night. He's the bassist in Aaron's band."

She nodded. "Yeah, he's a nice guy."

"Well, the elder Lewises are newly retired and are interested in learning more about horses, maybe getting involved in therapy. I was hoping you could hang around for another week or two after this, free of charge, help me work with them. I figured your background with your friend's business makes you a natural."

Shallie smiled at him, a full, happy smile. "I'd **love** to!"

He grinned back. "Okay, then, we'll see how it goes. I could pay you," he added.

"No need. Besides, I'm getting room and board."

"What about your flight? Can you change it?"

"Should be fine," she said.

"And your rental car?"

"I'll return it. Just have to work out the logistics."

"Now, about our meeting tonight. I'd suggest you make a list of whatever you know. Whatever info you can give Eli and the investigator."

"I'll do it right now." She'd been thinking about exactly that. She'd put together the little she could remember.

It occurred to her to call Russ. Because no one knew more about Christine Fletcher than he did. Even if that wasn't much...

In her room, Shallie began making notes about her mother. After almost an hour, she'd filled half a page on her iPad. Once more, she thought about getting in touch with Russ—and decided to try.

To her considerable surprise, he answered. To her even greater surprise, he was friendly. Shallie gave him a succinct version of what she needed and why. "I have to get this sorted out, Russ. I **need** to know. It's like...a hole in my life."

"Yeah, I can understand how you'd feel that way." He recalled that Christine had disappeared during the night, taken off in her car and was never heard from again. These were the few facts Shallie already knew. But he told her something she hadn't heard before. "I'm pretty sure," he said, "that it had to do with a call she got on the office phone that evening. From a Chicago area code." He chuckled. "I'm embarrassed to admit I eavesdropped from the hallway."

Shallie didn't think he sounded embarrassed at all. "Why didn't you ever tell me this?"

"For a long time you were too young and then...I kind of forgot."

Not great as excuses went, but Shallie realized there was no point in belaboring it.

"Anyway," he continued, "back to that phone call. Christine didn't say much. Then she suddenly rushed out, back to Room 2, and I barely had time to hide. I went in to check the phone number and even dialed it several times, that night and the next day. No one ever answered —so I deleted the number. I just thought having it on our phone might lead to... some kind of problem. And I was pretty sure my parents wouldn't want to know about it."

She was about to thank him and hang up when he suggested they get together sometime soon. His stammer and the invitation itself told her how lonely he was. How uncertain that she'd agree. She said yes, they'd arrange something soon, she'd be in touch. Shallie felt grateful to him for the information—and appreciated that he was making an effort to be friendly, to be useful, to create a bond. Their unpleasant past no longer worried her; they'd both changed, were still changing. She knew **she** was. And this new openness on his part clearly indicated that he was, too.

She added the new information to her list, then hurried downstairs and asked Cord if he'd mind printing off her notes.

She also told him about Russ and his interest in seeing her. "Good plan," he said. "There's a lot more you could end up learning. Plus, the guy could use a friend."

Then they went out for the next phase of that day's work. He planned to teach her how to teach, considering that she'd be dealing with his new clients.

CHAPTER NINE

Late that afternoon, back in her suite, half reading, half dozing, Shallie was startled by a knock on her door. Carly opened it an inch or two and peered in. "Sorry to interrupt, but can I talk to you?"

"Of course!"

As Carly entered, Shallie moved to the edge of the bed, where they sat side by side. Carly's voice was shaky. "You've probably guessed that I haven't been telling the truth, the whole truth and nothing but..."

Shallie wanted to tread carefully through this uncertain territory. "Go on."

"You might've noticed that those

people at the country music night—the
ones in that booth near the back—knew
something about me."

"I wondered." Shallie purposely didn't
make any comment or ask any leading
questions.

Carly then launched into what turned
out to be a lengthy and fairly complicated story. About her YouTube channel,
My 3 Dads, and how it included performances and updates, the money
she'd earned, the fact that her YouTube
name was, in fact, her real one, Charlotte.
She described the ongoing announcements she made in her videos—and
Shallie immediately clued in.

**So this was why Carly had avoided
DNA testing, avoided even bringing it
up with her "3 Dads"—or one reason,
anyway. The longer she put it off,
the longer her lucrative performances
could continue. Shallie hadn't discussed the necessity of the tests with
Carly yet, but knew the girl had to be
well aware of it.**

"Was the YouTube thing mostly about

the money?"

"Partly. I had nothing. And this turned out to be a way of supporting myself. And—" she shrugged "—I found out I'm good at this stuff. I've been singing. I get the music on YouTube and sing a lot of country-western. And I **like** doing it."

"I can tell," Shallie said. "And you have the talent."

Carly reached over to clasp her hand for a moment. "You're the only one I've told."

"The crappy clothes?" Shallie asked. "They were all part of the...act? So you had money but you didn't want to spend it on clothes or transportation or—"

"Yes." She took a loud breath.

"I'm guessing the Emmylou Harris song you did at Bailey's the other night you sang on one of your videos."

"Yes." Another breath. "Two of the girls who were there recognized me at the drugstore this morning. They tried to talk to me."

"What happened?"

She spoke quickly. "I ran back to the car. And I lied to Tina. Again. I have to tell her the truth soon, but I'm not sure what to say. Also I want Tina and Cord and all of you to know how grateful I am. I'm not sure what to say to Cord, either. Or the other two guys."

Shallie said, "Okay, I understand. What do you need me to do?"

"Be my friend, I guess. And my... adviser."

Shallie remembered what Emma had said in their recent phone call, how they'd talked about her ability to provide what Carly needed—support and friendship. Neither of which she'd received herself until **after** she'd left home. Except, to a limited degree, from Reba.

"I'll do what I can on the adviser front. I already consider us friends, and not just because of your mom."

"Will you go with me to tell Tina—and Cord?"

"Definitely." Shallie wasn't looking forward to that, but she was willing to do it.

More than willing; she considered it an obligation, although how and when they did that had yet to be decided. She got out Cord's list of questions, since this was the opportune time, and quickly went through them—which didn't seem to be a problem for Carly.

She glanced at her cell phone. "Listen, I have to go. Cord and I are meeting Eli at Bailey's in a little while. I'll tell you more later—and maybe you can give me some advice, too."

"Thank you," Carly whispered. "I'm so glad we met, so glad you knew my mom, so glad I can trust you. Shallie, I love you."

Shallie felt tears gather as she hugged the girl. "I love you, too. And you're right. You can trust me."

"Oh, here are some extra copies of your printout." As they prepared to leave, Cord handed her the two pages.

"Thanks. I know I could've emailed it, and I will email it to the PI. But I thought it'd be easier to do it this way for tonight, so I can make notes on our discussion."

They drove to Bailey's in silence, watching as the sun began its descent in the western sky. As always, Cord was struck by its generous beauty and felt pleased that Shallie seemed just as touched. When they arrived, Brynne greeted them with, "Your...friend is waiting. At the table over there."

Eli raised his glass of beer as they approached. "Don't worry, this is my only one. Have to set an example, you know."

"Yeah, yeah. Shallie, what would you like?"

Remembering his grandfather-inspired manners, Cord waited for Shallie to sit down before he did.

"A glass of white wine." She selected a West Coast Chardonnay from the brief list Brynne recited. "Good choice," Brynne said.

"She'd call anything you've got here a good choice," Cord muttered.

"Hey! I heard that," Brynne said. "And

by the way, anything you get here **is** a good choice."

"Okay, fine. I'll have a Corona. We'll order food once J.P. shows up."

"Let's move on to business," Eli said in what Shallie thought of as his sheriff voice.

She gave him the printout. "Here's everything I know. The Chicago information came from my cousin Russell at the Painted Pony Motel. We're planning to talk again. Or should I put the investigator in touch with him?"

Eli read over the pages and said, "Maybe later. Best if you talk to Russell by yourself first. Get him comfortable with all of this. Now, let me tell you about the guy I'm recommending. I've already run everything past him, and he's available **and** interested."

But before Eli could start discussing the case, Brynne returned with their drinks and a complimentary plate of sweet potato fries, accompanied by chipotle sauce.

Cord gave her a thumbs-up. After they'd had a few sips, eaten a few fries, Eli began. "This guy's a private investigator in Tucson. Name of Eddie—Eduardo—Gonzalez. Like I said, he's willing to get involved. I've known him since we were both at the police academy in Phoenix." He paused. "After the criminal justice program in Seattle, I spent a year there doing some extra training."

"So what kind of experience does he have with cases like this?" Cord asked.

"Lots—and he has a really terrific assistant, Melanie, who's **great** at on-line research. Between them, they've tracked down missing persons the cops didn't even know were missing. Guaranteed they'll see this as a challenge."

"Your recommendation means a lot to me," Shallie said. "Now, what do I have to do?"

"I'll tell him you're ready to go with this. Can I give him your phone number?"

She recited it, and Eli tapped it into his phone. "I'll ask him to get in touch with you, and you can email him this info." He paused. "Eddie will probably want to come here. Start from scratch as it were. You okay with that?"

"Where will he stay?" Cord asked.

Eli immediately said, "Don't worry. He can stay at my place. It'll be good to see him again, catch up on things. He'll be one of the gang."

"And speaking of the gang, guess who just arrived? Right on cue!"

J.P. and Trooper ambled toward them and took their usual places, with the dog lying half under the table. Brynne appeared a moment later, carrying a dog treat and a glass of draft.

While Cord quickly filled him in, Shallie said, "Thank you, Eli. I appreciate this so much."

"I'm willing to do whatever I can to help."

"Me, too," Cord said.

"And me—or rather, us, as well," J.P. told them, pointing at Trooper.

"Are we ready to order?" When everyone nodded, Cord waved Brynne over.

"It's on me," he said. They all objected, but to no avail. "Hey," he reminded Shallie. "You paid for our group last night."

They spent the next couple of hours enjoying their food and drinks, and discussing how things had changed in Painted Pony Creek. J.P. contributed a few ideas to the search plan—like tracking down Christine Fletcher's car, if possible. Maybe there'd be some information about her license plate hidden in some messy drawer in the motel office. And he suggested finding out if Russ remembered anything at all prior to the overheard phone call. He acknowledged that as an experienced investigator, Eddie would naturally pursue those options. "Can't resist trying to do my part," he said.

Shallie wrote down, "License number in office? Russ: any memory of what happened before phone call?"

At around ten they left, with Brynne giving Shallie an unexpected hug. "Bye, sweetie. It's so good to see you again."

She took Cord's credit card, and as soon as the transaction was complete, they were off.

Once in his truck, Shallie turned to him and said, "I know I keep saying thank you—but thank you, Cord. I'm **so** grateful for your help."

"I owe you this. And more..."

"Why?"

"You're a reminder of the past." Before she could disagree, he said, "That was poorly phrased. I meant it in a positive way, because we go back as friends. And I'm attracted to you." He knew she was aware of this—how could she not be? But he certainly hadn't recognized it eighteen years ago, with Reba complicating his emotions. This feeling had crept up on him in the past week. But what he'd said was true. He also realized that what he felt now was more than simply attraction.

"I'm not sure I buy that," she said. "Anyway, the past is past, if you'll forgive the cliché."

He grinned. "Yeah, I can forgive the occasional cliché. And can you forgive me for being such an idiot…that night?" He paused. "That night and a few others," he acknowledged, thinking of Reba singing "Piece of My Heart."

"You were in love with her."

"That was, what? Almost two decades ago? What I realize now is that I missed an opportunity with you."

He could hear her intake of breath. "Oh, Cord, if you only knew."

"If **you** only knew…" He put his key in the ignition.

"Wait. Don't start driving yet."

She released her seat belt and leaned toward him. Her arms went around his neck. And that was when they kissed. And kissed again.

On his way back to the station, Eli considered the evening and what he'd learned. Interesting situation with Christine Fletcher. Who knew if she was still alive? And if so, where? His own law experience told him she'd probably been living under an assumed name; fake ID was more readily available these days—and had been for years, much longer than a lot of people realized.

What he couldn't grasp was how she could've left two-year-old Shallie behind.

And if he remembered correctly, poor Della had been related to her and been kind enough to give Christine and Shallie a place to stay. Yeah, it was a wreck even then, but still...Christine had abandoned all of them, her child and her family, without a word.

There was certainly something desperate about her disappearance. He snorted at his own conclusion. Obvious or what? His first guess was something related to a man—a partner, either business or, more likely, personal. Could be money. Or both. A man **and** money.

One thing he knew, having looked through old records at the office, was that no one had called the sheriff at the time of her disappearance.

J.P. had made a good point about

pursuing the license plate number, if at all possible. The phone number was probably a hopeless cause. According to Shallie, all this new information came from Russell. So he'd kept his mouth shut all these years.

That sly old slob was certainly harboring some secrets.

And when it came to secrets, what about Carly? Definitely more there than met the eye, his or anyone else's, but he supposed they should leave the next move to her.

And then...Cord and Shallie. After tonight, he could hardly miss what was going on. He couldn't say he was surprised but pleased and...a little envious. He hoped their connection went somewhere, that it had a place to go.

No denying that Shallie was attractive. Beautiful, actually. Eli remembered her as shy and self-conscious, lacking confidence in her teens. She'd presented what he'd describe as a detached persona—one of those psychology terms he'd picked up from Investigator

Eddie. But detached or not, he'd always liked her and had sympathized with her situation. What a terrible life, and having the popular, self-assured Reba as her best friend must've made her feel even less sure of herself. And he, Cord and J.P. hadn't helped, obsessed with Reba as they'd all been. Then Reba had abandoned her, too.

Good to know where Reba had ended up—except for the sadness of her too-early death. And her husband, Carly's stepfather, was an asshole as Carly had no compunction in calling him.

He turned into the station parking lot to catch up on bulletins and messages, chat with Amos Edwards, the deputy sheriff on duty, and get in touch with Eddie to confirm. Then he did a bit of preliminary research on the Fletcher case, but came up with nothing new. He was committed to this now, determined to find out what had happened. He couldn't resist considering the possibilities. A new life lived under a new name? Kidnapping? **Murder?**

● ● ●

After that kiss—the kiss **she'd** started
—Shallie felt as if her life had changed. It
was like one of those defining moments
in the romance novels she sometimes
read. As if **this** was what she'd been
waiting for all these years. And the truth?
It was, she admitted. Despite a whole,
and in many ways gratifying, other life
with a man she'd loved, Cord was still
the one she longed for.

When Cord drove the rest of the
way home, they talked, but their conversation was admittedly a little awkward.

She felt as if life had led her back to
him. But she didn't want to pressure
Cord or make any demands. So their
comments were limited to the evening's
events until they reached a stop-light
on the edge of town and he reached over
to stroke her leg. Gratified, excited, she
leaned toward him and they kissed
again. Their kiss was cut short by the
changing light. But as soon as he'd

parked at the house, he turned to her.

So much all at once, and yet every moment, every kiss, was memorable. There was nothing casual about any of them.

"I think we should wait before we go on with this," she said. "Let me get used to the idea. I want to feel ready. Is that all right?"

The look on his face told Shallie he accepted her caution, and the gentleness in his eyes felt loving. "I feel ready," he said, "but I understand what you mean. And I respect it."

"Thank you. We'll continue where we left off. I promise."

After a quick good-night kiss and a moment with the dogs, she hurried up her set of stairs and prepared for bed. What did those extraordinary kisses mean? Besides attraction and desire. Was there more? Was there as much as she wanted, as much as she hoped?

Lying there in the dark, she relived their kisses over and over, waiting to dream about their time together.

• • •

Cord let the dogs out and sat on the porch without turning on the lights, staring up at a star-bright sky. What happened tonight had **stunned** him. Not that he hadn't hoped for this very thing. Or in a sense expected it. But the fact that Shallie had taken matters into her own hands—he grinned, remembering those hands on his face, stroking his hair, clasping his neck—changed everything. Did it mean **he** should start their next encounter? Their next embrace?

He'd take his cues from her, although he didn't care who set it in motion. He just knew he wanted it to go further. **All the way**, as they used to say in high school. To continue where they'd left off, as she'd put it.

His teenage feelings for Reba and his marriage to Jenna didn't even compare to what he felt now, and that was after only a few kisses. Until recently, he'd still believed Reba had been the love of his life. But he knew better now. Carly's arrival had awakened a lot of memories, and he'd come to recognize that his emotions, especially the ones he associated with Reba, were adolescent. He was ready for something new, something truly lasting. For **bigger** emotions. For Shallie.

It had to be getting close to midnight, and he'd scheduled a long day tomorrow. First a meeting with Mitch to discuss expanding the stables and enlarging the paddock. Then a phone call with his PR firm to hear about their latest ideas. After that, his next session with Shallie.

He got to his feet, stretching, and called the dogs, both hovering in the vicinity of the porch. "Okay, guys. Time to crash—and I don't mean that literally."

They dashed up the steps and he let them in, following close behind.

Cord knew he'd be dreaming tonight and he knew who'd be in his dreams...

CHAPTER TEN

Shallie had been at Cord's place for almost two weeks now. Monday morning she called Emma for one of their regular "catch-up conversations" and told her about the PI's coming arrival, plus the likelihood that she'd be working with the Lewises who'd be joining them that day, and about making an arrangement to see Russ. Then she mentioned Carly's confession a week ago and their plan to talk to Cord and Tina. Soon…"Put it off for now," Emma advised. "You've got enough going on." Shallie also suggested her friend visit Painted Pony Creek and Hollister Ranch when she could manage it, and Emma agreed. "And," Emma said, "it's your birthday on Friday!"

Not something Shallie really cared about at this point and hadn't cared about since her divorce. Other than Rob, who probably wouldn't acknowledge it, she knew Emma was the only person who'd remember, and that was fine with her.

Eddie called just afterward; he told her he'd received her notes and finally had a chance to study them. They'd start doing some research at their end. He'd see them on Friday night. (Oh, yeah, the twenty-first. Her birthday.)

Busy morning. And when she called Russ, he suggested coming by sometime midweek. She made a point of explaining she'd hired a detective to investigate Christine's disappearance. She described Eddie's background and skills. Russ said, "Sounds like a good guy, a good plan." Adding, "I'd definitely be willing to talk to him."

Shallie spent her remaining free hour reading a new horse book on Kindle—

actually an old one. She'd started rereading Walter Farley's classic, **The Black Stallion**, which she'd loved as a kid. It had given her so much pleasure at the age of twelve and even more now.

Then it was time to meet Cord for a quick lunch. He told her he'd introduce her to Len and Mary Jean Lewis when they arrived at two, but that he couldn't be there afterward; he had to attend a meeting Eli had organized with the local ranchers and farmers. "You might've heard that someone's been harassing them. Hasn't happened here yet, but this jerk or jerks—well, they've been letting animals out of their pens, paddocks, even barns," he said, "leaving them to wander around loose, risking death. They could be struck by a car, attacked by coyotes, abused or stolen by human predators." He explained that fortunately most had been recovered, although a couple were still missing. And, sadly, one sheep, a female who had "young'uns," as the farmer Perry Roberts put it, had wandered into the road and been hit by some kind of vehicle; at least the driver had stopped and immediately called Eli's office.

"I didn't know!" she said in horror. "How could someone possibly **do** this? Why?"

Nobody knew. It seemed to be out of sheer mischief or malice. Whoever was doing it hadn't, to Eli's knowledge, **directly** hurt any animals, but was interfering with their safety and with the livelihood of ranchers and farmers.

Cord was furious and determined to do whatever he could to help Eli resolve this.

After lunch, they met the Lewises—and Shallie was immediately captivated by their warmth, their easygoing charm and ready smiles. Len was a large man, with abundant gray hair, in good shape; Mary Jean was of medium height, had lovely bobbed blond hair and noticeably elegant hands. They both wore new-looking jeans and long-sleeved T-shirts with the logo of a women's curling club on the front. Mary Jean explained that she was a part-time coach, and that Len had always supported the team, attending most of their games. That impressed Shallie and so did their affection for the dogs, who responded with their usual enthusiasm. She asked why, since they were so natural and loving with animals, they didn't have any of their own, as they'd readily admitted.

"Soon," Len said. "Our lives are changing big-time now that we're both retired. I was in financial management and I'm thankful to be leaving it behind. From this point on, the only finances I'm dealing with are the family's." Mary Jean agreed, grinning down at Bandit, who seemed unwilling to leave her side.

"Her job—" he gestured at his wife "— was, if anything, more demanding than mine. She's a social worker and she mostly dealt with troubled and disabled kids."

Cord left for his meeting soon after, and the three of them spent the next two hours with the horses, making contact, bonding with the rescues in particular.

Mary Jean said she was "head over heels" in love with little Annie. Just like Shallie...

At various points throughout their session, the three of them talked, exchanging personal stories. Shallie told them she'd been abandoned in this town as a very young child and had lived here until her late teens and that she'd recently returned, after a failed marriage. She kept her summary brief, but predictably Mary Jean asked why she'd come back.

Shallie felt foolish, worried that she'd said too much, but in the end merely replied that she lived in Seattle, was on a "break," had known Cord years ago and wanted to do some horse sessions with him. She finished by saying she'd had some relevant experience thanks to a friend, loved animals and was fascinated by the work.

That answer didn't seem quite enough for Mary Jean, who probed into other reasons. Horse-training sessions were available in a lot of places, and Painted

Pony Creek couldn't have good memories for her, could it?

Shallie gave up. "You're right. One of the reasons I'm here is to see if I can learn more about my mother."

"I'm sorry if my question was inappropriate," Mary Jean said as Len frowned.

"No, it's okay. Obviously this is on my mind a lot."

"Let us know if we can help, if there's anything we can do," Mary Jean told her.

"Thanks," Shallie said.

After the serious part of the conversation, they shared the occasional joke or anecdote. Len was particularly fond of real-life "stupid criminal" stories, a number of which he was happy to share. Like the one about the idiot who'd locked his staff in a storage room while he made off with the company's profits; he'd collected everyone's cell phone— but hadn't realized the room had a landline!

As they all prepared to leave, the Lewises for their nephew's place and

Shallie for Russell's, she told them she'd met Ted at the Classic Country Night recently and had liked him. Mary Jean and Len didn't have kids themselves but were close to their nieces and nephews. Shallie invited them—on Cord's behalf, confident he'd be fine with it—to join them on the porch at four thirty or five for a drink and more conversation. About smart animals...and stupid criminals. She hoped their current criminal, the creep who went around releasing animals, would prove to be as stupid as some of the idiots in their stories, idiots who'd gotten themselves arrested...

Cord leaned back in his chair at the conference table in Eli's office. Eli sat at the head. Amos Edwards and Oliver Boone, two of his deputies, were on either side of Cord, while Mitch and fellow horse rancher, Miles Carey, sat across from them. Several others had joined the group, and the expression on every face was grim.

Eli briskly called the meeting to order, as he was wont to do. Cord had long figured Eli craved that sense of control, that way of encouraging (or more accurately, demanding) discipline. He summarized the situation, while Amos took notes on his lap-top, then asked for any other information. A few people added their own evidence: the gate to Miles's property was broken but his security system had sounded an alarm, and that was the end of **that** attempt, reminding Cord to recheck the effectiveness of his own alarm; Ellis Rogers mentioned empty beer cans on the road by his place.

Cord couldn't help remembering Eli's suspicions about his nephew—and desperately hoped Eric wasn't involved.

"Okay," Eli said. "We need to organize patrols. Deputy Edwards, can you take care of that?"

Amos nodded.

"We need to invest in more cameras and security equipment—all of you privately, if you haven't already. Your property insurance should cover at least some of that. We'll buy surveillance cameras on behalf of the department, too."

Everyone murmured agreement.

Cord excused himself when a text came in at three thirty. Shallie, asking if it would be okay to have the Lewises over for a drink late afternoon. They were looking forward, she said, to seeing him.

Of course, he texted back. **Tell them I look forward to seeing them, too. I'll be there in an hour or so.**

Cord had a good feel for the kind of people the Lewises were, and even when he'd left the ranch, he could tell that Shallie was getting on well with them.

He returned his attention to the group just as Eli described his plan to put out a bulletin on all available media. After that, the meeting came to a close. "Anyone want to discuss this further?" Eli asked. "We'll meet at Sully's."

"Yeah, I'm in," Cord said, "but only for about an hour. Have to get home to see a couple of new clients." Mitch wasn't joining them at Sully's because he had errands to do, which was why they'd taken separate cars.

The Lewises had arrived early. They'd spent the last forty-five minutes with Shallie, enjoying the warm sunshine and a cold drink, the dogs happily slumped at their feet. The three of them continued their afternoon conversation while enjoying their wine and nuts mixed with dried cranberries.

They were just discussing an article Mary Jean had read about consciousness in animals when they were interrupted. Carly appeared on the path to the porch and came stumbling up the steps, crying loudly. Between sobs, she managed to tell them she'd found a dog who'd been hit by a car on a little-used country road near Mitch and Tina's trailer. Tina and her visiting niece, ten-year-old Ashley, were with the dog right now, watching her; Mitch was out and he had their car, so he couldn't take them to the vet.

Len Lewis immediately offered to drive

over, pick up the dog, take them to the local clinic. Once he'd retrieved his car, Mary Jean got in the front seat, and Carly and Shallie climbed in the back, after they'd put the dogs in the house.

Shallie called Cord on her cell; he said he'd get in touch with the vet, Dr. Barbara Ferguson, and call back. A minute later, he gave her the vet's address and told her Barb was at her clinic waiting for them. He'd meet them there as well.

They arrived at the accident scene and Len carefully lifted the dog, a female beagle with no collar or tags, placing her across their laps. Tina and Ashley gently hugged the little dog goodbye and went home. The poor animal was whimpering but mostly silent, obviously in great pain. Shallie wanted to cry at her agony. She and Carly stroked her head and long soft ears, careful not to touch her injuries. Neither cared about the blood seeping into their clothes in spite of the towel Tina had draped over them.

"I hope she'll be okay," Carly said.

"Please let her be okay."

Shallie leaned over to hug Carly. "I'm sure she will be. She was lucky you found her. And I hear this vet is good."

"I **want** her to live," Carly said. "She deserves to."

"I know Dr. Ferguson will do everything she can and so will we."

Arriving at the clinic, they discovered Cord already there. Barb, a woman in her late forties with long graying hair, was instantly attentive, but the information Carly could provide was limited. Cord introduced everyone to everyone else, something Shallie had completely forgotten to do.

With Cord's help, Barb took the dog into an exam room; ten or so minutes later, they both emerged. The dog was young, Barb said, estimating about two years, not spayed and not microchipped. Her injuries were serious— blood loss, a broken pelvis, a broken paw. She was malnourished, too. She'd be in the clinic for at least a week.

Cord made the down payment and told

Barb's assistant, William, that he'd cover the whole cost. Carly objected and insisted she'd contribute; Shallie said she'd like to help, too, and even the Lewises wanted to kick in.

Barb told them she'd do the surgery tomorrow morning. Carly thanked her and said she planned to visit the next afternoon and maybe Wednesday, too. Barb lived nearby and tended to maintain fairly open hours.

On the way home, they decided to stop at Bailey's for dinner.

During their meal, Cord told them a little more about the current crime wave —the release of farm and ranch animals —and described his own plans to deal with the situation. "We're doing patrols. Amos at the sheriff's office is working out the schedules and the routes. Plus, Mitch and I will do regular checks on the property, even though we already have a good security system." It all made sense to Shallie, although she was distracted by Carly's emotional state. The girl was fidgeting, glancing around. Naturally, she was upset about the cruelty to animals Cord had mentioned and about the injured beagle, but Shallie felt there was more to her anxiety.

Exhausted though she was, Carly couldn't get to sleep for hours, and checking her cell phone didn't help. She got up when her alarm went off at nine. Tina had promised to drive her to visit the beagle that afternoon, but there were chores to do first.

Carly acknowledged to herself that she was truly happy being with animals— something she'd only begun to experience in her former life, with Dooley. This wasn't an interest she'd shared with Reba. Instead, it was something she had in common with Cord.

She tried to shut down that thought, figuring there was nothing genetic about a love of animals...

But J.P., too, was a proven animal-lover. Both potential fathers who understood her, understood something important about her.

She wondered if she could adopt the little beagle. And yet, with her own situation so uncertain, she understood that it wasn't practical. Or fair. Still, she loved the idea.

Tina spent the morning dealing with laundry, and Carly helped. "Thanks for taking care of my stuff, Tina. And Shallie's."

"Shallie wanted to do her own, but I said I'd handle it. I had to insist. Like I keep telling her, she's our guest. Our paying guest, at that."

Typical of Shallie **and** Tina.

After lunch, they drove into town to visit the vet's clinic and she felt so welcomed by Barb. "You deserve a lot of credit for this dog's survival. Come on back and visit her." Barb led them both to the recovery area. The poor little beagle was barely conscious, but the vet assured them she'd come through the surgery well. She also planned to spay her and administer the necessary vaccinations as soon as possible.

Barb opened the cage so Carly could

give her "little girl" a kiss on the forehead and ears, careful not to dislodge the IV. Then she and Tina wandered over to a local coffee shop, The Real Bean, where they ordered coffee, sat at a table for two and enjoyed the country soundtrack.

All of a sudden, Carly noticed that the two couples from Country Classics Night had entered the café. One of the girls—the one who'd tried to talk to her at the drugstore—approached and apologized. She introduced herself as Lindsey Morgan; they talked about music but Lindsey was discreet enough not to mention "Charlotte's" YouTube channel. The guy who seemed to be her boyfriend was fairly nice-looking, but obviously quite enthralled with himself.

He walked over and joined them at their table, ignoring Tina. But he acted way too interested in Carly, which clearly didn't please Lindsey. Or Carly for that matter. The boyfriend, if that was indeed his role, openly asked Carly for her phone number. She scowled at him and said she and Tina had to go. What a creep!

The current song, Dolly Parton's "Jolene," ended and Johnny Cash's "I Walk the Line" came on next. Suddenly, the guy grabbed Carly by the wrists, pulling her to a stand, saying, "Hey, I **dance** the line." He awkwardly swayed her around and between tables, despite her resistance, and to Lindsey's obvious embarrassment. Finally, Carly managed to yank herself free. "Don't **desecrate** Johnny Cash, you idiot. And don't humiliate your girlfriend."

Tina was already on her feet. "Smarten up, Eric! Do you want your mother—or your uncle—to hear about this?"

He gave her the finger, and Carly felt even more outraged, but didn't dignify his rudeness with a response of her own, merely sending Lindsey a sympathetic look. As they left, she asked Tina who this creep was. Eric Worth, she told her.

"You mean Eric Worthless," Carly muttered. "And who's his uncle?"

"That would be Eli Garrett—**Sheriff** Eli Garrett."

CHAPTER ELEVEN

The next morning, Carly asked permission to observe Shallie, Cord and the Lewises, who were already involved in their horse session. This time they focused on Annie, on expanding her confidence and teaching her some simple commands—walk, stop and stand, allow her face to be stroked. She was equally responsive to all four people (no doubt, Shallie thought, enjoying her new life). Cord said he was satisfied with everyone's progress, including Annie's.

Shallie could tell that Carly had enjoyed the experience; she, too, had connected with Len and Mary Jean, and they agreed that once their session had ended, they'd all get together again, either here or in Missoula.

At four, Shallie—feeling her life was just as scheduled as it'd been when she was working—left to visit Russ at the Painted Pony Motel. She brought some snacks, which Tina had helpfully provided, simple things like cheese and crackers and some cut-up veggies with dip. She knew he'd have liquid refreshments aplenty.

When she arrived, she was surprised to find him waiting in the office. Shallie made herself comfortable as he suggested—which was a challenge in that place. She would've preferred the floor to the ancient, hard-backed guest chair. He'd taken the only other one, a worn-out desk chair that still had a little padding. He'd placed the snacks and a bottle of bourbon, some brand she'd never come across, on the desk beside his laptop, which he'd moved there since her last visit, then poured her a partial glass, throwing in half-melted ice from a small dented bowl. He topped up his own drink.

Shallie glanced around the room, almost shocked at how spare and tidy it was now, compared to how it had looked when she'd arrived. What she remembered from the old days was a mess of papers and files, a guest book that always seemed to go missing, various shabby magazines, an overstuffed rubbish pail. Russ had clearly made an effort to do some cleaning and sorting.

She reached for a slice of cheese and took a small sip of her watered-down bourbon. He took a big gulp of his— likely **not** watered down and clearly not his first of the day.

Shallie felt self-conscious and, judging by his awkward expression, Russ did, too. The one subject they had in common was their shared past, so she started by asking him about Della and Norm, whose deaths had been so close together, and how he'd dealt with it. He shrugged, but didn't answer. Then he grinned. "Do you remember the time he got drunk and assigned the same room to three different customers? You woulda been around ten."

"Actually, yes," she said with a laugh. "What I remember most is how furious Della was. She had to talk all of them— one was a couple, right?—into not leaving. She not only gave two of them new rooms but gave everyone a discount."

She and Russ exchanged a playful smile at the memory.

From there they went on to recall several other humiliating incidents. Like the time the curtains in Room 5 fell down. And the plumbing disaster in Room 4— with water from a flooded toilet seeping under the door into the hallway.

Then, without any warning, Russ told her, "You've probably already figured this out, but I'm pretty unhappy. I have no idea what to do with my life. Never really did. The property's worth practically nothing. I get the occasional guest, don't have any employees. I don't have a college degree or real job experience. Haven't been anywhere. I've got hardly any friends."

Shallie felt a surge of compassion for him and, perhaps oddly, respect. His circumstances were troubling but his honesty was hopeful. She resolved that if she could help him, she would. She'd have to encourage him to come up with some plans, though, and be willing to change his life.

She mentioned Bethanne. He said they hadn't been in touch for some years. According to him, she'd been doing well, which Shallie already knew, with a husband, a business somewhere in Texas, but he suspected she'd taken "the long slide." They agreed they should try to make contact again, hoping she was still alive...

After that, she said something about Reba, about missing her, and he confided that he'd "had a huge crush on her back in the day."

Yeah, you and everyone else.

She brought him up to date; he hadn't heard about Reba's death—or about Carly, never mind the situation regarding the girl's unknown father and the three contenders for that position.

"Shit, I feel bad about Reba. And it's gotta be hard on the kid."

"It's very hard."

"Hey, maybe I should take bets around town. Who's this girl's dad? Personally, I'm betting on…Eli."

"None of our business," she said sharply.

At last, she broached the subject of Christine Fletcher, and he told her what he could recollect, but there was nothing she didn't already know, most of it from her childhood—except for the Chicago phone call, which she'd heard about in their previous conversation.

Shallie asked if he thought Christine had come from Chicago, based on that call.

"Never heard," he replied. "But I guess it makes sense. I never actually found out anything about her from Norm and Della." It wasn't a surprise that he didn't refer to them as Mom and Dad. "And nothing about her husband," he added. "Or **partner** as they now seem to say.

Who knows if they were even married?"

"You mean...my father?"

"Well, yeah." He raised the bourbon bottle, but she shook her head.

"He certainly didn't try to get in touch with me," she told him.

"My guess," Russ said slowly, "is that he's dead. I wonder if we can find out."

"I'm not sure why I never tried. Well... we don't even know his name. And, for me, it's always been about Christine."

"You've got this detective working for you now. Eddie, right? Bet he could find out in about five seconds."

"We'll know soon enough. I hope."

"Guess we will. This guy's going to come up with all the pieces and then put them together." An obvious comment, perhaps, but a fitting one. Christine **was** a puzzle.

"Now, what are your plans for the rest of the day?" she asked, almost sure she already knew the answer.

As expected, he said, "Not much." Taking a noisy gulp of his cheap bourbon, he said he watched a variety of shows on Netflix, one of his indulgences. He also got books from the small local library, mostly digital.

"Oh, yes, that's run by Susan, isn't it? Susan Robbins. What kind of books do you like?"

"Susan makes some recommendations. I mostly read suspense. Authors like Elmore Leonard, Lee Child, John Grisham, Linwood Barclay."

She told him she liked suspense, too, and listed a few of her own favorites.

"I also like nonfiction, adventure books," he said.

Adventure? The farthest possible thing from his own life. Of course, that was one of the needs books filled, wasn't it? Showing you a completely different reality...

On impulse she invited him to dinner—which she thought would qualify as a different reality from what his evening would otherwise have been. She **wanted** to do this, for him and for herself, too. She immediately added that she'd pick him up and drop him off. He hesitated and a moment later, agreed.

Cord got another unexpected message from Shallie; she was leaving Russell's place (aka the Painted Pony Motel) and confessed that she'd been presumptuous enough to invite Russ to dinner. At Cord's. Just like she'd done this past Monday with the Lewises. Was he willing to accommodate another guest? If not, she'd make some excuse and treat him to a meal at Bailey's instead.

He immediately texted back his agreement, wondering what this evening was going to be like. He'd never known Russ very well, hadn't seen him in years; his awareness of the guy these days was based on reputation more than anything. Russ was a veritable hermit in that dump of a motel, not someone who seemed interested in being part of the community. Cord added a suggestion to his text. **What if I invite Tina and Mitch, plus Eli and J.P., if they're available? They all used to know Russ.**

Sure. And we can't forget Carly, Shallie texted back.

Nope, no forgetting Carly.

Cord called Tina and Mitch. Tina answered. "That should be an...unusual evening," she'd said when he invited them. "I can't even recall the last time I saw Russ. Let me see if Mitch has any plans." Half a minute later, she was back on the line. "Mitch would like to come, too. Oh, and I'd be happy to cook." She told him she had a couple of lasagnas in the freezer—one regular and one vegetarian, both homemade. She'd also prepare a salad and some simple dessert. Cord put a bottle of Shallie's favorite wine (he'd stocked up) and a case of beer in the fridge.

Shallie came in with Russell soon after and made the reintroductions. "Cord, you and Russ remember each other, right?"

"Sure." He thrust out his hand in greeting. Russ's shake was more than firm, it was aggressive. Trying to prove something? That aside, Cord found him remarkably similar to the guy he remembered—a little heavier, a little grayer, just as awkward. But he seemed pleased to be there, which pleased Cord, too.

He supposed Russ wasn't a bad guy, never had been. The two of them hadn't been friends in the past, and given their age difference of several years, plus their circumstances, that made sense.

Carly followed them inside a few minutes later, claiming she'd been "answering email," but the expression on Shallie's face, quickly hidden though it was, made him wonder what the girl had **really** been up to.

"Russ," he said. "This is Carly. Reba's daughter."

Carly smiled at Russ and made a few cursory remarks; he seemed to be in shock, and Cord felt sure that was because of her unmistakable resemblance to Reba. He did manage to stammer, "I…I knew your mother. Way back."

She nodded abruptly and left to go pick flowers for a centerpiece, the dogs

trailing behind her, while Shallie set the
large and rarely used dining room table
and Tina put the finishing touches on
the meal. J.P. was just arriving with
Trooper, and Cord noticed that he and
Carly talked for a few minutes as the
dogs greeted each other.

J.P. shook hands with Russ as Cord
passed drinks around. Their conversation seemed almost animated, and Russ
paid constant attention to Trooper.
**Nothing like a dog to ease social
interactions**, Cord thought.

Carly obviously understood and appreciated that—no surprise, based on what
he already knew about her. Yes, he and
this girl had significant things in common, whether or not they were father and
daughter.

She returned with a selection of wildflowers. He recognized buttercups,
daisies and bluebells and reached into
an upper cupboard for a green glass
vase that had belonged to his grandmother. Carly arranged the flowers, very
artfully in his opinion, then set them in

the middle of the table.

Cord announced that dinner was ready and ushered everyone into the dining room. People chose their own seats—Cord didn't consider himself a social dictator. He did wonder how the inclusion of Russell would go. So far, everyone had been friendly, sharing anecdotes and laughing together, and Mr. Hermit seemed to fit in comfortably. Cord thought that boded well for the evening, but you never knew.

Eli found the evening lively and festive, **fun**—not a word he used very often. There was music, The GateCrashers' latest album, played at a nonintrusive volume. He enjoyed their songs and not simply because of the social connection. This album, called **The Lone Stranger**, featured all their strengths. Great playing, great voices, great harmonizing, plus an element of the traditional in their lyrics as well as their sound. Eli could tell how much Carly, swaying back and forth, delighted in the music—reminding him of her participation in that Classic Country Night at Bailey's.

He sat on one side of Russ, with Cord on the other, and they continued their conversation, which included general gossip about the town, complaints and news about local politics and, finally, made its way to Reba. At that point, Cord asked for silence and raised his glass. "To Reba, who in so many ways brought us all together as friends." Everyone echoed, "To Reba."

The idea of bringing them together as friends was a nice one, Eli thought, but her presence had initially divided what was already a close friendship. The toast should have gone **To Reba, who drove us apart as enemies and then** —No, never mind. That wasn't exactly celebratory or completely fair. All three of them, he, Cord and J.P., had played their own roles in what had happened.

He saw that Carly had tears running down her cheeks at the homage to her mother. Shallie and Tina, on either side of Carly, hugged her.

He was thankful that they offered her comfort. He wished he could do or say something, too...

He tried to catch her eye, smiling at her, hoping to establish more of a connection. It took Carly a moment to respond with a shy smile of her own. He immediately felt better. He appreciated the way she obviously fit into Cord's household and that she had good and growing relationships with Shallie and Tina. Both women were so accepting of her, so loving.

He helped himself to more lasagna of the surprisingly tasty vegetarian kind, and began to discuss their current crime situation with Cord, first doing Russell the courtesy of laying out the background for him.

After listening for a while, Russ piped up. "Have you figured out a motive yet? Isn't that where you should start?" Adding sheepishly that this was what detective heroes in his favorite suspense fiction and TV series usually did. He half apologized, saying that Eli, as a law enforcement professional, "obviously" knew what he was doing and that he—

"Thanks." Eli cut him off. "Yeah, we're trying to come up with a motive based on the evidence we've found, such as it is. Any thoughts?"

Russ looked more confident now and seemed more than willing to hold forth. "Okay," he began. "As someone hearing this for the first time, I'd say it sounds as though the **perp**—" Eli could tell how much he enjoyed saying that "—as though the perp is choosing random targets. As though he doesn't have a grudge against individual ranchers and farmers as much as against the entire town. Someone who hates this community. Or...it could also be someone with no purpose. Nothing valid to do."

"I can see both points," Eli said, thinking briefly but not seriously that the "no purpose" remark could apply to Russ himself. "But I lean more toward the first one. Or some combination. My guess is an angry young man." He paused. "Sorry, don't mean to be sexist, just

being real. Some kid who's resentful
and maybe feels trapped and is taking it
out on ranchers and farmers. And their
animals..."

"You told us about this before, but I
didn't realize how bad it is!" Carly, who'd
been listening quietly, as everyone at
the table was, burst out. "Sounds like a
total loser! An asshole."

"Hell, yes," J.P. agreed, and Eli chimed
in, adding, "That would certainly fit."

"And anyone who doesn't respect
animals," Carly said, "anyone who could
do this for **whatever** screwed-up reason, really pisses me off. Something
has to be done. And the rest of us are
counting on you to do it."

"Hear, hear!" Glasses were lifted again.

"And, J.P., that reminds me," Cord
said—obviously not wanting to go in the
Eric direction. "Are you willing to take
part in one of the patrols?"

"Definitely!" He nodded at Mitch, sitting beside him. "We were talking about
that earlier. So, Amos is organizing
everyone?"

"Yep. He'll give you a call."

"Uh," Russ murmured just as people were standing up to leave the table. "I'd like to help with the patrols. Can you ask him to call me, too?"

"You bet!" Eli said, satisfied with the evening from start to finish.

The night had gone well and ended well, Shallie reflected as she drove Russ back to the motel. He sat quietly beside her for about half the ride, then thanked her for inviting him, asking her to thank Cord, too. "This is the best time I've had in ages. I hope we can get together again soon."

"We will," she promised. "Plus I'll keep you posted on anything I learn about Christine. We'll make sure you meet Eddie, too."

"After you and I talked, I decided to start looking for Bethanne. I'll try to get in touch with her husband."

"I'm glad." Shallie was even more conscious of the fact that Russ was a decent guy, and smart. She regretted their complete loss of touch—and regretted some of her previous assumptions about him. His apparent self-involvement was more about his isolation and a fundamental loneliness; his lack of social comfort came from an understandable and lifelong shyness.

"Do you have anything to work with?" she asked. "Any more information?"

"No more than we already discussed. But I do have **time**."

"I'm glad you're using it—some of it, anyway—for this."

"Thanks." He paused. "Nice guys, Cord, Eli, J.P. I remember them, sort of. We weren't friends, but I liked spending time with them tonight. And believe it or not, I'm kind of excited about joining those patrols." He laughed briefly. "Never thought I'd become pals with the sheriff."

"Hey, no reason why not. That would be a useful connection for a businessman, in case someone tries to break in or rob you or something like that."

"I wouldn't need to be **friends** with

him in that case. I could just call 911."

"True..."

"I'm interested in getting to know all of them—and getting to know you better."

"Thank you. Me, too."

She dropped him off at the dark and dreary motel. He gave her a rather clumsy hug, then clambered out, her headlights providing him with a reasonably well-lit path to the office door.

Back at Cord's place, she saw him and Eli still talking. They told her J.P. had gone home and Carly had left with Tina and Mitch. They asked her to join them and she did, accepting a glass of wine. Eli let her know that he appreciated Russell's unexpected willingness to get involved with one of the patrols. "I hope I made that obvious."

Cord nodded.

"Is there anything new he was able to add to the Christine Fletcher situation?" Eli asked next.

"Nothing yet. Oh—I forgot to tell you both. Russ and I talked about Christine's husband earlier today. We assume he was her husband and my father, although my birth certificate just says 'Father Unknown.'" She grinned wryly. "Something else Carly and I have in common."

"We should learn more on Friday night when Eddie's here."

She and Cord walked him out to his car, then Cord suggested he and Shallie go for a ramble with the dogs.

"I hope he can find himself more of a life," Shallie said. "But this evening was a good start."

They returned to the ranch house, said good-night at the foot of the stairs, dogs hanging around them. When Cord reached for her, she moved into his arms. His kiss was everything she'd longed for, everything she'd learned to expect from him. "I'm falling for you," he whispered.

She wanted to respond that she'd fallen for him a long time ago and that she'd had to put it aside, had to escape. Because he hadn't fallen for her back then, but for Reba...Things were changing, though. She felt more and more sure of it. Her life had taken a different direction, away from him and from this town. But she was back—back where, twenty years ago, she'd hoped to be.

Cord, not sleepy at all, went downstairs to sit on the porch with a final beer; the dogs, of course, joined him.

This was a night of reckoning, he told himself. He knew he was falling in love with Shallie. He'd told her the truth about that. He just wasn't sure what would happen next.

They'd make love soon. Very soon. He was convinced of that. He decided he should just enjoy the building excitement, the anticipation. Or try to, despite his frustration. It wasn't as though he could draw on past relationships for guidance. Reba? Hardly. Jenna? That marriage was a disastrous mistake and it didn't bother him not to have stayed in touch. He still felt used by her.

He'd certainly had some examples of loving relationships in his immediate life, like his grandparents and Mitch and Tina. Bill and Mimi were more than grandparents, they were the parents he'd never had. As he'd intimated to Shallie, his own mother was nothing to him. Yeah, he could understand that after her husband's death, she might've given up, lost her mind, grown completely irresponsible—but didn't she have **him** to live for?

He had no idea where she was or what she'd done with her life and had never really cared, partly because his grandparents had written her off. About all he knew right now was that her name was Julie. There were no photographs of her in the house, not even a wedding picture of her and Toby.

As Shallie had said, his situation wasn't all that different from hers.

It occurred to him, for the first time, that he, like Shallie, could engage Eddie's services. Maybe he should try to learn more, find out where Julie was, who she'd become. No question, Shallie's determination to track down her own mother inspired him. And he felt encouraged by Carly's example in searching for her dad. Besides, whatever he learned about Julie, it wasn't as though he'd have to act on it.

And while he was considering the subject of missing parents...He could turn out to be Carly's dad—and the truth was, he hoped he would. Having her nearby, staying with Tina and Mitch, had given him an opportunity to know her and, more than that, to **like** her. At some point soon, he, Eli and J.P would have to pursue DNA testing. More than ever, he'd begun to crave that particular truth.

He felt he'd made two decisions that could be important to his life. He'd talk to Eddie about finding Julie, and he'd pursue the father issue. There was one more decision, but it wasn't strictly his. It was time he pursued a future with Shallie.

CHAPTER TWELVE

The sunlight was coming through narrow slits in the blinds as Carly woke up. She stretched, rotated her shoulders, flexed her hands and feet. Grabbing her cell from the small bedside table, she checked the time—only 6:48. She'd get up and sit outside for a while, do some serious thinking. Pulling on a pair of jeans and one of Susan's T-shirts (this one read "So many books, so little time"), she tiptoed to the kitchen, but she didn't need to worry about waking Tina and Mitch. They were already sitting there, drinking coffee and eating toast when they greeted her, and she told them she'd really enjoyed dinner at Cord's the evening before.

It was true. She'd loved seeing everyone, including Russ. He seemed nice enough but kind of an odd guy. When she'd first met him last night, he said he used to know Reba, but she'd learned from Shallie that he'd not only known her, he'd **lived** with her because Reba had ended up at that awful motel owned by his parents. Carly hadn't felt she could ask Russ for a lot of detail just then, sensing that it wouldn't have been appropriate.

But there had to be more Shallie could tell Carly about those days, about Reba in particular. Did Shallie know why Reba had come to the motel and why she'd left? Did it have anything to do with the fact that she'd obviously had three more or less concurrent relationships?

Accepting a glass of orange juice with ice from Tina, she went outside and sat on one of the wicker chairs near the trailer. Okay, what was she going to do? How much longer could she go on like this, essentially living a lie? Feeling guiltier by the day? Shallie knew what she'd been doing, but she had to confess to the others, starting with Tina and Cord. Then Eli and J.P., on separate occasions. She had to tell them about her YouTube channel, her search for her father, how she'd made money—through ads and viewer donations. Would they see that as exploiting them? The four of them, she and her three potential dads, needed to make a joint decision about DNA testing. It had to be done. But, embarrassing as it was to admit, she'd put off telling them the truth so she could extend her YouTube performances a little longer; the success of **My 3 Dads** was thrilling and she certainly couldn't complain about the money. But she'd begun to question her own motives…And no, it wasn't just the money, although she'd keep that going as long as she could. Who knew when she'd have another stable source of cash?

Thinking about all these questions, about the decisions she needed to make, left her feeling...kind of scared. And it made her miss her mother so much.

More than anything, she had to find out who her father was. They all did. She owed that to herself, to them...and to Reba.

She'd head over to the ranch house now and have a talk with Shallie—if she was up. Otherwise, Carly figured, she'd hang with the dogs while she waited.

She entered the house to an enthusiastic welcome from Bandit and Smoky. Cord called out, "Hi! Carly? I'm on the computer in the office."

"Hi, Cord. Yeah, it's me. I just, uh, came to ask Shallie about something."

"She's awake. She came down to get a coffee about ten minutes ago. Help yourself if you want one."

"Thanks!" Carly didn't bother with the coffee, but hurried up the stairs and knocked on the suite door.

Shallie answered and gestured her inside. "Good early morning, Carly. Everything okay?"

Carly immediately launched into an

explanation, telling her what she'd decided and why. "So, would you come with me to talk to Cord and Tina? Soon?"

"Yes. I already promised you that. And I think it's absolutely the right thing to do. When? We've got Eli's friend, the detective, coming tonight. We could try for the weekend?"

Despite her need, her plan, to follow through with this, Carly still had to consider how to phrase things, come up with answers to the questions she'd certainly be asked. A couple more days would help. "What about Monday?"

"Fine. I'm willing to make the arrangements, but it's probably better coming from you."

Carly nodded slowly. And nodded again when Shallie asked, "Do you want to go to the vet's clinic later this morning to visit our little friend? Cord and I were thinking we'd drive you there. See you back here around ten?"

"That would be great!"

Carly returned to the trailer to get her laptop, grab a muffin and more juice, then took herself to her favorite place under the spreading cottonwood tree, within sight of the paddock, and went on her YouTube channel. She announced in a solemn voice that the conclusion of her father search might be coming in the next few weeks. Without mentioning names—as usual—she said she'd become fond of all three candidates; she also talked about how grateful she felt to the people she was staying with and the fact that she'd become close to a former friend of her mother's. "I love this place and I can imagine living here." Then she sang "I Walk the Line." After the annoying incident with that Worthless idiot, she wanted to honor her beloved Johnny Cash.

After checking the news on her cell phone, Shallie went downstairs, empty mug in hand.

She'd received an email from Eddie, confirming his arrival; he and Eli would come over to the ranch if that was okay.

Downstairs, she told Cord that Eddie

was definitely on schedule for tonight, then asked him if he was still interested in going to the vet with her and Carly.

"Yeah. I can take an hour or two. We're expecting a delivery of oats, but Mitch'll be here to receive it. And I'd like to see that poor little dog again, see for myself that she's doing okay."

On the way to the clinic, they spoke about the dog, and Shallie felt more strongly than ever that Carly had a true emotional connection with the animal.

Once there, Barb gave them an update on the beagle's condition. She was healing well, but still needed another week or so under veterinary care. Cord and Shallie visited the dog, then chatted with Barbara, getting her opinion on the current crimes involving the illegal release of animals, which had become major news in the county. Barb said she was appalled, but thought it might be a matter of vindictiveness against the individual owners. Shallie knew Cord and Eli weren't buying that theory, but didn't mention it. Carly spent the entire visit with the beagle, talking softly and stroking those silky ears. She also paid attention to the other recovering pets.

Just as Shallie came into the recovery room to summon her, the Lewises showed up, also to visit the dog. They suggested meeting at Bailey's for lunch. As Len pointed out, the restaurant seemed to be the center of their universe —something that now made sense to Shallie.

Cord, Shallie and Carly got to the restaurant first and secured a table for five, since the place was already getting crowded. Brynne wasn't on the lunch shift. Instead they were greeted by a pleasant young man named Barry who told them he was from Detroit and had recently come here to "experience small-town prairie life."

The three of them waited to order until the Lewises arrived, which they did within fifteen minutes. Menus were consulted, meals chosen and conversation was, as usual, pleasant. Then Len made their announcement, his and Mary

Jean's. They wanted to adopt the beagle, but felt they needed to discuss it with the three of them first. He was looking at Carly as he said this.

Cord told them he considered it an "excellent idea." Shallie said she did, too, but thought Carly's opinion was as important as theirs, maybe more so.

After an emotional pause Carly responded with a sunny smile and gave her consent. And Shallie knew that was exactly how the Lewises saw it—as consent. They thanked her with relieved smiles of their own.

"I'm happy about it," Carly said. "I wish I could keep the little girl, but I'm... thrilled she'll be going to such a good home, with such good people."

Shallie reached over to clasp the girl's hand and saw tears in her eyes. "It's the best thing, Carly," she whispered. "The best thing for the dog, and for you. You'll know she's safe, happy, loved. And as the Lewises said, we'll arrange visits so you'll get to see her."

Carly nodded. She didn't eat much,

stirring her chowder repeatedly, not really looking at anyone.

Eventually, she spoke again. "I think we should get serious about names."

"Of course," Mary Jean promptly said and invited the three of them to dinner at Bailey's the next night, adding, "It is, after all, the center of your universe." Shallie liked the comment even more, hearing it a second time, and figured she'd be "borrowing" it from now on.

Mary Jean said they'd be treating and that everyone should come prepared with names. They'd like to include Tina and her husband; their nephew Ted might join them, too. "The more suggestions, the better," Len said, shaking his head comically. "It might come down to a vote."

"And," Mary Jean said with finality, "Carly's judgment should be the final one."

That evening, Eli came over with Eddie Gonzalez, and they all sat on the porch, where Shallie served drinks and salty snacks. Cord's immediate impression of Eddie was positive, and he could tell that Shallie's was, too. The man, who was tall and fit, with the look of a former cop, was confident but not arrogant.

Once the introductory small talk was finished, Eddie began by reviewing the information Shallie had sent him. He looked up from his notes and turned to her. "Melanie—you've spoken with her, I think?"

Shallie nodded.

"Melanie tracked down your father through various specialized databases we have access to. And...Kevin Fletcher's dead. He died five years ago."

Shallie gasped; Cord doubted she was truly surprised but seeing your suspicions turned into reality often left people shocked.

"Eddie, could you elaborate on the circumstances?" Eli asked. "Shallie, are you ready to hear them?"

She nodded again.

"Okay, the story is that he was a crooked cop, involved with organized crime in Chicago. So, it's not exactly unexpected that this is how he met his end, nearly twenty years after he apparently threatened Christine in that phone call and she took off and disappeared. Apparently, she had too much damaging information about him and his, shall we say, associates." He paused. "She might not even have been aware of just how much she knew."

"He found out she was at the motel?"

"Yeah, with a little help from his friends," Eddie said sardonically.

"So, those...friends, accomplices— eventually killed him," Eli concluded.

"I'd refer to it as an execution."

"Did my mother know about his... murder?" Shallie asked.

"Probably not. But since your birth certificate read 'Father Unknown,' we're assuming Christine already knew he was a threat, to you and to her. I'll email you some articles and other background on him that Melanie found. In fact, if I could use your computer, Cord, I'll do it before we leave. Oh, and Christine is never mentioned in anything I've seen."

"Do you have any idea where she is?"

"Not yet. Working on it."

"No problem with using the computer," Cord said. "I have another question for you." He told Eddie about his mother, Julie Hollister—at least that had been her name thirty-some years ago. He gave a brief summary of what had happened—his father's death in the military, his mother's negligence, which had led to the intervention of Child Services, and finally how he'd ended up here, raised by his grandparents. "Could you see what you can find out about Julie and where she is now? If she's still alive...I'll pay whatever it takes."

"Sure." Eddie turned to Shallie. "Are you okay with that? If we work on both cases at the same time?"

"Of course!"

Cord said, "I've never considered looking for her before. I always thought of her as the woman who basically abandoned me at a very young age. But

Shallie's search for her own mother has inspired me. Maybe it's a need for—and I hate this word—closure. And maybe I need to learn if there were any extenuating circumstances. Find out who she is, who she **was** and why she did it."

"Yeah," Eli murmured, "I think you **should** try to find out."

After Eddie had sent the emails, he and Eli left. Shallie said a hasty good-night, then rushed into the house, followed by Bandit.

Cord figured her reaction, her need to be alone, **had** to be connected to what she'd just learned about her father. That seemed obvious enough. He felt distraught for Shallie, but thought he should give her a chance to deal with it privately; he'd talk to her when she seemed ready, offer what advice and comfort he could. Which probably wouldn't be much, but he'd do his best.

To suddenly find out that your father was a criminal and possibly a killer...

Shallie escaped to her room. She was

horrified by what she'd discovered about her father. No, it wasn't a complete surprise—but worse than she'd expected. And she couldn't stop wondering if he'd murdered Christine. Maybe her body had never been found or identified.

Thinking about everything she'd just learned, she was almost terrified to learn more. She realized she should look at the material Eddie had sent, but decided she couldn't cope with it now.

As she got into her nightclothes, Bandit lay beside the bed. "You keeping me company, boy?" He wagged his tail as if he understood. It didn't take her long to fall asleep.

When she and the dog went downstairs the next morning, she remembered they were supposed to have Carly's meeting on Monday. Except... no. According to a text she'd sent at 6 a.m., Carly had put it off. **Wednesday**, she said now.

Cord handed Shallie a coffee and several sheets he'd printed out on Kevin Fletcher, corrupt Chicago cop. She sat down and read them quickly. Fletcher had been charged with racketeering, drug dealing, organizing a hit, and was on the verge of being tried when his "friends and accomplices," as Eddie had called them, delivered a hit of their own. No one was charged in that murder.

As Eddie had also said, there were no references in these articles to Christine or any other family. Including her.

Shallie studied the photo—and the man did look vaguely familiar. She could easily believe he was her father.

"I'm sorry," Cord said. "Life can be hard."

She understood. "You obviously had a difficult background yourself."

"Well, mine improved as soon as my grandparents got involved. I'm really grateful to them for everything. My mother—I can barely call her that— probably wouldn't have noticed if I'd simply disappeared from my crib."

Shallie raised her eyebrows. "Wow, there sure are a lot of screwed-up families out there."

"And many that aren't. Look at Tina and Mitch and their kids, for one. The Lewises for another. I happen to believe that you can recover from your past. You and I have—and Carly's on her way."

"That kind of recovery demands some responsibility from us, don't you think?"

"Definitely. I don't want to sound preachy, but I believe we owe gratitude to the forces—human or institutional or spiritual, whatever—that helped save us. We have to pass on to others what we've learned and received ourselves."

"I agree, but I'm not sure how."

"You've already done it for Carly. For Russ. For me. You've made a difference to all of us."

"And you've made the same kind of difference to me." **In more ways than you realize.**

"Listen," he said quietly. "If you want to talk about this, about everything you just found out, if you want to yell about it, cry…I'm here."

"Thank you, Cord. And if you want to talk to me about…Julie, please remember I'm here for you, too."

"We'll talk soon."

"And get together soon. If you know what I mean." She hugged him tightly.

"Oh, yeah."

CHAPTER THIRTEEN

That evening at Bailey's, Cord enjoyed the enthusiastic way everyone got involved in the Great Dog-Naming Event. Other than Shallie and Carly, they were all having local beer; Shallie had her usual Washington State Chardonnay and Carly drank sparkling water.

Various names had already been brought up and discarded. Brynne suggested a few, all vetoed, and finally said, "Call her Baby." At which Cord—predictably—rolled his eyes.

"What about something Western? Like Cowgirl," he said.

"Cow for short?" Brynne asked in a saccharine voice. Cord rolled his eyes again.

"How about...Sweetie Pie?" Tina said. Now they **all** rolled their eyes.

Mitch laughed. "A name proposed by a woman who likes to bake."

"Hey—should we go with Sweet Lady?" Ted broke into the Queen song, and Carly sang along; she even knew most of the words. Ted told her how impressed he was by the number of songs in what he called her "repertoire" and how well she performed. He said Aaron had mentioned including her in a gig sometime, after a few practice sessions.

"Thank you," Carly said, her voice almost a whisper.

"Your singing is lovely." Mary Jean looked at Carly. "I have an idea. I think we should name her **Carly**. Since you're the one who found her."

"Thank you, but no." Carly shook her head. "Why don't you name her Holly? Short for Hollister, as in Hollister Ranch."

"I like it!" Mary Jean said excitedly

and Len raised his glass. "Holly it is," he said.

The others raised their glasses and chanted, "Holl-ee! Holl-ee!" Cord chanted as loudly as anyone, a broad grin on his face. He felt deeply moved by Carly's suggestion, grateful that she'd acknowledged this place he loved.

Brynne joined in the applause, then brought them a round on the house. "In honor of Holly and her new family. Now, what about ordering dinner, you guys?"

Driving back to the trailer with Tina and Mitch, knowing she faced a difficult conversation in a few days, Carly settled into the backseat. She stared out at the dark, gloomy sky lit only by a few stars that appeared among the clouds. "Hope it doesn't rain tomorrow," Mitch was saying.

"It's not in the forecast," Tina said. "What's on for next week?"

Mitch replied—something about buying wood and making repairs to a length of fencing. Tina said she planned to do some cleaning, then weed and water the garden in front of the trailer. But tomorrow she'd relax...

Carly loved hearing ordinary talk about ordinary things. It had never really been part of her life. Instead, her mother and stepfather had argued constantly about which task was whose and who should pay for what.

Mitch went on to say that early the next afternoon, he and Cord were going on their first patrol; Amos had emailed them today with details. **Nothing ordinary about that**, Carly told herself.

When there was silence again, a warm, comfortable silence, she told them how much she appreciated their kindness. How she felt she had two mothers now, Tina and Shallie, and that Mitch had to be one of the world's best dads. Tina reached behind the seat and clasped her hand. "Thank you, sweetie. Now, let me ask you a question. How do you feel about Holly going to the Lewises? I know you love that little dog."

"I'm actually fine with it. In fact, I'm happy because I do love her. And Len and Mary Jean are great." She paused for a moment, seeking the right words. "I think it was meant to be."

Monday night, Cord was exhausted. First there'd been the stall cleaning, then the training session with the Lewises (although Shallie was handling a lot of that), a conference call with his PR group—and most tiring of all—a second patrol of local ranchland with Mitch. They'd run into Russ and another rancher en route. Russ had binoculars, a magnifying glass, a camera and who knew what else. Cord was pleased to see he was taking this seriously, and Shallie was just as pleased when he told her.

He went to bed earlier than usual, thinking about the coming news regarding Julie. He was looking forward to it in one way, not at all in another. He had no idea what to expect. Compared to Shallie, he knew a lot about his past. But there were still unanswered questions.

Like…had his mother **ever** loved him?

Up in his room, one dog underfoot, since Bandit had apparently taken to sleeping in Shallie's room, he felt oddly powerless. His past was in Eddie's hands, his future in Shallie's.

Cord fell into bed, determined not to think about her—or Julie.

He dreamed that night, and although he rarely remembered his dreams, this one remained with him, still vivid when he woke up. In it, he was surrounded by animals—dogs, cats, horses, even a coyote and a deer—and they were all talking to him. Bandit, Smoky and Holly the beagle were telling him he had to say **yes** to Shallie, to whatever she asked. The cats said he should adopt one of **them**. According to the horses, the local criminal would be caught, and soon. They also told him he needed to become friends with the Lewises.

In the light of day, it actually all made sense. Except maybe the idea of taking on a cat; the dogs might not go for that. He got up to perform his first chore of the morning—making coffee, the good kind.

Shallie had been dreaming about him. Dreaming that they'd made love, **powerful** love. The first time in her bed, the second under a tree at the edge of a meadow.

Her images of these encounters were vivid and sensual. So was her memory of how she'd felt. That this was unsurpassed—and that she wanted to make it real.

What would Cord think if she suggested starting their day by reliving her dream?

Cord was pouring his second coffee when Shallie came down, Bandit yawning beside her. She seemed a bit shy, certainly not typical of her. He fed and put the dogs out, but at their loud insistence, let them back in.

He noticed that she hadn't bothered to get herself a coffee, although she knew she could help herself at any time. Not typical, either.

All of a sudden, she said, "Let's do it now." **It?** Do it? Despite the high school vernacular, he wondered if she'd meant what he thought she meant. If she was referring to what they'd promised each other last night.

Clearly she did. She got up, grabbed his hand, hardly giving him a chance to put his mug down, and led him, unprotesting, up the stairs, Bandit in pursuit. "Do you have time for this?" she asked.

"Time? Of course! For you...For this."

Inside her room, he closed the door to shut Bandit out. Then he took hold of her arms and they tumbled onto the bed together. He stroked her, she stroked him, between deep, passionate kisses. Their clothes came off with little effort. He whispered a question about birth control. Should he get a condom?

"Yes. I'm on the pill, but it's never a bad idea."

He left the room and quickly returned with a packet of condoms. And then it started…He brought her to a long drawn-out climax, kneeling between her legs, thrilled at her gasps and moans. Followed by more kisses, more excitement. He worshipped her breasts with his hands, his mouth. She poised herself above him—and, as he later put it, the rest was history. **Their** history.

Yes, they had a history and, he now believed, a future. He was prepared to dismiss past expectations, past hopes, in favor of a growing sense of **future** hopes. And love…

Cord lay in bed beside her, arm resting lightly across her waist. She glanced at him, feeling an unfamiliar contentment. She'd certainly made love before, but she'd never felt so…invigorated.

Was this it? Was Cord the real, the enduring, love of her life? Not merely an adolescent fantasy anymore. And yet, was that fair to him? She didn't know how serious he was, what he wanted from her, what he was willing to give her. Other than great sex.

Or what she was willing to give him.

A lot to consider here. Was she pre-pared to take a life-altering chance—if this **was** a chance? Relinquish not only her job, which she was prepared to do, but her dream of working with Emma? Her long-established life in Seattle?

Shallie realized that Cord had no intention of leaving this ranch, this town. Painted Pony Creek held his history, his work, his friends and his community.

But even if Cord seemed ready to make a commitment, there was always risk. The risk of being hurt, of disappointment and betrayal, she reminded herself, remembering why she'd left Rob. He'd betrayed her in the most basic way—by being unfaithful.

She appreciated many things about Cord, including the concern and res-ponsibility he'd shown when he'd checked with her about birth control.

He dressed and went downstairs with a final kiss and she put her clothes back on, too, then phoned Emma. Couldn't reach her but left a vague message saying, "It finally happened," leaving her friend to intuit the rest.

Time to get some coffee and breakfast, then go out to meet the Lewises and Carly. A morning session today, since Mary Jean had a dental appointment in their hometown that afternoon. As things turned out, Cord wasn't able to join them. Just before they arrived, he got an urgent call from a woman named Kelly who worked with a rescue group and had saved Annie, the shaggy little horse now in his barn. She had another horse, also neglected, that she'd found wandering down a nearby road a week ago. Could he come and get her as soon as possible? Kelly had limited space and resources. He and Mitch were setting out to pick up the horse immediately; Mitch was busy attaching the trailer to Cord's SUV.

Carly told him he'd better **not** come home without the horse, an opinion seconded by Shallie and the Lewises.

They spent the next two hours working with Chief, the formerly abused racehorse. He'd lost much of his fear, and Mary Jean said she could see him as a therapy horse, partly because he'd have needs in common with his "clients."

Afterward, they took Carly to visit Holly, inviting Shallie, too. At the vet's they learned that "the little girl" could be released in another two days, which coincided with the Lewises' planned trip home on Thursday. Carly gave Holly a kiss on the nose and rubbed those long silky ears. "You'll always be welcome to see her," Mary Jean said. "In fact, we'd love it if you both came to our place. It's only about two hours away."

"Absolutely," Len agreed. "And if you need a ride, we can work something out."

That afternoon, Shallie kept obsessing over her fear that her father had killed her mother. She was descended from a corrupt and murderous man and...And when she wasn't focused on that, she continued to think about her feelings for Cord.

She found some release from the intensity of her thoughts in emails and texts—to her disappointment, nothing from Emma yet—and by spending half an hour reading. She sank, once again, into the comfort of **The Black Stallion**, which she understood in a whole different way now. Eventually, she dozed off with her cell phone playing blues on low volume.

The commotion downstairs woke her about an hour later. She rushed into the kitchen to greet Cord and Mitch, then went outside with them to meet the new horse, named Patience by her rescuer. Carly and Tina were already oohing and aahing over her, another small, shaggy mare, dappled gray with a darker mane and tail. As Shallie joined them, she could already see that this one seemed more ready for affection than Annie had originally been.

Tina wondered aloud whether she'd been "released" by their local criminal, but Kelly had placed ads and sent out announcements, with no response from an owner.

They received word from the Lewises that they were picking up Holly tomorrow morning, a day earlier than expected, and would stop by the ranch on their way home to Missoula.

And according to a message on Shallie's phone, tomorrow night she and Cord were heading over to Eli's place to meet with Eddie again. Eddie preferred face-to-face contact when possible. It sounded as if he'd made **some** progress.

Wednesday morning, Carly didn't get out of bed although she was wide-awake. She felt guilty as hell, no other way to describe it. She'd postponed the Big Meet with Cord and Tina; Shallie must be disgusted with her. She hadn't gone back on her You-Tube channel, either, leaving her audience in limbo.

It was her task to set up the meeting. Should she take all of them to Bailey's? Or stay in the privacy of Cord's home? Perhaps she should leave it up to them. She'd ask Shallie for her opinion.

She reflected that so far, she'd learned some major things during her time here. She reached for her notebook, which she fancifully called a "journal," and started to write them down.

1. There **are** good people in this world. Good people and good places.

2. I have to be stronger, more courageous, get this meeting set up. OK, Friday. For sure.

3. Back when she lived here, my mom had some good friends, like Shallie. I'm happy about that. Talking to them makes me appreciate her—and miss her— even more.

4. I need to talk to Russ again, see what he can tell me about her, the town, Shallie. He's weird but not a bad guy.

5. I love Shallie and Tina and Mitch, and I want them always to be part of my life. And Cord has been **so** good to me. Eli and J.P., too.

6. I love and adore animals. I'm so glad I learned this about myself. Dooley was special—but so are Holly, Bandit, Smoky the horses...

7. Music is my other passion. My loves, my future, my life will be about animals and music.

8. I'm grateful to so many people here. This search has turned out to be such a good thing.

9. I'll be OK with any of those 3 guys as my dad...I could love any and all of them. And, whichever one it is, I'll have another bonus—2 new uncles.

She hated ending on an odd number, thought for another minute.

10. My life is going to be good, happy, worthwhile.

That pretty much covered it, that last one. With an unaccustomed sigh of satisfaction, she closed the notebook and slid out of bed.

CHAPTER FOURTEEN

Early that afternoon, Carly was ready and waiting to say good-bye to Mary Jean, Len—and Holly. They'd promised to drop by once they'd picked up the dog, and Carly was waiting on the porch after lunch, planning her announcement for Cord and Tina. Yes, she'd moved the Big Meet again. Friday, no further excuses or delays.

Shallie had just joined her, dogs crowding around, when they heard the Lewis SUV coming down the drive. They parked and got out, as did Ted. He removed Holly from a brand-new dog carrier.

The beagle trotted unsteadily to the porch. Carly could hardly keep herself from breaking into tears—a mixture of sadness and joy for the "little girl" who'd been granted such a wonderful home. She was heartened, too, by the way Cord's dogs approached Holly, how sweet they were with her. She suspected Holly needed more socialization, of both the canine and human kind. Hugging her carefully, she whispered goodbye as she stroked those adorable long, silky ears.

Cord and Tina had emerged from the house a few minutes earlier; they and Shallie took their turns with the dog. While the three of them were engaged in that, Ted began a conversation with Carly, telling her he'd spoken with Aaron and the others, and they'd arrange a rehearsal soon. She was thrilled and told him so. Then as Ted returned Holly to her carrier, Carly kissed Len and Mary Jean goodbye. She felt that, with them, she'd gained more parents, more family.

Today she'd promise Shallie that she'd set up the discussions with Cord and Tina, followed by the ones with Eli and

J.P. Unhappily, it had somewhat be-latedly occurred to her that if Eli turned out to be her dad, she'd be related to the Worthless jerk—a prospect that horrified her.

As they waved goodbye to the depart-ing vehicle, Carly murmured, not for the first time, as she was well aware, "I just **love** that little girl."

After a moment, Tina pulled her aside, saying she had a suggestion. "I have a friend named Meg," she began. "She's in her sixties and recovering from cancer surgery and now she's undergoing chemo, which means regular trips out of town. She needs help looking after her two cats. Her kids do what they can but they're not local and they're usually the ones who take her to the cancer center for treatments. I sometimes go over to her place, but I think it would be perfect for you. Giving Meg that kind of support, helping animals **and** people, would be **perfect** for you," she repeated.

Carly enthusiastically agreed; so did Shallie. They'd have to arrange rides, but they'd sort that out.

Between Tina's suggestion and Ted's offer, Carly felt she had more proof than ever that her life was meant to be about animals and music **and** helping people in the community. Maybe she could even find ways to combine them!

The next evening, when Shallie and Cord drove to Eli's for their second meeting with Eddie, she wondered what his place would be like. The house turned out to be small and spotless, the furniture basic, carpets a plain gray. It certainly wasn't the stereotypical cluttered mess she'd half expected.

They sat down in surprisingly comfortable chairs around a polished dining room table that actually had a cloth on it and a plant.

Eli served them each a beer, no snacks.

Eddie then handed around folders, one labeled "Julie," the other "Christine." "All right," he said, "we'll start with the easy one. Julie."

Shallie heard Cord's sudden and no

doubt unintended gasp. **Easy?**

"It wasn't hard for Melanie to get the information on Julie, primarily because of the military background. So, Julie Hollister married Christopher Daniels four years after Toby Hollister's death. Chris is a marine and they're living in San Diego. They have an eighteen-year-old daughter, Kathleen Daniels."

Shallie heard another gasp, one he tried to disguise with a cough. **He had a half sister.** About the same age as his possible daughter. "Do you think Julie would want to hear from me?" he asked a minute later. Shallie figured he'd had to wait until he could control his voice.

"I'm guessing she would, but I can look into it if you like."

Cord nodded. "Please."

Eddie went on. "Now, Shallie, Melanie's learned a few things about Christine, and we're continuing the investigation."

"Thank you." Shallie's voice was as tense as her posture.

"Okay, what we've found out is that when she left Painted Pony Creek, she got herself down to Florida. She left by car, we know that, and maybe she sold it along the way or maybe when she arrived—to avoid having the license plate identified and probably to get some cash. And here's the big news. Thanks to my brilliant assistant, we've learned that she changed her name, which as I told you earlier is a lot easier to do than most people think, even back then. But there's usually information left behind—if you know what I mean. And if you understand how to look for it. Which Melanie does. Christine became Sharon. Sharon Sutherland. She lived in Florida. Near Orlando."

Shallie just nodded. What else could she do?

"What we learned next is that Christine Fletcher, living as Sharon Sutherland, connected with Reba Shannon in Florida about fifteen years later. Which is how Reba ended up here in Montana, and specifically at the motel."

"But **how** did they connect?"

"They were both working at the same

motel near Orlando."

"**Motel?** Oh, my God." Shallie covered her mouth. "I don't know whether to laugh or cry."

"So, Christine, aka Sharon, was a waitress at the motel restaurant. The place was—and still is—called Sunny Days. Reba, meanwhile, was handling the desk. They met during dinner one night, when they were both off, and became friends, saw each other regularly. Then Christine asked Reba to go to Montana, to this town and the motel, to check up on you. To see how you were doing and report back to her. Christine Fletcher paid her what she could."

"Oh, my God," Shallie repeated. "I think I **am** going to cry."

Cord intervened with a question of his own. "How did you and Melanie get these details?"

Eddie grinned. "A lot of it was simply good luck. Helped by the fact that I know an investigator in Florida, believe it or not."

"Oh, I believe it," Eli murmured. "So,

you hired him?"

"Yeah. This guy, Tony, went to the Orlando area and researched various motels, interviewed people. And discovered there were still a few employees at a particular place—the Sunny Days that I mentioned earlier—who remembered them both. And I guess Christine wasn't totally discreet at the time, since one of the staff overheard some of their conversation..."

"So then what?" Eli asked.

"Then Christine disappeared. Five or six months later. Probably a combination of feeling reassured that you were doing okay, Shallie, and fear that there were still criminal types out there searching for her. Melanie's continuing to follow up. At this point we don't even know if she's still alive."

On their way home, Cord and Shallie were silent. When they arrived, he invited her to sit on the porch with him, talk about what they'd learned. "I think we're both still numb," he added.

The dogs were happy to be allowed out with them, and Cord got a second beer for himself and Shallie. After a sip or two, he said, "Eddie was right. Mine was the easy one, comparatively speaking."

"Not **that** easy. Anyway, I think you should get in touch with her. And you have a half sister! Let's invite them here or—" She blushed. "I'm sorry. I mean, it's not my call or any of my business."

"I feel it is." Although he couldn't clearly explain why. "Here's an idea. Once I've established contact, maybe I'll see if we can meet her—or them—someplace halfway between here and San Diego. And if you'll join me..." He hoped with an almost painful intensity that she would.

"I'd like to," she said. "Let me know."

"Eddie's impressive, isn't he? And Melanie, too. You really are fortunate to get these results and to get them so fast."

She gave a slight shrug. "No way of knowing where Christine is, though. Or who she is. Of **if** she is."

"He'll find out. Meanwhile, let's go for a dog walk." It was becoming their evening ritual, one he'd never enjoyed more.

Their walk was relaxed, as always, except that they heard a coyote in the distance. Cord muttered, "Good thing these dogs are well trained and not chasing after that critter."

As soon as they got back, they hurried inside and Shallie threw her arms around him, raising them from his waist to his shoulders. "Upstairs?" she whispered.

"Oh, yes!" And so they went.

Another night with Shallie! Cord felt so grateful, so fortunate. No question, their lives were filled with complications, but in some ways those complications had brought them together.

Their sexual encounter was possibly even better than the one before. The excitement, passion, **warmth**—he'd never experienced anything quite like this.

They woke at the same time, probably because one of the dogs had begun pawing at the door. "Hey, cut it out!"

Cord said. "Maybe you're not as well trained as I thought you were."

Shallie laughed. "It's okay. He can come in. I don't mind."

"No. I'll go down, do the dog thing, make us coffee." He dressed quickly, then gave her a long, slow kiss.

She reflected that last night had been a good one. And once they'd reached her room, it became a great one. It wasn't only the passion between them. It was also the emotion, the empathy. Everything she needed in a relationship. That and trust...

The Lewises were gone. How much longer could she justify staying here? Unless she and Cord made a commitment to each other soon...She wanted exactly that, but a commitment wouldn't be simple, for a whole host of reasons. They'd have to talk about it.

Before she could get out of bed and dressed, there was a knock at the suite door. Cord, she assumed as she called, "Come on in." But no, it was Carly bringing her a large mug of coffee.

"Hi, Cord gave me this to bring up to you," she said, handing it over.

Shallie took a grateful sip. "So, how are you this fine morning? At least I hope it'll be a fine morning."

Carly smiled. "I'm good. But can I speak to you for a minute?"

"Of course! You know that."

"Well, I talked to Tina last night, and I just talked to Cord. They're both willing to meet with me. With **us**. Tonight."

"Good. What time? And where? As if I even have to ask."

"Seven. You guessed it—at Bailey's," she replied with a smile. "On me, although they don't know that yet. Oh, and I've included Mitch. I'm not sure how much he understands about my…situation, but I'm sure he's heard some of it from Tina."

"Are you positive I should be there?" Shallie asked, already a little anxious about the Big Meet.

"Yes! Please! I can't do it without you!"

Shallie nodded. She finished her coffee and asked, "And how do you feel about this? You sure you're okay with it?"

"I am. I'm kind of nervous, but I feel as ready as I'm going to be."

"I'm so glad," Shallie said. "Give me a chance to get dressed, check my email and head downstairs. We'll catch up later."

She had to wonder how the others— especially Cord—would react to these revelations. Would he feel betrayed, angry, upset with Carly? And with her, if he guessed or realized she'd already known most of this?

Shallie, still yawning and sipping her coffee, got dressed, but wasn't quite ready to make her way downstairs. She'd agreed to be at the Big Meet tonight, mainly because Carly's request had seemed so desperate, but she wasn't really prepared for it.

Didn't matter. Moral support was all she needed to offer...

Everyone relevant to this particular discussion would be there. Act One, as Shallie thought of it, to be followed by

Acts Two and Three, aka Eli and J.P.

She checked her cell and saw that Russ had left her several text messages. **Call me**, he'd written. Then, in a second one, **I want to run something by you**. Finally, **I know it's early, but CALL ME.**

She did, and he answered after the first ring. "Hi, Russ. What's so urgent?"

"Listen, I've been turning this place upside down, looking for anything on Christine. And...I found something."

"**What** did you find?"

"Not ready to tell you. I need to look around some more. But I promise to show you tomorrow."

Shallie wanted to ask why he'd been so insistent on talking to her if he wasn't ready to share what he'd found. She had to grit her teeth not to shout at him. But she figured that was typical Russ. Everything on his terms. "Fine."

"How are things with you?" he asked.

"Okay," she replied, more curtly than she'd intended.

"Yeah? So are you seeing Cord Hollister? Uh, like boy-friend-girlfriend, I mean." He paused, managing an embarrassed chuckle. "Lots of us voices from the past, huh?"

Her relationship with Cord was the **last** thing Shallie wanted to discuss with him. "Gotta go."

"Let's do lunch tomorrow," he said.

"Sure. Why not?"

"At Bailey's?"

Although she realized it was a good thing for Russ to leave the motel on a more regular basis, Shallie felt she was spending enough time at Brynne's. And she'd be there for the Carly revelations tonight. Besides, if he had something to show her, it was more practical to simply meet at the motel. "Why don't I pick something up and bring it over?" she suggested. "Maybe pizza from that outlet on Main? I hear the food is decent."

"Around noon?" he said.

"Okay. See you then."

The day passed quickly, despite the lack of a schedule or serious work, other than a couple of hours spent acclimating

Patience, the little rescue horse, to her new home. She and Carly did have a brief discussion that mostly consisted of Shallie encouraging the girl, reminding her this was the right thing to do. They visited with the other horses, went for a stroll with the dogs—and then Carly showed her **My 3 Dads**.

Shallie was impressed—and told her so.

"This is incredible!" she said. "Everything about it! Your singing—no surprise there. Your comments and the way you tell your story, the videos, the way you've organized everything. And you look gorgeous. In spite of those clothes."

Carly laughed at that last remark.

Cord and Shallie drove to Brynne's together, while—as usual—Carly went with Tina and Mitch. It was going to be another mild and almost balmy night with more than a hint of humidity. They hadn't experienced heavy rain since the evening Carly had shown up.

However, he had something more

critical to discuss with Shallie right now. This was his chance to ask her, in advance, what Carly's meeting was about —although he could guess. Sort of. All she'd said when she invited him this morning was that it was "important" and "personal" and also "concerned him."

But he figured if anyone knew what that meant, it was Shallie.

Carly had obviously, **more** than obviously, been hiding things. Her history, the little they knew, checked out according to Eli, who'd examined her birth certificate. Exactly as expected. Mother: Reba Diane Shannon. Father: Unknown. Issued in Orlando, Florida.

"Well," he began. "What do you suppose Carly wants to discuss with us? She's set up a pretty formal way to do it, so I have to wonder—"

"I don't want to be rude," she broke in, "but it's not my place to tell you. Anyway, you'll hear soon enough."

"Fine, we'll leave it for now."

He could hear her take a deep breath. "I talked to Russ today," she told him, staring straight ahead. "And he says he has something to show me. Something to do with my mother."

The fact that Russ had evidence of some kind (if he really did) struck him as interesting—and potentially valuable.

"When are you going to find out what he has?"

"Tomorrow. I'm having lunch with him."

"I hope whatever it is will be useful. Nothing too unexpected, at least not in a bad way. Nothing that'll distress you." He wished he could be there with her, to lend any support or offer any help he could. "I'd join you if that would help but tomorrow's one of my patrols."

"Thanks, I appreciate the thought. But Russ will probably do better if I'm there on my own. This time, anyway. On another subject, I should mention that Carly will want to talk to Eli and J.P., as well. Separately."

"She told me. Makes sense."

"The timing is up to her. She has to arrange when to see them."

He nodded.

They were silent after that. As they reached Main Street, Cord ventured one more question, hoping she wouldn't consider it presumptuous. "Would you be willing to stay on for another week or two? I've heard from some tentative clients...A couple of veterinary students interested in training therapy horses."

"Yes," she replied immediately. "I'd love to! Plus, it'll give me a chance to see where the parent search goes— for both of us. And even more for Carly. Plus, I want to learn everything I can about working with horses and clients. And...I want to find out what's going on between us. If it's something that might last." A moment later, she said, "I'm just trying to be completely honest with you."

"I know." He wasn't sure what else he could say, other than **I want to find out, too**. And a moment later, he **did** say that, even though she already knew it. Still, some things couldn't be said often enough...

Not quite seven yet, full daylight,

though clouds were continuing to form. No sign of the darkness that would descend on them a few hours from now.

As they drove along Main, he saw several people he recognized and slowed down to wave at them. "Okay, here we are," he said unnecessarily, pulling into Bailey's lot. "Tina and company are already present and accounted for, I see."

When they walked into the restaurant, Brynne met them at the door and led them to a relatively isolated table—as isolated as it was possible to get. Which meant near the kitchen. The other three were already seated.

After the formalities of greeting and ordering, and Brynne herself had served their drinks, Carly said, "I'm the one who called this meeting, so...I guess I should start. And by the way, dinner's on me."

Despite everyone's protests, she persisted.

She began, sounding like she'd practiced this speech. "You already know that Reba Shannon was my mother.

And Cord, as you also know, you might be my father. Same is true for Eli and J.P. I've reached a point in my life where I **need** to know. I imagine you guys feel the same way."

Cord nodded vigorously. "I do." And he meant it. He was sure Eli and J.P. would, too, even if they hadn't before. It was time to get this settled.

"That's part of what I wanted to talk about. The other..." And she launched into a complicated story that involved a YouTube channel called **My 3 Dads**, with various musical performances— including classic country songs—and the accumulation of a shocking amount of money.

Neither Tina nor Shallie seemed surprised. Even Mitch didn't appear too startled.

And was he? Cord asked himself. Well, yes. Shocked. At least she'd indicated in her description of **My 3 Dads** that she'd been extremely careful to protect their privacy, careful not to reveal details of their lives, and once they learned who her father actually was, she'd consult with him, Eli and J.P. about how much to say.

All this new and astonishing information left him with conflicting reactions, opposing emotions. He couldn't help feeling disturbed, even a little betrayed, that she'd made private information public—and profited from it. Yet he believed Carly's reassurances about her discretion, which would be easy enough to check. He also understood her nervousness.

At the same time, her revelations made him feel something else. An unexpected **pride**. Pride in the fact that, at her age, she'd pulled this off. Pride in her honesty and courage, her enterprising spirit, her talent.

Carly now went on to explain that she wanted all three of her potential dads to agree to DNA testing and, of course, she would, too. After that...who knew?

Cord knew. If she was his daughter, he'd do anything and everything he could for her. He'd be a true father, a good father, make up for what she'd lost and lacked in the past. And if J.P. or Eli turned out to be her dad, he'd be an honorary uncle.

Again, Tina and Mitch said nothing; neither did Shallie.

Cord decided it was time to make something clear. "Carly, whichever one of us is your dad will be privileged to learn that. And the other two will be an important part of your life, too, as your honorary uncles." A little formal, perhaps…"All of us will do our best to make your new life here as happy as we can."

Carly nodded, not hiding her tears.

Brynne had obviously noticed the confidential nature of their discussion, not interrupting but keeping an eye on them. Still, four friends stopped by their table, obviously not as sensitive as Brynne to their need for privacy. Finally, Cord waved at her and she brought over their appetizers and fresh drinks. The conversation grew lighter and there was a sense of relief all around.

The only thing that still bothered Cord

—and he guessed it was his traditional upbringing—was that Carly really did pay. In cash.

The rain had started, nothing too heavy, but to Cord it seemed fitting.

He and Shallie spoke little during the drive, but the atmosphere was relaxed, comfortable.

After the evening they'd just had, he was left with various impressions, various feelings rocketing through him. First, a residue of his earlier shock. He was tempted to check out Carly's YouTube channel, but decided he should control his curiosity for now. He realized that he felt a bit afraid of learning what had been said about him, not by Carly, but by her fans and supporters, even though she'd assured him she'd never used his name. He also felt relief that the mystery of her paternity was going to be solved.

Another thing—considering the money she'd made, he should put her in touch with his accountant, Mitch and Tina's son-in-law, for financial advice. Or suggest that she call Len.

In addition, they'd need to arrange for DNA testing. He'd look into what that involved.

He'd have to focus on his business, too, especially at this time of year, since most of his clients arrived between April and October. He had to connect with his PR team again, plan some events for his website, organize upcoming clients, work with the new horse.

Then there was the whole Julie situation. Not to mention Christine Fletcher...

And Shallie. Most of all Shallie.

She'd admitted that she wanted to see if there was anything serious between them. Despite his inevitable fear of another betrayal, another disappointment, his connection with her—connection in every sense—felt the closest he'd ever been to what he truly wanted. Without Reba's lies and duplicity or Jenna's exploitation.

It suddenly occurred to him that although he and Shallie had spent a lot of time together (like tonight, for instance), they'd never been on a **date**. Or was that too dated (ha!) a term, too old-fashioned a concept these days? Too juvenile? Too…unequal?

No, he decided, it all depended on your expectations and how you handled them. The fact was, any time he and Shallie went out together, they encountered his friends, neighbors, acquaintances. There was no opportunity for the kind of discovery an old-fashioned date could provide. Time to change that.

He glanced at Shallie. Her eyes were closed. "Uh, Shallie, are you awake?"

"Yes." She smiled over at him.

"Can I ask you a question?"

"Of course!"

"Would you go out with me?"

"What?"

"On a date, I mean. An old-fashioned, real, honest-to-God date."

She giggled and he was delighted by the sound. "Have we reverted to high school or something?" she asked.

"No." He laughed, too, then explained

what he'd been thinking.

"Where would we go?"

"How about somewhere outside of town? I was thinking about Silver Hills. There's a nice inn there, with an elegant restaurant. That's not a slight against Bailey's, mind you. Her place has its own charm. I'd just like to go somewhere that would give us some privacy, a little solitude. If you like that idea."

"I love it! My answer is an unqualified **yes**."

Feeling a rush of excitement, he said, "I'll make the reservation. And the animal-care arrangements."

Carly climbed into bed, wearing another long T-shirt of Susan's, this one with an I Love New York logo. The first thing she did was haul out her makeshift journal. She wrote the date at the top of a fresh page, chewed the end of her pen for a moment, then began to write.

Today was the beginning of the beginning. A **new** beginning. I truly believe that. I'd be happy if

Cord turns out to be my dad. Or
if it's Eli or J.P., that would be
really good, too. Cord would
still be in my life. Like, my uncle.
I hope he and Shallie get
married! Then she'd be my
mom—or my aunt.

I was so worried about how
dinner last night would go—and
it was so good. Nobody freaked
out about the YouTube thing—
or the $.

I know I keep saying this, but
I just **love** the people I've met
here. Including Len and Mary
Jean. I adore the animals. I'm
thrilled about the chance to get
more music experience, to learn
from Aaron and Ted and the
others.

I feel so lucky, and a month
ago I couldn't have said that.
Didn't think I'd ever be able to
say that.

I've heard about "gratitude
journals" for years. They seemed

totally pointless, in my life,
anyway. Now I finally have all
kinds of things to write in one!

She closed the notebook, attached the pen by its clip and set the book on her nightstand. Next, she found a country-blues station on her laptop and let it play softly, lulling her to sleep.

Once again, Russ called **way** too early, abruptly waking her from another vivid dream about Cord. This time the two of them were riding crazy-fast across a field. He was on Chief. She was on the Black Stallion...

Russell's voice was practically trembling. "Hey," he began. "I'm ready for our get-together. And I **do** have something else to show for my search." He paused, as though waiting for a comment from her. "You're going to be really happy with it," he finally said.

"Thanks. We're still good for lunch?"

"Yeah. I can't wait till you see what I've got!"

"Me, neither. Pizza still okay with you?"

"For sure!"

When their call ended, Shallie got up, rousing Bandit, who'd fallen asleep beside her bed again. "Okay, my little man. Let me put on some respectable clothes and then down we go."

Tail wagging, he met her at the door and they hurried downstairs, Shallie careful not to trip over him—or trip him up. Cord, who'd been in bed with her during a night of sleeping in each other's arms, was already in the kitchen and busy making coffee, the usual scenario. He smiled. After some serious kissing and hugging last night, they decided they were both too tired for anything else, following the emotionally exhausting discussion with Carly. Tonight, though...

She moved toward him and he leaned forward to kiss her, a kiss that lengthened as she responded, putting both arms around him, her tongue meeting his. Before their embrace and their kiss could go too far—Tina would be joining them any minute—she released him and accepted the coffee he handed her. As he let the dogs out, she filled their bowls.

When the pack of two reemerged, she pointed to their breakfast and said, "There, dum-dums, as Brynne would say." They didn't have to be told twice.

Cord shook his head in mock disapproval. "She calls **us** that—or at least Eli, J.P. and me—not her canine guests."

"True. Well, speaking of dum-dums but not really, guess who's already phoned me?"

"Russ? Jeez, it's barely nine."

She yawned for effect, then said, "I'll help out with the horses this morning, and then I'll drive over. I can drop Carly off downtown if she wants."

"Downtown?"

"You know what I mean."

"I'm sure she'll be thrilled about visiting Main Street."

Shallie ignored his sarcasm. "Well, I'm not sure about **thrilled**, but it's up to her."

"Any further word from Eddie?" he asked.

She shook her head. "Nothing yet. You?"

"Me, neither. Want to sit on the porch with our coffee. And some toast?"

"I'd like that."

Once they were seated in what had become "their" chairs, Bandit and Smoky on either side, he said, "I'll make a reservation at the place in Silver Hills today. Any evening that is or isn't good for you?"

"Nope. Whatever you choose will be fine." She gave him an exaggerated wink. "Like I have **so** many commitments in this town."

"One more question. How would you feel about spending the night at the inn?"

"My answer is **yes**. Another unqualified yes. Does that take care of it?"

"Oh, yeah!" He grinned and she loved it. Loved the way his mouth widened and his eyes crinkled. "Exactly what I was hoping to hear."

"Now, let me get that order of toast I promised you." As he stood to go inside, both dogs came to their feet. "Guys," he said, pointing at them. "Don't need your help. Stay out here and entertain your guest." Minutes later he was back with two plates of buttered whole wheat toast, small bowls of jam and peanut butter on the side.

And then they left for the barn to feed the horses and turn them into the pasture, except for Patience, the new addition. They spent an hour with her; she was already comfortable with them.

As they returned to the porch, Mitch and Tina arrived with Carly—who was happy to accept Shallie's offer of a drive "downtown." She had plans to visit The Real Bean, possibly get together with Lindsey, and Shallie was pleased she'd made a friend. Their conversation in the car was jovial and didn't touch on what had happened the night before. Shallie dropped her off near the café, said she'd text her about the pickup time, then went directly to the pizza place. Damn, it was lunchtime. She should've called in her order, but ended up waiting only twenty minutes and walked out with a small veggie pizza and a large chicken parm.

Driving the still-familiar route south of town, Shallie reached the motel, encountering next to no traffic. Needless to say, there weren't any other cars in the lot. Russ kept his decrepit old station wagon—inherited from Norm—in a falling-down garage behind the building. Sitting in her rental, she waited for several minutes, nervously wondering what to expect. Would this really be the clue they needed? Or would it add to the confusion about Christine Fletcher? Would it make her feel better or worse, more optimistic or disheartened?

Carrying the pizza boxes, she walked to the office door—which opened immediately. Russ gestured her inside.

They sat in the office, which had been further cleaned up, somewhat decluttered and reorganized since she'd last been there. They started with the pizza and a glass of bourbon Russ insisted on (hers with **lots** of ice). Shallie was more than a little impatient to have this conversation, but left the timing up to him. Finally, after he'd finished almost his entire pizza and she'd eaten half of hers, leaving the rest for him, he said, "You ready?"

It was all she could do not to shout, **Yes! I've been ready for hours.** But she simply nodded.

First he removed the remains of their meal, then poured himself another drink. He reached inside the top desk drawer and carefully handed her a crumpled sheet of paper. "I found this inside a cardboard box in the basement," he said. "No envelope. She must've left it the night I overheard that phone call." He paused for a moment. "Tell you the truth, I didn't expect to find **anything** down there."

It was a handwritten letter. From Christine to Della and dated September 12, thirty-three years ago, when Shallie was two.

Dear Della,
Thank you for being such a good sister—and wonderful aunt to

Shallie. And thanks to you and Norm for understanding the danger we're in.

My husband is after me again. He called here this evening. So I'm leaving **now** and trusting you with Shallie's care. Try to get in with foster services to help pay for her needs. As you know, I have no money to leave you, just have a few hundred dollars in cash. I've left her birth certificate, as well. Please give it to her once she hits her teens.

I don't know where I'm going, but I do know I won't be able to get in touch. At least not for years. If ever...

Please tell her I've always loved her and always will. She'll be on my mind forever. And please let Shallie know I'm doing this **because** I love her. I'm doing it to protect her.

Thanks to both of you for letting me stay here and for being the

family my daughter and I needed.
Love
Christine

Shallie felt completely shaken. "But to be honest, none of this is…totally unexpected. Still, I should pass it, or at least a copy, on to Eddie."

Russ agreed. "Uh, I have something else for you."

Shallie could hardly imagine what that might be; having this letter was more than she'd ever dared hope.

He took another object from the drawer, this one a frayed and discolored photo packet. She accepted it, hands trembling.

She opened it. The photos—just five—were faded and the edges torn. Unbelievable as it might seem to most people, she'd never seen a picture of Christine Fletcher before. But this was unmistakably her. Reddish-brown hair, eyes the same color and shape as hers… The resemblance was clearly there. **My mother.**

One of the photos showed Christine holding a tiny baby. Had to be her. **Had** to be. Shallie turned it over to look at the back. "Christine and Shallie" was written in Della's best handwriting, followed by the date: Feb. 10, 1984. She turned over another one; this time she was sitting by herself on the bedraggled gray sofa (no doubt still in Russ's living room); she wore a too-large frilly yellow dress, the frills rather limp. "Happy 2nd Birthday, Shallie! June 21."

There was one picture of the twins, sitting on either side of Christine on that same sofa. Another of Norm with his arm around Della. And a final one of Della bouncing Shallie on her knee.

Putting the photos down, Shallie knew she was going to cry. She sniffled and dragged the back of one hand across her face. She'd finally seen real evidence of her childhood, her earliest years. And the letter from Christine had changed some of her feelings about this woman, her mother. Who hadn't simply deserted her. Who'd **loved** her.

"The pictures and the letter—they're for you to keep. You could scan them or get Cord to do it and email 'em to Eddie. But they're yours." He shook his head. "I have no idea why Della never gave you these photos. She probably forgot she even had 'em."

"We'll never know. Doesn't matter anymore." The tears were more persistent now. "Thank you," she said in a shaky voice.

"Here." He stood up to get the box of tissues on his desk. She accepted one with another "Thanks," and gave Russ a hug. He returned it, his own arms loose around her. Then he stepped back, picked up his glass and held it out. "Here. For strength," he joked. "Not that it ever gave **them** much strength."

Shallie forced a laugh and took a small sip. "I should go. Carly's waiting for me. I'll send her a quick text that I'm on my way." She did, then glanced up at him again. "Russ, I'm so grateful."

"Hey, we'll see each other soon. And meanwhile, I'll keep looking."

CHAPTER FIFTEEN

On her brief walk to the café once Shallie had dropped her off, Carly checked her cell, leaning against the building's corner. No emails from anyone she cared about. A few ads and sales "alerts," the usual stuff, which she deleted. As she scrolled through news highlights, she suddenly heard a distressed sound from behind the Bean. A high-pitched shriek. Then, "Quit it! I **know** you did it. Don't threaten me!"

The girl's voice sounded familiar. Was that **Lindsey Morgan**? Carly wasn't sure, but darted into the narrow alley between the Bean and the flower shop next door, phone held in front of her. She slipped behind the building, where the garbage and compost cans were kept. And yes, it was Lindsey. With Eric Worth standing directly in front of her.

Eric was muttering something about how Lindsey "better not say anything." At least, Carly saw with relief, he wasn't touching her. She ran toward them, yelling, "Let her go!" He kind of scared her, but she acted instinctively because Lindsey needed her help.

"Get lost," he snarled.

"No, **you** get lost! 'Cause I'm calling the sheriff. And you know what's going to happen then."

Eric spat in disgust, narrowly missing Lindsey's shoes. "Bitch!" He turned abruptly, shoving her away, and raced out of the alley. "Both of you! Bitches! You don't know anything. Can't prove anything."

Carly took her friend's arm. "Come on. We're getting a coffee." She led her inside, selected a table near the back, then hurried to the counter to order two coffees and a plate of chocolate chip cookies. Not the healthiest—and probably not as good as Tina's—but this was a time for comfort food.

Once they'd relaxed for a few minutes, Carly clasped Lindsey's hand. "So what's going on?" She'd begun to guess some of it, but why leave to guesswork what evidence could provide?

Lindsey closed her eyes for a moment. "You know, the whole thing about animals—cows and sheep and horses—being released from their pens and paddocks? Not stolen, but...let go? Well, I just found out that Eric's behind it."

Carly made what she considered a heroic effort to stay calm. Not to react. Still holding Lindsey's hand, she said, "Tell me **how** you found out."

Lindsey sighed. "His cell phone, of course. He had photos on it, selfies of him basically committing the crimes, and he was stupid enough to leave it on the table here while he went to the bathroom. And it wasn't only him. Some of his loser friends, like Jeff Nolan and Freddie Lansing, were part of it, too.

They're in a few of the photos, so I know who they are." After a tearful pause, she shook her head. "I'm sure he's already deleted the pictures."

"We can't ignore this," Carly said decisively.

Lindsey nodded.

"All right, I'm going to get Eli's cell number from Cord right now, and then I'll call him, make an appointment for us. Okay?"

Another nod.

Carly texted Cord with a vague message and received Eli's private cell number minutes later. No questions from Cord, just the info she'd requested. She left Eli a voice mail, explaining that she and Lindsey urgently needed to meet with him. He got back to her in a minute or so, and said he'd see them at the office in half an hour.

Fortunately, Shallie turned up as they finished their coffee—Carly had missed her text. Lindsey told her what had just happened, how threatening Eric had been and that Eli was expecting them at

his office. Shallie immediately offered to
drive them. No questions on her part,
either. Her only comment was a muttered remark about who the **real** "gatecrashers" in this town were. "And I'm
talking about farm gates and paddock
gates, but I'm sure you get that." Despite
the situation, Carly had to smile. She
was more grateful than ever for Shallie's
unwavering support and her sense of
humor. Her love, when you came right
down to it. She was also convinced that
she and Lindsey were destined to be
friends.

Carly had no idea how this official visit
would go and felt nervous about it—
especially since they were providing the
sheriff with proof that his nephew was
guilty of a crime, currently the town's
most notorious—but there was no other
option.

They left the café, and the two of them
piled into Shallie's rental.

Eli had been waiting for them. His
admin, Kathy Roberts, who was Perry's

cousin, ushered the girls into the private room he'd reserved for their conversation —and he wasn't surprised to see that Shallie had accompanied them.

Once he'd heard the story, he had to admit, to himself, anyway, that none of this was the shock Shallie and the girls had probably expected. He should've had a serious talk with his sister, Sara, a lot earlier. Should've had a major confrontation with his nephew. Well, it was coming now.

He wished he'd acted on his suspicions, wished he'd taken them even more seriously.

During their discussion, he took careful notes. Then assured the three of them that this would be dealt with—**firmly** dealt with, and Eric's misdemeanors, plus those of his "gang," had just come to an end. Lindsey seemed worried about repercussions, and Carly knew that was because she and Eric had dated for a while, but Eli told her not to worry. He said she could call his private number anytime. Carly, too.

"Um," Carly began awkwardly. "Can I ask what Eric's family situation is?" She shrugged. "I don't know anything about him, other than that he's an asshole. Sorry! He's your nephew and—"

"No need to apologize. His father took off years ago. No one has any idea where he is."

"He always told me his dad was a hundred percent out of the picture," Lindsey put in.

"True," Eli said. "Zach Worth was a useless piece of shit." He glanced at Shallie. "Sorry. My turn to apologize. I swear too much."

Shallie grinned. "Not a problem for me. And sometimes it's the most appropriate response."

"And this is one of those times," Carly said.

Shallie stood. "We should let you get back to work, Eli. Let us know if there's anything else you need from us."

He nodded. "Thank you for your honesty and courage," he told the girls. "I know it was hard to report Eric—for a number of reasons."

"Courage?" Carly repeated, sounding a little panicked.

"Don't worry, everything's going to be fine." He tightened his mouth. "I'll make **sure** of that."

When they'd left, Eli thought through his plans. First, he'd go to Sara's and insist on seeing Eric. Then he'd seize his cell phone; if Eric had deleted the photos, Eli's deputy Oliver would be able to recover them. He was a tech geek who had some very handy skills.

Charges might have to be filed, which meant Eric would need a lawyer. In the interim, until he knew where everything stood, he'd place the kid under the equivalent of house arrest. When he was finished with Eric—for tonight— he'd have to pay visits to the rest of his nephew's so-called friends; Lindsey had listed their names. Then, tomorrow, he'd contact the various ranchers and farmers who'd been affected by their actions, who'd made complaints. He supposed there was a possibility they'd settle for reimbursement, apologies and serious community service from Eric and his companions. Not that **he** could suggest it; a decision of that kind was up to them.

Eli got in his patrol car and drove the five minutes to Sara's place on Sky Street, off Main. She worked the first shift at a county day care and should be home by now. Yep, her car was in the driveway. He parked behind it, then stepped out, walking slowly to the house. He felt deluged by emotions, contradictory ones—intense anger toward Eric, pity for Sara, even pity for her son. Fury at Eric's father, the jerk who'd abandoned his family. Embarrassment for Sara, for Eric's younger sister, Hayley —for himself. Everyone knew the kid was his nephew. He'd been thinking for some time now that he should've taken a more paternal role, but his work hours had made that difficult. And Eric's behavior had only recently become a problem, which Eli had to admit was no excuse.

Well, things were about to change.

He straightened, then banged loudly at the door. When Sara opened it, she said, "Oh, hi! You should've told me you were coming. I'd—"

He gave her a quick hug. "Never mind that. Where's Eric?"

She seemed surprised by his tone. "He's in the basement, watching TV. I think..."

"Could you get him? We need to have a conversation, and I need you to be present."

Her eyes grew large, her expression scared. "O-okay," she stammered. "What's wrong?"

He shook his head, wondering if the little bastard really was in the basement. Or hiding out with one of his loser friends, like Jack "Ass" Martin, as he was known, or Freddie Lansing. But he could hear stomping on the basement stairs and loud complaints that were obviously coming from Eric. Sara was keeping her voice down.

Eric slammed open the door and hurled

himself through. Eli guessed he was half-drunk. Or half-stoned.

"Yeah?" he shouted in a belligerent tone. "What the hell do you want?"

"Eric!" Sara said.

"Oh, I think you know." Eli turned to Sara. "Is Hayley up in her room?"

She nodded.

"Good. Okay, everybody, sit."

Sara and Eli did; Eric refused and remained standing.

"Fine," Eli said. "First things first. Give me your cell phone."

"No way! You have no right to—"

"Oh, yes, I do. In fact, I can arrest you and I'm about two seconds away from doing it."

That was when Sara started to cry. "What's **wrong**?" she asked again between sobs.

Eli turned to face her. "I'm sorry to tell you this, Sara. But your son appears to be guilty of a serious crime. He's the one who's been releasing animals— with the assistance of his so-called friends."

"Damn it!" Sara shrieked, and that was heavy-duty swearing for her. "Give him your phone, damn it! **Now!**" Tears were rushing down her cheeks.

Frowning, Eric reached into his back pocket and handed over his cell.

"Your password?"

He recited the numbers and Eli quickly got in and found the photos—which were exactly as Lindsey had described. Hard to believe he hadn't deleted them. Clichéd though it was, maybe he **wanted** to get caught?

"Ready to make a confession?" Eli asked.

"Yeah. I did it. Don't blame my friends. It was all me."

"I doubt that, and these pictures are evidence to the contrary. But I do believe that you're the ringleader here. **Why**, Eric?"

"Yes, why?" his mother sobbed.

"I guess I'm just an asshole, like everybody says." There was no hiding the tears that had begun to seep out.

"You realize charges will probably be

filed, and that means you'll end up in court. I'd say there's a good chance of jail. At the very least, you'll have to compensate the people whose lives you've affected. Some of those animals **died**, you jerk!"

"I'm sorry! I didn't mean for that to happen!"

"Then what was the point?"

"I just wanted to...I don't know." He paused. "I hated seeing them trapped. Behind those fences and stuff..."

Was this bullshit? A rationalization of sorts? A convenient lie? And even if it was something Eric actually believed, Eli doubted any of his accomplices had that kind of motive.

Eli couldn't help wondering if Eric's comment meant he felt trapped himself. Just in case there was some truth to that implication, he added, "Another thing we'll request is a psychiatric assessment and likely a therapist. Your friends will be facing the same pro-cedures."

Sara nodded. "Yes! He needs help and

I can't do it!"

"Don't worry. We'll take care of it." He turned back to Eric. "Anyone else involved, besides the guys in the pictures? And don't bother trying to protect any of 'em."

Eric shook his head. "Just them."

"All right. I'll be making a few other visits tonight. Now, here are the rules. You do not leave this house. You will give your mother your keys. I'll keep your cell phone. You will not communicate with anyone unless or until I give you permission. And you will apologize to Lindsey and Carly—by written letter, which you will pass to me. Do you understand?"

"Yes..."

"I'll see if I can take tomorrow off," Sara said in a tremulous voice.

"You shouldn't have to, Sara. But it's up to you." He walked to the front door. "I'll be in touch. Soon."

Then he left, after giving his sister another hug. Eric ignored him. Eli felt only compassion for Sara—and even greater fury toward Eric and his piece-of-shit father.

Nothing more he could do here to-night. Time to make a few other visits…

Carly got up Saturday morning, feeling both relieved—because Eli was taking care of the Eric Worthless mess—and excited. She and Tina were going over to Meg Simon's house so Carly could meet her and the cats.

She dressed quickly, choosing another Susan T-shirt (she sure owned a lot!). This one appropriately proclaiming that "I Love Cats and They Love Me," with the sweetest photo of a young woman surrounded by tabbies and Persians and a Siamese.

As soon as she got to the kitchen, Mitch poured her a coffee with exactly the right amount of cream, then returned to his crossword puzzle book. Thanking him with a smile, she took an invigorating sip. Tina walked in then and said she was making scrambled eggs and toast.

"Thanks, Tina, but let me help."

"No, no. This won't take long. Why don't you help Mitch with his puzzle instead?"

"If I can…"

He moved the book in her direction. "This one's all about popular music. That should be right up your alley. Now, who sang 'One Too Many Mornings'?"

"Mitch! It's Bob Dylan, of course."

"Hey, just funning. I knew that. How about 'Hallelujah'?"

"It's a Leonard Cohen song! Probably his best known." She began to hum the first lines.

Their puzzle solving went on until Tina presented them with plates of cheesy scrambled eggs and toast. "How come you know so much about all these old-time songs and musicians?" Mitch asked. "They're our generation, not yours."

"Well, for one thing, they're classics. And…I learned them from my mom." That was part of why she loved those songs and it was one of her most important memories.

"We only met Reba a few times," Tina said.

"You would've loved her if you'd had a chance to really know her."

Tina nodded, a thoughtful nod, then changed the subject. "I see that Russ, over at the motel, is getting out more. He knew Reba from way back. You met him, remember? That night at Cord's?"

"Oh, yeah. He's a little...odd, but—"

"Always was."

"But he seems decent."

"He is. He's just kept to himself too much. I'm glad to see him discovering life again."

"I'll bet what made the difference is Shallie coming back to town," Carly suggested.

"I'll bet you're right."

"What time is Meg expecting us?"

"Around ten," Tina replied, "so we'll leave at nine thirty. Anything you need to do before we go?"

"Not really."

"Okay." Mitch clasped his hands on

the table. "Give us a quick rundown on the Eric Worth situation."

"If you're okay with doing that," Tina said, "we'd like to hear."

Their request startled Carly, but she realized Shallie must have talked to Cord yesterday afternoon, and he'd probably told Mitch some of it, and naturally Mitch had told Tina.

She began with her visit to the coffee shop, ending with the trip to Eli's office. They asked the occasional question, then congratulated her on taking action. "Smart and brave," they agreed, which embarrassed Carly, who thought Lindsey had been the brave one. It also reminded her of Eli's remark about courage.

By now, it was almost time to leave. Carly went to retrieve her purse, tore a few pages from her "journal" to make notes if needed and put on a little make-up. She and Tina got into the SUV, chatting in their usual friendly manner. Carly recognized again how much she loved her, loved Shallie—and that suddenly made her miss Reba so much more.

She tried not to let herself dwell on her loss very often. She didn't understand why her mom had never mentioned Shallie, at least by name, and why Reba had never explained how she'd ended up in this small town, in that dump of a motel. But their meeting—hers and Shallie's—seemed...fated. She gathered from Cord that Reba had been Shallie's protector, a mentor of sorts, for the months she'd been in Painted Pony Creek. And now Shallie was doing the same for **her**.

"We're just about there," Tina said, interrupting Carly's thoughts. She turned into a driveway near the edge of town. The house was small but charming. It had redbrick walls, a well-kept garden, a porch with an old-fashioned swing, and windows with traditional-looking shutters.

"Oh, I should mention. The cats are Logan, a large orange boy of about six, and Plum, a gray tabby with the biggest eyes you've ever seen. She's three or so. They're healthy and lovely, and on Barb's recommendation, Meg doesn't let them out—what with the coyotes and cars around here and all."

"Makes sense to me." Coming from a big city with its heavy traffic, she'd always believed in keeping cats inside. And that way, they'd provide Meg with more companionship, too.

She and Tina approached the door, up a short flight of steps, and Tina knocked. A minute or two later, Meg opened it. She was probably in her late sixties, attractive but too thin. Her hair, which she'd lost to chemo, was starting to grow back, looking sparse and spiky. Her smile was warm and reflected in her eyes. "Hi, Tina! And you must be Carly. Hi, darling." She reached forward, enfolding first Tina and then Carly in a hug. "Come on in and meet the fur babies."

As they followed her, the cats—precisely as described by Tina—came rushing toward them, and Carly immediately bent to stroke Logan, then picked up Plum who was purring madly. "Hey, sweeties! I'm so glad to meet you." Glancing up at Meg, she said, "They're adorable!"

"I think so, too."

Meg had them sit in her living room, with its fireplace and antique chairs. When coffee or tea had been declined by her guests, she turned to Carly. "You've probably heard that I'm going through chemo for breast cancer."

"I...didn't know the details. Just about the chemo." She felt her eyes fill with tears. "My mom died of breast cancer."

"Oh, God, I'm so sorry!"

"Thank you. She got diagnosed too late." And part of the reason was that Reba had ignored her symptoms and avoided seeing her doctor...

"I've been lucky—if that's a word you can associate with cancer. It hasn't spread and the chemo seems to be working. Afterward, I'll be having radiation." She glanced down at Logan, sitting by her feet. "Listen, Carly. I'm so grateful you're willing to help me out, supporting me, supporting my pets."

Carly stood up and hurried to Meg's chair, leaning over to hug her carefully. She could feel her protruding ribs, her fragile shoulders. "And I'm happy to be doing this. I'd be happy to do it for other people—and animals, too."

"Does that mean you'll be staying in Painted Pony Creek?"

The question was unexpected but shouldn't have been. "Uh, I hope so." She didn't want to expand on her situation, not yet, anyway, and Tina obviously hadn't.

"You'll be going to the county high school?"

"Yes, I hope so," she repeated. She hadn't given it much consideration, but regardless of which man turned out to be her dad, regardless of where she ended up, she planned to continue her education. Or rather, resume it.

Unlike her mom…

"Good." Meg nodded. "My kids attended that school and so did Tina's. And they all went on to live successful lives. Now, you've met my feline community. Do you have any questions for me?"

Carly took out her pages and pen and made notes as Meg gave her the cats' feeding and care instructions.

Meg went through her treatment schedule. "My next chemo's in four days at a cancer hospital in Missoula, and every two weeks after that. I'll be away overnight on my chemo days, staying with my son or daughter. I'll leave you their contact info."

After the comment about staying with her family, Meg explained that she'd been a widow for six years. "We're very close, my kids and I, especially since my husband died."

Carly murmured her condolences.

"He died of cancer, too. Melanoma. I still have a hard time with losing him, and so do our kids."

Again, Carly couldn't prevent her tears.

Meg lurched to her feet and came toward her with Tina's help; she knelt— a laborious process—and slid both arms around her and kissed her on one cheek, then the other. "Carly, I get some of what you're going through. Your mom —and at such a young age for both of you. Anytime you want to talk, let me know."

"I will! Thank you..."

Tina hugged Meg, too, her own eyes noticeably damp.

"Aren't we a huggy group today?" Meg joked.

"Hey, that's better than muggy," Tina joked back. "We'll see you soon, okay? And we'll see Logan and Plum in a few days."

Meg handed Carly her house key, attached to a cat-shaped ring, before they left. "This is your copy. The fact that I'm giving you this tells you how much I trust you."

"Your trust is not misplaced," Tina said quietly. "I guarantee it." Carly looked up at her gratefully.

"I'll need your help when I'm away for treatments," Meg continued, "and for a day or two once I'm back. Is that okay? Also, I'm willing to pay you..."

"No!" Carly insisted. "I **want** to do this."

Carly sat on the floor to kiss the cats goodbye. "Love you," she whispered. "And love your mommy." After their protracted farewells, human and animal, Carly and Tina got into the car again, and at Tina's suggestion, stopped at Bailey's for lunch. They were served by Miranda and enjoyed more back-and-forth joking—and their large order of nachos. "I'm thrilled to be doing this," Carly told her. "And I'm going to sing lullabies to those adorable critters! But —" she frowned "—how will I get to the house? You won't always be able to drive me."

"Don't worry. Like I said, we'll sort something out."

Carly decided to simply trust her.

Cord was serving himself and Mitch some chili, left over from yesterday's dinner, when he got a phone call.

It was the two veterinary students from

Montana State University, Karen Christie and Joey Knight, who'd been in touch a few days earlier. They would arrive in a week, Karen said, if that was okay. She also repeated that they'd read some of the more recent material on his site, regarding therapy horses, and this was an area of interest for them.

After a moment's hesitation, he agreed with their plan and said he'd get back to them about lodging. The options? Have Shallie move into his room so the guest suite would be available? He wanted to do that, but was she ready? Having Karen and Joey stay at the elegant but expensive Big Sky Inn on the other side of town, as many of his clients had, was another possibility. However, they were students, with limited resources, as Karen had pointed out when they'd ended their conversation. Or— and this never would have occurred to him before—maybe they could get a couple of rooms at Russ's motel cleaned up, with repairs made as needed. Cord was willing to assume the cost. He'd ask

Shallie what she thought; in fact, he'd ask Mitch and Tina, too.

Mitch felt it was a reasonable plan, if Russ consented. And there was no way of knowing whether he would until someone—preferably Shallie—had spoken to him.

As they finished their lunch and their discussion, Tina and Carly reappeared, and Shallie came in right after with the dogs, having taken them for a long ramble.

"Chili, anyone?" Cord offered.

Tina and Carly had grabbed a salad at Bailey's, while Shallie said she'd eaten a late breakfast and wasn't hungry yet —but she'd take one of Tina's blueberry muffins. "I'll have one, too," Mitch agreed enthusiastically.

Cord began by asking Carly about her morning with Meg. "Loved it! Love her, love the cats." She gave a quick shrug. "We'll have to work out rides, though. And Meg, Tina and I will need to set up a schedule."

"I admire you for doing this," Cord said,

and both Mitch and Shallie chimed in. "Whatever we can do to help, we will. And that includes driving you there." Nods all around.

"Now on another subject, Shallie, those new clients I mentioned are con- firmed." He paused. "This couple—not sure if they're a couple in **that** sense— they want to pursue horse therapy. As I said earlier, I'm hoping you'll be able to stay another couple of weeks." He realized they'd never really discussed the duration of her stay—beyond the original two weeks and then the exten- sion to work with the Lewises. "You're still on leave from work, right?" He wasn't clear on the arrangements she'd made; she'd never really said. Was it a longer period than he'd assumed?

"Right. And yes, I can do that. I love that they're interested in working with therapy horses!"

"That's a major reason they're coming here," he replied. "We're developing a reputation in that area. I have another question, though. Obviously I can't make the guest suite available to them. And don't even suggest sleeping in the den." He didn't bother to mention the junk room, which had been his bedroom as a boy. "The Big Sky Inn is far too costly. But what would you think about approaching Russ, ask him if he'd be willing to get a couple of rooms fixed up? I'll help absorb the cost, plus their stay."

Everyone and, most important, Shallie, applauded the plan. She said this would be good for Russ and volunteered to help clean, as did Tina and Carly. Mitch offered to handle any small repairs. "I'll call him right now," Shallie announced. "If he's agreeable, we'll start next week."

She called. He was, and plans were made.

The next morning, Cord had just finished his first long coffee in the kitchen, dogs fed and "outed," as Carly liked to call it, when the phone rang—Ted Lewis. "Hi, Cord. How ya doin'?"

"Okay. You?"

"Same. Listen, I have a favor to ask.

Could The GateCrashers have a small concert at your place in August? The twenty-fourth? Two reasons. It'll be part of the celebration for Tina's sixty-fifth birthday, which is on the twenty-third—"

"Holy crap!" Cord interrupted. "I'd forgotten all about that."

"Oh, trust me, there are plenty of us who would've reminded you, including Tina herself, I'll bet. The other reason is that we're all really impressed with Carly and want to officially include her."

"Great! Yeah, we'll definitely do that. What about rehearsals?"

"We'll set up a few—maybe one or two at your place?" When Cord murmured a yes, Ted continued, "Would you let her know? Also, if Carly has any songs of her own..."

"I'll tell her, and I'll encourage her to start writing songs, if she hasn't already."

Cord tried calling her. No answer, so he left a message, then hurried out to the stables.

Still in bed, Carly received Cord's

message and almost burst into tears yet again. Had she ever cried more in her life? But for completely different reasons that had nothing to do with feelings of grief and rejection. It was the kindness of these people, their boundless generosity.

She pulled on her stretch jeans and a blue-and-green-plaid cotton shirt, one of the few pieces of clothing she had that used to belong to her mom. Then she flounced into the kitchen, self-conscious and at the same time ecstatic.

"Hey," Mitch said, raising his cup. "You look happy as all get-out."

"I am! Did you hear I'm going to be singing with The GateCrashers?" She didn't mention Tina's birthday, since she wasn't sure if this was planned as a surprise.

Tina didn't mention it, either, merely smiled as she poured her a coffee with, as usual, the perfect amount of cream. "Aaron told me. Plus, they want you to write a song or two of your own."

"I know! And I want to!"

"Any ideas?" Mitch asked.

"I'll get serious about it today. When we come back from cleaning the motel..."

Tina smiled again. "Good for you, kiddo! And I'll lay odds that there'll be something about animals in at least one of your songs."

Cord-like, Carly rolled her eyes. "Gee, am I really that obvious?"

"Yep," Mitch said cheerfully. "Sure are."

"Don't worry," Tina threw in. "We like it!"

Carly's phone buzzed. She put down her mug when she recognized the Lewises' number. "Hello? Hi, Mary Jean! I heard about the concert today. I'm so excited. I'll give Ted and Aaron a call this morning."

"We're **all** thrilled. And so, of course, is Holly. We'll be bringing her to the concert. We're looking forward to it. Ted's going to confirm the precise date, and we'll stay at his place for the week-end. We'll get together for dinner with you guys, too. We'll go to the center of your universe."

Carly couldn't help giggling. "Sounds good and see you then."

Song topics. Animals, all kinds of them. Ranches. Western beauty, Western life, which she now felt she'd begun to understand. Mothers, one in particular. Fathers. Friends. Love...

CHAPTER SIXTEEN

Shallie checked her car rental information online. She'd had the car for more than three weeks now. She hadn't honestly expected to be here that long—although she'd been willing to consider the possibility. Better return this thing to the rental agency, today if possible.

She'd rented it at the airport in Billings, and driving there and back meant about six hours. She and Cord had talked about it; he had an important meeting at the sheriff's office, but suggested Tina might be able to do it. Before she could ask Tina, she got a call from Russ.

"What are you doing this week?" he asked.

"One thing I need to do is return my rental to the airport. I'm not sure who's—"

"Why didn't you ask me? I can do it. I'll drive my car to Billings with you, then take you back."

"Thanks! That would be a huge help."

"Hey, it's not like my schedule's over-booked—or booked at all," he added wryly.

Shallie still found herself a little sur-prised when he expressed that kind of self-deprecating humor.

"When do you want to go?" he went on to ask.

"What about today?"

"Works for me. Why don't we meet here, 'cause I'm closer to the highway? Nine thirty?"

"See you then!" She started to thank him a second time, but he'd already hung up.

Half an hour later, she pulled into the motel parking lot. Russ was already in his car, waiting. They set off a moment later. He was a slow, careful driver and she frequently lost sight of him in her rearview mirror.

Arriving at the airport, Shallie turned in her car, then waited at the entrance while he parked his, thinking they'd find a restaurant inside for a quick lunch. When he finally showed up, he asked if they could walk around the airport for a while first, confessing he'd never flown before, never been anywhere but Painted Pony Creek and its surrounding area. "We'll have to change that," Shallie said. If she did return to Seattle, she'd invite him to visit...

Russ commented on almost everything they passed, stopping to read the arrival and departure boards and to gawk at staff in their uniforms. Half an hour later, she finally succeeded in getting him to choose a place to eat, and they had lunch at a chain bar with windows looking out on the tarmac. He was so fascinated by the loading and unloading of planes that conversation was minimal— although Shallie did manage to arrange a day for the motel-cleaning project. Monday, they decided.

Driving home with him, she was afraid all their talk would be of airports and airplanes, but then he brought up Christine and Bethanne. "They're the big questions for us, aren't they?" he said. "We need to find out what happened to both of them."

"We do. You and I have had enough losses in our lives."

He nodded. "The way Della died, and then Norm so soon after—it still bothers me, too. But at least there was no mystery there." That seemed to be enough personal conversation for him, and he flipped on the car's radio.

Eli had sent out word the night before that he planned to hold a meeting at his office at ten thirty. He'd invited the ranchers and farmers who'd been affected, in any way and to any degree, by his idiot nephew's actions. He'd also included most of the people involved in the patrols, except Russ, who was driving to the airport with Shallie. Cord and Mitch, for instance, would have a valuable role to play; they knew the community and its landscape well, they knew Eric—to the extent that anyone could—and their opinions were respected.

Once everyone was seated, with Deputy Amos Edwards at the opposite end of the table, Eli began the meeting. He recounted the information concerning Eric and how his guilt had come to light, then said his nephew was at Sara's but would join them now, if anyone wanted the opportunity to talk to him personally.

"As you all know," Eli said, "he's my nephew. But that means **nothing**. This isn't about family. I called you all together to see how you feel about Eric Worth, what he's admitted to doing—which includes recruiting the rest of them. And since this is a community issue, I want to see how, from your point of view, it should be handled." Eli paused. "Do you want to launch lawsuits against him and the others? Do you want to see charges filed? You could choose to pursue theft, damage to property, cruelty to animals...What do you see as the right thing to do?" He paused again. "Eric's virtually under house arrest and prohibited from contacting any of his companions in crime."

There were whispered conversations around the table. Mitch sat back, arms folded, and Eli guessed he'd go along with Cord's preference.

Finally, Miles Carey spoke up. "Okay, here's what I think. First, this is a messed-up boy, which isn't entirely his own fault."

Eli nodded grimly.

"Not blaming you or Sara," Miles went on. "We all know his father did a lot of damage. But Eric's almost an adult now, and it's time for him to act like one."

"I agree," Cord said. "None of us wants to see his life destroyed and Sara's life damaged. I'd insist on what would basically be a form of probation. With supervision. He needs to pay for what he's done, and the best way is to have him do some work for all his victims.

Make sure he learns what we do and gets to know animals. That he understands he affected the entire community because of his actions."

"Hey, I forgot to tell you something," another rancher named Clarence Todd said next. "I got my missing calf back! My son found him nosing around the barn door. What a relief! I can't even tell you..."

"Good to hear," Eli said. "**Really** good."

Everyone echoed that sentiment, and Amos added, "I think that leaves only one animal unaccounted for at this time." He glanced at his notes. "A pet donkey belonging to your neighbor, Joanne Berg, and her little girl." Looking up, he said, "She's told me how much Caroline misses Eeyore. I know we'll all keep an eye out."

"My son and I will do another search," Clarence promised. "Joanne couldn't make it to the meeting today, and she asked me to speak for her."

After a brief silence, Cord turned directly to Eli. "How capable do you think the

418 LINDA LAEL MILLER

little bast—sorry—**Eric** is of recognizing the wrong he did? How capable of redeeming himself, staying on the straight and narrow?"

"I'm probably not the best person to say," Eli replied. "But he'd need to be supervised. Check in regularly with our office. Amos, you up for that?"

"Oh, yeah."

"He'd have to return to school. He dropped out during his final year of high school. Sara and I both talked to him, and we had him see the school counselor but Eric just wasn't...receptive. He said he needed a 'break,' but oh, yeah, he's going back to school this fall."

"I'd add a psychiatric assessment to that, and therapy if necessary," Cord said.

"I already told him as much," Eli responded. The discussion continued along those lines, and then a vote was taken. Everyone present was willing to accept the terms that had been outlined—with the proviso that this would be Eric's one and only chance.

Eli was grateful, saying he and Amos would make their agreement known to his nephew. He was determined to help Eric, to hound him, whatever it took. The boy's companions in crime would receive the same treatment and they'd all be obliged to avoid contact with each other.

In other words, his nephew was getting a second chance. Oh, boy, that kid owed him! And speaking of what was owed...

He pulled Eric's letter of apology to Carly from his pocket and handed it to Cord.

The cleaning session at the motel on Monday morning went as planned, and Carly actually enjoyed it. She and Tina worked on a room together. They'd chosen Room 5, which seemed to be in better shape than most of the others. They vacuumed the ancient rug, dusted, polished the bedside table and rickety desk, and made the bed. Fortunately, there were clean, if very old, sheets and covers hidden away in a closet. Carly went out to pick some wildflowers; she arranged them in a vase she found in Russ's tiny kitchen and placed it on the desk.

Russ and Shallie selected another room across the hall.

All four of them inspected both rooms and declared themselves satisfied. Then they pitched in on the already improved office. Mitch was going to come over later to repair the old sign with its burned out lights.

Shallie suggested Russ consider getting a part-time cleaner soon, and he said he'd think about it.

Then he went out in his "crapmobile," as he called it, to pick up pizza for their lunch. Afterward, Tina drove Carly and Shallie home.

That afternoon, Carly decided to draft a song or two—or at least try. She sat, as usual, under her favorite tree, cradling her laptop.

Her first song had to be about her mother, about the two of them and how their lives together had been. Okay, first stanza.

Life can be hard.
Life can be cruel.

She needed something to rhyme with
"hard"—**card?** That made no sense.
Lard? Come on! She'd change the first
line:

Life can be full of pain.
Life can be cruel.
People treat you with disdain
And call you a fool.

Not bad, she thought.
Next stanza. She'd work out the tune
when she was finished, with the assistance
of Aaron and the others.

Life was cruel to my mother.
It was cruel to me.
People are cruel to each other
And won't just let you be.

Pretty good! And true…as she'd often

seen and experienced.

> **Mom, Mommy, I miss you
>   so much!
> I miss your love, your voice
> And I miss your touch.
> I wish I had some reason
>   to rejoice.**

> **But...I do. I know it.
> Life has brought me comforts...**

She stalled. Memories and thoughts of Reba overwhelmed her with grief, the grief she'd tried so hard and for so long to push aside. To ignore. To move past. But it couldn't be done. The grief was for both of them, for Reba and for herself. Despite everything that was happy and promising in her life now, despite everything that felt uplifting, depression was dragging her down.

She supposed that, ironically, part of what made her feel so **bad** was the contrast between her present and her past. Between her new sense of purpose and her ongoing grief. Between the love she'd begun to feel for the new people in her life—and the pain and loss that had come before.

She had to admit that another benefit of her YouTube channel was the way she'd been compelled to think about her mom—as well as the dads. They'd all known Reba, all loved her. And being here, in Painted Pony Creek, seeing them regularly, felt like a chance to learn more about her mother, through them and through Shallie...

She wondered if Shallie was back, if they could talk. She hit Save and packed up her laptop, then walked to the ranch house.

Cord was sitting on the porch with his canine companions, taking a break—checking his cell and having a mid-afternoon beer. "Hi!" he called out. "How'd it go?"

"Good. Um, is Shallie still at home?"

"As far as I know."

And then Carly made an abrupt decision. "Do you have a minute?"

"For you? Always. What's up?"

"Just...want to talk to you. But first I want to say that whether you turn out to be my dad or not, I'm really, really grateful for everything you've done to help me. You've all become so important to me. You and Shallie, Tina and Mitch... Eli and J.P."

"You're important to all of us. And not just because of Reba, but because of who and what **you** are, how you've dealt with the incredibly hard circumstances life's handed you."

"Thanks." She took a shaky breath. "I've been thinking about my mom a lot lately. I try not to. But I can't help it. I'm depressed and I can't talk my way out of it right now."

Cord sat forward. "What can I do?"

She wanted to respond, but couldn't, not yet, as tears crowded her eyes. **Again.** "I...I loved my mom," she finally managed. "Still love her. And sometimes the grief just hits me."

"I understand," Cord said quietly.

"We all have hard times," Carly told

him, "I realize that. We all have losses and go through grief. I'm not comparing. But..."

"Your situation is especially difficult. First because you're so young, and Reba died so young, at a very vulnerable age for you. And not knowing who your father is—that doesn't make it any easier. But like I said the other night, whichever one of us is your dad will step up. And then you'll have two uncles, as well."

That was a thought she'd had a number of times now and hearing him say it made her smile.

"You know, my mom...Reba didn't tell me a lot about any of you guys. Or about Shallie. I don't really understand why. All she told me is that you or Eli or J.P. is my dad." Carly had to hesitate for a minute. "She was already in the hospital then. And...and never came out. Stage 4 when it was diagnosed. I spent all my time there." She couldn't disguise her bitterness when she added, "Duncan, her husband, hardly even bothered to show up."

"Man, I wish I could have a private— shall we say, conversation—with that asshole in an alley somewhere."

Regardless of everything, she had to smile again. "I wish you could, too. And I'd want to be there."

"Unlikely it's gonna happen, more's the pity. But let me tell you again—you can count on me. On **all** of us."

"There's something else I should tell you. Something Reba told me. This was about a week before she died. The thing is, she didn't **plan** to get pregnant, whatever anyone else might think. She said she really did love all you guys, in different ways. And she knew she messed up. She also told me she had a close friend here, when she was living at the motel, but they lost touch. I guess that would've been Shallie."

Cord nodded. "Thanks for telling me—"

"That I was an accident? Unintentional?"

"You were her daughter, she **loved**

you, and nothing matters more than that."

"I agree." Carly bit her lip, almost hard enough to draw blood. "I loved her, too."

"Should I ask Shallie to come down?"

"In a little while. But if you don't mind, I'd like your opinion about the kind of plans I should make."

"Even if I don't turn out to be your dad? You want my opinion now?"

"Yes, please."

"Number one. Get registered at the county high school here. I know for a fact that it's a good place."

"Oh, 'cause you went there?"

"Isn't that proof enough?" He rolled his eyes, just as she'd known he would. "Seriously, it's well regarded throughout the state. High SAT and literacy scores and all that."

"I'd have to get my transcript, right?"

"Should be easy enough."

"I'll email my old school tomorrow. I did manage to finish tenth grade—with good marks."

"Doesn't surprise me. But I'm im-pressed." He sounded as if he genuinely was. "With all the pain and disruption in your life…"

Carly bowed her head. "So, I'll need to apply there?"

"You do. Use this address for now."

"Have they got a music program?"

"I believe they do. Look it up. I'd definitely want to see you enrolled in that."

She pulled down the neck of her T-shirt to reveal the musical note tattoo. "You know why I have this?"

"Because you're a musical genius?"

"No, but I'm really interested in music, and people seem to think I have some talent." She raised her hand when he seemed about to interrupt. "The main reason is that my mom used to sing to me, at night and in the car and when we went for a walk. All the songs she loved. I didn't tell you that before."

"I didn't hear her sing very often. But there was one night in particular…" His voice trailed off.

"We sang lots of her favorites together. Johnny Cash, Patsy Cline, Bob Dylan, Reba McEntire—"

"Of course," he broke in with a laugh.

"And many more."

"Again, I'm not surprised by what you've told me. But I'm very moved. And I get the tattoo thing now."

"I had it done a few months after she died. It's to commemorate her and to... celebrate our history."

"You still want to talk to Shallie? To be honest, when it comes to dealing with emotional stress, I think she'd be more helpful than me. But you and I will talk later, okay? Whenever you want."

"Okay," she responded and he called Shallie on his cell.

Shallie came down a few minutes later; she and Carly exchanged a long hug.

"What can I do?" Shallie asked, exactly as Cord had. "I'm available to talk anytime you need. You know that."

Carly nodded. "Thanks," she whispered. "I've been feeling bad. About my mom."

"I'm going to suggest setting you up with a therapist I used in Seattle. You can do Skype appointments with her. Would you like that?"

Carly nodded again.

"All right, consider it done."

"Oh, by the way," Cord said, "Eli asked me to pass this on to you." And he gave Carly an envelope. "Let me know if you have any...concerns."

That comment about "concerns" made her wonder, but she wasn't really worried.

Other than her relationship with her mom, she'd never connected with people in a more profound, loving way. Fate, or whatever it was, had finally served her well.

Back under her favorite tree, Carly closed her eyes against the sun. Since the letter Cord had given her came from Eli, she could guess who'd written it. Tearing open the envelope, she pulled out a single sheet of paper, unfolded it and glanced at the signature. Yes, indeed. Eric.

The message was carefully printed by

hand.

> Dear Carly,
> I'm sorry. That's all I can say.
> I was a jerk to give you and
> Lindsey a hard time. You guys
> don't deserve that. I'm sorry for
> all the hurt I caused everyone.
>   I don't know what's wrong
> with me.
>   I'm getting a second chance.
> That's what my uncle Eli says.
> I'm not going to blow it. I'll be
> working with the ranchers and
> farmers I was so unfair to. I'll
> get to learn about animals. And
> I'm going to find that missing
> donkey, I swear it!
>   Please forgive me. I want your
> forgiveness and Lindsey's. I will
> see you around but won't talk to
> you unless you want me to.
> Eric Worth

Despite the lack of details, Carly finally
had a sense of who this boy was, what

he'd gone through, what he hoped to become. What he **could** be.

She decided not to reply at this point. Checking her cell, she saw a text from Ted Lewis. Rehearsal Thursday night. Time to finish her Reba song and do a little work on the tune—then start her next one.

CHAPTER SEVENTEEN

Friday—and almost time for their date. Shallie hadn't been on one for years and was both excited and a little anxious about this evening.

Cord had told her they'd leave at five; he'd made arrangements with Mitch and Tina as well as Carly regarding horse and dog care. The vet students had arrived that morning and offered to help, especially since their lodging was free. Joey and Karen, in their midtwenties, seemed competent and knowledgeable, as Shallie would've expected; they were also charming and friendly. When she asked whether the motel suited them, they both declared it was "perfect" (well, hardly), and mentioned how much they'd enjoyed meeting Russ, who planned to buy them dinner that night.

Shallie thought, with pleasure, of how busy Carly had been the last few days and how happy she seemed. The rehearsal—which took place on the porch and which she and Cord sat in on—had been completely enjoyable. Aaron, Ted and the rest of the band were obviously delighted with their new roles as her mentors, especially in preparing the song about Reba, which she'd titled "Mother and Nature." Shallie had been affected by its emotion and liked the simplicity of the music.

Carly'd had her first Skype session with Loretta, the therapist; they planned to talk again. "It really helped me," she'd told Shallie. "My feelings are...clearer, you know? She said that grief isn't a simple thing and that it doesn't matter how long ago the person died. Grief can come back anytime and hit you hard."

"After my divorce, I experienced grief, too, a different kind of grief, but she helped me in much the same way."

Carly had shown her the letter from Eric, another positive sign.

Cord said Eric had been working with Miles Carey for several days, checking in with Amos, behaving more respectfully in general...

All good news.

Shallie packed a small bag with a change of clothes.

She threw in the sexiest nightgown she'd brought with her, although it was actually more practical than sexy. And included her usual range of reading material. She **never** wanted to be without something to read. Would Cord be offended by the fact that she might not be paying constant attention to him? No, she decided. Not based on what she knew about him.

This evening would also be their private Fourth of July celebration. Yesterday, they'd gone as a group—with Mitch and Tina, J.P. and Eli, Carly—to the festivities, including fireworks, at the small park not far from J.P.'s house. "It was either this or poker," Eli had joked. "We drew cards, and I got a four of hearts, so this won."

For tonight's dinner, Shallie planned to wear the one "fancy" dress she'd brought, a sleeveless black sheath, and her only pair of heels.

She offered to share the driving, but Cord said he'd be fine; Silver Hills was only an hour and a half away, and the trip was slow-paced, relaxed.

"Any news on Carly?" he asked.

"I'd say she's doing well. I've learned a lot about her and I get the feeling that she's learned a lot about herself. She's really connected with Mary Jean and Len, and the situation with Meg Simon is so good—for both of them."

"That's the impression I had, too. And the concert is a great opportunity for her, a real boost."

Shallie nodded. "She and I talk just about every day, and right now, the concert's one of her main topics. That and her mom, and how much Reba would love the fact that she's discovered music in a big way." They were just turning into Silver Hills as Shallie finished her thought. "Remember how we couldn't recall if Reba did much singing when she was here? Turns out it was one of the things she and Reba did together."

"Yeah, she mentioned that...And I'm happy they had that connection. I'm having more conversations with her these days," he added.

Shallie had noticed with pleasure that their interactions were more frequent.

"We've talked about Reba some, the concert, Holly—and her opinions of certain people. She has a great sense of humor."

"So do you," she said, and they smiled at each other.

When they arrived at the inn minutes later, Cord parked in the lot; they went immediately to the onsite restaurant and were seated near a window. Shallie felt good, not a hint of any doubt. It was easy to tell that this place was special. The predinner drinks were lovely; Shallie had perhaps the most delicious Chardonnay she'd ever tasted, and Cord said the local craft beer was "exceptional." After that, they shared an appetizer of sustainable Pacific shrimp and scallops, followed by creamy mashed potatoes, salmon and asparagus. She said she made no exceptions for meat but would be pescatarian tonight.

Dessert? Although Shallie said she couldn't, Cord asked for two decaf coffees and an order of the fruit tart special to split.

Shallie told him—and it was the truth— that this was one of the best meals she'd ever had, not adding that the company was a large part of that.

"I hope this will be one of the best **nights** you've ever had."

She didn't respond or meet his eyes, but she hoped so, too...

They retrieved their bags and walked toward the front desk to check in.

And right there in the lobby, she dropped her purse and bag, slipped both arms around his neck and kissed him—

briefly but it was enough to arouse her.

When they entered their room, Shallie felt as if she was an inexperienced twenty-year-old again, despite her marriage and a short-lived relationship or two, and all the times she and Cord had been together. Throwing their bags on the floor, they surged into each other's arms and he kissed her deeply. She kissed him back with the same passion, and they tumbled onto the bed.

Until these recent weeks with Cord, she hadn't kissed **any** man since before her divorce from Rob.

She and Cord were gentle the first time. They slowly removed each other's clothes. She'd already kicked off her heels, which had never been all that comfortable, anyway.

The intensity of kissing and touching continued, and it wasn't long before she took him in her mouth. His excitement had the same effect on her. Then he brought Shallie to a climax unlike any she'd ever had—she was sure of it.

This was good sex, which only

continued to get better.

Then they took the conventional approach, with him on top, and that worked for both of them, too.

He sighed, stroking her breasts, kissing her lips. "You know what I think this means?" he asked. "Not just **this**, but every minute we've spent together?"

"What?" And she couldn't help sounding a little breathless, anticipating his response.

"That I'm in love with you. Completely, deeply, truly in love. And maybe..."

"Maybe I'm in love with you?"

"Yeah," he replied. "Is that possible?"

"Oh, yes," she whispered. They drew close again, her arms around his neck. "You know I always wanted you, back then," she said. "I was jealous of Reba because you loved **her**. Even though— or maybe because—she was my best friend."

"I see that now. I also see how stupid I was," he muttered.

"Never mind. Different place, different time. Different me."

"Well, yes and no," he said with a smile. "Now, should we have a glass of wine, relax in bed?"

"I'd like that." So he ordered wine from room service, and they made themselves "decent," then settled with a glass each. She'd expected to do some reading, but he turned on the TV and she found herself caught up in one episode and then another of a British mystery series.

They cuddled together, holding each other tightly—and it was more about reassurance, about comfort, than sex.

But the next morning...

J.P. felt he and Carly had put off their meeting long enough. He knew Cord and company had already had theirs and Eli would soon.

His initial thought had been to leave the planning of their session to her, but now he didn't want to wait any longer, wanted to set it in motion.

He'd received Trooper from a women's minimum security prison about two hours away in the town of Elm Ridge. He was almost certain Carly would be willing to accompany him there. And with Cord and Shallie away until this afternoon, as he'd learned from Mitch, today would be an opportune time.

He drove to the ranch house and let Trooper out, following him to the porch, where Carly was sitting with Bandit and Smoky. She was listening to something on her cell, some podcast or other.

"Hello there, Carly," J.P. called loudly, and she finally looked up.

"Trooper, hi! Come on over!" Pause. "Oh, hi, J.P."

He chuckled at that. Spending too much time with Brynne?

He watched her entertain all three dogs, then said, "I have a suggestion if you're interested. I'm going to visit Trooper's training facility, and I thought you might like to join me. We can stop for lunch on the way back...and talk."

Carly frowned at him, as if she knew exactly what she meant by "talk." Finally, she nodded. "I'd love to see where he was trained. Is it far from here?"

"A couple of hours. It's at the Elm Ridge Women's Prison. They have various dog-training programs there for inmates. They train service dogs, like Trooper, therapy dogs, Seeing Eye dogs, search and rescue dogs. It's a huge success for everyone involved. It really helps the inmates with rehabilitation, helps the animals, most of whom are rescues and, of course, the new owners, like me. Or like I used to be."

"Wow! And this is all done by... prisoners?"

"Yes, and as I said, everybody benefits. Sometimes it's hard to know who's rescuing whom." He smiled down at Trooper. "Some of the inmates even end up working as dog trainers when they're released."

"Wow," she said again. "Will I meet **his** trainer?"

"Yep. I heard she's getting out at the end of the month, so I'd like to see her, show her what a great job she did with Trooper, what a difference she made.

And I want to thank her."

"What's her name and what's she in for?"

"Her name is Jennifer. And you don't need to know why she's there. Trust me, it wasn't murder or anything like that. This is a minimum security prison." The crime, in fact, had been financial fraud.

"Oh-kay." She stood up, dusted her hands and sent Cord's dogs inside. "Tina's in the house. Let me go tell her and get my bag."

J.P. figured they'd arrive by twelve thirty or one, spend an hour or so, then go to a local place for lunch. He returned to his car and put Trooper back in, holding the front door as he waited for Carly. The day was bright and warm, but not **too** warm, the sun still reaching its zenith. Ideal July weather.

She climbed in, and once he'd exited the driveway, he saw her take a notebook from her backpack. At first she just held it on her lap. Some twenty minutes later, she started writing; he glanced over and noticed what looked like...a poem? No, it was a song! He realized that as soon as he heard her humming quietly to herself. Some lines were crossed out, some words circled.

"This is one of your songs?" he asked. "Do you want to read me what you have?"

She took a moment to consider his question, then began to read.

"The animals I know
Are the animals I love
It's as simple as that
Here and in the world above.

"I'm rhyming lines two and four. **Love** and **above** aren't the best, but I can't come up with anything better. Dove? Shove? Don't think so."

"I think it's okay," he reassured her. "It makes the point. Love lasts beyond death."

She nodded slowly. "Yeah, that's actually what I'm saying in the next verse.

"If I loved them once,

I love them still
Even if they're gone

"To their graves—I'm stuck there. Need something to rhyme with **still**."

"On the hill," J.P. suggested. "Maybe not the strongest choice, but…"

"**To their graves on the hill.** I like it. Next I've got—

I love my Dooley and our Holly,
   Bandit, Smoky.
I love Trooper and Logan
   and Plum.
I also love the horses.
And the animals all love me
back—they're not dumb!"

J.P. laughed.
"I have another stanza," she said.

"They and the animals in
   my future
All of them bring me pleasure.
They've changed my life and
will change it more,

Each one of them a treasure."

She gave a shrug. "Well, **pleasure** and **treasure** is a little obvious. I might change them later."

"Don't think you need to, but I'm no expert on songwriting. I'm impressed with what you've done," he said, and he wasn't just being polite. "Any ideas about the kind of music?"

"Something kind of lively. Maybe like that one by Shania Twain, 'Man! I Feel Like a Woman!' or '9 to 5' by Dolly. But The GateCrasher guys will have some input."

He smiled at her. "Thanks for letting me join in. I'm looking forward to the concert."

She smiled back. "I am, too." Then she watched the landscape for a while, the Rockies in the distance, the forests with their different shades of green, the pastureland interspersed throughout.

"Those mountains are so...majestic."

"Material for another song?"

"Why not? I could use the word **rock**!"

"Speaking of songs," she said a moment later, "could we listen to the radio for a while?" When he said yes, she flipped it on and found a country station.

According to a road sign, they were approaching the outskirts of Elm Ridge. Carly felt satisfied with her songwriting progress and had enjoyed the drive. Of her "three dads" she knew J.P. McCall the least, but now that had begun to change.

They parked in the front lot of a building that looked to her rather like a condo. An older one, anyway. J.P. got out first and had Trooper stand quietly while he put on the dog's harness. They could hear dogs barking excitedly not far away and Trooper went on alert, whimpering a little.

"Calm," J.P. told him—calmly, of course—and the dog settled down.

The three of them walked past a yard enclosed by chainlink fencing, and they watched several women throwing tennis balls for the dogs to catch and bring back. Carly said this must be playtime. He agreed, describing it as a break — forgive the word, he said with a grin — for all concerned.

He led her to a guard stand, identified himself and her; next they were ushered inside, where they went through the process again. This time, a correctional supervisor named Margaret Colton greeted them in a friendly fashion and brought them over to meet Jennifer, who was in a lounge with two other women, all casually dressed, and the dogs they were currently working with.

J.P. shook Jennifer's hand and introduced Carly. Trooper wagged his tail at the standard poodle mix and the Australian shepherd, who responded in the same way. Jennifer introduced Laura and Mary, plus the dogs, Rooney and Bruce.

Then, J.P. freed Trooper from his leash, and tail thumping even harder, he darted over to Jennifer, reaching her in seconds, resting his head on her knee. She slid her arms around him, hugging him, murmuring the same endearments Carly always did. "Oh, my handsome boy! How are you? Jen's missed you." She glanced up at J.P. "He's doing okay?"

"As you can see. And so am I—thanks to him. And, by extension, you."

She turned to Carly. "He's retired, you know. Trooper, I mean," she said with a giggle.

"I do know. But in some ways he's still on the job."

"Sure is," J.P. agreed. "It's just that now he has the time and leisure to make friends."

"And he's got **lots**," Carly put in.

Jennifer nodded. "I'll bet he does." Her colleagues smiled and nodded, too.

"Would you mind talking to Carly about the kind of work you do?"

"We'd be happy to!"

Thrilled, Carly took the opportunity to ask questions and wrote the answers in her songwriting notebook. Answers that had to do with the various kinds of training. One point the women made repeatedly—and it reminded her so much of the comments Cord made about working with horses—had to do with the love and connection between trainer and dog.

Jennifer told them, with neither pride nor embarrassment, that she was getting out soon and hoped to pursue a career in the "dog world."

Carly and J.P. thanked her and the other women, who all hugged Trooper, and wished them the best. They strolled back to the car after the exit procedures.

"I'm so glad we did that!" Carly said eagerly. "Thank you, thank you!"

"Now, what about lunch? There's a nice place with a patio not far from here and we can bring Trooper. Sound all right?"

"Oh, yes."

The restaurant, called La Fiesta, was attractive and no doubt got plenty of business from friends and relatives of women in the prison.

They chose a table with a giant umbrella that provided some necessary shade.

Trooper and J.P. were obviously known there and the dog was immediately served a bowlful of water. Carly studied the mostly Tex-Mex menu. They chose that day's special, enchiladas with a bean, cheese and vegetable sauce, plus chicken tacos.

Once they'd finished their meal, Carly decided it was time. Without prelude she told J.P. the whole story—which she was quite used to telling now.

He didn't interrupt or ask any questions, merely said he was prepared to undergo a DNA test and would be overjoyed if he was her dad.

And he told her he was grateful to her for returning Reba to him.

On the way home he dropped her off at Meg's, prepared to wait in the car, but Carly invited him inside, saying, "We should probably leave Trooper here, okay?"

"Sure. We'll give him a rest from socializing."

As she knocked on the door, then let them in, Carly told him Meg had recently come home from chemo and always felt weak for a few days.

Meg was in her living room, a somewhat emaciated older woman resting on a lounger. Carly bent to hug her and introduced J.P. as a "family friend." That was true enough. He sat with Meg as Carly did her cat duties—after she'd had him meet Plum and Logan, whose names he recognized from her song.

"Carly's wonderful, isn't she?" Meg said, her voice frail. "We haven't known each other long, but she's so good to me and my sweet cats. She's like another daughter."

J.P. nodded. "She loves you, too. It's easy to tell."

They spoke about a range of things, from the town's history to their personal histories. He told her about Trooper and how he'd taken Carly to visit the women's prison where the dog had been trained. Meg loved that story. She told him about her husband, dead six years but still so missed. "You don't get over that kind of loss. Carly and I talk about it quite a lot."

"I know Carly understands."

"We understand each other," Meg said.

Their conversation was interrupted twice. First by Carly offering to make them coffee or tea. Both declined. And then by a playful cat racing around, showing off a toy mouse. "Good work, Logan," J.P. praised him, to Meg's evident delight.

By the time he and Carly left, J.P. was prouder of her than ever, proud of her generosity, her empathy. She hugged Meg goodbye. Then Meg held out her arms and J.P. hugged her, too.

Saturday afternoon, Cord and Shallie arrived home and parted with a final kiss at the foot of her stairs.

Cord went to his own room and discovered he had a message. From Eddie. Fortunately, he reached him immediately—and Eddie got right to the point. "I have Julie's contact info. I'm emailing it. And she **would** like to hear from you. She's also open to meeting halfway. Maybe Seattle."

"Great!" And he decided that it was. All of it. He'd begun to hope for this very thing. Probably more because of Shallie's influence than anything else. In spite of his previous feelings, his in-difference, he was ready to meet Julie, even excited about it. And he had a sister! Never mind that she was about the same age as his maybe-daughter…

And, in addition to everything else, there was Shallie's connection with Seattle.

"Any news on Christine Fletcher or whoever she is now?" he asked.

"Nope. But we're not giving up."

"I'll let Shallie know, and please keep us informed."

"You bet."

He waited in the kitchen until she came down again and told her what he'd learned. He was glad to see her com-posure about the Fletcher situation—and pleased that she responded so positively to the road trip. "We can stay at my place! And you can meet Emma," she said. They agreed to invite Carly. And just after they discussed this, Carly and J.P. were at the door. She told them with great enthusiasm about where they'd been, adding that they'd also had "the talk," their own version of the Big Meet.

Cord described the trip they were planning and asked if she'd like to join them.

"Yes! I've never been to Seattle. And I'd love to meet your...Julie." She frowned. "I'll have to check with Meg and see if she's going to need cat care."

"If she does, I'm sure Tina will help. Or maybe Lindsey, since she drives and has access to a car?"

"Besides," Cord pointed out. "I still have to call Julie to make arrangements and set up a time."

"If necessary," J.P. said, "I could drop in on Meg. I'm sure I can deal with the cats—how hard could that be?"

"Well..." Carly seemed to be deliberating on his potential cat-handling skills. "I know she'd love to see you again..."

"Give me a call if she needs me."

J.P. left then, after congratulating Cord on reconnecting with his mother. That evening, holding his breath, Cord called the number Eddie had given him. A woman answered on the first ring. "Julie?"

"**Cord?** Oh, my God! Oh, my God, it's you."

"Sure is."

"You have no idea how much I've wanted this, how **long** I've wanted it. I've felt a lot of guilt over what I did—and what I didn't do—all those years ago. But...I never felt I had the right to contact you." More than once, he could hear her gulping down sobs.

He acknowledged privately that he wouldn't have been emotionally prepared for this before, and barely was, even now. "Well, we're finally in touch." Kind of a lame remark, but it was the only thing he could manage for a minute or two. He'd never dared to imagine this...He was talking to his **mother**!

Feeling oddly shy, he asked, "Would you be interested in having me visit?"

"Of course! I'd like nothing better. And

I'd love for you to meet my husband, Chris Daniels, who's a lieutenant at Everett Naval Base, and our daughter, Kathleen."

"I'd like that, too. And would it be okay with you if I brought the woman I'm… seeing? Her name's Shallie. As well as a young friend of ours?"

"Totally okay!"

"And are you okay to meet in Seattle? That way, we can do a road trip…make it a bit of a vacation, as well."

"Totally okay with that, too."

Then they considered times, choosing the third week in August. She said Chris could take a few days off. Perfect timing, Cord thought. Karen and Joey, his current clients, would have left by then. And school wouldn't start for another couple of weeks.

Cord and Julie promised to keep in touch, to call each other every couple of days.

When the call ended, Cord felt staggered, as though he was living in an alternate reality. His mind kept repeating the same thoughts over and over. **I'm going to see my mother. And meet my sister.**

Half an hour later, he, Shallie and Carly were sitting at the kitchen table with laptops and several road maps, courtesy of Shallie. "How traditional," Carly scoffed at the maps—but that didn't stop her from taking a surreptitious glance now and then.

CHAPTER EIGHTEEN

The trip would be Wednesday to Sunday, August 14th to 18th—two days' travel and three in Seattle.

They left at six and stopped in Missoula for breakfast with Mary Jean, Len and Holly. Then the Lewises took them to see one of the town's most famous attractions, A Carousel for Missoula, with its hand-painted ponies. "How could we **not** go there?" Carly proclaimed.

She posted on her YouTube channel, with a video of the merry-go-round, referring to the trip as "an out-of-state visit with one of my potential dads." She was no longer trying to make money from the site, as she'd informed Shallie and Cord; for now, she just wanted to keep in touch with her fans.

She was, as she repeatedly told them, stunned by the magnificence of the Rockies.

Meanwhile, she'd received a text from Lindsey, who'd visited Meg's place to change the litter, feed and play with the cats. Meg was currently out of town undergoing tests, as Carly knew. But the surprising thing Lindsey revealed about this visit was...**Guess who showed up? Eric! With his uncle Eli—in uniform. They found out about this from you guys. Anyway, Eric was decent to me, very polite and kept his distance, and was really good with Logan and Plum**.

Carly was surprised but not really shocked to learn this.

They reached the outskirts of Seattle at eight thirty that evening, and Shallie took over the driving. Her 1920s apartment building was in the Waterfront neighborhood, Carly remembered from their night of making travel plans.

Tired though she was, Carly stared intently out the window. Between the still-bright sky and the streetlights, which had already come on, it was well lit outside. What a beautiful city!

Shallie said she'd called her friend Emma, who lived in the same building, to tell her when they expected to arrive. She'd explained earlier that she hadn't given up or leased her apartment yet. Carly had noticed the…inquiring? troubled? look Cord sent Shallie's way when she said that. Carly didn't consider herself the most observant person on the planet but could hardly miss the fact that he had serious hopes of a perma-nent relationship with Shallie. She hoped Shallie would make up her mind—fast!— get rid of her life in Seattle and move in with Cord.

Carly was charmed by the low-rise, not the kind of building she was familiar with, and loved the idea that people had lived here for generations. Through the Roaring Twenties, the Depression, the Second World War and on. Shallie parked in the nearby lot, texted Emma and, carrying their bags, they walked to the front entrance.

Emma was waiting at the door, a tall, very pretty woman with shoulder-length blond hair and a vivacious manner. Shallie made introductions, then Emma hugged each of them in turn. She suggested Carly stay at her place—she had a sofa that converted to a bed— which appealed to Carly and no doubt to Shallie and Cord. It was something of a relief, if Carly was honest about it; she wanted them to have their privacy.

"Let's get ourselves organized," Shallie said. "And then we'll plan something for dinner."

For dinner that night, the four of them decided on takeout from a seafood restaurant Emma recommended; she said she had plenty of wine, beer and soft drinks.

The meal was as good as promised, in Cord's opinion. The shrimp appetizers, salmon main course with a vegetable stir-fry—it was all delicious.

In a very short time, he'd come to like Emma Grant, to feel a connection with her due to their shared interests and, even more, her closeness with Shallie. He noticed Shallie's approving smile as he and Emma spoke, and that only added to the sense of rightness he felt about this new friendship. He could very much see Emma as part of his life, his personal community, in the coming years.

"Dessert, anyone?" Carly asked. "We have brownies **and** ice cream. Don't they go together **perfectly**?"

Go together perfectly. A good summary of how he felt...

The next morning, Shallie made coffee, grateful that Emma had supplied her kitchen with the basics, and plenty of them.

She brought Cord his coffee in bed. Stretching, he said, "This is true luxury. Only one thing missing." He sent her a meaningful glance.

"We were both too tired last night."

Too tired for more than a few kisses. Too tired to do more than lie asleep in each other's arms. "Tonight for sure."

"I'll hold you to that. And just plain hold you." He took a sip. "I can hardly remember what crappy coffee tastes like anymore."

"I was never an expert on it." She paused, looking around the bedroom. "I wish the dogs were here."

"Me, too, but I can do without them bugging me for this and that."

"You like it!"

He shrugged, then outlined their day. "So the plan is that we're seeing Julie and family tomorrow, and today we're going to visit Emma's stable, right?"

"Right. We'll take it easy this morning, do some sightseeing and go to Emma's after lunch."

And that was how their leisurely morning went. Shallie acted as tour guide, choosing the sites she thought Carly in particular would enjoy. They started with a Seattle underground tour, which Shallie had always found fascinating, then they **had** to visit Pike Place Market. And that was followed by a trip up the Space Needle, where they had lunch while gazing out at the city. "We're seeing Seattle from top to bottom," Cord joked. "Or rather, from bottom to top."

Following that, Shallie drove them to Horses Help in nearby Bellevue. Emma rented the property and the stable; she had one full-time assistant, Avery Bridger, whom Shallie knew well, and a part-timer, a young man named Drew Samuels, who was studying physiotherapy. Both were present that afternoon but only Avery was there to greet them. She explained that Emma and Drew were in the paddock behind the stable, working with two experienced horses and a couple of kids, one of whom, a girl of nine, had cerebral palsy. The other, a boy in his teens, had been seriously hurt in a car accident and was recovering his ability to walk.

The group, including Avery, stood by the fence and watched. Carly's eyes were huge. Cord was paying careful attention, and when the session was over, when the horses had been returned to their stalls and the kids picked up by their parents, they all gathered in the stable. Napoleon the cat joined them, or rather, joined Charley the horse. Both Shallie and Carly got photos of the twosome nuzzling each other.

They greeted all the horses and asked questions. Carly ran back to the car to get her notebook, turned to a fresh page and began writing down Emma's responses.

Cord talked to Emma about doing something jointly, as a visiting expert, at Hollister Horses. Shallie added her encouragement. "I've been trying to get her to visit," she told Cord.

"You're welcome anytime," he said. "We'll discuss it later. But right now, I see you have another client coming in."

A middle-aged woman using a walker moved toward them.

After welcoming her, Shallie and company said their goodbyes and left. They'd invited Emma and her staff over for a home-made dinner, so they needed to stop at the local grocery before returning to the apartment.

Friday morning, they set off to meet Julie Daniels and her family, who were staying in Tacoma. Shallie was familiar with the town, about half an hour from her neighborhood.

Cord appreciated her handling the transportation, since he felt he would've been too nervous to drive. He was going to meet his **mother**. Just that knowledge brought his thoughts—but not his feelings—to a complete halt once again. His mother. A woman he had no memory of. Not only that, he was meeting her new (well, not **so** new) family.

He hadn't wanted to see any pictures of Julie, old or current, although he certainly could have requested some from her or checked online. He didn't really understand why he felt that way. To create a completely new start? To avoid expectations? To avoid prejudgment?

He was thankful that Shallie and Carly would be there to act as buffers, if that was the right term. Or perhaps as distractions...He knew he'd value their observations, and he'd be interested to hear Carly's opinion of his new half sister, a girl close to twenty years younger than he was.

"What should I say when I meet Julie?" he asked. He'd run through a number of possibilities in his head, but nothing seemed quite fitting.

"How about hello?" Carly said, and glancing into the backseat, he couldn't tell if she was being sarcastic.

"Carly!" Shallie objected. "This is serious."

"I know, and I **am** being serious. What's the other option—goodbye?"

Cord laughed before Shallie could remonstrate with her again. "She has a point," he said. "This is either going to be another beginning or another end."

"See?" Carly said in a snippy voice. "But to go with that hello, why don't we pick up some flowers for her?"

They did, at the first plant shop they saw. He wondered why he and Shallie hadn't thought of that. But instead of a bouquet, he chose three elegant orchids, one a soft pink, one a lilac color, the third a pale yellow.

They reached the motel soon after, a well-kept low-slung building painted white with dark green trim. It featured a patio and a garden lush with ferns; Cord wasn't a gardener, but he could appreciate its beauty.

As they reached the unit's entrance, the door opened wide before he had a chance to knock. A slim woman, maybe five foot six, wearing her brown hair loose and straight, stood before them.

Cord couldn't stop staring at her. Eyes the same blue as his, hair lighter, the same cheekbones. She'd be in her midfifties. He knew she'd been twenty when he was born, and after he turned two, they hadn't been part of each other's lives.

She'd obviously dressed carefully for the occasion, wearing a black skirt,

simple black sandals and a silvery top.
Meanwhile, he was in jeans and a light
denim shirt, sleeves rolled up. Oh, well.
He hoped to make his impression based
on character and conversation, not
wardrobe.

"Cord?"

"Julie." Too soon for a hug. He thrust
the orchid he was carrying toward her
and she placed it on a side table in the
narrow hallway. Carly and Shallie held on
to the other orchids. "Hi, you're Shelley?"

"Shallie," she and Cord said simul-
taneously.

"And I'm Carly. Um, a friend of theirs."

They moved into the main room,
where they deposited their orchids. Two
people were waiting, a fit and very handsome black man with close-cropped hair
and muscular arms, and a slight, lovely
girl with shiny dark hair and huge brown
eyes.

The man stood up, held out his hand
and introduced himself. "Chris Daniels.
And I know who you all are," he said
with a smile. "This is our daughter,

Kathleen."

The girl threw her arms around Carly. "I'm **really** excited to meet you! So, you're a friend of Cord's."

After a heartbeat's worth of silence, Carly nodded. "Well, it's a complicated story, but...yeah."

Chris offered everyone coffee—Cord figured he wanted to end an awkward moment—and Carly said emphatically that she'd have one "with lots of cream."

Kathleen seemed surprised by that, but Chris grinned. "Coming right up." He moved into the suite's galley kitchen, complete with fridge, coffee maker, the works.

Julie invited them to sit at the table; their coffee was served—with plain milk for Kathleen—accompanied by a large platter of muffins and brownies. Good thing they hadn't had much for breakfast. Afterward, the others acknowledged that he and Julie needed time alone.

Despite the importance of this private meeting, Cord felt nervous when they left for the front patio and sat in two of the Adirondack chairs in the shade.

Julie began with a deep, shaky breath. "You're my son and I'm your mother. It's not simply a biological connection, although it must feel that way to you." She paused, eyes closed. "I loved your dad, and I loved—**love** you. I screwed up. I know it." Her eyes opened wide at those last words.

"Wait," Cord said. "You were very young and you'd just lost your husband to a senseless accident."

"But I had a **child**." Tears filled her eyes. "You."

"My life's turned out okay."

"I can't tell you how thankful I am for that." She stared down at her hands as she spoke. "I'm a good wife to Chris and a good mom to Kathleen. You're right, though, I wasn't capable of that, or the mom part, anyway, all those years ago. And my grief at losing Toby...It made me insane. I had no control over myself anymore."

"I'm sorry—for both of us." Cord

thought he could understand a little of what she'd been through all those years ago. He felt his resentment begin to lift —it was almost a physical sensation.

"I'm also sorry I blamed your grand-parents for never letting us regain contact."

"You can't blame them, Julie. They did what they thought was best for me."

She sighed again. "I agree. You're right. I was a mess, and I turned your life into a disaster with my neglect— until they came along." Wiping her eyes, she said, "I should be, and I actually am, very grateful to them. And look at you now! You're such a success. Eddie Gonzalez told me—and then I checked you out online. Didn't have the nerve to do that before..." She smiled up at him. "Oh, and I like your girlfriend."

"So do I," he said, smiling back, not ready to explain the complexities of his relationship with Shallie. "Listen, we'll talk more, lots more, but it's getting noisy out here. Let's go join the others."

• • •

The remainder of Friday and then Saturday didn't afford many private conversations—a few brief ones, in which Julie discussed the details of her recovery and described her current job as an organizer with a charity that helped the homeless.

But their meetings and the opportunities they did have to talk felt like a genuine beginning. He needed a chance to absorb everything, these new experiences and feelings, and thought she did, too.

He and Shallie returned to her apartment Friday night, while Carly stayed with Kathleen. They'd spent the day together, doing whatever teenage girls did.

Saturday, they were all in a sociable mood, prepared to have fun. And they did.

Cord had been worried about too much intensity, but after that first hour with Julie, he was more relaxed than he'd expected. He invited the Daniels family to visit the ranch soon.

Carly and Kathleen took off for the afternoon and returned at suppertime with several of Kathleen's friends.

That evening, Cord and Chris handled barbecue duty on the balcony of Shallie's apartment, while the women made salads and dessert. Emma joined them, and the girls were fascinated with her work, admiring pictures of the horses.

Cord supposed that in some ways, it was like any other casual, pleasant summer get-together, and yet...It was and it wasn't. Pleasant, yes, but very much **not** like other events.

He was genuinely pleased that the trip had gone so well, genuinely thankful to Julie and her family—and to Shallie and Carly.

Sunday morning, they were on their way home. Carly admitted to herself that it **was** home. At least, Cord's place was for now, although she was actually living with Tina and Mitch. Whatever happened, however things turned out, Painted Pony Creek was her hometown. And she had only good feelings about that, about her future.

Everything was so different from what her life had been. She wasn't naive; she knew she'd face difficulties again. Everyone did. Disappointment, grief, regret. But she felt far more prepared to face them.

She didn't pay as much attention to the unbelievably beautiful landscape, highlighted by the brilliant early-morning sun, on their return trip.

During a too-brief stop in Spokane, she checked her cell. Another text from Lindsey. Yesterday's visit with Meg's cats had gone well—and Eric had shown up again. Eli had only dropped him off this time, hadn't stayed, but had come back an hour later to pick him up. She said her conversation with Eric had been friendly; he'd told her he was interested in continuing with the pet support group, as Lindsey and Carly were now calling it.

She also got a text from Kathleen, who said she was excited to have met her, they'd keep in touch, see each other soon.

One of the things Carly had learned in Painted Pony Creek was that life provided opportunities. You had to recognize and value them. She didn't want to sound all "positive thinking" — but it was true.

Hmm. Might be a song there...

CHAPTER NINETEEN

Tina's sixty-fifth was on the twenty-third of August, a Friday. The party and concert were taking place tonight, Saturday evening. As far as Shallie could tell, Tina wasn't aware of the extent to which this party was in her honor, probably figured it would be a handful of people, a few drinks and appetizers on the porch. One of her daughters, Caroline, was busy keeping her occupied in the trailer.

Carly and The GateCrashers had managed to fit in another couple of rehearsals, and Shallie knew she felt confident about her ability and her contributions. She'd be singing her own creations, the song for Reba, plus the animal one, and she'd do a special version of "Happy Birthday" for Tina. Of course she'd also join in on a number of other songs.

The audience would include Tina's family and friends, the Lewises with Holly, Russ, and many more. Unfortunately, Julie, Chris and Kathleen couldn't make it, although Cord had invited them; Chris was on a special deployment to help fight a growing wildfire in the state.

Bailey's was handling the food, mostly appetizers, and drinks, setting up a small bar. Brynne had obtained the liquor license and also arranged for a quantity of nonalcoholic drinks, finishing up with coffee.

Fifty or sixty people were expected. The performers would be up on the "stage"—Cord's porch. Mitch and the musicians were in charge of the sound. And Susan had put together an exhibit of photographs reflecting Tina's life.

It was now four o'clock, and the party had a six o'clock start. As Shallie observed, everything was prepared and under control. The lineup of songs was complete. The final rehearsal had been at Bailey's the afternoon before and if the cheers and applause they'd received were any indication, Tina's concert should be a rousing success...

Cord had rented dozens of portable chairs from a place in Billings; they'd been delivered that morning and set up on the lawn facing the porch, although people could sit on the grass if they preferred. Russ had come over to help with arranging the chairs and was now assisting Brynne and her two servers. J.P. offered to watch the dogs, while Eli and his deputy Amos were providing security.

Shallie figured that even if Tina knew more about the party than they realized, there'd still be some surprises.

At five thirty guests began to arrive; Carly, Shallie and Lindsey helped seat them. Brynne and her staff, with the assistance of temporary server Russ, were handing around appetizers and drinks.

The Lewises were among the first, and Len was immediately drafted by Mitch and Aaron for a final check of the sound system. Cord had taken on the role of general oversight, handling whatever was needed, directing traffic—cars were parked along the sides of the long drive—and answering questions.

Mary Jean took care of the gift table, where people placed their wrapped packages and cards, while Caroline and her daughter, Ashley, were still keeping Tina entertained in the trailer.

There sure were a lot of people involved in pulling this off—and a lot of guests. That told Shallie how beloved Tina was. She went over to the photo exhibit to study it one more time. Pictures, black-and-white as well as color, of Tina's early life, her wedding, a portrait of her and Mitch and their children... Carly joined her, a nostalgic expression on her face.

They waved at Eli and Amos, who stood at the edges of the crowd, and then at J.P. who had Trooper, Cord's dogs and several others under his control.

What a night this was going to be! For maybe the thousandth time, Carly told Shallie how lucky she felt to be part of this community.

The party was about to start, Cord announced as Susan headed over to the trailer to fetch Tina and the other family members.

Ten minutes later, she led her mother out to a burst of applause. Everyone stood. There were shouts of "Happy Birthday, Tina!" and "Yay, Tina!"

Tina seemed overwhelmed, raising her hand to her mouth; Mitch moved it aside and kissed her fervently—which brought more applause—then led her to a chair in the front row. Cord said that once Tina was served and given a class of champagne, everyone else should line up and get further snacks and drinks.

An hour of eating and greeting later, Aaron went to the mic and said the concert was now officially underway. People settled in to listen.

Carly climbed up to the stage and took part in the first few songs—"Walkin' after Midnight," "Jolene" and "Ring of Fire." Then Aaron said that Carly Shannon, whom most of them had met, was going to end this set with a newly written and very personal song of her own called "Mother and Nature."

When she'd finished her performance, the applause went long and loud, with Cord, J.P. and Eli cheering the longest and loudest of them all. Shallie, standing beside them, had to cover her face to hide her tears—tears of sadness for what she and Shallie had lost and joy for what they'd found.

The break gave their friends and neighbors a chance to chat, to score more food and drink, to hug Tina and wish her the best of birthdays. Carly heard someone say, "You're a senior citizen now!" Tina just rolled her eyes—seemed to be a habit around here.

The next and final set began with Carly's animal song, unquestionably a hit with this group. And it ended with her special version of the birthday song.

"Happy Birthday to you.
Happy Birthday, dear Tina,
We all love you!
From the smallest cat to
The biggest horse
Every one of us is on course
To wish you the greatest day
And the best in every way.
Happy Birthday, dearest Tina,
We...all...love...you!"

The audience sang along the second time through, ending in a shout that could have shaken the leaves from the trees.

Tina was openly crying, and she and Shallie rushed over to hug Carly. "You know," Tina said, "you're always saying how lucky **you** are to be with all of us. Well, we're just as lucky to have you in our lives. **Both** of you."

By then all three of them were crying.

A lot of tears tonight, Shallie thought. Almost as many tears as cheers. She couldn't help a slight grin at her inadvertent rhyme.

Cord joined them then, with a kiss on the cheek for Tina and Carly, and slid his arms around Shallie. She sheltered there, with a feeling of gratitude that these people were in **her** life, too. Especially Cord...

As the evening wound to a close, Eli approached Carly, asking if she'd be willing to meet with him the following day. He knew he'd let this wait far too long. "If you're available, we'll go to Sunday brunch at Brynne's. I'll pick you up at eleven." He knew he sounded more abrupt and businesslike than he'd intended, but he didn't want to reveal the slightest hint of anxiety. If he turned out to be Carly's father, he had to be ready for the changes that would bring. And if he didn't...the disappointment.

"Okay."

The house and driveway lights had been turned on, and he helped escort the remaining guests to their cars. Cleanup had begun—the chairs and tables, to be picked up by the rental company on Monday, the leftover food, the sound system and instruments...

Brynne brought him and Amos a beer each, and then Cord came over, asking for one, too. The three of them sat on the porch steps, dogs asleep at their feet. Eli was tempted to tell Cord about his arrangement with Carly, but it was too private to share with a colleague, even if that colleague was also a friend.

The next morning, Eli showed up at eleven sharp, to find Carly waiting for him. There was little conversation as they drove to Bailey's; he saw immediately that Brynne wasn't on duty. Too bad, but not unexpected, given the night she'd just put in.

He and Carly had coffee and the brunch special—scrambled eggs with pancakes. Their talk was slow to start, but once he'd made the overtures, by referring to her meetings with Cord and J.P., she launched into a point-by-point summary of everything he'd suspected and some of which he already knew. The family history, her hitchhiking journey, the YouTube channel and the money she'd made as a result. This public aspect of her recent life, and the money she'd made doing it, took him aback. But he didn't hold it against her, recognizing that it was about survival. Different kinds of survival. Financial **and** emotional.

She ended with, "I assume you'd be willing to do the DNA test?"

He nodded emphatically. "All three of us are agreed on that. Might've taken us a while, but..." They discussed logistics for a few minutes, then moved on to last night's party. She told him she'd helped Tina open her gifts and described some of them—books of all kinds, including a couple of celebrity cookbooks, several bottles of champagne, fancy bath products, jewelry and much more. She made a point of adding that Tina had **loved** his gift, a beautifully photographed history of Montana. He appreciated her telling him this.

They both seemed relieved that they'd had their discussion, that this step had been taken. "Father or honorary uncle, I'm part of your life. We're in each other's lives. And I'm happy about that."

"I am, too." And as they got up to leave, she clasped both his hands.

When he drove back to the ranch, Shallie and Cord were sitting on the porch, apparently engaged in a confidential exchange. Eli wanted to bring up the DNA test details, but this didn't seem to be the time. He'd call later.

He simply waved and took Carly to the trailer.

When Carly left Eli's car, she discovered that Tina was waiting for her, sitting in one of the garden chairs.

"How was it?" she asked.

"Good! Nice brunch and we had The Talk. We're all okay with DNA testing." She grinned at Tina. "You're probably thinking it's about time, huh?"

"Not for me to say. Still...I'm glad it's

happening." The older woman glanced down at her hands for a moment. "I have something else I need to discuss with you. Susan just found out she'll need to move out of her apartment for a little while. She told me last night. The management's doing a major overhaul of the plumbing in her building, and it's expected to take two or three weeks, maybe longer."

"You mean she wants to move back here?"

"If possible. She's aware of your situation, though, and figures she could stay with a friend, maybe alternate between a couple of them, if necessary."

"You mean couch surf? That's not fair to her! She needs to be here, with you. Maybe I can sleep on Cord's downstairs sofa. Or on Shallie's floor."

"You've already had so many disruptions in your life," Tina began. "And—"

"I'm doing really well. Loretta, my therapist, says so, too. Don't worry, okay? Let me talk to Cord and Shallie."

She did, later that afternoon. First with

Shallie, who said **of course** she'd share her room. Then with Cord, who told her they'd work something out.

Cord carried a glass of wine up to Shallie's suite, both dogs racing ahead of him. "Hey, don't make me spill this," he warned them. The door was open; he saw that she was at the small desk, working on her laptop.

"I'm drafting a possible blog," she told him. "Emma suggested it. What's going on?"

"Blog about?"

"The growing use of animals for therapy. Mostly horses and dogs, but others, too. She'll put me in touch with some of her clients to interview. And I can talk to the Lewises, plus Joey and Karen. When the blog's done, it'll go on her site." She paused. "It could go on yours, too, if you want."

"Please. And you'll let me know if I can help?"

"Oh, yes. I'll interview you, as well. Now, what's going on?" she asked again as he handed her the glass. "Whatever it is evidently requires liquid assistance."

He brought up what was happening with Susan—and Carly's possible displacement.

"She can stay here," Shallie said in a firm voice. "No problem at all."

"I have another—"

"Proposition?" She laughed, obviously remembering their earlier conversation.

He joined in her laughter, remembering it, too. "Kind of. Move in with me, and we'll let Carly have the guest suite."

"But—"

"Any clients can stay at Russ's motel, at reduced rates. In fact, I'm going to encourage him to do more renovation, fix up the rest of the place."

She was silent for a painfully long moment. "I know we've talked about this, me sharing your room..."

"More than once. Including earlier today." He'd mentioned it as a "future possibility" as they'd sat on the porch— although he'd actually meant "near future."

He knew her well enough now that he understood her loyalty and honesty, how strong and steadfast she was. There was no resemblance between her and Jenna, none at all. He also knew that, although they loved each other, her divorce—not to mention the fact that she'd lived with a history of abandonment—was something of an obstacle. He just hoped that the love she'd already shown him would allow her to take this first step toward a real—and permanent—commitment.

Her response was disappointing. She took a sip of her wine. "Can I think about it? Can I tell you tomorrow?"

"Fine." He realized his voice sounded rather sharp and tried to soften it. "Completely up to you," he said. "But you already know what I want."

"I'm sorry. Are you angry? Upset?"

He shook his head. "I'd better go see to the horses." He left, but the dogs stayed behind.

Shallie wondered what to do. She tried to

work, but kept returning to his question, with its potentially life-altering answer. Should she ask her best friend for advice? Emma would say **"Go for it!"** Should she trust her own instincts about Cord—which said "yes." Or her doubts, which said "maybe."

Yet her instincts had been positive about Rob, too. They'd been wrong, not at first but eventually.

This **was** different, though. Because her feelings for Cord had been part of her life for so long—even if they'd mostly resided in the background.

Those feeling were at least as big a reason for being here as her search for Christine and her hope of becoming Emma's business partner.

Another sip of wine. Hard not to fantasize about doing the same kind of work for Hollister Horses but on a permanent basis. Quitting the job in Seattle, leaving the apartment and starting over. With Cord. Revisiting—and revising—the past.

Damn it, she loved the man! When

had she become so scared of taking a chance?

She took one of those deep breaths that presaged an announcement. Or in her case, a decision. An answer.

And it was YES!

She'd tell Cord this evening, and there was one obvious way to do that.

She turned off her laptop, shooed out the dogs and left the suite, stopping in the kitchen for a refill—then headed up to his room.

Cord was ecstatic. No other word would do.

Shallie wanted to be with him, share his room. His life?

Surely this was another beginning! In so many ways...These last months were the best he'd ever spent. Shallie, Carly, reconnecting with his mother, the addition of therapy to his business. And his friends were as important as ever.

So, what **didn't** he have? What was he lacking? Anything?

Certainty, he supposed, but he trusted

that would come.

They spent what he could only describe as a passionate night together. They made love three times, each better than the one before.

They hadn't repeated their proclamations of love, not yet, but he was confident that wasn't far away. And he **felt** it, was sure she did, too.

Despite Reba, despite Jenna, who were part of his past. Cord's love for Shallie, and hers for him, were about the present and the future. As she herself had said, the past was past.

Shallie was thrilled by Cord's reaction — and her own. It all told her she'd made the right decision.

They informed Carly the next morning. Then he, Tina and Mitch worked out the logistics, which were easy enough. They'd move Shallie's stuff to his room that morning, help Carly move hers into the suite, and Susan would return to the trailer tomorrow. Tina and Mitch were delighted, and Shallie figured that had to do with more than just the arrangements regarding Susan.

She'd noticed Tina's subtle encouragement of her relationship with Cord, and knew her approval was assured. Mitch's, too.

Shallie and Cord met Russell for lunch at the center of the universe—or their universe, anyway, as the Lewises had described it. They discussed Cord's suggestion of refurbishing the remaining rooms and making the motel the official Hollister Horse destination. Russ had a cleaner now; it turned out that in a conversation with Susan a couple of weeks earlier, he'd mentioned his need for someone to help out. She'd recommended Elaine, a part-time assistant at the library who was looking for more work. He'd interviewed her and hired her on the spot.

At lunch, Shallie also suggested renovating the office and hallways. And the outside. Cord explained that he'd be willing to invest, and he thought J.P. would, too. They'd make some basic profit-sharing arrangement. Russ told them he was more than happy with everything; this was a whole new life for him. He said he was becoming part of the community in a way he'd never been before. And he thanked Shallie for her kindness, her encouragement.

Shallie was moved, knowing that her presence in Painted Pony Creek had made a difference.

CHAPTER TWENTY

Eli talked to Katie Fairfield, originally Katie Dupree, a nurse and ex-girlfriend of Cord's, about getting DNA tests done. She recommended using blood samples, which she said she'd be willing to take and submit to the lab situated in the county hospital. As sheriff, he was familiar with that lab, which was also used for criminal cases.

Katie agreed to meet them, together with her husband, Dr. Zach Fairfield, at Cord's place for that purpose. She warned him the results would probably take at least a month, since medical and criminal cases had priority—a fact he was already well aware of.

They met at Cord's late Friday after-noon; Katie collected the samples, and then she and Zach settled in for a relaxed hour or so. Well, **sort of** relaxed. It seemed to Eli that they were all determined to avoid talking about this important next step. Including Katie, whom he'd informed of the situation.

He hoped they'd get a response by mid-October...

He reflected that this evening was typical of the Fridays they often spent at Cord's. Except that Shallie had become a regular participant—and more than that, the two of them appeared to be a couple now. A real couple, although Cord hadn't confided in him or J.P. about that yet.

He saw their relationship as good news. It had made sense to him practically from the day of her arrival.

This was the first Friday in September, and so much had already changed. Obviously Carly's arrival was a big part of that; she had a role in their lives and in their town, and now she was attending the same high school they had.

Once the DNA results were in, even more would change.

Eli knew he had to present a positive outlook. And he did. He believed his own declarations—and those of Cord and J.P. However things turned out, they'd be okay. They'd talked about it. And they'd talked with Carly, alone and as a group.

Cord's place tonight offered the usual welcoming atmosphere; Eli enjoyed the time they spent with Katie and Zach, who stayed for a drink, then left before supper to get home to their kids.

A bit later, Lindsey came over, and so did Mitch, Tina, Susan and Russ. The barbecued ribs and veggie burgers were tasty, conversation was light, silly jokes were exchanged.

But, enjoyable though it was, the evening ended early.

Carly was in a constant, if low-level, state of anxiety about the coming DNA results, but knew there was nothing—nothing!—

she could do to hurry them along.

That aside, things were going well. She was in her first full year at the county high school, and to use a favorite saying of Reba's, **so far, so good**. She and Lindsey were both in the eleventh grade, same home room, and Eric Worth was in twelfth—repeating it, since he'd dropped out the previous year. Thankfully, none of his companions in crime were at the school anymore. With Shallie and Susan's guidance, the pet support group had been officially registered as Montana Pet Support, MPS for short. **Better than PMS**, as Carly had said, and that became a popular joke—among the girls, anyway. In fact, she sometimes wondered if the guys even got it.

With Tina's help and again Shallie's, Carly had assumed the role of administrator. "Good for your résumé," one of her new teachers said. But it provided a lot more than that.

They had several additional clients now—and **clients** was the term they used, although of course no money changed hands. One was a friend of Meg. Sandra had suffered a serious fall and lacked mobility. She had a beagle she adored—Holly the Second!—but this one was an older boy named Tex. Like Holly, he, too, was the sweetest little creature, and Carly fell instantly in love.

And there was Miles Carey's elderly father-in-law, who insisted on preserving his independence by living in a small apartment above a store on Main. His dog, a midsize part-Lab rescue named Linc, needed regular walks. Surprisingly, or maybe not, Eric had taken that on. He went over every weekday morning before school, and the old man's grandkids did the other shifts.

A third new client was a single mom, Alexa, with three-year-old twins; she needed assistance with her five (five!) cats.

Four MPS "clients" so far...

Susan Robbins was spreading the word, via a blog she'd done, posters in the small library, conversations with patrons.

And that odd but nice guy, Russ— Shallie's cousin or whatever—had said he'd help with transportation or any- thing MPS needed.

The program was gaining a strong reputation. Shallie, Cord, Tina, Eli, J.P., **everyone** seemed to congratulate her constantly.

Early days yet—another favorite Reba saying—but her classes were going well, especially English and music. She was making new friends, and she loved having her own large room at the ranch house, loved knowing Shallie and Cord were together. Outside of her anxiety about the DNA results (but it wasn't as though that could go **badly**), she'd never been happier.

And an unexpected bonus—when Susan moved in with Tina and Mitch for her temporary stay, she offered Carly some of the T-shirts she'd left at the trailer. She said Carly should take her pick, take as many as she wanted. Hard choice, since Carly liked (and had worn) them all. She chose the cat-love T-shirt, plus the So Many Books one and then the one celebrating The GateCrashers. No need to be greedy, she told herself. In exchange, she gave Susan the Horses Help T-shirt she'd received from Emma, figuring she could easily ask for—or buy—another.

Cord and Julie spoke every two days, as they'd promised. She'd told him that last month's forest fire had been devastating, but successfully vanquished. She and Chris hoped the damage to woods, farmland and a number of small towns could be repaired, recovered from, although they knew it would take years.

He'd told her about the situation with Carly and the DNA test. Julie regularly asked if he'd "heard anything yet."

"Trust me, I'll let you know," he always said.

Her other regular question was when (not if) he and Shallie were getting married.

Same response.

• • •

Shallie's most recent call with Emma, a day ago, had ended with what was becoming a standard question. "So, when are you two getting married?"

Standard response: "Don't know."

"Come on! You're meant to be with him. You're such a great couple!"

"Perhaps..."

"And you're basically living together as it is. Make it official already!"

"We'll see."

Then their call moved on to other subjects. Emma described her new therapy clients and mentioned that many of the people Shallie had met were continuing to improve. In turn, Shallie told her about Cord's newest clients, a couple from Chicago who were staying at Russ's motel. She went on to say that she and Cord had talked to Russ about fixing up more rooms, making his motel the "residence of choice" for Hollister Horses' clients. And, as Cord had sur-mised, J.P. was interested in getting involved, investing in the motel and its renovations.

Emma asked about Carly, and Shallie found it easy to respond. Everything was positive—doing well at school, loving her music program, planning another concert with The GateCrashers, which made her a celebrity among her fellow students. The pet support charity had brought her happiness and satisfaction.

And what about Shallie's own plans? Emma asked. Was she thinking about returning to Seattle if she wasn't sure about marrying Cord? "I miss you so much," she added.

"I miss you, too. We'll talk soon, okay?" Shallie said hastily. "Gotta run."

She didn't really have to, but during their conversation, she'd suddenly realized this uncertainty couldn't go on. She couldn't continue in a state of indecision regarding her future. After all, she still had a job, her unpaid leave extended for another month, and an apartment in Seattle. She and Cord had to determine exactly where their relation-

ship was going. Marriage? Shallie moving here? Some kind of arrangement
with her living part-time in both places?
Although she couldn't imagine him being
enthusiastic about **that**. And honestly?
Neither was she.

Despite their history and genuine
connection, great sex, a shared sense
of humor...she still had doubts. Fleeting
ones, perhaps, but self-protective ones,
mostly at this point based on Rob's
unexpected betrayal. And yet, had she
ever loved anyone more than Cord? Had
she ever **trusted** anyone more?

Cord, out in the stable that afternoon,
was perturbed by Shallie's text—mostly
because it was so abrupt. **Need to see
you. 5 p.m. okay? Porch, with drink**.

That sounded rather alarming, but he
immediately texted back. **Sure. See you
then**.

At 4:45 p.m., he was sitting on the
porch with two dogs, one beer and a
waiting glass of wine.

She hurried outside, apparently surprised he was already there. "Oh...hi."

He picked up the wineglass, held it out to her, then gave her a chance to settle in one of the chairs, greet the dogs, take a sip. "All right. What's so urgent? You okay?" he asked.

"I'm fine. Well, not really."

He leaned forward, frowning. "What do you mean?"

"I need to know where we are. In terms of our relationship. We're living together —sort of. Sharing a room, anyway. Not to mention sleeping together. But how serious **are** we?"

"I'm serious," he said. "Totally and completely." He had to stop, breathe deeply, so conscious of her beauty, her nearness, her scent. "I'm in love with you." He paused again. "I told you that night in Silver Hills, remember?"

She stared down at her wine, at the dogs, the wooden slats of the floor— anywhere but at him. Then she glanced up. "I do remember. And I remember what I said. That I might be in love with you, too."

He nodded, recalling the moment. Not that it was ever far from his mind. "But when we talked about this earlier, I got the feeling you weren't ready..."

"Now I am. I want to be with you for the rest of our lives. I love you. And," she added, "I realize I'm not afraid anymore. Because I trust you. I just needed your reassurance that—"

He reached across to embrace her, accidentally knocking the glass out of her hand, wine spilling on her jeans—but fortunately not on the dogs. "Sorry! I'll go get you a towel and another drink. But answer my question first. Will you marry me?"

"Hey! I was going to ask! The answer is yes, but as Carly would say, how traditional of you—thinking the man has to be the one to propose."

"Carly does tend to see **traditional** as a negative. We'll do a mutual proposal, okay? But I'll go refill your glass first so we can toast to our future. Or is that too traditional?"

She laughed. "Who cares? Could you

bring some food while you're at it? And some dog treats?"

He returned with a tea towel draped over his arm, carrying her wine, plus a dish of corn chips and guacamole. And a couple of dog chews, which he handed out. "Good enough, you guys?" Their wagging tails said it was.

Once she'd dried off her jeans and he'd arranged everything on the table, he held out his arms. Shallie stood up and practically fell into them; he sat back in his chair, with her on his lap. After a series of kisses, quick ones and slow, he set her down. "Now, about that proposal..."

"Yeah. Gotta do this right." She picked up her glass and raised it to his. "Cord Hollister, you're the man I love. Will you marry me?"

"Yes, Shallie Fletcher, I will. And now it's my turn to ask the question—even though you've already answered it with yours. Will **you** marry **me**?"

"Yes!" She giggled, pointing at the dogs. "You can't back out now. We have two witnesses."

"I have no intention of backing out. I love you," he said. "You make my life complete in a way it's never been before."

Serious again, she told him, "You've done the same for me."

They sorted out some plans that evening.

They'd have the wedding on the Friday before Christmas, they decided. Short notice, but they'd send out the invitations in the next few days. And they'd have an informal party here on the Saturday of Thanksgiving weekend.

Then, their planning as complete as possible for now, they went to bed—to **really** celebrate.

The following day, they talked about selecting a best man and a maid of honor; certain wedding niceties would be observed. Shallie's maid of honor would be Emma; Cord said Eli and J.P. should draw cards to decide who should be the best man. Or maybe he'd just skip right to Trooper—as his "beast man."

The GateCrashers would be hired to provide the music for both events with, naturally, an original contribution or two from Carly.

Shallie tried not to think about the DNA tests. She hated the now-common expression, "It is what it is," but...It would be what it would be. She'd come to recognize that what she hoped for was not only to be part of Cord's life but Carly's, as well.

The invitations went out by mail and email, and responses were coming back quickly.

These days she was helping Carly with MPS by driving her to some of the appointments, writing a blog about the charity, which Susan—with whom she was becoming good friends—posted on the library website. MPS now had nine area clients. She also continued to work with Cord's horse people.

They'd made a number of decisions about the wedding. The ceremony itself would be in the Painted Pony Creek

Community Church, followed by a
reception at Bailey's. She and Carly
ordered dresses, fairly informal but long,
hers an off-white, Carly's a pale blue.

In mid-October, she flew to Seattle,
planning to spend three days there. She
resigned from her job, meeting former
colleagues for dinner that first night.
Julie flew in for a couple of days, and that
meant a lot to Shallie.

She gave up her apartment as of
month's end, offering Julie Daniels, as
well as Emma, any furniture, electronics
and kitchenware they could use. The rest
was picked up by a local charity.

Shallie didn't keep much—clothes,
some books, which she shipped to herself in Montana, a few personal effects
and jewelry.

She loved seeing Julie again and was
beginning to feel a new depth of connection. With Shallie's agreement, Cord
had shared the news about their engage-
ment. Now Julie told Shallie repeatedly
how happy this made her, that she
already adored her as a daughter-in-law

and was convinced no woman could be better for her son. "We'll definitely plan to be at the wedding," she promised. "And the Thanksgiving party if possible."

When Julie drove her to the airport on Sunday, she handed her a small sealed package. "I called Cord and told him I'm giving you this to bring home. It's my wedding ring, from his dad."

It was all Shallie could do not to open it midflight.

Eli, J.P. (and Trooper) met Cord for brunch at Bailey's that same afternoon to discuss what they called "the best man thing." They listed the alternatives. Draw cards as suggested by Cord. Find out if they could **both** take on the role. Recommend someone else? No way!

But if Shallie had **two** maids of honor, they could do the two-best-men scenario, couldn't they?

Brow wrinkled in a frown, J.P. wondered if they were being childish about this, like grade-school kids competing in a school-yard. Eli disagreed. "No.

Because we're friends. Close and long-time friends. In fact, we fought for this friendship—"

"Fought **about** it, anyway."

They grinned and Eli continued. "The three of us are important in each other's lives. I truly believe that. I've always believed it, especially after that Christmas."

"The one orchestrated by your grandfather," J.P. reminded him—as if any of them could have forgotten. "And you know I feel exactly the same. But we do have some time before this has to be resolved."

The conversation wandered in different directions. How well Russ was doing with the motel renos and J.P.'s pride in the venture. How much Eric had progressed; Eli gave credit to a long list of people—including Carly and Lindsey and the pet support group. Sara. And Eric himself.

"Hey, he knows you'll kick his ass from here to beyond if he screws up again."

"True. But I honestly think he **wants** to

be the person he should be. By the way, I saw Sara and Hayley last night, and I could tell they're a lot happier these days because Eric's doing so well."

J.P. nodded. "Let's just hope he stays with it." He paused. "Any news on that missing donkey? The one with the storybook name?"

"Eeyore." Eli shrugged deeply. "Not yet, but Eric told me just a few days ago that he hasn't given up hope. He can't forgive himself for that—or the dead sheep."

"He's right. Pretty bad.," Cord said.

"He's making up for it the best he can."

"So, what happens now?" J.P. asked.

Shaking his head, Eli murmured, "Don't know. It's like an unsolved crime. Maybe Eeyore was killed, worst-case scenario. Or rescued, best case. We put out the word a month ago, but got no response."

J.P. sighed. "Too bad. Should we try doing another patrol?"

"I don't think so, and this isn't the best time of year for it, either." He hailed

Brynne who, without asking, brought them each a local dark ale, plus "a Trooper treat" that she slid under the table.

"Thanks," they said and Trooper lashed his tail excitedly.

"On the house. I heard you talking about that poor animal and—"

"Not necessary to give us a free beer. But we'll take it. Any suggestions?"

She pointed at Trooper. "What about involving this little man?"

"We've asked the owner if she has a dog who might recognize his scent. She doesn't."

"Maybe Shallie or Susan could do a blog about it," Brynne said."

Eli nodded slowly. "Good idea." But he had a better one. He'd ask Carly. Her YouTube channel could be a real opportunity in a situation like this.

Okay, that meant there were two questions he wanted to settle as soon as possible—the damn best man (or men) thing and the whereabouts of Eeyore. And, of course, the DNA result, but that he could do nothing about.

After lunch Eli invited himself over to Cord's; fortunately, it was a Saturday. Cord had more clients coming in, although not until Monday. Late afternoon, the two of them went riding—Eli hadn't done that in ages—and stopped to sit on a rock outcropping, inhaling the scent of fall, reveling in the beauty of the early-setting sun.

"So, on the topic of who's going to be your best man..."

Cord seemed confused. "What about it? Up to you guys. Does it really matter?"

"Sure does, and you should get that."

Sigh. "I'm fine with either of you. Do whatever you want."

"No," he protested firmly. "It has to be what **you and Shallie** want." He stared into the trees for a moment. "Like we discussed, how about if J.P. and I both do it—and Shallie has a second maid of honor?"

"I'll ask her."

That was the end of that particular subject for now. They were soon distracted by a host of other problems, questions—and a few jokes.

On her late afternoon return from Seattle, Cord met Shallie in baggage claim at the Billings airport. She'd brought two suitcases from the apartment, filled with the clothes, memorabilia and gifts she was keeping. After a long welcome-home kiss, he hauled her suitcases to the car. The small package from Julie was tucked in her purse. She'd have to find the right time to give it to him—perhaps over dinner.

Once in the car, they kissed again. "I missed you so much," he murmured. "I can't wait to hear more about the trip— and to get you home."

"I missed you, too. I never want to leave you again." They'd exchanged regular phone calls and texts while she was away, but that wasn't the same...

At Shallie's suggestion they stopped to visit a restaurant with an attractive dining room, lavishly decorated with flowering plants.

After a few minutes of conversation about her time in Seattle and how things were in Painted Pony Creek, she said, "I think we could use a glass of champagne, don't you?"

"Sure! To celebrate your home-coming." He raised his hand to attract the waiter's attention. Once their drinks arrived, they raised their glasses. "To us," he proclaimed.

"And to celebrate...this." She reached into her purse and pulled out the packet, then opened it to reveal a velvet box. "Julie gave me this for you. It's her wedding ring from your dad."

"Yeah, she told me." Cord actually felt tears well up, spill over—and they were nothing he was ashamed of. Shallie gently brushed his cheeks with one hand.

A minute later, he said, "Why don't we invite Carly to be our ring bearer at the wedding?"

"Yes!" She nodded vigorously. "I love that idea!"

Gazing down at the simple gold ring in its velvet box, he said, "This will bring so many parts of my life together. You and me, Carly, my family."

"Yes," she said again. "You ask her, okay?"

"No, we should do it together."

And that night they did. He also explained the best man "issue"—and Shallie immediately said she'd see if Tina would be her matron of honor.

She called Tina, and in a matter of minutes heard an enthusiastic "Of course!"

Carly wrote a brief entry in her journal.

> Another reason to smile! I'm going to be the ring bearer at Cord and Shallie's wedding! Cord did say he knows it's a really "traditional" thing, and that he's not officially my dad (yet?) and that I might consider myself too old for that kind of role.
> I told him and Shallie that none of those things matter. I'm

just so honored by this. I know
their wedding will be one of the
happiest days in my life.

That evening, Eli went to Sara's for
dinner, delighted to find the whole family
in a good mood. Still, he watched Eric
carefully and sensed that his nephew felt
a bit nervous, but when Sara proposed
that they play an old-fashioned board
game, they all joined in. Hayley chose
Monopoly, which Eli hadn't played in—
what? Twenty years? At least. And, for
her age, Hayley was a better-than-aver-
age player and deserved the win she
achieved.

After goodbye hugs with Sara and
Hayley and a handshake with Eric, the
boy followed him to the door, asking
for a confidential discussion. Keeping
his voice low, he said that one of his
companions in crime had texted him a
threatening message. "Who is it?" Eli
asked bluntly. "Threatening how? Give
me details."

Eric shook his head. "I'm not sure

that's a good idea. I just wanted you to know about it."

"Do you want me to do something or not?"

"Uh. I guess we should leave it for now. I'm not really scared—more pissed off."

"Okay, I'll have to go along with that. But you call me the second you hear from this jerk again. If you do."

Eric nodded, a gloomy look on his face.

"Listen," Eli said. "You've been doing really well. We're all proud of you."

"Thanks, Uncle Eli. I mean that. I owe you and Mom and Loretta—you know, my therapist—and a bunch of other people for that. I feel like I have a future now."

"You do, damn it!"

"You don't have to yell at me."

Eli sighed, relieved that Sara and Hayley had gone upstairs. "Sorry, I know. Just keep in mind that you have a second chance here." He clasped Eric's shoulder. "You've got a lot of potential and we're all counting on you."

But as he climbed into his car, he couldn't help worrying that this former so-called friend of Eric's was going to be trouble.

Sunday, Carly made an announcement about Eeyore on her YouTube channel, and then it occurred to her to offer a reward. She asked Eric what he thought. He said he couldn't afford it, but otherwise would do whatever was necessary to get that little critter found. If she fronted the money, he promised he'd eventually pay her back, although it wouldn't be for quite a while. She dismissed that, and with his not always helpful comments, wrote a piece about Eeyore, offering a thousand-dollar reward. He seemed impressed with what she'd written and agreed to contact Joanne Berg, the owner, to ask for a photo. He received it within the hour, and the post went out. Granted, this would go continent-wide or wider, and Carly knew there'd be hundreds if not thousands of comments. But she agreed with Eli that it might be their best chance of tracking down the animal.

The money didn't matter to her. These days, she had enough, and since Len had started helping her with investments, she had **more** than enough.

Responses to her YouTube piece started coming in almost immediately, including quite a few local ones. She insisted Eric review them with her, and he said she didn't even need to ask.

Eric sat at the dining room table, where she'd set up her laptop, examining each response with her. She shouldn't have been shocked, but she was, by the number of scammers. **You live in Alabama and you "found" him...really? On the highway? What, he was hitching a ride? Oh, and you'll ship him back here if I send you the money first?**

Delete. **What kind of dum-dum do you think I am?**

She was outraged but amused. Eric just seemed embarrassed, probably because he'd done his own share of scamming—and worse.

But after sifting through a couple of hundred responses, they came up with one that seemed credible. A woman, Ruth Cooper, who lived about six miles from Painted Pony Creek, claimed she'd found Eeyore or a donkey resembling him. Or rather, one of her dogs had. The donkey had been by himself in a nearby field; he was disheveled and stumbling. She'd assumed the animal had been dumped or abandoned and brought him home. She included a photo, but it was difficult to tell with any certainty if this was Eeyore...

They made an arrangement with Ruth to go and see the donkey the next afternoon after school, before calling Joanne.

They did that with Eli's approval; he drove them there and went in with them.

Meeting Ruth was a gratifying experience. She, her kids and her husband had a genuineness, a quality of kindness, that affected all of them. And the fact that a number of obviously much-loved animals seemed to be running around their home appealed to Carly.

Ruth suggested that Joanne come to her place to determine whether this was, indeed, Eeyore—and she said that if it was, she absolutely would not accept the reward.

Carly asked if she'd be willing to donate it to MPS, and Ruth gave her immediate approval.

Eli followed up with Ruth and Joanne the next day, meeting both of them at Ruth's—and yes, this **was** Eeyore. He was clearly familiar with Joanne and showed her unmistakable affection; not only that, Joanne described a couple of scars he had before she even went out to see him.

Eeyore was going home.

Again, Eli felt proud of Carly. She was the one who'd brought this reunion about. And he was pleased with the strides Eric had made as a pet support volunteer.

So, yes, things were going well. Life

seemed almost too good—and that always worried him. It probably said more about his own disappointed hopes than anything else. There'd been enough in his life to prejudice him against excessive optimism, as he thought of it.

He hated to admit this again, but he was a little envious of Cord, one of his two closest friends. In actuality, he felt glad for him **and** envious. But he was determined to be stoic about it.

Cord was worried about Eli's glum demeanor lately, and his apparent lack of enthusiasm about the community, an enthusiasm that had always defined him.

It would be awkward to bring any of this up, despite their longtime friendship. They didn't usually share personal things of this kind with each other, didn't usually discuss emotional concerns.

Jeez, how "traditional." How masculine. At least according to the stereotypes and no doubt to Carly. He decided he'd do what he could for Eli, without being obvious about it.

For a few years now, he'd had the suspicion—the **strong** suspicion—that Eli was interested in Brynne. Any chance he could do something to encourage a relationship there? He'd ask Shallie, trusting her emotional responsiveness more than his own. But at least he could tell Eli that she was fine with the double bridesmaid/double best man scenario, that Tina had happily agreed to be matron of honor.

At the end of October, the day before Halloween, Katie Fairfield set up a conference call with Carly and all three men to tell them that the result was in.

"Okay, everybody, I'll get right to the point. The DNA evidence says, and says conclusively, that...Cord is Carly's dad."

And once Katie made the announcement, Carly's happiness, already at a high point, completely lit up her life, like a brilliant sun in the noon sky.

Cord was her dad!

The two of them had been sitting

together to hear the news, Cord's phone on speaker. He threw it down so they could exchange a long hug. Then Carly ran to tell first Shallie, and then her "second mom," Tina, while Cord accepted J.P. and Eli's congratulations.

CHAPTER TWENTY-ONE

Even though—or probably because—certain decisions had now been made, there seemed to be more planning than ever. Shallie was constantly making lists, comparing notes with Cord, getting opinions from her friends. And, of course, from her daughter-to-be.

One thing she'd decided was that she'd return to her graphic arts work; she'd help Cord, Russ, Susan and Carly with advertising and websites. Cord had his out-of-town PR group and Carly was certainly familiar with YouTube, but Shallie could contribute art, design and logos, and help set up the pet support website. Not that she intended any of that to be a moneymaker; it was simply a matter of doing something for family and the people she'd come to consider her friends.

Another plan—photography. It was an interest that had recently grown, and she was going to experiment, taking pictures of this beautiful country, with all its strengths and paradoxes, its people and their love of the land.

She'd have to buy a new and more sophisticated camera.

Then, on November first, she received an unexpected call from Eddie, telling her he had a possible lead on Christine Fletcher—emphasizing the word **possible**. When he described what he knew, or might know, it sounded to Shallie like another bizarre saga. He said that a former staff member at Sunny Days, the motel in Orlando, had contacted Tony, his investigator friend, to say she thought she'd seen "Sharon Sutherland" a couple of months ago, although she and Sharon hadn't spoken. "No idea why she'd go back there, or what her name is now, but

Tony's on it and we're not letting this go. Melanie's doing another online search, too."

Later that evening, she, Russ and Cord considered various potential circumstances over a drink at Bailey's. Had Christine/Sharon left something behind? Could she be looking for another job? Was she, for whatever reason, nostalgic about the place, considering she'd lived there for quite a few years. And the most basic question of all—was it even her?

"We'll have to leave it to the professionals," Cord concluded.

Shallie confessed that she was worried about the increasing expense, but they both told her it was more important to track down Christine and assured her they were willing to help. Especially generous of Russ, since he didn't have a lot of money to throw around.

"I can't imagine what name she'd be using now," Shallie said. "I don't know enough about her to even guess. Probably a random name she came across on her travels."

Then something occurred to her. Would Christine **dare** use Reba's name, either her first or her last? Did she know her one-time friend had died? The fact of Reba's death would've been easy enough to find out if Christine had access to the internet and she probably did.

Horrifying as the thought of stealing Reba's name was, Shallie decided to go online herself, see what—if anything—she could learn. She didn't mention it to the others, although it was something she might bring up with Eddie.

She did ask Russ if he'd had any success with his search for Bethanne, but figured she would've heard. He'd told her he hadn't found even a trace of his sister, and the husband hadn't res-ponded to a message he'd sent via Facebook.

Talk turned to the wedding. Russ told them that renovations on the motel were progressing, and that the contractor recommended by J.P. was doing a fantastic job. "And he's speedy, too!"

So, any out-of-town visitors who needed accommodation could stay there, as his guests.

Susan's part-time library colleague, Elaine, was still working as the motel's cleaner and was helping with administration.

Another important aspect of the Thanksgiving party was that Cord, Eli and J.P. had stuck to their resolve, motivated by Carly, to announce the DNA results there, to friends and other family members. This was partly because all four of them were still adjusting. And as Carly had said, why not make a dramatic event of it? This was their new truth, a truth they needed to share, and it had to be given the importance it deserved.

Shallie and Cord agreed it made sense to include this announcement in their celebration. So far, none of them had talked about the DNA results with friends or even relatives, everyone holding it close.

She reflected on something else for a

moment. Another possible change in the future they were shaping, she and Cord. They hadn't yet talked about having children, a conversation that needed to happen soon...So far she hadn't stopped taking her birth control pills.

Both she and Cord were in their mid-thirties, so from a biological perspective, hers, anyway, the timing might be getting a little urgent.

She'd talk to Cord about it later tonight. In bed.

After they'd made love, with gentleness and the deepest affection she'd ever felt or experienced, she asked him.

Cord replied that he'd always wanted a family, a child or children, and had assumed it would happen. How did **she** feel?

"I **do** want a baby but it wasn't something Rob was ever interested in," she admitted. "I thought he'd change his mind—"

"His loss. But I want children and I want them with you."

"I want that, too! And we should do it soon..."

"We can afford to wait," Cord said. "A little while, anyway."

"Not too long," she warned, repeating the thought she'd had earlier that evening about their ages.

"Let's take the next year to decide," Cord suggested.

Shallie guessed their decision would be made well before that, probably by Christmastime and their wedding. And she was almost positive she knew what it would be.

Cord loved her and he wanted a baby in their lives soon. He started for the stables midmorning, gripping a second coffee, the dogs trotting alongside. Shallie was working on her laptop and, since it was Saturday, Carly was presumably still asleep.

Today was a calm and colorful fall day, and he hoped they'd be able to take advantage of it. There wouldn't be many more of them this year.

He realized Mitch hadn't appeared yet, which was unusual. But it **was** Saturday and he decided to give the older man a break.

He put his cup on a railing when he saw Susan Robbins running toward him, the dogs dashing over to meet her. She ignored them. "There's something wrong with my dad!" she shouted when she was within hearing distance.

Cord reacted immediately. "What? What's wrong with him?"

"We tried to phone you," she panted.

Of course! The one time he'd forgotten his cell...

"We think he might've had a heart attack."

Cord asked her to shoo the dogs inside, since he didn't need them getting in the way, and to tell Shallie about Mitch—then ran at double speed to the trailer. The door had been flung open, and he yelled for Tina, who came running from their bedroom.

"You called an ambulance?"

"Yes. On their way."

He hurried back to the room with her, asking, "What are the symptoms?"

"He didn't get up at his usual time, but I didn't worry about it. I went in to see him again five minutes ago—and he's having trouble breathing!"

Mitch lay in bed, his breathing erratic. Cord recognized that he was suffering from shortness of breath, a common heart attack symptom.

He'd learned CPR years before and started to perform it, pumping Mitch's chest, alternating that with mouth-to-mouth resuscitation.

He could hear the ambulance arriving, siren blaring, and asked Tina to direct the paramedics inside. At almost the same time, he heard Susan, Shallie and Carly rush in.

The two young paramedics, a man and a woman, continued the CPR, checked Mitch's vitals, then laid him on the gurney. Fast and efficient, they got him into the ambulance, accompanied by Tina.

Cord said they'd drive to the county

hospital, meet Tina there, and shortly after that, he set off, with Shallie, Carly and Susan. Carly told them she'd try to get in touch with Lindsey and Eric to arrange for cat coverage at Meg's. Both her friends responded quickly (and now she did think of Eric as a friend, which would've been a shocking idea a couple of months ago); both wished Mitch well and said not to worry about MPS or Meg's cats, that they were on it.

At the hospital, the group spent about three hours in the waiting room, trying to comfort and reassure Tina. Many tears, much hugging.

Cord knew, they all did, that Mitch was only seventy and had always been in good health. His own thoughts had instinctively and immediately reverted to his grandfather's death—of a sudden heart attack. Cord had been trying to stave off the memory. He'd told Shallie about Bill's death in their conversation the day she'd arrived, and she obviously remembered. She kept her arm around him and whispered that his grandfather would be proud of him, whispered words of encouragement. Susan sat in the same position with her mother, after calling her sisters. Caroline and Elspeth showed up as soon as they could, family members trailing in after them.

Meanwhile, Cord called Eli and J.P. and they came, too. As did Russ after Shallie sent him a text.

The small waiting room was soon filled to crowding with Mitch's family and friends.

Eventually, one of the surgeons walked in, still wearing his scrubs; he asked Tina if she'd prefer that he speak to her privately. "No," she insisted, this was her family.

The doctor nodded, then said, "Mr. Robbins had what we consider a minor heart attack. It's the damage to the heart muscle, or muscles, that determines the severity of the incident. He has a blocked artery and we've dealt with that by inserting a stent." He then asked if anyone had questions.

Susan did. Would her dad be on any

kind of medication?

Mitch would be on beta-blockers to reduce his blood pressure, the surgeon explained, and he'd be receiving very specific physiotherapy. As far as Cord was aware, Mitch hadn't ever had high blood pressure before—but what did he really know?

There'd be another important change, this one to his diet; he'd have to avoid saturated fats and high-sodium foods...

He and Tina would meet with one of the hospital dieticians to discuss these restrictions, and Mitch would need regular medical exams and tests.

One final caveat. He'd have to restrain his physical activity.

Cord took that to mean Mitch's work at the ranch was finished. Not that Cord was giving him a choice; he refused to risk his friend's life. So Mitch would have to consider himself retired.

Cord could only feel grateful that Mitch had survived and that his prospects were good. He'd continue to pay him—a pension, as it were, well deserved after all the years of working for his grandfather and then him.

This wasn't the time to worry about assistance with the ranch. But...maybe he could hire Eric for a while? Part-time? He'd see what Eli thought.

On the drive home from the hospital, Shallie, sitting in front with Cord, told him that she'd learned nothing—less than nothing— about Christine Fletcher in her newest online search. It was what she'd been doing on her laptop that morning, she went on to say. She even described her theory, although in retrospect it sounded pretty weak, that Christine might have stolen some part of Reba's name for her new alias.

Carly and Susan in the backseat both had earphones on. Good. Carly didn't need to hear this.

Cord shrugged. "No crazier than any other theory we've come up with."

"Maybe..."

"What about Russ? Any success with his search?"

"Nope. I talked to him for a few minutes at the hospital. He tried to get hold of Bethanne's husband again, but no luck there, either."

Their conversation shifted to their concern about Mitch and their relief that his outlook was positive as well as the changes this would bring to his life.

Over the next week they took turns visiting Mitch. Shallie drove Carly to the hospital in the afternoons or evenings, when she wasn't in school and didn't have MPS responsibilities. More than once, Mitch asked Carly to sing for him, and his favorite choices included "Hallelujah" and her animal song. Inevitably nurses, other patients and their guests gathered around, some joining in, all of them applauding.

Shallie loved loved seeing how happy it made him—and Carly.

One evening when she and Cord were visiting, he asked them for what he called a favor. He said he knew they'd already made wedding plans, but could he give Shallie away? Kind of old-fashioned, he acknowledged. Still, he'd done it at two previous weddings, with his daughters Caroline and Elspeth—so didn't that mean he'd be good at it? Besides, he loved both Cord and Shallie, and it would mean a lot to him. And with Tina being the matron of honor ...It all seemed to fit, didn't it? They laughed and instantly agreed.

This wedding seemed to be getting more complicated and more traditional by the day. But she valued Mitch's request, his desire to be an integral part of the most important event in her life so far. And it wasn't as though she had— or **ever** had—a father of her own to assume that role. Norm Schafer came the closest but he hadn't exactly been what you'd call an adequate dad.

A week later, Mitch was home again, settled in bed for the next few days. By then Cord had regular help from Eric, two afternoons a week and Saturdays. He told Shallie he was pleased by Eric's newly positive attitude and his willingness to learn, and he knew that much of the money he was paying the boy would go to the ranchers he still owed. Brynne had also recommended her waiter, Barry from Detroit, who claimed that he was "thrilled to get a real Western experience."

So, back at the ranch, as Carly had started to say, things were fine. For the moment.

Shallie felt it was very much an in-between time. Above all, waiting to see Mitch's condition improve. Waiting for Thanksgiving and wedding plans to coalesce. And she was intent on making progress with her photography and other new projects.

As Thanksgiving—and their party—drew closer, she noticed that their moods lightened, their fears lessened. But she couldn't put a halt to her worries about Mitch; naturally, Cord felt the same. Mitch's close call had made them more aware than ever of the uncertainty and brevity of life, of the need to cherish each and every day.

And ultimately, what was Thanksgiving about if not gratitude for life itself?

Shallie received another call from Russ, saying he had something else to show her. He didn't know what it meant, he said, if it meant anything at all, but could she come over to look at it? Now? She knew from experience that he wouldn't reveal anything he considered poten- tially important except in person.

She immediately drove to the motel, where he was waiting to let her in.

"So, what is it?" she asked, realizing she sounded impatient. "I mean, thanks and what is it?"

"Like I said, it could be useless. Here." He took a postcard, in almost pristine condition, from his desk and handed it over. "I actually found it in a book of Della's, if you can believe that. She was never much of a reader, but...Post date's 2004. The year Della died."

The front was a photograph of Hemingway House in Key West, with its colony of cats. The card was addressed to the Painted Pony Motel, and on the back someone had printed a brief message by hand.

> S. WOULD LOVE THIS PLACE.
> GIVE POSTCARD TO HER IF
> YOU CAN. HOPE SHE'S WELL.
> LOVE.

No signature, not even any initials.

Could this **possibly** be from Christine Fletcher? There were two hints. The reference to "S," clearly a girl or woman, and the fact that it had been sent from Florida, where she'd had a long history. Was Christine saying—and this would've been fifteen years ago, Shallie reminded herself—that she lived or had been living in Key West?

"Maybe it **is** from Christine," Russell said. "Anyway, I'd say it's more grist for Eddie's mill. And didn't you say there'd been a sighting in Florida?"

"Yes, at or near the motel where she used to work in Orlando. I'll courier this to him," Shallie said. "And he can pass it on to Tony."

She brought home the postcard to show Cord and Eli over lunch, and they agreed it was worth sending to Eddie. Shallie made the arrangements at the small courier office on Main—actually a kiosk at the drugstore—then met Carly at Meg's.

On their way home, she told her about the postcard. What seemed to impress Carly most was the information about the cats. "Wow! So they're all descendants of Hemingway's cats?"

"Yeah. And his wife at the time, Pauline. Oh, and the cats are polydactyl." Shallie had made a point of looking up Hemingway House for her own information.

"What's that?"

"It means they have an extra digit—like a thumb."

"Cool! So can they open packages and type and stuff like that?"

"I'm sure some of them can."

"But if it was...your mom, why did she send **that** card?"

"I guess to let me know, in an indirect way, where she was at the time, which was about fourteen years ago. But right now?" She shrugged. "Could be any-where. Or nowhere."

"It's Eddie's job to find that out, right?"

"Right." And by then they'd reached the house.

CHAPTER TWENTY-TWO

Friday of Thanksgiving Weekend

They were all gathered around the dining-room table—Cord and Shallie, Carly, Brynne, Tina and Mitch—finalizing plans for tomorrow's party.

Brynne went through her menu, the bar list, quantities. "So, we're expecting about sixty guests," she said.

"Yes," Shallie confirmed. "From near and far." Julie and family would be coming from San Diego, Emma from Seattle, Eddie from Tucson.

Brynne smiled at that. "Okay, I think we're covered."

"Don't forget the bourbon for Russ,"

Shallie said.

"And we'll provide the dog treats," Carly put in.

"I figured," Brynne said with a laugh. "I love that dogs are welcome."

Cord laughed, too. "I'm sure you wouldn't expect any different."

"Not here, I wouldn't." She paused, looking up. "Is that a phone I hear?"

"It's my cell," Shallie answered. "Now, where did I leave it?"

"In the kitchen, I think." Carly jumped up to get it. "Yeah—and it's Eddie calling."

Shallie answered seconds before the call could go to voice mail. "Hi, Eddie! Hope you're not canceling on us."

"No way. But...are you sitting down?"

"Um, no."

"Sounds like you have people over. I suggest you and Cord go into another room for a few minutes."

"Hold on. We'll call you back," she said breathlessly.

She leaned down to say in Cord's ear, "We need to talk to Eddie. Privately."

He stood abruptly, saying, "Excuse us, everyone. Be back shortly."

Up in their room, hands shaking, Shallie hit Redial. Cord's arm was around her waist as Eddie answered.

"Cord and I are by ourselves now," Shallie told him. "I'm putting the phone on speaker."

"Good. I've been in touch with…" He paused, but somehow Shallie knew whose name he was going to say. And he did. "Christine Fletcher."

Shallie couldn't stop shaking. "Then she's…she's still alive."

"Sure is."

Cord moved her gently toward the bed; they sat down as he continued to hold her close.

"Is she…all right?" Shallie hardly knew what to ask, what to say. Her **mother**! After a lifetime of grieving, searching, wondering…

"She is. And she asked me the same about you. I was happy to report that you're doing very well."

"Where is she?"

"Key West." Shallie immediately remembered that postcard. "And she's married to a guy named Doug Elliot. So her name's Christine Elliot now."

"Th-thanks."

"She'd like to speak to you tonight. And she and Doug would like to visit, fly in tomorrow if possible. She doesn't want to wait. Is that a problem, with your party and all?"

Cord whispered in her ear. "Tell him it's fine."

She nodded. "That'll be okay. But give me an hour or so before she calls." She turned to Cord. "Where would they stay?" she whispered.

"Don't worry. We'll figure it out," he whispered back.

"I'll have her call at five, your time," Eddie said. "And I'll see you tomorrow. By the way, is it all right if I tell Eli—in confidence, of course—since he's been instrumental in getting this search set up?"

She glanced at Cord and said, "Yes. And it's fine for him to tell J.P."

Then the call was over, and she collapsed onto the bed. "Could you let everyone know I'll see them later?"

"What about telling Carly?"

"You and I will tell her this evening."

At precisely five, her cell phone rang. Shallie had spent the intervening hour thinking about the questions she wanted to ask and rehearsing her own responses to the questions she thought Christine was likely to ask.

Despite having waited and hoped so long for this very thing, she wasn't ready, couldn't possibly be.

"Hello?"

"Shallie? This is Christine Elliot. Your... mother."

She couldn't speak yet. A moment later, she managed to say, "Mom."

"It's me. Oh, Shallie, baby, I've loved you all these years. I've missed you so much."

"Me, too, Mom. But why didn't you try to get in touch with me earlier?"

"For a long time I was worried about

your safety. And later—I didn't want to disrupt your life. I didn't know what you'd chosen to do, but I knew you'd succeed at anything you did."

"Thanks, Mom. But you knew that how?"

A moment's silence. "I just did. I've always had complete faith in you."

Shallie didn't understand what that faith was based on but she supposed her question was one that couldn't be answered in any logical way. She changed the subject. "So you're flying here tomorrow? You and Doug?"

"We already bought the tickets. But Eddie told me you're having a big party. Is it still okay? We could always change the tickets."

"No, it's fine. When do you get in?"

"Early evening. We'll take a limo from the airport—"

"All the way here? That's expensive!"

"Not a concern. However, it means we won't get to you until later. How do you want to do this? Meet us someplace the next day? And would you like to talk now or wait until tomorrow?"

"Come to the party," Shallie said, feeling reckless. "And we'll talk tomorrow night. Catch up on our lives." That's **thirty-three years of catching up**.

CHAPTER TWENTY-THREE

Saturday of Thanksgiving Weekend

Cord's house was ready, logs in the living room fireplace lit, decorations in place, food and drinks ready for their guests. The buffet-style meal would consist of classic Thanksgiving fare, including turkey slices, gravy and cranberry sauce, salads and more. Brynne and two of her staff would do any serving and take care of the bar. Champagne would be the drink of the evening.

Cord and Shallie planned to make their announcements after dinner.

Meanwhile, The GateCrashers were setting up in a corner of the large room.

Couldn't have a party without them!

Shallie felt nervous, more nervous than she thought she'd ever felt before, her emotions a tangled mess of excitement and fear, uncertainty and hope. Every few minutes she found herself glancing around, although she knew they wouldn't arrive for some time. The Elliots were planning to meet Eddie at Eli's place, where he was staying, and he'd bring them here.

Eli and J.P. approached her with their fingers crossed—which made her laugh. One on either side, they kissed her cheeks and murmured encouragement. She'd also told Russ, who was astonished and said he was "absolutely thrilled." He told her he'd invite the Elliots to stay at the motel. Shallie couldn't speak for them, of course, but couldn't help feeling that seemed appropriate—even though they obviously had money. She noticed that Russ, too, did his share of glancing around.

Shallie and Cord had discussed the

final order of events and decided to let Carly make the first announcement. Just before she walked to the front of the living room, they poured some mock champagne into one of his grandmother's crystal flutes, which Cord presented to her.

She made her way slowly to the small table that functioned as a podium, set up with a mic borrowed from The Gate-Crashers. "Hi, everyone," she began. She raised her glass. "To my friends, neighbors and family." Glasses in the audience were raised in return. "You know me as Carly Shannon." Silence. "But today I'm officially Carly Hollister." There were gasps of surprise and bursts of applause. She glanced over at Eli and J.P., standing off to one side, near the large front window. Trooper, of course, lay beside them. "I'm Cord's daughter, Cord and Reba's. Many of you will remember my mom. The DNA tests we had done, with Katie Fairfield's help, proved that Cord is my father, proved it once and for all. I love the men I used to call 'my three dads'—Cord, Eli Garrett and J.P. McCall—but now I have one dad and two uncles."

The three met her at the front of the room and bowed, and the applause brimmed over.

"Thank you," she said. "Thank you!" With a cautious sip, mic in one hand, she told her audience, "I also love this ranch, this town—and the people here."

Then she moved back into the crowd, receiving hugs and best wishes.

Cord and Shallie allowed about ten minutes for Carly's reception before they went to the podium. "We want to thank you all for being here," Cord said. "First, though, let me say we're very, very proud of Carly."

"And we hope to see you all at our wedding next month," Shallie finished. People were cheering and raising their glasses again.

Carly leaped up to join Cord and Shallie, grabbing the mic from him. "You know what this means, right? Cord's my dad and Shallie's my **mom**!"

The ovation seemed unending.

She lifted one hand. "We're about to be upstaged by Holly Lewis, the cutest dog in the world." Holly, off her leash, was trotting toward them, lovable ears flapping, tail wagging. Oohing and aahing from the audience. "**She** wants to congratulate me, too!" Carly and the dog walked to the back of the room, where they met the Lewises.

Eli and J.P. had asked to say a few quick words, as Cord's best men and best friends; he and Shallie had agreed. The two of them advanced toward the microphone, and Eli spoke first. "Cord has been one of my two best friends for most of my life—and here's the other one." He placed his arm around J.P. "Now, Shallie is best friend number three. She's one of us. And Carly is my honorary niece."

Eli leaned toward the microphone. "Same goes for me. And Carly's my niece, too!"

Surprisingly, Eric Worth pushed his way to the front, begging to have his say. Cord glanced at Shallie; she nodded.

"You probably think I've got a lot of nerve getting up to speak, but...I **owe** these guys," Eric said, dashing a fist across his face. "Cord and Shallie and especially Carly have been friends. And I owe my uncle Eli. And my mom...Thank you!"

Russ came up to the stage then and took the mic from Eric. "I know this isn't supposed to be a public speech-making thing. I just want to say that I consider myself part of Shallie's original family. She's my cousin, so now I feel I'm part of her new family, too. The best thing that's happened to me in years was Shallie coming back to Painted Pony this past June. It changed my life. Thank you, Shallie."

Not surprisingly, this brought applause, too.

As he finished, Julie hurried toward Cord and Shallie and asked in a low voice if they were okay with her speaking. "Definitely," he responded.

"Thank you," she said, swallowing

visibly and stepping up to the make-shift podium; Cord passed her the micro-phone.

"I'm Julie Daniels. At one time I was Julie Hollister. I was married to Toby, Cord's dad, and then...he died. Cord ended up living here with his grand-parents." There were more than a few gasps from the audience. "On behalf of my daughter, Kathleen, my husband, Chris, and myself, I want to say that we offer my son, Cord, his wife-to-be, Shallie, and his daughter, Carly, our love."

Bringing Lindsey with her, Carly rushed over to Kathleen, hugging her tight. The three young women maneuvered their way through the crowded room, edged past Brynne and went into the kitchen to talk.

Cord announced a short break, and that was when The GateCrashers began tuning up, and Aaron said that any comments they had would come in the form of songs.

The first was "Girl from the North Country," followed by the ever-popular "I Walk the Line" and "One of These Days." Carly sang "Mother and Nature," the song she'd written about Reba. Aaron then asked her to perform her newest number. The music started, and she turned to grin at the band. "Here we go.

"I love them all
My new mom and my dad,
My uncles, too, and all
    my friends
Who've kept me from
    feeling sad.
Friends like Kathleen and
    Lindsey
And even Eric.
I love Tina and Mitch and Susan
And...
Sorry, Eric, couldn't find a
rhyme for your name.
But, hey, I'm not to blame!"

That brought laughter and a few hoots.

"I love M.J., Len and Holly,
Meg and her cats—and oh,
    golly.
The GateCrashers!"

She gestured toward them, which once
again generated applause and cheering.

"I love Painted Pony Creek.
Here you'll find whatever
    you seek.
I love every dog and cat
    and horse
Love my new school—

"Well, I don't know where to end. What
rhymes with **school** other than **fool**?"
People were shouting out alternatives.
"Cool!"
"Rule."
"Tool."
"Pool!"
And from Eric, **"Ghoul!"**
Not her best song, Cord thought, but
very much a performance. And he knew
the emotions were real.

"All right," he said, regaining control of the crowd. "Enough creative contributions. I suggest that those of us who are of age grab a glass of champagne—sparkling water, fake champagne or juice for the young'uns—and toast ourselves. Toast each other."

But first everyone toasted him and Shallie. Again. And after that, Carly and her "uncles."

Cord reflected with satisfaction that a new country life had just begun. **Their** country life, his and Shallie and Carly's, was being celebrated, and no one had more to celebrate than he did.

Everyone was chatting, laughing, all enjoying each other's company. There was music playing in the background, various CDs they'd chosen, and a few of the younger people were dancing.

Then Shallie caught sight of Eddie standing near the back of the crowded room. He was escorting a woman in her midsixties, classically attractive, and an elderly man using a walker. She nudged

Cord; they instantly recognized Christine from the photo Eddie had texted.

Cord and Shallie looked at each other. **This is it.**

As they approached, Doug shifted farther back and Cord stood beside him.

"I don't think introductions are necessary," Eddie said in what Shallie thought was a somewhat misguided attempt at humor.

Christine leaned closer to her. "May I please hug you?" she asked in a hoarse whisper.

"Yes, Mom!" Their embrace began tentatively, then grew more intense.

Shallie was conscious of her mother's slender form, her height—the same as hers—the light scent of her perfume, the softness of her blue wrap. And most of all, the comforting feel of her arms.

Releasing Shallie, Christine said, "Let me quickly introduce Doug. And I'd like to officially meet Cord. Who's going to be my son-in-law! Oh, and Russ. Then can you and I talk somewhere private?"

"We'll go upstairs to the office. And

you can meet Carly up there, too," Shallie suggested, since she assumed that, too, would be an emotional encounter.

"I hope to meet your friends at the wedding—if we're invited," Christine said mischievously.

"Of course! In fact, I'll give you an official invitation."

Cord and Doug had been talking and came forward now. Cord spoke briefly with Christine and Shallie with Doug, who told her how much he'd heard about her, especially in the past few days.

Shallie then gestured to Russ, standing a few feet away; he approached and she stepped back so they could have a moment alone—although she did hear him offer Room 2 at the motel and heard Christine say, "There are some good memories there, and this will allow me to overcome the bad ones. So I accept on behalf of Doug and me."

Shallie and her mother sat in Cord's office upstairs, a second chair pulled close to the desk. Tina had come in with a tray, bringing each of them a glass of champagne. "I can guess who you are. I'm Tina and we'll talk soon." Both Shallie and Christine nodded. "I think you'll need this," Tina said, putting down the two glasses—and a box of tissues.

"So," Christine murmured. "I gather from Eddie and his associate Tony that you know some of my background. Let's start there. But first I have to say it again, I love you, baby, and I've loved and missed you all these years."

"Me, too," Shallie half sobbed, leaning over to clasp Christine's hand.

"You know I left this town because I was afraid, for you and for myself. I was afraid of my husband...and his cronies. He turned out to be a crooked cop, involved with the mob in Chicago..." She shook her head forcefully, then settled her gray-blond hair behind her ears. "I'd figured it out a few years earlier. That's why your birth certificate says 'Father Unknown.'" With a wry smile, she added, "I guess that's accurate, since I **hadn't** really known him. In any case, I felt I had to get out, that **you** and I had to get out. His threats were escalating."

This revelation was no longer new to Shallie but remained terrifying.

"My half sister, Della, was kind enough to take us in, and then I got a threatening call from Kevin, and I had to escape, I knew she'd be willing to look after you. She and Norm. And Eddie did inform me that they died sometime ago. I'm sorry about that."

Shallie nodded, not bothering to point out that the Schafers were mostly in it for the money. It didn't matter now, and there'd certainly been moments of kindness.

She studied Christine, who still, in some ways, resembled that thirty-year-old photo—the classic profile, the slenderness, the expressive eyes. "I didn't even know what you looked like," she said. "Or anything about you. Until Russ found a few pictures. And a letter you'd left for Della."

Christine stared at her. "She never

showed you the letter I wrote, saying that I loved you and I was running away as much for your protection as mine?"

"No..."

"**Damn it!** I'm sorry."

"It's not important now. And I have seen the letter, thanks to Russ." Christine smiled faintly.

"Tell me what happened after you left," Shallie said. "I mean, I know some of it, but I want to hear it from you."

"I think Eddie told you, but I changed my name and found a job in a motel near Orlando. That's where I met Reba Shannon, who came here to Painted Pony Creek at my request to meet you, see how you were."

"Yes, and she became my best friend for a time."

"She reported that to me, let me know you were doing well," Shallie had to clear her throat before she could continue what she needed to say. "I think you know that Cord has a daughter by Reba. Eddie told you that, right?"

Christine nodded.

"Her name is Charlotte but she goes by Carly. And…Reba died two years ago."

Christine hid her face in both hands. "Eddie mentioned that, too. I can't get over it."

"We're all still sad about Reba," Shallie said gently. "But we both love Carly."

Christine nodded. "I look forward to meeting my **granddaughter**."

"I tried to contact Della about…oh, fifteen years ago," Christine went on, "with a message for you. A bit indirect, but I was still afraid to be too explicit… I assume you didn't hear about that, either? My postcard?"

"No, but I'd already left by then." She looked at Christine curiously. "How did you end up in Key West? Oh—and again it was Russ who unearthed that postcard. He found it in a book about Florida."

Christine nodded. "I had the book shipped to her."

"That explains it."

"I left Orlando because I had another scare. I thought I saw one of Kevin's…

associates. I went west for a while, then came back to Florida." She lifted her shoulders. "I just like it there. I decided to try Key West, see if I could find a job. I did, as a server in a bar. That's where I eventually met Doug."

"He seems nice."

"He's wonderful. Older than I am—obviously. A widower, no kids. And he has enough money that I no longer have to work. He also trusted me from the start. I explained my complicated history, which he accepted without question, and I began using my real name again. We're happy together."

"I'm glad." And she was. "How exactly did Tony find you?"

"He had an age-progressed photo of me—one of the group of photos Russell found—and started by asking in the local bars. Lo and behold..."

"Good detective work," Shallie said, smiling.

After a moment, Christine asked, "Can you ever forgive me, my sweet Shallie?"

"Yes. I already have." She felt no

hesitation in saying that. "I'm just so happy to have you back in my life."

"I am, too! And I refuse to waste another second, another day. I don't think, at Doug's age, that we can move here, but I'll visit, have you come to us, keep in constant touch."

"I'm still overwhelmed," Shallie said. "My life feels surreal. **Everything** I wanted I now have." She used one of the tissues Tina had left to wipe her eyes and handed one to Christine. "You know something else? Cord found his mother, too, a few months ago. Again with Eddie's help. He hadn't seen her since he was two."

Christine closed her eyes. "Does that sound familiar or what?"

They went through Shallie's history, most of which Christine had already learned.

Then Shallie said, "I'm going to bring Carly in, okay?"

She took a sip of her champagne and stood up, first grabbing a blank invitation from the top drawer before she headed for the door.

Christine nodded and swallowed some champagne, too. "Could you have Doug join us?"

She was almost relieved to step away for a little while—simply because the emotions she felt were so **strong**, so new and unexpected. She needed time to absorb them...

Downstairs as she looked for Carly, she was stopped by Russ. "Did you hear Christine say they're going to stay at the motel? In Room 2!"

Shallie nodded.

"God, I'm totally stunned. And incredibly happy," he said, a bewildered expression on his face. "It's like my past isn't separated from my present anymore. Do you know what I mean?"

She nodded again.

"The only thing is...she asked about Bethanne. I had to tell her Bethanne's disappeared, or in any case we've lost touch."

"That must've been upsetting," Shallie

told him. "For both of you."

"It was. Anyway, I'll let you do what-ever you need to do now, and I'll drive them...home."

She saw Cord, saying goodbye to a few of the guests. He hurried toward her, saying, "Carly's still in the kitchen. I'll get her."

"Oh, and could you help Doug upstairs, too?"

Carly had to yawn; it was almost eleven now. She badly wanted this meeting— and yet, she didn't. Maybe she was a little envious that Shallie had her mother back? Maybe...What a parent-and-child reunion these last few months had been! She reminded herself that this was the woman who'd sent Reba here, who was therefore indirectly responsible for **her** existence.

Cord brought her over to Shallie, who took her hand and led her upstairs. Carly said, "I'm truly happy for you."

She must not have sounded completely convincing, since Shallie's response was

"Don't forget. This is—or will be—your **grandmother**." That hadn't occurred to Carly yet.

They walked into the office, still hand in hand, and Shallie said, "Mom, this is Carly." **Mom.** It seemed so...strange to Carly's ear. "And this is Doug, her husband."

She studied Christine Fletcher—no, Elliot—an attractive older woman with something of Shallie about her. Or the other way around, she supposed. Without prompting, she released Shallie's hand and walked over to the desk to embrace Christine and then Doug. "I'm excited to m-meet you," she stammered.

Shallie left, with the obvious intent of giving them privacy—but not before handing Christine a wedding invitation. Carly had seen her fill it in downstairs.

Conversation was easier than she'd expected—or feared. Reba's name came up almost immediately, and they exchanged memories. Of Reba and Christine ("Sharon Sutherland" as she had been back then). The nights Sharon

and Reba had spent exchanging anecdotes and confidences at the motel bar.
Christine's gratitude that Reba had been
willing to come here, to reassure her
about Shallie.

Carly talked about the music Reba
had taught her and made her love,
showing Christine her tattoo. She mentioned some of the books they'd read
together. The fun they'd had. She spared
Christine the uncomfortable details
about Reba's marriage. But she did
disclose that when Reba was dying,
she'd told her about this place and her
three potential dads...

Christine and Doug seemed to find that
fascinating.

Soon after, Doug announced that,
considering the time—after 2 a.m. in
Florida—they should head over to the
motel now, and could she ask Cord to
help him down the stairs?

When she returned with Cord, she
kissed Christine. "Bye...Grandma."
Smiling, she added, "Bye, Grandpa."

CHAPTER TWENTY-FOUR

Shallie felt that the weeks before the wedding seemed to hurtle by, moving faster with each passing day.

The church was booked; Cord and Shallie had spoken with the minister, ordered flowers for the church and discussed the reception schedule, menu and bar with Brynne. The GateCrashers would start their set at eight and play for an hour.

Christine—she had to get used to calling her Mom—and Doug had left but not before promising to come back for the wedding. Christine also asked if they had honeymoon plans; when they said no, she invited them to visit Key West and stay with them, sometime in January or February. That timing worked well, and they accepted gratefully. **First thing I want to do is go to Hemingway House**, Shallie had told them.

Her dress and Carly's had arrived, and she made no demands or even suggestions about what her attendants should wear.

She and Cord had bought the wedding ring she'd give him during the ceremony.

Shallie had decided to take Cord's name, to become Shallie Hollister. There was no longer any reason to keep "Fletcher," not with a dead and dangerous father, a stranger yet, being the source of that name.

And...she'd gone off the pill.

They were as ready as they could be for the ceremony—and for the next stage of their lives. Their life together.

The day before the wedding, out-of-town guests had started to arrive. Like the Lewises (who'd boarded Holly for the occasion), Emma, Eddie, Julie and family, and, of course, the Elliots.

Cord hosted a "guys' night" at Sully's, while Shallie had a "girls' night" at Bailey's. He'd laughed when Carly made a sarcastic remark about how "traditional" they were being. That was still one of her favorite insults.

The next morning, after a night of love that they both felt foretold a lifetime of loving, Cord woke up, not in the least tired or groggy. He went downstairs to make coffee, do the dog duties and bring Shallie a cup. Awake now, she sat up, leaning against a stack of pillows, and kissed him.

As she took a sip of her coffee, he said, "This is the most important day of my life—and that's saying a lot after this summer."

She nodded. "Everything, my whole life, makes sense to me now, and so much of that is because of you."

Tradition (that word again) would suggest that they should have slept in separate rooms—or at least beds—the night before their wedding. But Cord had no interest in that. And neither did Shallie. He'd had every intention of starting their married life with the same joy they'd already learned to antici-pate. Why skip even one night of being together if they didn't have to?

Locked in each other's arms, they took advantage of not having to be up early today...

Sometime later, there was a knock at the bedroom door. "Hi, it's Tina and Carly with breakfast for you!"

"Breakfast in bed," Carly said with satisfaction.

What a nice start to the day.

At two, they arrived at the church. At three, the service began. Cord was grati-fied but not surprised by the number of guests as he walked to the front to join his best men.

They watched Tina and Emma make their way down the aisle, followed by Carly, carrying a small silk pillow hold-ing the rings.

Then, her arm in Mitch's, Shallie moved slowly toward the flower-covered altar and the man she loved. On her way, she waved at her mother and Doug in the front row on the left, and then at Julie, Chris and Kathleen on the right.

The readings, the hymns and a short sermon came next. Then the most important part, the exchange of vows. Reverend McPhail asked Cord, "Do you, Cord Tobias Hollister, take Shallie Fletcher to be your wife, to have and to hold from this day forward, for better, for worse, for richer, for poorer, in sickness and in health, to love and to cherish, until death do you part?"

Cord repeated the vow.

Shallie did the same when it was her turn. "I, Shallie Fletcher, take you, Cord Tobias Hollister, to have and to hold from this day forward, for better, for worse, for richer, for poorer, in sickness and in health, to love and to cherish, until death do us part."

Carly, smiling and tearing up at the same time, brought them the rings, and they placed them on each other's fingers. And finally the reverend said, "You may kiss the bride."

Cord did exactly that, whispering, "Hey, Shallie Hollister. My wife."

And she whispered back, "Hey, Cord Hollister. My husband."

It was done! They were married. This was the woman he would love all the days of his life; they would not only love but support each other, share joyful times and sad ones. Perhaps share a family if that was meant to be.

Their lives had brought them to this moment, and whatever else happened, they would have each other.